ACTS OF DESIRE

"Acting is simply projecting passion," Shreve murmured. His fingertips caressed her temple as they tucked away a wisp of hair. He brushed her cheek, the corner of her mouth, her lower lip with feathery kisses. "Not pretending passion, but real passion. Acting is bringing your experiences into play."

Miranda set her teeth as his warm breath played over the side of her throat. Her skin felt hot and prickly. Without her being aware of what he was doing, he guided her back toward the bed. His mouth slid down the side of her face to nibble at her earlobe.

The backs of her knees came in contact with the mattress. "Shreve," she whispered. "Shreve, I don't think —"

"Ssh," he cautioned. "Experience. All you lack to make you a great actress is experience."

He kissed her deeply as he held her tightly against him. She sighed, drowning in his eyes, aching for more. . . .

DISCOVER DEANA JAMES!

CAPTIVE ANGEL (2524, $4.50/$5.50)
Abandoned, penniless, and suddenly responsible for the biggest tobacco plantation in Colleton County, distraught Caroline Gillard had no time to dissolve into tears. By day the willowy redhead labored to exhaustion beside her slaves . . . but each night left her restless with longing for her wayward husband. She'd make the sea captain regret his betrayal until he begged her to take him back!

MASQUE OF SAPPHIRE (2885, $4.50/$5.50)
Judith Talbot-Harrow left England with a heavy heart. She was going to America to join a father she despised and a sister she distrusted. She was certainly in no mood to put up with the insulting actions of the arrogant Yankee privateer who boarded her ship, ransacked her things, then "apologized" with an indecent, brazen kiss! She vowed that someday he'd pay dearly for the liberties he had taken and the desires he had awakened.

SPEAK ONLY LOVE (3439, $4.95/$5.95)
Long ago, the shock of her mother's death had robbed Vivian Marleigh of the power of speech. Now she was being forced to marry a bitter man with brandy on his breath. But she could not say what was in her heart. It was up to the viscount to spark the fires that would melt her icy reserve.

WILD TEXAS HEART (3205, $4.95/$5.95)
Fan Breckenridge was terrified when the stranger found her near-naked and shivering beneath the Texas stars. Unable to remember who she was or what had happened, all she had in the world was the deed to a patch of land that might yield oil . . . and the fierce loving of this wildcatter who called himself Irons.

DEANA JAMES

ACTS OF PASSION

ZEBRA BOOKS
KENSINGTON PUBLISHING CORP.

ZEBRA BOOKS

are published by

Kensington Publishing Corp.
475 Park Avenue South
New York, NY 10016

First printing: April, 1992

Printed in the United States of America

To—
Jory and Charlotte, Dusty, W. C., Elmer, Barb, and the
rest of the WWA

Sheridan was wonderful.

A special thanks to Dee Brown,
author of The Fetterman Massacre, *upon
whose research the opening and closing chapters
of this book are based.*

THE PLAYERS

Act I

With the 2nd Cavalry at Fort Gallatin, 1866

The Colonel	Benjamin R. Westfall
The Colonel's Wife	Maud Mary Butler Westfall
The Captain	Francis Drummond
The Captain's Wife	Ruth Taylor Drummond
The Glory Hunter	Brevet-Colonel Robert E. Clarendon
His Friend	Major Reed Phillips
The Scout	Hickory Joe Magruder
The Trader	Adolf Lindhauer
The Children	Miranda Drummond, Age 13
	White Wolf's Brother, Age 10

Act II

In Chicago and in St. Louis, 1869

The Sons of Thespis	
Romeo	Shreve Catherwood
Juliet	Sheila Tyrone *née* Bessie Smith
The Comedian	Frederic Franklin
The Wardrobe Mistress	Ada Cocks
The Bit Players	George Windom
	Mike Lonigan
The Stowaway	Miranda Drummond, Age 16
The Owner of the *Queen of Diamonds*	Connal O'Toole
The Pinkerton Detective	Parker Bledsoe
The Matron	Mrs. Mortimer
Her Orderly	Big Hettie

Act III

In Chicago, Washington, D.C., and Wyoming, 1883

The Actress	The Magnificent Miranda
The Actor	Shreve Catherwood,
	Romantic Star of Three Continents
The Brigadier-General	Benjamin Westfall
His Wife	Ruth Drummond Westfall
His Stepdaughter	Rachel Drummond Westfall
The Senator	Hugh Smith Butler
The Arsonist	Archie Doight
The Detective	Henry Keller
The Shopkeeper	Victor Wolf *née* White Wolf's Brother
The Wife and Mother	Blue Sun on Snow Lindhauer

Act One
The Wyoming Territory, 1866

One

Let slip the dogs of war!

A trooper arched forward in the saddle. His scream of pain and fear was drowned in the war cries joined in half a hundred throats at the top of Lodge Trail Ridge. Falling against his horse's neck, he clawed at the shaft buried deep in his back. On the right his comrade toppled from his horse without a sound, an arrowhead protruding from the side of his neck.

"Whip 'em up, men. Make for the fort!" Capt. Francis Drummond drew his saber and pulled his horse aside as the first of the heavily loaded water and wood wagons thundered by. The ostlers needed no urging. Their bellows blended with the war cries, as they cracked their long bull-hide whips over the backs of their teams. The mules surged against their yokes and galloped over the frozen ground for Fort Gallatin.

Sioux warriors, some swinging rawhide lassos, charged down the slope. Deliberately they slammed their ponies into the sides of the troopers' mounts. The detachment of U.S. Cavalry sent to protect the woodchoppers' train staggered. Some horses went down, their riders with them, struggling with stirrups and reins, helpless before their attackers.

In the center of the melée, Drummond swung his saber as a noose settled over his stallion's head. Wellington, the big mahogany bay, reared against the pull as the Sioux swept by. The size of the Indian pony was nothing compared to the heavy army mount, but its speed hitting the end of the rawhide dragged Drummond's horse off the trail. Straight for the captain's back another Sioux galloped screaming, swinging his war club around his head. The heavily dressed stone whirred in the air.

"Daddy!" Rising from among the rocks high up on the ridge on the opposite side of the road, Miranda Drummond's high-pitched scream was lost in the din. "Daddy! Watch out! Behind you!"

Realizing that she could not be heard, she sprang up and began to scramble over the rocks. Immediately, she was jerked back, falling heavily on her hip, her skirt caught in the hands of her playmate. "Let me go! They're going to kill him. Daddy!"

Paying no attention to her demands, White Wolf's Brother dragged the struggling girl back behind the rocks. Frantic to get to her father, Miranda squirmed around and pounded on her companion's shoulders and head with her small fists. "You let me go. I've got to get to my daddy."

"You can't help him. Ow! Mirry! Stop! You'll just get in his way."

Below them Francis Drummond caught the war club on the edge of his saber and turned it aside. Thrusting the long-knife into the belly of his attacker, he spurred his horse into the side of the pony. Down the creature went under the superior strength and size of the grain-fed army stallion. The fall tore the saber from the wound, and with the return stroke, Drummond slashed Wellington free of the choking lasso.

"Let go! Let go, I tell you! I've got to help him!"

Miranda sobbed. Desperately she twisted and tore in White Wolf's grasp, prying at his fingers locked in her heavy wool skirt.

"You can't help him. You'll be killed."

Suddenly remembering that she and her friend were on a hunting expedition, she reached for her precious rifle. With trembling fingers she shoved a tiny .22 cartridge into the breech. "I'll shoot them."

Wolf released his hold on the skirt to grab hold of the rifle. "Not with that. You couldn't even shoot through their buckskins."

"But—"

A series of horrifying yells carried up to them. Miranda twisted around and peered over the rocks. Wolf slapped a hand on the top of her blond head and pushed her back. "Keep down! Don't let them see you! They'd kill us too quick to talk about."

But Miranda threw her companion's hand off and eased up. Francis Drummond galloped at the back of his men. A yelling warrior, a pair of eagle feathers streaming from his long black locks, slammed his pony into Wellington's shoulder. Even as the stallion staggered and broke stride, Drummond ducked the war club, driven full of nails and grisly with matted skin and hair. Teeth bared with effort, the captain rose in his stirrups.

Blood spurted from the attacker as Drummond's blade slashed through the buckskin jacket, trade shirt, skin, and muscle clear to the bone. The Sioux warrior screamed and reined his pony away. Ululating wildly, a second spurred his mount to come up on the captain's other side. Hickory Joe Magruder, Drummond's scout, tossed a quick shot over his shoulder that toppled the Indian out of the saddle and into the icy ditch. The last of the wagons lumbered over the ridge.

"Ride for it, men!" Drummond wheeled Wellington

across the trail, slashing the chill air with his bloody saber. The excited stallion curvetted, rose, then came down tossing his black mane and champing the bit. But the Sioux were already reining their ponies in and falling back. The men of the Second Cavalry broke off their fighting and galloped hell for leather up the trail.

Miranda would have risen to her feet to cheer, but White Wolf's Brother started dragging her away from the hill. "We've got to get back to the fort as fast as we can. If your ma or my pa finds out we've been playing this far away, we'll wish the Sioux had caught us."

The thought of their parents' ire was like a cold shower of reality. Forbidden to leave the fort much less trek out across the narrow valley and up the ridge back, their punishment would be painful if they were caught. Blond braids flying behind them both, the two sprinted down the shoulder of the hill and into a stand of scrub cedar. There Miranda Drummond, tall for thirteen and longer legged than the half-breed Cheyenne, stopped to catch her breath before wading through the snow still knee-deep in the thicket.

"Wasn't he wonderful?" she panted when Wolf had caught up. "Just like Jeb Stuart. He was so brave. What a fight!"

"I didn't get to see much," the boy grumbled. "I had to keep wrestling with you all the time."

"If you'd let me shoot —"

Her companion's disgust was monumental. "That's a varmint rifle. It wouldn't bring down a coyote much less a Sioux in buckskins. You'd have to shoot somebody in the eye with it and then it'd just make him mad."

"Who made you so smart?"

"I'm smart enough to know I didn't want to get scalped."

"If it was your daddy doing their fighting, you'd

14

have wanted to shoot."

"My daddy doesn't fight. He trades."

"I'm going to be like my daddy some day."

"You can't. You're a girl. I'm the one who's going to be like his daddy some day."

She pulled a face at him. "We might as well go back to the fort. We won't find anything to shoot after all that noise."

Half an hour later, Pvt. Arnold Richardson on guard duty at the sally port pulled the children inside and slammed the gate. Dropping the bar across it, he confronted them. "Goldangit, yuh told me yuh wouldn't go past th' woods. And what do I see? I see yuh sprintin' down th' hogback."

"We're sorry." Miranda hung her head.

The short, fat private, no taller than she, stooped so he could see her face. "Yuh scared me near t' death." His earnest face was white over his curly brown beard. "Near t' death. This is th' last time I let y'all kids out for anything at all. Don't come round beggin' no more. Hear me! It's too dangerous out there."

"We won't ask to go again," White Wolf's Brother promised solemnly.

"See that yuh don't. Adolf'll beat me t' death—t' death if he ever finds out." He thought of the straight-backed heavy-shouldered German mercantile trader, whose blond Indian son rode everywhere on the wagon seat with him. "And yer dad—" He swiped a hand across his mouth. "Godalmighty. I'll be court-mar-tialed."

"Is my father all right, Arnie?"

Richardson wet his lips nervously. "He's cut some, but everyone of 'em looks like they've been run through a meat grinder. I didn't sign on fer nothin' like this. I swear if I'd a known—"

15

With a gasp Miranda dashed away.

"Francis. Oh, Francis." Ruth Drummond put her slim arms around her husband's chest and held him tightly.

"Sweetheart." He rested his cheek on the top of her head and molded her to him. For a long minute they touched at every part. Then he gently loosened his grip. "I'm sweaty and I stink."

"But you're alive." She clutched him even more tightly. Her fingers splayed over his broad back. "You smell and feel just wonderful. Just wonderful." She tilted back her head staring up into his dear face. It was pasty beneath the dark, weathered skin. A court plaster covered a scratch on his cheek. His trouser was crusted with blood, and a white bandage gleamed through the slit.

One corner of his full mouth turned up into a deep dimple on his weathered cheek. He kissed her. "I know you're crazy."

"I had to be to marry you." She kissed him back then broke off the kiss to guide him toward the horsehide settee.

"This thing's an abomination," he groaned hoarsely. His arm slipped down from her shoulder until his fingers were pressing against the swell of her breast beneath her arm. "Let's just go right to bed."

"Francis, your wound — "

He grinned and again the dimple flashed. The excitement of battle still surged through his body. "I count on you to kiss it and make it better."

"Daddy!"

Both of them turned as Miranda burst in through the door. Their only daughter and the love of their life, she flung herself into their arms. "I heard all about it.

16

From Private Richardson. Indians, he said. Oh, you're hurt!"

Drummond wrapped his free arm around her and hugged her close. "Nothing but a raiding party of young bucks."

Beside him his wife muttered. "I hope you're right."

He sought to reassure her. "They were after the horses. They even threw a rope around Wellington's neck."

Miranda grinned up at him. A dimple identical to the captain's tugged up at the corner of her mouth. "Bet you scared them good."

Drummond hesitated. He did not want to tell his daughter the detachment had run for their lives. Yet he had never been anything but honest with her. "We got the wagons over the hill and then we retreated, sweet baby. We didn't take any chances."

"But you could have beaten them if you'd stayed, Daddy."

"Maybe. Maybe not." He frowned down into his wife's worried eyes. Against his hip, he could feel the moderate thickening of her waist. She was filled with life, life he had put there. The life of the son he longed for, or if not a boy, then another beautiful daughter as fair as Miranda. "I couldn't take any chances. I've got to take care of my girls."

His wife lifted her mouth to his kiss, her heart full, her eyes brimming with tears.

Miranda did as she had done since a very tiny child held in their arms. She stretched up on tiptoe, put her arms around both their necks, and kissed them both at the same time. Their three mouths joined as they hugged each other hard. When they pulled away, all three had tears on their cheeks. Overcome as much by strong emotion as weakness from his wounds, Drummond swayed against his wife.

17

"Francis, please sit down."

"Yes, Daddy, sit. I'll put on water for a hot bath." Miranda disengaged herself from her father's arm. "But I still bet you could have beaten them, Daddy. You were wonderful. Slashing with your sword and reining Wellington right and left."

Francis frowned. "Miranda, you seem awfully well informed about the battle."

She froze. A red stain climbed in her cheeks. "I—I asked Private Richardson, Daddy. He told me the story."

"I've told you to stay away from enlisted men."

"Wolf was with me." She, too, had learned never to lie more than absolutely necessary. Before her father could question her further, she dashed into the small kitchen and began to pump water.

Francis Drummond frowned as his wife helped him to sit on the settee. Then she put her cool palms on his cheeks and kissed him with deepest tenderness, and he forgot everything else in the world.

The dance the week before Christmas was a new tradition at Fort Gallatin. Three enlisted men had been impressed into playing their musical instruments. They sounded quite good considering that they owned a pair of fiddles and a banjo. Fort Gallatin was as yet too small a fort to have a regimental band.

The hostess was, of course, Maud Mary Westfall, the post commander's wife, although she had done nothing herself to prepare the refreshments, nor to decorate the quarters. The strings of blue juniper berries and the strips of cloth tied up in bows to the branches of the spruce tree had been done by the wives of the other officers. Ruth Drummond had dressed a china doll in an angel's robe with white cardboard wings and placed it on the top of the tree.

18

Colonel Westfall's wife suffered from a deterioration of the spine. The overbright eyes, with which she watched the dancers, were attributable to a low-grade fever that never cooled. Set deep in her sallow face, they watched everything that passed between her husband and his staff, but most especially between him and the wives.

Tonight her eyes were trained especially where her husband waltzed with Ruth Drummond. Her lips thinned as she watched him smile down into the face of a woman ten years her junior, a healthy, beautiful woman, a woman with masses of blond wavy hair and big blue eyes.

Seated in a high-backed chair, braced with pillows, and covered by several bright paisley and woolen shawls, Maud Mary could only watch. She moved her wasted limbs fractionally. Pain streaked through her hips and up her spine. Her thin hand clenched beneath the rich wool, her fingernails cut into her skin.

"May I get you a cup of punch, Mrs. Westfall?"

With a sigh she looked up. Bvt.-Col. Robert Clarendon stood at her side. His smile was obscured beneath the blue-black walrus mustache that blended with his heavy sideburns. He had newly come from an eastern fort. "Why thank you, Colonel Clarendon."

He bowed formally and moved away. Her gaze returned to the half-dozen couples revolving in the cleared space of the living room of the bachelor officers' quarters.

The waltz ended and the dancers applauded. Benjamin Westfall made no move to return Ruth to her husband. Instead, he called to the musicians to begin again. His smile engaged her though she stepped back with a nervous glance over her shoulder.

Maud Mary's brows drew together. She drew in her breath sharply as her husband arbitrarily pulled Ruth

19

into his arms and began to sway back and forth with her. The young woman's full skirts swept between his trouser legs. Not even an inch separated their bodies.

Maud Mary sighed unhappily. Benjamin loved to dance. He had loved to dance with her until this foul condition developed after her last miscarriage.

Clarendon bowed as he placed her cup in her mitted hand. "Lovely party, Mrs. Westfall. Just the thing to raise our spirits out here on the lonely frontier at Christmastime."

Her smile of acknowledgment was thin. Her eyes remained on her husband and the woman in his arms. "Thank you."

Clarendon chatted on as Westfall guided Captain Drummond's beautiful young wife in the short circle prescribed by the small room. "Wish I'd been in charge of the wood and water detail," he remarked loudly. "Great chance missed there."

"I beg your pardon." Ill she might be, Maud Mary was no fool. Trained in protocol by her mother and her father, Congressman Hugh Smith Butler, she thrived on the conflicts and intrigues, the petty jealousies and petty ambitions of the Washington political scene. Because of her health, she had endless hours wherein she had little else to do but read and write. More often than not, her reading matter had become the daily reports of his officers and her writing, the reports that her husband abhorred.

Both she and her husband saw Fort Gallatin on the Montana Road as a stepping-stone into Washington politics. To that end she worked with feverish dedication to write reports to impress his superiors as well as letters to her father's colleagues praising her husband's work. Promotion to the rank of general with appointment to a prominent position in the nation's capital was the next stop for them both.

As she digested Clarendon's words, she stared at him, an air of speculation in her look as she analyzed his motives for making his statement.

Mistakenly thinking he was speaking to an uninformed woman, Robert Clarendon took a fortifying drink of the potent punch and continued unabashed. "I said that a great chance was missed there."

"A great chance?" She allowed herself a small smile at the man's jealousy. Francis Drummond was a brave man and a good officer. Although several men had been wounded, two badly, the captain had lost only one man to the hostiles. She had written the report herself.

"Indeed. He missed his chance to attack and carry the fight. It would have been a good fight. The eastern press would have picked up on it immediately." Clarendon stared mournfully at the dancers. Then he smiled down at her. "A man could be promoted very quickly."

Maud Mary's look did not alter even as she realized that Clarendon was not simply jealous but ambitious. The two went well together although they could be dangerous. "But he was outnumbered. His force could have been wiped out. He could have been killed."

"Of course, there's always that chance." Clarendon rocked forward on his toes. "But not likely. Not likely they'd have been wiped out, either. Trained cavalrymen against savages. Why a single troop of regulars could whip a thousand Indians."

"But he did not have a troop."

"He missed his chance," the colonel repeated obdurately. "With eighty men I could ride through the entire Sioux nation."

"You think he made a mistake." Maud Mary's dark eyes bored into him.

Suddenly Clarendon was aware that he spoke to the colonel's lady. He had heard stories about her shrewdness, her intelligence. He had even heard rumors that she helped Westfall from time to time. Her father was some sort of politician back east. He pulled in his pugnacious chin. "Well, I wasn't there, of course. I'm sure he did his duty as prescribed."

"And what would you have done, Colonel Clarendon?"

He took a deep breath. The dance had ended. The musicians had their heads together whispering. The small room had gone quiet. Her question had dropped into the silence. His mouth worked under the heavy black mustache. "I would have charged immediately. That would have taught them a lesson they wouldn't soon have forgotten. Attack! Attack immediately. Drive them back to the hills." His eyes flashed. "These savages have no place among civilized people. The quicker they learn it and get out of the way, the better."

Westfall moved to his wife's side. His gaze was measuring, speculative. "You certainly present the attitude of many U.S. congressmen, Mr. Clarendon."

The brevet-colonel nodded proudly. "It is my own, sir. The people of the United States have a right to these lands. If the hostiles cannot depart in peace, then they'll have to be driven off."

Ruth Drummond poured her husband a second cup of coffee. "Maud Mary is sick again. She woke up in the middle of the night with a putrid throat and shooting pains."

"Poor lady."

Ruth turned back to the stove, to stir the bubbling oatmeal. "She sent an orderly for me, but I don't want to go."

He looked at her over the rim of his cup. One eyebrow arched in question. He waited.

Ruth banged the spoon against the edge of the pot with unnecessary force. "I don't like the way her husband dances with me."

Francis stared at the contents of his cup. Ruth made good coffee, a clear brown brew, not too weak, not too strong. He drained it and set the cup down. "I didn't like it, either."

She swung around. They stared at each other helplessly. Both had been career army for fourteen years. He had married her as soon as he had graduated from West Point. Their daughter had been born the next spring. She had followed him faithfully from post to post, loved him with all her heart, never complained about the hardships, the toil, the uncertainty, the danger.

Underlying and running through all those were the bitter problems of being the beautiful wife of a junior officer. Bachelor officers flocked around her. Worse than bachelor officers were those who were not bachelors but whose wives had left them, taken their children, and gone back home. Worst of all were those who flirted with her under the accusing eyes of their wives living in the tight community on the post. Tact of the highest level was required at all times because all too frequently those whom she had to fend off controlled her husband's duties, his assignments, his promotions, and ultimately his career.

Francis grimaced. "He's got good taste."

"Maud Mary's an invalid," Ruth said quietly. "She's not going to get any better. Poor lady. I really admire her. But her husband makes me ill. She writes all of his reports, does so much of his work for him, and he repays her by embarrassing her."

Francis shrugged cynically. "They both want the same things. He's just looking around."

Ruth wrapped her arms around her waist. "That certainly makes me feel wonderful. I don't want to go over there."

He leaped to his feet and began to pace around the tiny kitchen. "Christ! Do you think I want you to? A man makes overtures to my wife and I let him get away with them. I'd like to call him out." He caught her by the arms and stared down into her eyes. His expression was tortured. "You know that, don't you?"

"I know." Her head was bowed. He could not look into her eyes.

He heaved a sigh. "You don't have to go. Just send a message. Say that Miranda's sick."

"Miranda! Ha! She's healthy as a goat. Maud Mary would know why I wasn't coming. And she'd tell Colonel Westfall."

"Christ," he murmured again. He dropped his hands helplessly. "It's a mess. Shall I get out when this tour is done?"

She shrugged. "Not if you don't want to. Another six years and you'll have your time in. By that time we might be in Washington."

"Or Death Valley."

She laughed a little and raised her head. Their eyes met laughing at their favorite joke. They would be in Washington—or the worst place they could think of. "At least we wouldn't be freezing. The mercury's frozen in the bulb on the thermometer."

He put his hand on her belly. "I want what's best for our son."

She put her hand over his. "I do, too. So I guess I'd better get about three layers of clothes on and go over to stay with Maud Mary."

"I'll come over in two hours to escort you home. If he's there, I'll stay and talk about how much I love you and how good you are to me. Maybe he'll take the hint."

"Save your breath. He knows. Everyone on the post knows." She kissed his unhappy mouth. His arms closed around her and the kiss deepened. Desperately, they strove together each seeking and giving the other assurance with their passion.

Benjamin Westfall himself opened the door for her. Smiling a welcome, he pulled Ruth in. The furious wind and driving snow blew her into his arms. "It's so terrible out there," he observed. "So good of you to come out in all this. You're a true friend to her. To me." His dark eyes scanned her wind-bitten cheeks. "She's very sick."

"Then I'd better get to her side." Ruth hurried into the center of the room where she began to undo her garments and unwrap her head. Westfall followed her. As he stepped close, she draped her muffler and coat over his outstretched arm.

"Ruth —"

"Ruth? Is that you?" a hoarse voice called from the bedroom.

"Yes, Maud Mary. I'll be right in. Just let me get my coat off."

"My throat's killing me." As if to testify to her condition, the colonel's wife began to cough. Deep hacking convulsions scraped out of her throat. "Oh, God," the sick woman moaned. She coughed again. "Oh, mercy."

"She sounds bad," Ruth whispered.

"The doctor said it was pneumonia," Westfall confirmed. "Pneumonia, with complications." A certain flat tone in his voice might have been resignation.

"Poor dear."

"Ruth," came the importuning call.

Maud Mary's every breath rattled out of her lungs.

25

Her fever was so high that she drifted in and out of consciousness. Ruth brought in buckets of snow to put compresses on her wrists and forehead. At the same time she boiled compresses and taped a hot mustard plaster to the woman's hollowed chest to try to ease the catarrh and loosen the cough.

The post's doctor had left quinine, but it seemed to do little good. When he called again to examine his patient, he shook his head. Motioning to Ruth, he led her to the door and turned his broad back to the patient in the bed. "Too many ills. Too many wrongs in that frail engine. I can only treat one at a time and my supplies are few."

She stared at him wide-eyed. His face was raw from the icy wind, his lips beneath his mustache chapped and peeling. His breath smelled of whiskey and his bad stomach disorder. She steeled herself not to pull back as he leaned forward to whisper.

"I don't have the proper instruments. My skill with women is negligible. I can treat broken bones and wounds, the diseases and problems of young men." He glanced significantly at Ruth's thickening waist as he took her hand. Gravely, he shook his head over her skin blistered from wringing out hot compresses. "I would not admit that to anyone but you, dear lady. The first spring thaw you should go to your mother. I beg you do not wait too long." He rubbed his thumb reflectively over the backs of her fingers. "I'll give you some salve."

She pulled back her hand, her body trembling. "I cannot leave without my husband."

"Then perhaps he should take leave and go with you."

She nodded. "Perhaps so. If you would recommend —"

"Ruth — Ruth —" Maud tossed in the bed and suddenly sat up. "What are you two whispering about?"

The doctor spun around as if he had been shot. "Dear Mrs. Westfall. What a relief to see you yourself again." He hurried to her bedside. "I was just giving Mrs. Drummond instructions for your care, but perhaps they will not be necessary."

Maud Mary sank back on the bed. "Oh, I know you think she's pretty, too. All of you are half in love with her."

"Now, ma'am —"

"She's a good woman. Too good for the likes of you. Leave her alone."

"Mrs. Westfall, I assure you —"

"Leave her alone." Maud Mary turned her head away. Her eyelids fluttered closed. "All of you."

He stared at her, a flush creeping into his cheeks. "I'll leave you some more quinine, Mrs. Drummond. See that she takes it," he remarked loudly. "Obviously, she is still in the grip of delirium."

Two

O villainy! Ho! Let the door be lock'd.
Treachery! Seek it out.

Maud Mary drifted into a restless sleep after taking the quinine from the doctor's own hand. Cheek propped on her fist, Ruth watched the older woman's slumber. How strange that she had thought Mrs. Westfall to be her enemy! Instead, the colonel's wife had revealed herself to be a sympathetic friend.

Ruth wondered whether she would have had the courage to regard someone in her position as a friend. If she had seen Francis dancing too many times with another woman, would she have been able to see the woman's side? She shuddered at the thought that Maud Mary Westfall must have seen many such episodes in the course of her marriage. She understood perhaps better than Ruth the social life and politics of an army post. Her pity and concern for the grievously ill woman grew.

And with them grew a deep resolve to avoid Colonel Westfall at all costs. The front door opened belowstairs. Her eyes flew to the clock ticking imperturbably on the shelf. That would be Francis. Had he knocked and she had not heard him? Tucking the covers more securely around her patient, she tiptoed out the door.

Her heart sank as she saw Westfall mounting the stairs. He smiled. "My dear Ruth. How is my wife?"

"Oh, much better. She's passed into a light sleep. If you go in and sit by her side, she'll probably wake up at any moment."

He nodded. "Then she is better."

"She sat up and spoke to us while Doctor Peters was here." Ruth stepped back in the doorway, determined not to leave the slight protection that Maud Mary's room might offer.

Westfall came to the door, his smile everything that was warm and sincere. "I'm sure it was all because of your good nursing." His eyes never left his wife's face, pale and drawn in the lamplight, as he reached out to close his fingers around Ruth's wrist.

"Thank you, but — really — I only did what the doctor ordered. Colonel Westfall —"

"Benjamin. My first name is Benjamin. You call my wife by her first name. Why not me?"

"I don't know." Ruth looked down at his hand, then back at the bed. Why had her patient, after being restless and wakeful at the slightest sound, suddenly fallen into a deep sleep. "Girls —" Her voice rose slightly. "Girls call each other by their first names."

"And you are just a girl, aren't you?"

"Nonsense. I'm a married woman with a thirteen-year-old daughter."

"You're raising your voice. I'm afraid you'll disturb your patient. Come away with me." Before she could even draw back, he had pulled her out into the hall and closed the door behind them.

"Maud Mary shouldn't be left alone."

"She'll be all right for the time being. I won't leave her for more than a minute or two. At least not at this time." He led her down the hall to the window at the back of the house. Snow whirled in utter blackness be-

29

hind the dingy lace curtain. "I must talk to you, Ruth."

She shivered as a gust rattled the windowpane. "My husband will be here any minute. In fact, I thought you might be him when I heard you open the front door."

"We'll hear him when he comes." He put his free hand around her shoulder, drawing her ever closer to him.

She tried to stiffen. "I really need to go downstairs and get bundled up for the trek back across the yard. I imagine the temperature has dropped considerably in the last couple of hours."

"Ruth." He lifted her hand. His dark eyes stared into hers before turning her palm up. "You've scalded yourself," he murmured. "Your lovely skin is blistered."

"I — The water for the compresses. I had to —"

"Ssh." He inclined his head. Before she could draw away, his mustache tickled the tender palm, his breath cooled it.

"Colonel Westfall."

"Let's not play games, my dear Ruth. I felt you tremble when we danced together last night."

"No, sir. I tell you, you misunderstood. My baby"— she wrenched one of her hands away and clapped it to her middle—"you must know that a baby —"

"I don't know," he murmured sadly, his eyes never leaving her face. His expression became melancholy. "I don't know. Maud Mary has never given me any children."

"The life is very hard. Perhaps you should consider—"

"Oh, I've considered. I've considered everything." His other hand pressed meaningfully into Ruth's back. He was stronger than she. In another instant she would topple against him.

"Your wife—" she reminded him, a desperate note in her voice.

"She will not last the winter." His arm was like a bar across her back.

"You mustn't say that."

A knock sounded on the door downstairs.

Westfall's saintly expression changed to one of annoyance. "I can only suppose that that will be the gallant Captain Drummond."

Ruth pulled herself free of his arms and hurried to the top of the stairs. "I asked him to come fetch me before it got too late."

He followed at her heels. His voice sounded unnaturally loud in her ear. "And of course he came as ordered. A good soldier. He always obeys orders."

She turned, trying to read his feelings in his set face. His eyes had a peculiar light. The knocking came again louder. She hastily dropped her eyes to the worn stairs. "I don't want to keep him standing around. We've both got to get back home. Miranda's alone."

Westfall detained her, covering her hand on the bannister. The palm that pinned her was hot and rough. "My dear, your loyalty to your husband does you credit, just as does your friendship to my wife."

She did not want to look at him for fear that her disgust would show in her face. Feeling distinctly sick at her stomach, she stooped slightly to catch up her skirts. Something more was required. She must answer his compliment in some way. Finally, she swallowed hard. "I am as my parents reared me, Colonel Westfall."

"Benjamin, please. I want you to be my friend as you are my dear sick wife's. Please don't forget to be."

The knock sounded again, heavier, as Francis tried to make himself heard upstairs. "He'll wake your wife."

Westfall took his hand away. "Then go to him. I'll stay with her. Good night."

"Good night." Ruth flew down the staircase and across the downstairs hall to open the door and let Francis in.

"It's routine, sweetheart."

"But the weather. How can a train be coming at this time? It's only four days till Christmas."

Francis shifted his wide shoulders uneasily. "Supplies. Mail. Ammunition. The weather's been good. The snow's almost melted."

"But after what happened just three weeks ago — Oh, Francis, I'm afraid."

To soothe her, he took her in his arms. "Now, I've got to go. It's my duty. I've been ordered."

"Are you in command?"

"No." He hesitated. "Clarendon."

Ruth shuddered. "How many?"

"Fifty mounted infantry. Twenty-seven cavalry."

She began to weep helplessly. Her feelings were too raw. He patted her shoulders and hugged her.

"Why, sweetheart —"

She pulled herself together. "I guess it's just the baby." She looked up at him tears swimming in her eyes and wetting her cheeks. "Is Joe going with you?"

At last he could offer some measure of reassurance. "I should say so. He wouldn't let me out of his sight. I owe him money from the poker game last week."

"I'll feel safer with him at your back."

She put on her coat, even though he told her not to. Arms around each others' waists they walked to the east gate. The weak sun shone through the veriest hint of white mist. The horses' breaths made puffs of clouds beneath their muzzles.

Clarendon came forward to tip his hat. "We'll get

them today, Mrs. Drummond. When we come back with the wagons, we'll be heroes."

Ruth's fingernails dug into Francis's hand even through the leather gauntlet. "What's he talking about?"

He frowned warningly at the other officer. "No danger. We're just to go out and escort the train. Just do our jobs. Nothing fancy."

"Ah, good morning," a voice called behind them. Westfall came striding over the frozen ground, his boots crunching. He presented himself before them nodding and smiling. "Good morning, Captain Drummond. Good morning to you, my dear Mrs. Drummond. Sorry to take your husband away from you even for a moment so close to Christmas."

She managed a smile. "I understand, Colonel Westfall."

"Of course. Part of the job. Part of the life. Captain Drummond, you are to report to Colonel Clarendon, implicitly obey his orders, and never leave him."

Drummond saluted. His sergeant held Wellington as well as his own horse. With a smile he put his arm around Ruth's waist. His hand slipped between the buttons of her coat to press against her belly. He kissed her while his fingers pressed against the gravid mound.

"It's too soon," she whispered against his mouth. "Be careful and come back to me, Francis. You'll feel him kick."

A trooper yelled encouragement. The others took up the cheer. When they broke apart, Francis waved cheerfully. Ruth blushed and shook her head.

"Very affecting," Westfall remarked, his face expressionless. To Clarendon he said, "Be sure to come back heroes."

"Right, sir. I intend to do just that." Clarendon snapped a salute and swung into the saddle. The line

33

of mounted men swung out. "Column of twos. Forward! Ho!"

Hickory Joe Magruder in his buffalo robe, fur hat, and bushy beard looked like a great mounted grizzly bear bringing up the rear. "Don't worry none, Miz Ruth," he called. "I'll watch his back."

She caught his gnarled hand where it rested on his thigh. "Do that for me, Joe. Oh, and please, please, be careful."

She stood by and watched them ride away. As the gate closed behind them, Benjamin Westfall stepped to her shoulder. "I'd appreciate it if you'd be with my wife for a space of a few hours, Ruth. She's been very restless, now that she's beginning to feel better."

Miranda thought she had never seen anything more gallant than the men of the Second as they rode out of the east gate. When the last man had passed through, she and White Wolf's Brother ran after them talking to Hickory Joe. Excitement sang along her veins laced with anticipatory terror.

As the first soldiers topped the rise, she halted. In her mind she could hear the war cries of the Sioux, see her father's saber flashing in the cold air. Sudden fear, premonitory and awful, seized at her heart. Tugging her red wool muffler from around her neck, she waved it round and round her head. "Daddy! Daddy! Be careful!"

Francis heard her. Turning in the saddle, he swept off his white hat and waved it in return. "I will, Miranda. Take care of your mother."

The first of the troopers mounted the crest and began to ride down out of sight.

Maud Mary smiled wanly as Ruth brought her a cup of hot tea. "So good of you, dear."

34

"I'm glad to do it."

"Did I hear a commotion?"

Ruth nodded. "The escort for the supply train just rode out."

The general's wife tasted the tea. It was perfectly steeped, just to her liking. She took a reviving drink. "I have unusual hearing. I suppose it's brought on by the fever." She looked at Ruth over the rim of the cup. "Sometimes I can hear people talking in the next room."

Ruth's eyes widened. She opened her mouth to speak, then closed it tightly.

Maud Mary smiled a little grimly. "Sometimes I can hear the horses stamping and moving around way down in the stables. It is most disturbing."

Ruth stirred uncomfortably. "I can imagine."

The older woman took another sip of tea. "I must get my strength back. Benjamin depends on me for so much of the paperwork."

"We all depend on you for so many things."

Maud Mary tried to straighten her back. A faint groan slipped between her lips. Her face twisted. She stared at Ruth. "You are all leaning on a frail reed I'm afraid."

For a minute the younger woman was silent trying to think what to say. At last she decided on a neutral statement. "Colonel Westfall has been so anxious about you. He's had several of the officers' wives in to nurse you."

"But you most especially."

The color drained from Ruth's face as silent, bleak communication passed between her and Maud Mary. Each knew the other's thoughts and at the same time recognized that they were better left unsaid. Neither could afford the luxuries of jealousy and affronted honor. They were totally dependent on the men who

35

owned them. The silence grew.

Maud Mary's teacup clattered in its saucer. "Do I hear shots?"

"Shots!" Ruth sprang up, spilling the tea she had fixed for herself. "Oh, no!"

"My dear—"

"Francis just rode out."

The color fled from both faces. Ruth flew down the stairs and out through the door onto the parade ground. Once outside she could hear them, too. Rifles barking like small angry dogs in the distance. Soldiers were hurrying out of their barracks and climbing the icy ladders to the palisade.

On the headquarters porch Westfall was already conferring with his other five officers. "—nothing to be alarmed about. Clarendon has his orders."

Maj. Reed Phillips objected strenuously. "Sir, we've got to send a relief column?"

"We have no reason to think that they need relief." The colonel's smile was bland. "The hostiles have been known to fire sporadically."

Phillips reddened. Young Brevet-Colonel Clarendon had become his fast friend. He tried again. "Permission requested to mount a scouting party to ascertain the cause."

"Permission denied."

"But, sir—"

Westfall waved him to silence at the sight of Ruth's frightened face. "My dear Mrs. Drummond, you're out without a coat."

She halted her headlong flight. Suddenly self-conscious as they all turned in concern, she thrust her hands into the pockets of the wool dress. "I'm sorry, gentlemen. I was concerned—"

Westfall came off the porch to take her hand. "There's no cause for concern, I assure you—"

"Horse! *Horse!*" The sentry's call stiffened them all around.

Reed Phillips led the junior officers in a dash toward the east gate. "Let him in."

"It's Wellington!" Miranda's scream from atop the palisade dropped Ruth to her knees. As if she had taken an arrow, she fell, clutching at her middle. "Wellington!"

Westfall angrily scanned the wall. "What's that child doing up there?"

Even as Miranda was scrambling down the ladder, the gate swung open. In sight of the fort, the stallion slowed. Limping he came, his left foreleg up, blood running down over the white stocking, dripping off the hoof.

Miranda dodged the trooper and dashed out through the gate. "Wellington!"

"Come back here!" Westfall's grab for her came too late. He rounded on the unfortunate guard. "Stop her! Damn it, trooper, you let a child out of that gate."

His harangue was drowned out as Ruth screamed again. *"Miranda!"*

The child ran on heedless. The stallion saw her coming, threw up his head. His nostrils drank her scent. Strong in them was his own blood. He snorted. He took another step, another, holding his foreleg up like a hurt dog. His head dropped.

"It's her father's horse," the man explained as if that excused his lapse.

"It's Drummond's horse," another agreed. "God help them!"

"Francis!" Ruth had pulled herself to her feet. Tears streamed down her cheeks; sobs tore from her throat. Clutching her belly, she stumbled across the great distance to the gate. Her eyes were fixed on the figure of her daughter where she had now reached the stallion,

37

unmistakable because of his mahogany bay coloring.

"Wellington. Oh, Wellington." Miranda held out her hand. She had never been allowed to do more than touch the horse's shoulder. He was a cavalry mount after all and no child's pet.

The stallion snorted in pain. His eyes showed the white ring. In the distance rifles barked. He laid back his ears and hopped forward, bearing his weight on the right foreleg.

"Wellington, where's Daddy?"

As the horse moved past her, heading for the fort, Miranda could see the feathered shaft sticking out behind the point of the shoulder. It twitched and blood welled around it with each pained step. Francis Drummond's daughter began to shake. Fearfully she looked at the brow of the hill.

"Miranda!" Her mother was stumbling toward her.

Reed Phillips dashed up to catch the stallion's bridle and exclaim. "He's shot! Arrow! It's Sioux all right! Goddamn! Oh, goddamn!"

Others dashed up behind him exclaiming and cursing. "We've got to ride out."

"Listen to that firing."

"They've been ambushed."

"No." Colonel Westfall's voice fell like a thunderstroke on Ruth's ears. She screamed.

Phillips spun around. "Why the hell not?"

"Major Phillips, you are out of control."

"That may be, sir, but—"

"We cannot leave the fort undefended. Clarendon knew not to pursue. He may be pinned down, but we cannot ride out into we know not what."

"Those are your men out there, sir. They're expecting you to come to their aid."

"I am in command here. You will cease this conversation immediately, or it will go into your record. We have a fort to defend. We cannot desert it or leave it undermanned because we hear stray shots being fired."

"But the horse—"

"That will be enough!"

Ruth clapped her hands to her mouth as the horse was led by her. Miranda, who had walked beside him, confronted the group. Furious color flooded her cheeks. Her hands were doubled into fists at her sides. "You've got to rescue my father."

Westfall stared at her, his face stony. "Take her back inside the fort."

A trooper stepped to her side, but she refused to budge. "You've got to ride out and save my father and his men," she repeated. "They've been ambushed just like they were before. They need help right now." Her steadfast determination coupled with the desire of every man to go to the aid of his comrades almost won the day. The junior officers poised on the balls of their feet waiting for the word from their commander.

The valley beyond had been silent for several minutes. Then a flurry of shots began again.

"It's not too late. You can go. You must go. P-please." Suddenly, her nerve broke. Tears streamed down her face as she twisted her hands. In that minute she became the child she was, intruding in the affairs of men. "Please save my daddy."

"Miranda," Ruth called from inside the gate, her voice thick with woman's tears. "Come back inside, baby."

The men stood silent. The firing stopped.

"Back inside the fort." Westfall turned on his heel and led them in. The trooper led the stallion down the parade ground in front of the officers' quarters to the stables. The gate swung shut. The bar dropped into place.

Miranda screamed. "You're not going out! You're not going to save my daddy!"

"Mrs. Drummond, will you please control your daughter?"

The command was like a douche of cold water flung in her face. It steadied Ruth. "Miranda, you're embarrassing me — us. Your father would not be proud of you. You are a soldier's daughter. You are expected to obey orders."

"But they're not going to help." She swung around on them now. Practically the entire force at Fort Gallatin was assembled on the parade ground by that time. A tiny blond fury with Francis Drummond's blue eyes assailed them. "You're cowards. Every one of you. Cowards. Cowards. Cowards! He'd go for you. You know he would. He'd go for you."

"Miranda." Ruth tugged at her arm. Emotion and fear were making her feel faint. She swayed. "Miranda, please help me."

At the appeal the girl turned. "Oh, Mama. You're sick."

"Yes, I'm sick. I need you to help me to quarters where I can lie down."

Instantly the girl put her arm around her mother's shoulder. "You're out here without a coat. You'll catch a cold."

For the first time in that dreadful hour, Ruth began to shiver. Miranda led her past the commanding officer's quarters.

Maud Mary had dragged herself to her feet and now actually stood on the porch, her arms wrapped around the supporting post. "Bring your mother in here, Miranda."

Ruth could feel Benjamin Westfall's eyes on her. Feelings that frightened her with their power, thoughts so awful that she cast them aside even as she thought

40

them, suspicions that horrified, all whirled in her brain. Beneath her heart her baby kicked. Francis's child. She had promised him that he would feel the child when he returned. Now he would never return.

"No." She spoke the word louder than she meant to. It was not an answer to Maud Mary's kindness. She modulated her voice. "No, you don't need to try to take care of me. I'll be all right. Miranda and I will be all right."

A squad of volunteers led by Adolf Lindhauer rode over the hill two hours later. There had been two hours of awful silence.

"What the hell's going on?"

One of the trappers scratched his head. "Damnedest thing I ever did see. Do you supposed they was all carried away."

Lindhauer shook his head. His butter-yellow hair fanned out around his shoulders. "The Sioux wouldn't take the corpses. They'd take the horses, if they was alive, and the guns and clothes, but they wouldn't take the corpses."

"Then where in the hell are they?"

Almost the length of the valley, they found the place where the troop had left the road. The slope up to the crest of Lodge Trail Ridge was torn by the horses' hooves.

"Looks like they went up fast," Lindhauer remarked.

"Hear that." Another man pointed to a copse of rocks. A horse whinnied weakly.

"Do we dare?"

Lindhauer shrugged. "I haven't seen anything to be afraid of yet. If we hear one whoop, or see one feather, then we hightail it back to the fort. Every man for himself and devil take the hindmost. Agreed?"

Cautiously they rode, stiff in the saddle, their shoulders hunched against the feathered death that could come at any moment from anywhere. Under the hoof of one of the horses, a stone turned and rolled clattering and knocking down the slope. They all froze, fearful that the small sound had alerted a Sioux or Cheyenne.

The shadows in the shortest day of the year were already falling when they found the first of the dead ponies. Past several half-frozen carcasses the whinnying of a horse in pain brought them to a small declivity in the ridge. On the slopes of the declivity lay more bodies of Indian ponies. And in a circle no more than forty feet in diameter somewhat protected by rocks lay the slaughtered men of the Second. Their horses lay dead around them except for a bay gelding who threw up his head and whinnied piteously.

"Jesus Christ."

One man leaned out of his saddle and vomited at the sight.

"Why'd they cut 'em up like that?"

Lindhauer spoke, his voice thick with bile he had trouble swallowing. "Mutilate the body and your enemy can't enjoy Paradise. See they're all together in it. Sioux and white. But our men"—he wiped at the corners of his eyes—"they can't see, nor taste, nor hear. They can't reach for a gun with the hand cut off, or put a foot in a stirrup. They can't take p-pleasure in a woman."

"Goddamnit."

"What are we gonna do?" The man who had been sick had managed to right himself in the saddle.

"We'll take a count, make a list of those we know and get the hell out of here."

The minutes ticked by as they hurried from body to body.

42

"This horse's got both legs broke and more'n a dozen arrows in him. Shall I shoot him?"

"Hell, no. You'll bring every hostile within hearin' back." Lindhauer's face contorted in pain and anger. "Slit its damned throat."

The other man gulped. "I can't do it."

Lindhauer drew his own knife, a wicked eighteen-inch bowie, and pushed his companion aside to put the suffering animal out of its misery. "Hell, Custis, why'd you volunteer for this detail anyway?"

"For old Hickory Joe." Tears trickled down the grizzled cheeks. "And I ain't found him neither."

"Hickory Joe Magruder." Lindhauer brightened. "If anyone could of made it, he could."

"Do you think so?" The other three gathered around him like children.

"Maybe. Leastways, he'd sure have taken a hell of a lot with him."

They looked around them. "No dead Indians here."

"But they were here." Lindhauer walked a few feet out of the circle until he came to a dark stain on the bare earth. He kicked at it with his foot. "Lot of blood spilled here."

With a wild light in their eyes, they looked beyond the bodies to the dark spots that dotted the surrounding ridge.

Custis, who had wept once, began to weep again. "Bless 'em. They sure did do us proud."

Lindhauer cleared his throat. "Everybody through."

The others nodded.

"Then mount up. We'll ride just below the skyline back to the fort. If some of our boys made it, that's the way they went."

Three

The valiant never taste of death but once.

They found the bodies of six more men in a small declivity a couple of hundred yards nearer the fort. In a circle of Indian ponies, they lay, mercilessly mutilated.

"Ah, God. Poor ol' Hickory Joe." Custis dropped to his knees beside what was left of his friend. "Oh, goddamn! Joe."

"Sergeant Long's here, too." Lindhauer shook his head. "Look at the cartridge cases. Damn! That Henry repeater was sure a fine weapon."

"If'n they'd all had 'em—"

"Bless that little lady's heart," Lindhauer interrupted, "here's Captain Drummond. Poor little Miranda."

The darkness had begun to fall. A wolf howled somewhere to the pale sliver of moon.

"We got to take Hickory Joe in, Adolf." Custis stood up. He began to pull his saddle off his tired horse.

Adolf shook his head. "They'll be all right till morning. It's so cold they're damn near frozen solid right now."

"Ring around the moon," one man offered. "Storm's coming."

44

"Yuh done heard the wolf. He's roundin' 'em up. They'll be a pack here by midnight. I ain't leavin' Joe to 'em." Solemnly, he turned to his friend. "Help me get him across my horse."

"Custis—"

"If'n yuh cared so much about that little girl, seems like yuh'd want to bring her daddy home."

Adolf cursed wearily. His friend lay at his feet. The wolf howled again, closer this time. Another answered. Following Custis's lead he stripped his good saddle off his skewbald and dropped it on the ground. It could lie there better than Francis Drummond.

"There is the very real and present danger that Red Cloud will attack the fort." Westfall looked at the faces of his staff and hastily dropped his eyes to the map. Their expressions, one and all, accused him. Reed Phillips looked as if he would do murder.

At the same time Westfall was conscious, as they were, that their numbers were shockingly reduced. The absence of Clarendon with his cocky hell-for-leather pronouncements and of Drummond with his calm analytical statements had somehow stolen their voices.

Phillips bit each word off and spat it out. "Probably so. They must think we're a bunch of lily-livered cowards. Our own men killed within hearing of the fort. Clarendon was pinned down and no effort made to rescue him."

"That will be enough, Major Phillips."

"Poor Clarendon." Another man spoke for the first time. "He wanted to come back a hero."

"He should have been," Phillips muttered.

"He disobeyed orders," Westfall announced. "Under no circumstances was he to take the men up onto Lodge Trail Ridge."

They all looked at him and then at each other. Each remembered Clarendon's bravado and Westfall's encouragement. "Come back a hero," the colonel had said. They had all heard him.

"Colonel Clarendon wouldn't deliberately disobey —" Phillips began.

"I shall so enter it in my report." Westfall folded his arms daring them to question.

Phillips's mouth tightened. He was a career man, and a career man did not lightly contradict or question a superior officer, even if he knew that the officer was clearly at fault. Now was not the time, with the very real danger that they might all be dead before the end of the week. For now he would swallow his anger. The time would come to let it out.

After a moment's sullen silence, Westfall continued, his voice for the first time betraying real concern. "On one score you are right, Major Phillips. Red Cloud will certainly be encouraged by this success."

Phillips coughed behind his hand. The colonel was a coward for sure. He had seen many like him. Soldiering a desk, shuffling papers, until someone transferred them into a situation they could not handle. "I don't think you've got much to worry about on that score. Red Cloud's no fool. He knows he can't break in without terrible loss of life. The number of ponies lost on Lodge Trail Ridge indicates —"

"But dead ponies don't mean dead braves," a younger man interrupted.

Phillips looked him straight in the eye. "Dead warriors would have been carried away. Many fell without losing their ponies. Clarendon and Drummond gave a damn good account of themselves."

"I only meant —"

"You are correct, Major Phillips." Here Westfall could see a possibility for alleviating the situation. He relaxed slightly. "Our men gave a good account of themselves. The troop will receive a citation."

"And Captain Drummond." Suddenly, the major was remembering the way Westfall had danced with Ruth Drummond a few nights ago. He took a deep breath and let it out slowly. Such a suspicion was monstrous.

"Of course. He was leading some of his men back to the fort when they caught him. He will certainly receive a citation." Westfall did not notice the new light in the eyes of his second in command. He looked around at them all for approval. "And others as well. Sergeant Long, for example. The point is that the good account was given. Still Red Cloud might try an attack."

"Against the howitzer, sir?"

Westfall tugged at his pointed beard. "We are probably safe enough for the time being. However, I propose to send messengers to Fort Laramie to ask for relief."

"As soon as the storm abates."

The howling wind had found all the chinks in the log structure. The officers wore not only their uniforms, but their heavy overcoats as well. Outside on the posts, the guards drew only half-hour watches on rotation. Longer would have meant the man might freeze to death.

"Of course, the storm. Red Cloud will not attack in the storm. He would lose more men to the elements than to bullets."

"Did Daddy give a good account, Mr. Lindhauer?"

Awkwardly, the German knelt in front of Miranda, taking her hands in his. His son White Wolf's Brother stood at his shoulder. The boy's eyes were swollen from crying. "He gave the best account, Miss Miranda. The best account."

"Did they hate him when he died?"

He blinked. Her eyes were dry. Her lips tight and pinched. She looked like Francis Drummond. The stern little face had been stripped of childlike character. "Well, I don't suppose they liked him much."

"Did they" — she swallowed — "hurt his body?"

Adolf shot a look over his shoulder at his son. The boy was so blond like himself that he frequently forgot that his son had a Cheyenne mother. "What've you been telling her?"

The boy drew back at the anger in his father's eyes.

"He's told me what the Indians believe about their dead."

Adolf looked back at the stern little face. "Miranda, you just remember your daddy the way he was."

"Don't worry about that. I always will. But I want to know what happened to him."

Adolf shook his head. Rising to his feet, he set his big square hands on her shoulders. "He's dead. He was killed. And he took a lot of his enemies with him."

She looked up at him, her eyes accusing. "You won't tell me."

He shook his head. He looked at Ruth. "I'm sorry, Mrs. Drummond. I don't know what else to say."

Ruth had regained her courage. She and Francis had discussed what she must do in the event that this happened. "You've made us both feel better, Mr. Lindhauer. We know all we need to know. F-Francis fought bravely and died as a good soldier should. He was very good at his job."

"That he was, ma'am." Lindhauer put his arm around his son's shoulders. "We'll be going now."

"Get a well-deserved rest." Ruth followed him to the door. "You were brave to go out and bring him back."

"He would have done the same for me." Lindhauer

and White Wolf's Brother hunched their shoulders and plunged out into the raging blizzard.

Miranda knew the way to the hospital. She passed it every day. Still walking along in bright sunshine was quite different from fighting her way through roaring wind and whirling snow. People had become lost in Wyoming blizzards and died only a few feet from their own doorsteps. She had heard the cautionary stories in Adolf's store. She had shivered in horror and nodded solemnly as she promised never to go out.

She could not see the building through the window. Still she knew it was there. Her father's body and Hickory Joe's had been taken there.

She had to see him.

Major Phillips's wife and a friend of hers were sitting up with Ruth. Miranda could not hear their soft voices over the howling wind, but she knew they were there.

People were with her mother, but no one was with her daddy. She could not leave him there alone. Shivering, she dressed in layer upon layer of clothing. Noiselessly, she slipped out of her room and into the back of the house. Since the front door faced north, the back would be in the lee. She could go out without the wind blowing too much in.

The very house itself was cold. She was feeling the bite on her nose even before she slipped outside. If she followed the path — But there was no path — only drifting snow knee-deep.

The night was white. Utter whiteness cloaking the blackness. No moon, no stars. She threw a look over her shoulder. The house had disappeared. Immediately, she faced front. Straight on. Straight on to the headquarters, then turn to the left. She could not miss headquarters. It was too wide. She did not think how she would get back.

The icy cold blasted through her clothing, through her boots. She wiggled her toes with each step. *Wiggle your toes, so your feet won't freeze.*

A light pierced the whiteness. Headquarters. She found the porch with her hand. Following the edge, she came to the corner. As she walked she had been trying to think how many long steps to the hospital. Twenty? Twenty-five?

Ducking her head she plunged forward, counting out loud. Before she had gone ten steps, she saw the light.

Someone must be there. She would be discovered. Would he tell? She had no choice. She could not retrace her steps. She could only go forward.

Once on the porch she hesitated fractionally. Surely, if she told whoever was in there, what she had come for, he would not deny her. Her mittens slipped on the frozen knob, gripped again, turned it.

The wind blasted the door open and pushed her into the room. The flame wavered, then steadied in the chimney of the kerosene lamp. Miranda pushed the door closed, then slumped back against it, eyes closed, shoulders hunched, shivering uncontrollably.

After long minutes she realized she was alone. Fearfully, she looked around her. An ordinary desk stood on her left, a couple of chairs, another desk in the center of the room, and behind it a long table with a long line of thick black books, the light faintly glimmering on the gold lettering on their spines. No fire showed through the grate of the rounded stove. The room seemed warm only in comparison to the outside.

An open archway yawned black on the left and a closed door across the room. Crossing to the lamp, she lifted it. The kerosene sloshed in the well and the flame sank. Lowering it, she turned it higher.

Her father. She had come to see her father. The quest had become more than a whim. It had become necessity. Until she saw him, she could not believe he was dead. Adolf could have made a mistake. He might be out on the trail somewhere, hurt, in desperate trouble, trusting in her to rescue him.

Just before the arch she halted, hearing the sound of snores. A man or men were sleeping in there. Sick soldiers lay in their cots in the hospital. Probably the orderly had gone to bed there also.

She tiptoed silently back to the desk and then behind it to the closed door. The doorknob was so cold it was a shock to her fingers. Resolutely, she turned it and pushed. The room behind it was dark, very cold, and empty except for a couple of sturdy tables, higher than ordinary, and a washtub.

Shuddering so that the flame wavered and the kerosene sloshed, she hurried through the surgery. At its end was another door. At first when she opened it, she thought the room behind it was empty. Fearfully, she raised the lamp aloft. Then she saw them—three blanket-wrapped forms side by side on the floor.

Her heart beating fast, she approached them. What if she had to look under each blanket? She had never seen a dead man before, much less three dead men. Even as she hesitated, she recognized Adolf Lindhauer's distinctive red and black saddle blanket. Her father lay beneath it.

Her teeth were chattering as she went down on her knees and set the lamp down by his shoulder. In the dimness she saw something white and leaned forward. His bare feet thrust out from one end. The sight brought the tears streaming. Her father's feet were frozen. No one had bothered to cover them. For several minutes she stared at the body.

Then with shaking hands she pushed the blanket aside.

Despite the need for quiet, she could not hold back the thin scream. He had been scalped. A knife had slashed just above his hairline and his blood had clotted in the remaining fringe to turn it brown. His eyes were set open and black, the iris muscle relaxed so that the pupil filled the space. His mouth pulled back from his teeth as if he grinned in death.

"Daddy," she whispered.

Beneath the point of the jaw a jagged cut began a second dark mouth. With trembling hand, she pulled the blanket farther down. His head had been almost severed from his body.

"Oh, Daddy. They hated you. They hated you. They hated you." Like a mantra she recited the words as the sight imprinted itself in her brain. It was a sight she would carry to her grave.

When the rushing tears had obliterated everything, she sank forward, her forehead pressed to her knees. Her grief welled out of her. A river of tears, harsh sobs shaking her entire body. He was really dead. The Indians had killed him. Knowing him to be a great warrior, they had tried to destroy his spirit as well. Just as White Wolf's Brother had told her.

She might have lost consciousness; she might have only cried mindlessly. Hands closed over her shoulders, lifted her.

"What y' doin' here?"

She looked into the bearded face of a young, frightened soldier, the orderly.

"You ain't supposed to be in here. What y' doing?"

She shook her head wearily. "My father—" she croaked. She had cried away her voice.

"Jiminy. Y're the captain's daughter."

"I had to see him."

52

"But, miss, he ain't no fit sight for a lady."

The tears welled again. "He's my father."

The orderly was a boy, only five years older than she. He looked over her shoulder at the mutilated face. His own face turned green. He snatched up the lamp and caught her by her arm. "Come on. Let's get outta here."

She followed docilely. She had done what she had come to do, seen what she had come to see. Her first tearing grief had expended itself.

He shut the door to the surgery and bent over to poke up the fire in the round stove. When it blazed up, he came back to her. "How'd y' get here?"

"I walked."

He glanced toward the window. "Walked? Y're crazy."

"I'll leave."

"No! My god, no. You ain't goin' anywheres until it's light enough out there to see."

She thought about that for a minute. "But if my mother finds me gone, she'll be worried."

"Y' should of thought about that 'fore y' came," he told her sternly.

"I thought I could slip back in just like I slipped out—without her knowing. I know I can if you'll just let me go." His homely presence was reassuring her, driving the terrible thoughts out of the front of her mind.

He crossed his arms over his chest. "I ain't lettin' y' outta here till the storm lets up or daylight, whichever comes first."

She looked at the clock on the wall. "It's a long time. Please let me go. I found my way over. I'm sure I can find my way back."

He shook his head. "Jist sit y'rself down by the fire. The minute it clears off enough to see I'll

53

take y' myself."

"You don't have to do that. I'm sure—"

He pointed to the chair beside the stove. "Sit down!" She dropped into it.

They sat in awkward silence for several minutes. He looked at her somberly. "I'm sorry about y'r pa."

"Thank you."

"I guess y'll be goin' back east soon."

She had not thought about that. "I guess so. My mother's folks live in Chicago. My father"—she choked, but recovered—"my father's people are all dead."

"He was a brave one."

"Thank you."

"The scoutin' party just brought in three bodies— him and two others. Shows y' how much they thought of him."

"Yes."

"It's too bad. None of us know why so many officers went on that trip anyway."

She had been staring into the heart of the fire, allowing it to mesmerize her as its heat warmed her chilled body. His words slid slowly into her numb mind. "What did you say?"

He shrugged. "Jist that we can't figure why so many officers went?"

"He was ordered."

"Yes'm."

The orderly had folded his arms across his chest. She could see he did not really care to know the answer to the question he himself had raised. Suddenly she wanted to know very much. Unfortunately, she knew he could not tell her.

"We'll be leaving on the first wagon train."

"My dear Ruth." Westfall put his hand on her arm. "There's no need for you to do so. You and Miranda must stay with Maud Mary and me. You won't be crowding us at all. It can't be good for you to travel with the baby coming."

She turned away to pace the office, more to avoid contact with him than from any nervous compulsion. "I must leave. You know the regulations."

"But I'm the base commander. I can make allowances for you."

She shook her head. "I don't want favoritism. Francis wouldn't have wanted it for me. Besides, I want to go home. To be back in Chicago when my baby is born. My mother and father will help me."

Westfall watched her, his eyes angry. He had not counted on her being so stubborn. "You might lose the baby."

She gave him a withering look. "The post doctor has already said that he's not equipped nor prepared to perform anything but the most routine delivery. I'm taking less chance traveling now than I would if I were to stay."

"To take a young girl out in this weather—"

"Miranda is healthy as a young goat. Are you forgetting she walked through the blizzard to the hospital the night Francis died? I still get sick thinking how close she came to being lost. But she didn't suffer. I was the one who almost died when I found her gone."

Westfall frowned. "She's a handful. All the more reason to stay here. You'll need someone with a firm hand. Someone with authority to keep her in line. I'll be happy to stand in for— That is, I'll be happy to help you. You shouldn't take on all that responsibility yourself."

Ruth shuddered. "Don't you see? I must get her out of here. She spent the night in the hospital with an orderly and a couple of sick men. Anything could have happened."

"She ought to have been whipped for doing something so stupid."

Ruth wrung her hands. "But she had her reasons. They were awful reasons, but they're part of the problem. She had to see her father's body. Adolf's son had told her that the more severely mutilated the bodies were, the more they were hated and feared. She wanted to see the honor done to her father's body." She began to laugh shakily.

Westfall cursed fluidly.

"The sooner I get her away from here, the sooner she'll begin to lead a normal life."

"The cold—"

Ruth shook her head. "When the supply train leaves, Miranda and I are leaving with it."

She started for the door, but Westfall was there ahead of her to bar her way. "Ruth."

"Don't! For heaven's sake." She held up a pleading hand.

He caught it and drew it in against his chest. "Ruth, you must know how I feel about you."

"Colonel Westfall—"

"Benjamin. Please call me Benjamin."

"No."

"I don't ask you to love me now. Of course you cannot. I wouldn't honor you if you did."

"I loved Francis with all my heart."

"Of course you did. You were ever his brave, his gallant wife. Never complaining, making a home for him on the wild frontier. Cheerful, loving, a companion as well as a wife."

"*You* have a wife."

He looked at her with liquid eyes, taking her other hand and clasping them together between his. "Maud

Mary and I have been together for over twenty years."

Ruth stared at him, her face revealing her disgust and amazement. "Then how can you speak to me like this?"

He smiled. "Like what? Have I said one word I shouldn't? I've only asked you to stay so that I — an old friend — may help you."

She shook her head. "I'm confused. Please let me go. Please let me."

Keeping her hands imprisoned in one of his, he slid his arm around her waist. "I only ask that I be allowed to offer a shoulder to comfort you. Every officer feels most keenly the suffering of the wives and children of the men who fall under his command."

"Colonel Westfall." She looked up at him through a mist of tears.

"I would feel better about our friendship if you would call me Benjamin."

She hesitated. She was so miserable and so afraid. She bowed her head. "Benjamin."

He sighed. His smile flicked up the corners of his mouth. "That's right. Oh, Ruth, how I want to be your friend."

"Then you'll help me to leave?"

"Ruth, why don't you just leave everything to me?" He drew her in until she was leaning against his chest. He could feel her body trembling against him. He tightened his arms fractionally. Her breasts, enlarged from her pregnancy, pressed against him as did her belly. She was rounded and soft, not yet ungainly as she would be in her last months, the perfect figure of a woman. He dropped a light kiss upon the top of her head.

The thermometer inside the wagon dropped to forty

below and then the mercury froze in the bulb.

"Sit back under here with me," Ruth commanded as Miranda knelt up to stare through the peephole in the back of the supply wagon.

"There's buffalo out there. They're wallowing in the snow. Hundreds and hundreds of buffalo."

"They won't bother you, if you don't bother them." Ruth half sat, half lay on a pallet in the wagon. Her daughter scooted into a place beside her and she wrapped them both snugly in the buffalo robes. "Stick your feet down against the little stove, so you won't get frostbite."

"Are we going to freeze to death?" Miranda blew a fog breath into the air.

Ruth closed her eyes wearily. She would not be surprised. For her daughter she said, "We'll make it. The men won't let us freeze."

"How can they stand it?" She was thinking of the driver on the wagon seat.

"They're brave and strong. They got through with the supplies. Now they're going back. And we're going with them." Ruth began to feel drowsy. Was she really freezing? She did not feel as though she were. She gathered her daughter more tightly against her side.

"I don't see why we couldn't wait at least a month."

Ruth thought of Benjamin Westfall. Twice, he had come to her quarters late at night on the pretext of sitting with her, so she would not be alone with her thoughts. She pressed her daughter more tightly against her. "A month wouldn't have made it any better. I have to get you home. Back to Chicago."

"But Mama—"

The baby kicked strongly against her side. "Did you feel that?"

"Oh, yes."

"Your little brother or sister is halfway here. If I wait

58

even six weeks more, I'll be too big to travel. I want him or her to be born at home, just like you were." Ruth kissed Miranda's cold forehead. Sometimes she put too much onto her daughter's young shoulders. Now was one of those times. "I don't want my baby born in the place where its father died."

"Oh." Beneath the buffalo robe, Miranda slipped a gloved hand out of her mitten and laid it on her mother's stomach. The baby kicked again, more strongly. She smiled. "I hope it's a baby brother."

"I hope so, too."

"Whatever it is, it will look just like Daddy, won't it?"

Ruth closed her eyes against the tears. She seemed to have an unending supply. "I wish it would with all my heart," she murmured, as Francis Drummond's face smiled at her on the backs of her eyelids. "I wish it with all my heart."

Act Two
Chicago, 1869

Four

One may smile, and smile, and be a villain.

"Love is a smoke rais'd with the fume of sighs; being purg'd, a fire sparkling in lovers' eyes."

Miranda leaned forward in her seat; her mouth dropped open; her moist palms pressed against her thighs careless of the delicate silk of her skirt. She had never seen a more beautiful man in her entire life. To her it seemed that for all of her sixteen years she had been waiting, sleeping, and dreaming of him and him alone—the man who posed on the stage in front of her.

Raven black hair, long and wavy, brushed the shoulders of his maroon velvet doublet. Black black eyes seemed to find her face in the audience, to speak a line of love just to her before moving on. Silver gray trunk hose covered his long legs, his calves and thigh muscles clearly defined beneath the clinging material. He smiled.

Her heart stepped up its beating.

His teeth flashed white before he spoke. *"I have lost myself; I am not here; this is not Romeo. In sadness, cousin, I do love a woman."*

Miranda swallowed hard. A man so beautiful. Of course, he would love a woman. Her heart fluttered

63

as she struggled to control her disappointment.

He pivoted. His arm swept up to the audience in the balcony. The slashed maroon and silver gray fell away exposing a white silk sleeve with lace and ribbons cascading from the wrist. His fingers curved as if to caress. *"She'll not be hit with Cupid's arrow."*

Miranda put her hand to her burning cheek. The girl he loved did not love him. She could hardly believe that anyone could be so stupid. He was the most beautiful man in the world. He turned back to face his friend and she caught a glint of gold. He wore an earring in his left ear. She could not get enough air into her lungs. She was going to faint. The corset that her mother had made her wear had seemed nothing when she had been laced into it. Now she felt it clamp her ribs like a vise.

Unable to forget the girl whom he loved, Romeo left the stage distraught, followed by his friend. Miranda slumped back fighting for breath. Her heart was pounding, her blood singing in her veins. She pressed her hands to her burning cheeks. Thank heavens the theater was dark.

Oh, mercy.

She bobbed forward again. He strode back on to discover that the girl he loved was going to a supper that he could not attend. His family was fighting with another family.

Miranda could feel herself begin to sweat. She wanted to rise and beg him not to go. He would be in deadly danger. When he left the stage vowing to go alone, she clenched her hands in her lap and gathered her feet under her. Her fighting blood was up.

Fortunately, the next scene was between a couple of women. Miranda was able to relax and look around her. She did not bother to strain to understand their words. Some of them she had never heard before, and they were put together in such strange order that she sometimes had to guess what the people were trying to say. Rather than take the trouble, she took the opportunity to remind herself that she was attending a play, the first one she had ever attended. Of course, actors on a stage did not talk like real people. Romeo was played by an actor.

Her feelings about the evening were mixed. The procurer of the tickets for herself and her mother was none other than Col. Benjamin Westfall. When he had appeared in her grandparents' parlor, she had been surprised and suspicious. Since the terrible Christmas of three years ago, she had tried to forget everything that had happened. Except her father. She would never forget him.

Evidently, Colonel Westfall had not forgotten them. His own wife was dead and he had come to find her mother to take her to the theater. That he had included Miranda in the invitation had been at her mother's insistence. Life in Chicago with Ruth's parsimonious parents had not offered many opportunities to broaden Miranda's cultural horizons.

In the spill from the footlights, Miranda found wrinkles in her skirt. She must have clutched it during the last scene. Hastily, she tried to smooth them. It had been her mother's dress, hastily made over so Miranda would have something grown up to wear. It was delicate silk. Miranda pressed it out on her thigh, hoping she had not ruined it.

The conversation on the stage caught her attention. The girl was only fourteen years old, two years younger than Miranda. Her mother had told her she was going to be married.

Miranda smiled. This play was going to be like her mother's novels that she read surreptitiously. She had it all figured out now. The girl would meet and marry the beautiful man who was coming to the party.

Sure enough only a few scenes later, Romeo took the girl's hand. *"My lips, two blushing pilgrims, ready stand to smooth that rough touch with a tender kiss."*

Miranda felt the kiss to the bottom of her soul. She must have sighed aloud because her mother nudged her in the ribs and the woman in the seat in front shifted irritably. Thereafter, Miranda sat up very straight and tried not to get caught up in the story.

They did get married in secret, of course, just as men and girls did in her mother's romances.

Then, Romeo was challenged to a duel with swords. He stripped off his jacket, and his shirt was open down the front almost to his waist. He had black hair on his chest which made Miranda blush and peek through her fingers. But when he began to fight he was so swift, so graceful, so strong, so dangerous, that she forgot everything but her fear for him and his beauty.

Unfortunately, he had killed the girl's cousin, so the end of the play was not as she had guessed. The stupid girl pretended to poison herself. When Romeo thought she was dead, he killed himself. *"Here's to my love."*

Miranda thought her heart would break.

Romeo clutched at his throat and then at his heart. He sank to his knees. *"O true apothecary! Thy drugs are quick. Thus with a kiss I die."*

Tears that had started as a stray trickle became a flood. She was sick with the thought of him — so beautiful, so strong, so young — so in love that he could not bear to live. Not Romeo. She had forgotten Romeo. The handsome actor had become a real person merging himself into the person of his character until she had fallen hopelessly in love.

Ruth Drummond smiled apologetically at Benjamin Westfall as she pushed her own handkerchief into her daughter's hand. "She's never seen a play before," she murmured. "The seats were wonderful, but I think a little too close. A bit farther away and she might have been able to control herself better."

He nodded with a show of understanding. "I take it from her tears that she enjoyed it."

"I think she did. Did you enjoy it, Miranda?" Ruth prompted.

She shook her head, mopping at her eyes. "It was too sad."

The actors came forward to take their final curtain calls. Members of the audience were already filing up the aisles. Miranda rose transfixed to look up into the face of the actor as he bowed over the footlights. She had not applauded once, only sat stunned, weeping. Now ushers were passing down the aisles lighting the lamps. She did not feel her mother pull gently at her arm. Instead, she swayed toward Romeo, one hand half extended.

The actor looked down into her eyes. His smile was wide, his teeth flashing white under the trim black mustache. He winked at her.

Suddenly, she felt wonderful. He was alive. It had only been a play after all. But Shreve Catherwood was the most wonderful actor and the most handsome man she had ever seen.

"I have waited for your tears to dry, my dear Ruth."

"Benjamin, I don't —"

"You can't have any objections now," he reminded her. "There are no obstacles. The fact that I've come here should demonstrate that I want to marry you." A portrait of supreme confidence, he stood straight and tall, heels together, shoulders back. His neatly trimmed beard was gray with a snow-white streak to the right of his mouth. His hair likewise was gray, his hairline receding at the temples. Although he would be considered distinguished, his cheeks were slightly sunken and deep parallel lines grooved his forehead between his eyes.

Ruth bowed her head to conceal the tumult of emotions. Like destiny he had appeared on her doorstep. He was at least twenty years older than she, an old man really. Was his body as old as his face? She could not forget Francis's young, sleek body nor the terrible days before and after Francis's death.

"Ruth." Westfall's voice sounded unnaturally loud in her ears. "You must consent. Think what I can offer you."

In three years, she had met no one else. For fourteen years she had lived the challenge, the sheer excitement of the frontier life with Francis Drummond. Abruptly, she had been forced into a lonely bed at night and an intolerable sameness that her parents considered well-ordered. Many a night she had believed her spirit had died and lay in the grave beside Francis in the valley in Wyoming.

Benjamin Westfall put his arm around her. She closed her eyes as actual pain slid beneath the skin of her thighs. He was tall and strong. He smelled like a man. Her father smelled of the cedar press in which her mother kept his clothing.

His warm breath brushed her hair. She shivered. He felt the slight tremor beneath his fingertips. Lips to her ear, he whispered, "I'll take care of you as you should be taken care of."

"Benjamin, I —"

His fingers splayed across her shoulder, pressing her close, caressing her. "We'll have a house of our own. You won't be living in your parents' house on their charity which I can only guess has not been generous. Your daughter, that beautiful child, had never been to a play until last night. I can give her and her baby sister so many advantages. I can give you so many advantages."

Ruth felt tears prick her eyelids. Since Francis's death, not only Miranda but she as well had had little. Her parents, though well positioned in society, had little real wealth. Lately, her mother had delegated more and more household chores to Ruth as if she regarded her daughter as some sort of unpaid servant.

Her father insisted that she turn her small widow's pension over to him to manage for her. From it he dispensed a meager, grudging allowance. He never tired of telling her that her marriage to the young West Point officer had been ill considered. Marriages for love very seldom benefitted the parties involved. On the other hand, if Colonel Westfall offered for her, her father would consider that marriage a different matter entirely.

In that minute she decided. Still she delayed. She would play a close game. Her pride demanded that she not appear too eager. "I must think about it. It's a big step."

"Don't." He caught her shoulders and shook her gently. "Don't think. Be daring. Be brave. I remember your bravery, Ruth. You were a perfect soldier's wife. You can be again."

She shook her head. "I doubt that very seriously. When I married Francis, I was a young girl eager for adventure. I didn't mind hardships so much. Now that I'm a matron of thirty-four, I want my creature comforts." She smiled up at him. "I couldn't stand a trip over the frozen wasteland with the thermometer at forty-below."

He assumed a stern demeanor. "I should never have permitted you to make that trip. I will always regret that you left as you did. No one will ever ask that of you again."

The time had come for plain speaking. She stepped out of his embrace and faced him soberly. "Why do you want to marry me, Benjamin?"

A small smile lifted his thin lips. "You won't believe that I love you. That I've always loved you."

She shook her head unsmiling. "I believe that you wanted me once."

He nodded. "I did that."

"But I don't believe that you loved me then." She watched him closely. "And I don't believe that you love me now."

He spread his hands helplessly. "I had hoped to be so romantic. And here you are demanding the truth."

"I would prefer it."

"Very well. You shall have it." He guided her to a chair and seated her in it. When she was comfortable, he took a deep breath with the air of a man unburdening himself. "I need you to marry me."

She started. "But why?"

He began to pace around the room. She followed him with her eyes, noting how his face reddened. His mouth beneath the neatly trimmed mustache worked agitatedly. "The business with Clarendon has never died. Reed Phillips—damn his eyes—has never let it. I have defended myself before a court-martial and won, but still it haunts me."

"But what can anyone say? You made a decision that you thought was for the greater good."

He dropped into a chair beside hers and took her hands. "You see that, do you? Thank the Lord. You remember what a glory-hunter Clarendon was. You remember how he was ordered not to ride after the Sioux. If there was blame, it lay with him. Not with me. You can see that even though your husband died so tragically. But others call me coward, say I should have ridden out to rescue them,

70

risked the entire troop and perhaps the fort itself."

"Oh, Benjamin."

He rose again, a man possessed, pacing back and forth across the rug, repeating the story to himself as he must have done time and time again. "And the stupidity of the whole thing is that the fort is gone, burned by the Sioux as the army deserted it. The trail it was to guard is closed by treaty with that murdering Red Cloud." His face darkened with fury. "It should never be. I stand condemned in men's eyes while those savages are free to overrun the land."

"But what can I do?"

He swooped toward her. "Don't you see? You can marry me. Your presence as my wife will smother the gossip. If you forgive me, Phillips will look a perfect fool."

Ruth dropped her eyes to her lap. Did she forgive him? It was over three years ago. And she had tried not to think about it. As the hurt had faded, so had the half-formed suspicions. She had even forgotten about Clarendon's glory-hunting. If anyone was to blame for Francis's death, it was he. Yet it all seemed so long ago. She made a helpless gesture. "Are you sure that all this is necessary?"

He drew back and spread his arms. "You have noticed—I am sure—that I have the same rank. I should have made brigadier by now, but I have been passed over. With your approval tacit in your marriage to me, my superiors will take notice." Now he came to stand over her. The intensity of his burning gaze made her drop her own. She could see only the polished toes of his shoes. "It will be the making of my new career."

She had not forgotten the rate of promotion in the army, nor the reasons why some men were never promoted. How ironic that she had allowed herself to be pursued by this man rather than ruining Francis's chances! Now she was being called upon to save another career.

She sighed at the death of a little romantic dream. When he had written begging to visit her, when he had first appeared at the door, carrying flowers, taking her and her daughter to the theater, she had held out hope that perhaps the embarrassing declaration that he had made to her three years ago had been the truth.

So much for love. He had not really remembered her with undying emotion. His wife had died at last, his reputation had been blackened by his constituency, and he had thought of Ruth Drummond as a possibility for making everything right again. She folded her hands together, covering the gold wedding band that Francis had given her. It had never been off her finger. "Will you please come back tomorrow?" She raised her eyes. "I must discuss this with Miranda."

He frowned incredulously. "But she's a child!"

Ruth remembered that he had no children. Undoubtedly, intimacy would be expected of her. She smiled wanly. "She's almost grown. Sixteen."

He opened his mouth to speak, thought better of it, and abruptly closed it, pressing his lips together.

She rose and escorted him to the door. There she placed her hand on his arm, touching him for the first time voluntarily. "Please try to understand. My older daughter has been a great comfort to me in these past three years. She's taken so much of the responsibility of raising Rachel onto her young shoulders. I was so unhappy for so long. Without her, I would have lost heart."

He smiled stiffly as he lifted her hand to his lips. He could never forget the child who had been the first to call him coward. "I suggest that you don't let our future rest in the hands of a sixteen-year-old girl. She loves you as she should. But will you consider this? In all likelihood given the romantic tears she shed last night, she will be marrying in a couple of years. What will you do then?"

Ruth struggled with that frightening thought. "I had hoped she would go to school."

"An excellent idea. A good girls' school would be very wise. And also very expensive." She saw the pained expression flit across his face. "And I can be by your side to ease the way."

She bowed her head. "I hadn't thought about that."

"Don't ask her permission," he said with the air of one issuing a command. "Just tell her what we have decided. Believe that she will want you to be happy again."

Miranda stared at her mother as if Ruth had suddenly grown a second head. "He wants you to marry him!"

Ruth smiled tremulously. "That's right. He wants to take care of you and Rachel and me. Miranda, listen to me. He's a well-to-do man. He can take us to the theater often. You enjoyed the theater when we went the other night."

"The play was sad."

"But some plays are not," Ruth rushed on desperately. "Some are funny. Some are romantic and heroic. Some are nothing but music and dancing with people wearing beautiful costumes. You'll get to see all different kinds."

"I don't think I care that much about seeing plays."

"It's not only plays. Listen, sweetheart, he's offered to help me send you to school. You will learn all the things you need to know to be a wonderful wife for a fine ambitious young man. He'll be a father to you and a husband to me."

Miranda stared aghast at her mother's flushed face.

Instantly, Ruth dropped her eyes. "But he's so old."

"I'm not so very young myself."

Miranda's frown deepened as memories long buried arose like ghosts from the corners of her mind. The day her father had died, they had all heard the shots. Wellington had come back with an arrow in his shoulder. More shots had been fired. Her father and Hickory Joe.

She had begged and begged, but Benjamin Westfall had refused to order the men to ride to the rescue. Her young jaw set. "He's a coward."

Ruth hunched her shoulders. "No. Don't say that. He's not. Oh, no. You mustn't say that."

"It's the truth."

"You can't know that."

"I remember."

The face Ruth raised to her daughter was drained of color. Even her lips were white. "You were too young to understand," she pleaded desperately. "He had more responsibilities than just F-Francis, your father. He had to think of us all. If he had left the fort undefended, we might all have died."

"They were on their way back. White Wolf's Brother told me. His father found them a long way from the others. If that coward had ridden out and rescued them, then they could have come back and help him defend the fort."

Ruth put her hands over her ears. "I've forgotten all that," she wailed. Tears began to trickle down her cheeks. "I don't want to remember. It doesn't help to remember. It won't bring Francis back."

Miranda clenched her fists against her mother's distress. "He could have saved my daddy. But he was a coward."

"He wasn't," Ruth denied steadfastly. She did not dare think as Miranda was thinking. The course of

74

those thoughts would lead to others far worse. She began to sob in earnest. "And anyway, none of that has anything to do with me. Nor you. We had no control over what those men did so long ago."

"Mother—" Miranda put her arms around her mother's shoulders. "Please. I didn't mean to upset you. Don't cry so."

"You don't understand." Ruth's voice rose. Like a dam bursting, the feelings she had repressed for the sake of her daughters, for her own sanity, came pouring out. "You don't know how it was. You were just a child. We could have been raped and scalped by the Sioux."

"Mother, please."

Ruth tried to swallow her sobs, but they were too powerful to hold in. "I know you saw your father's body. Well, think about this. What happened to him could have happened to you and me. And Rachel would never have been born."

For long minutes the older woman sobbed her heart out in her daughter's arms. At last she managed to get herself under control.

Miranda tried once more. "Mother, I don't think you should have seen him at all. Look how upset he's made you. You can't marry him. He's bad for you."

Ruth's face hardened. "That's enough, Miranda. I don't want to hear you say another word against him."

"But, Mother—"

Ruth rose. The tears for Francis were forgotten before they had dried on her face. "I didn't want to say this to you because when I'm done you'll think badly of me. So far you've been able to live your life in black and white. You think in those terms—like a child. You're too young to see compromise and accommodation."

"Mother, I'm not a child."

"Then don't behave like one. Just listen." Ruth threw back her shoulders. "I've lived here with my mother and father for three years. But I don't want to live here any longer. I've been absolutely miserable for every day of those three long years."

"Mother!"

"Surprised, aren't you? I'm glad to hear that. At least all that acting I've been doing hasn't been wasted." Ruth smiled grimly. "I love my mother and father and I honor them. But they drive me absolutely crazy."

"We could move," Miranda pleaded weakly.

"Oh, yes. We could move. We could live in a tiny little cottage somewhere on a miserable back street. That's all your father's pension would entitle us to. I'd remake my dresses for you until finally I wouldn't have any more garments to remake and we would have to dress you out of the poor box. We'd go to church on Sunday and that would be all. We would never receive an invitation to anyone's house. And you would never meet anyone fit for you to marry."

"I'm too young to get married."

Ruth caught her daughter by the shoulders. "But you won't be much longer. I married your father when I was seventeen. Seventeen! You'll be seventeen in just a year. Don't you understand? The way your grandfather keeps us tied here on his charity—" Here her voice fairly dripped bitterness. "You've never been to the theater, and it's only a mile from the house. And when you finally got to go, you had to wear a dress that was old when your father died."

"I don't mind."

"I mind!"

"But this man—"

Ruth swiped her fingers across her cheeks. "I'm going to marry him. He'll take care of me and you and

Rachel. And anyway. You're already sixteen years old. Soon you'll be leaving me to start a home of your own."

Miranda stumbled back, as her mother brushed past her and hurried from the room.

When Benjamin came that night, Ruth was dressed in her newest dress, a pale gray polished cotton, since her period of mourning was officially over. She had spent the afternoon pacing the floor. Her anxiety had grown. Now that she had made up her mind, she was desperate to marry him. What if he had changed his mind? What if he did not come? More than once, she was tempted to send her father's single servant with a summons.

By the time Westfall came into the parlor, she was near collapse. The hands she held out to him trembled with relief. Her voice shook. "Benjamin Westfall, I will marry you."

"Ruth." He held her at arm's length staring into her eyes that glittered with barely controlled tears. Then he smiled thinly. "I have waited long to hear you say that." He pulled her into his embrace, kissing her firmly on the mouth. When they broke apart, he was still smiling. "I take it your daughter was agreeable."

"Not exactly. But I hope she'll see reason."

"Perhaps if I talked to her—"

She shook her head. "I think we should give her time to adjust to the idea."

"Then shall I speak to your father?"

Ruth smiled for the first time. "Yes. I should like you to speak to my father and my mother as well. And I want to be with you when you do. I'm going to enjoy the sight of their faces."

Five

Few love to hear the sins they love to act.

"You should go away. You're not good for my mother. Last night she cried so hard she made herself sick."

Benjamin Westfall scowled into Miranda's determined face. Short of stature and running to flesh around the waist, he was barely an inch taller than Francis Drummond's daughter. He cleared his throat gruffly. "Women cry for a number of reasons. One of them is happiness. I suspect she felt wholehearted relief that she wouldn't have to bear the burden of you and your sister alone any longer."

Miranda lifted her chin imperiously. "I am not a burden. Neither is my sister. I take care of Rachel."

He held up a placating hand. "Responsibility, then."

"Our mother loves us."

"Of course, she does." His sigh was exaggerated. He was bored with the interview already. Why was he wasting his time arguing with some stupid child? Ruth had consented. Her parents had been almost insultingly happy to hear that their daughter was going to marry and leave their house. They had even hinted that an early spring wedding would not come too soon.

"Mother loved my daddy," the girl continued, her blue eyes flashing.

Westfall stiffened; his eyes narrowed. Mention of any of the men who had died with Clarendon put him on the defensive. "No one said that she didn't. To marry again is not to say that the first spouse was unloved. Quite the contrary. It shows how happy the surviving partner was with the first."

"My father was wonderful."

Try a little sugar for the annoying little fly. Westfall locked his hands behind him and assumed a semi-official stance. "I remember him well. He was a good soldier."

"He received a medal."

"At my recommendation. I cited his gallantry on the field." *Let her chew on that.* His statement silenced Miranda, but her eyes remained cold.

Hoping he had mollified her somewhat, Westfall played his trump card. "Your mother will have a life of luxury. I'm a wealthy man." He snapped his mouth closed on that statement. He would be damned if he would discuss his financial situation with this child. He did not require her permission. The longer he stood there, the more he felt like some pimpled swain begging a hostile parent for his daughter's hand.

Miranda sniffed. "We have everything we need right here." She was lying, but she tamped down her conscience. Under no circumstances should her mother marry this man. "We're all very happy."

Westfall shook his head. "Perhaps you believe you've got everything you need. After all, you've never known anything but privation and want."

"We're happy," she insisted stubbornly.

"You could be happier. So happy that you and your sister will look back on all this as a bad dream. You and

79

she can have the very best. Beautiful clothes. Good schools. A chance to meet young men of consequence."

"I'm too young to be thinking about men."

"But you'll be seventeen very soon. And your mother is very concerned about your prospects. She and I have already discussed them."

She knew he was telling the truth. Her mother had said much the same thing to her. Still she could not forget her hatred for this man. Arguing with him did no good. "You can't marry her."

He blinked at the absolute statement from one so young. How dare she? *"Can't,* young lady. Young girls don't say *can't* to their elders. Perhaps you'd better understand one thing right here and now. You don't tell me what I can and can't do. I'm the one who'll tell you what I intend to do. I am marrying your mother."

"You can't. You're a coward."

His eyebrows flew up. He could feel the hot color rise in his face. His heart began to pump harder. "I suggest you take that back immediately, if you know what's good for you."

"I won't take it back. It's the truth."

"Who told you that?" Had his enemies spread their lies in the good homes of Chicago?

She lifted her chin. "I didn't need to be told. I was there."

Slightly relieved, he struggled for control. "You were a child. You didn't know what went on."

She shook her head. Her blond braids switched across her shoulders. "I did. I might have been only thirteen years old, but I'm not an idiot. I heard the shots. I saw Wellington come back."

"Wellington?" *A witness?*

"My father's horse."

Westfall opened his jacket and pulled forth his cigar case. His hand was steady as he selected one and then

80

found a match. Lady's parlor be damned. He needed this. When he had blown a cloud of smoke into the still air, he answered. "Of course, your father's horse. Well, let me tell you that when your father's horse came back without him, your father was already dead. The arrows that wounded the horse shot the rider out of the saddle."

Her eyes accused him relentlessly. Her voice rose. Her fists clenched. "He wasn't dead. I told you. We all heard shooting later, closer. He was coming home, fighting for his life. If you'd gone out to meet him, you could have saved him. But you let him die."

Their hatred for each other was a tangible thing. His eyes damned her as they had damned the prosecutor in the court-martial. Blood pounding in his temples, he drew the calming smoke into his lungs. "I had to think of the rest of the fort," he said evenly. "I had a duty to the rest of the men, the civilians, the wagon trains that would be coming up that road."

Her lip curled disdainfully. "You were afraid you'd get killed. You're a coward."

He stubbed the cigar out in the case and closed it with a telling snap. "No. I'm an officer. I know my duty."

"Then why didn't you go to the aid of your men? Why did you let them get killed? Did you want them to get killed?"

The question struck deep, ripping at the scar tissue over his conscience. His face turned dark with blood. His control snapped. Drawing back his right arm, he slapped her.

She saw the blow coming and snapped her head back so only his fingertips grazed her cheek. Unfortunately, in the act of dodging backward, she stumbled over a footstool and ended on the floor, one foot up in the air, her skirts and petticoats ruffling around her knees. The mark of his fingers scarcely showed against the blaze of anger that suffused her face.

Even as he had struck her, he had tried to pull back. What had come over him? If he struck this child, her mother would never marry him. Muttering an apology, he reached his hand down to help Miranda to her feet.

Misinterpreting his gesture, she threw up her arms to protect her head and tried to scramble away from him. Too late, he had put a foot on her skirt. With a cry she caught the heavy wool in both hands and tugged. Her strength staggered him back, and she sprang to her feet.

"You hit me!"

He shook his head. His hand shook as he straightened his tie and shrugged his shoulders inside his coat.

"You hit me!" she cried again louder.

He held out his hands, placatingly. "I shouldn't have done it, but you deserved it."

"Deserved it? What did I say?"

He did not want to remember what she had said. He straightened to the attack. "Obviously your education has been lacking. You were yelling insults, lies—"

"You hit a girl." Her voice rose. "You knocked me down! You really are a coward."

"I didn't knock you down. You tripped. Keep your voice down."

"Coward! Coward! Coward!"

He lunged for her, caught her by the arms, and shook her. Her braids slapped against her shoulders. "Shut your mouth! I am not a coward. You're a bad child. Bad children need discipline. Your mother needs me to control you. Obviously, she's had her hands full with you. You need a man's hand." His own tightened until she cried out.

Thoroughly frightened now, his grip bruising her who had never been struck, much less manhandled, she looked frantically toward the door. Tears were coursing down her cheeks. Why weren't her mother and grandparents coming to help her?

The lack of objection from the rest of the house had not gone unnoticed by him as well. He smiled nastily. "The very first thing I'll do is put you in a good school. Somewhere far away. New Orleans is nice. It has some very strict Catholic schools for girls. They'll knock that impudence out of you and replace it with Christian teachings."

"N-New Orleans." She had never been separated from her mother nor her baby sister.

"Or Boston," he continued, warming to his idea. "Excellent schools—really emphasize deportment and discipline."

"My mother won't let you."

His smile widened. "Yes, she will," he sneered. "Do you think she can't hear you pitching this temper tantrum? You're a terror. She's obviously lost control of you. No wonder your grandparents are so eager to get rid of you."

"They're not."

He released her and stood back, his arms folded. "Where are they then?"

She made a dash for the door.

"Go ahead. Run to your mother," he called after her. "But I suggest you run to your room first and think about all this. You won't get anywhere with your wild stories. Your mother'll just be happier to agree with me when I tell her what you need is a good school."

Miranda jerked the door open and fled down the hall.

The clock in her grandfather's hall struck one. Miranda sat up in bed and threw back the covers. She thrust her feet over the edge of the bed. Even before they touched the cold floor, she began to shiver. For a full minute she sat shivering, doubting herself.

Fear chilled her more than the cold room. If she pulled her feet back under the covers and lay down again, no one would ever know. On the other hand, once she went out through the back door, she could never return. She hesitated. The tip of her big toe touched the floor. The contact sent shivers through her.

She threw back her head remembering. The fires of injustice began to kindle within her. Her mother had not seemed too upset about the slap. She had put her cool hand on Miranda's cheek, a sorrowful expression on her face, but her grandfather standing shoulder to shoulder with Westfall had all but congratulated the colonel, telling him that a girl needed a firm hand.

Suddenly, she wondered about her mother's childhood. Had more than love driven her to marry Francis Drummond at the first opportunity? Had her grandfather "disciplined" his daughter as Westfall had "disciplined" Miranda. She shuddered. The sudden insight made her all the more aware of Westfall's power. Her mother must be desperate to escape.

Resolutely, Miranda stabbed both feet onto the floor. She had nothing to lose. Not really. She was going to be separated from her family anyway. Westfall would send her to some strict school in Boston and everyone would heave a sigh of relief.

She would not go. She would remember her father. And someday—Someday she would come back and rescue her mother and sister. Someday she would find a way to avenge her father's death. She would disgrace the coward who had left him to die. She would destroy him.

Muttering her resolutions to herself, she tugged on first one layer and then another of clothing. The wind off Lake Michigan was strong and cold. Two pairs of stockings, her winter boots, a stocking cap, and a muffler around her ears and under her chin.

Her main worry was money. In all her life she had never had more than a nickel in her possession. No use to take her reticule. She stuffed her underclothes into a small grip and snapped it closed.

A sad smile played about her mouth. The drawers of the wardrobe were almost empty. Only a couple of summer dresses remained beside her mother's silk dress she had worn to the theater. She really had nothing to leave behind. Almost everything she owned was on her back and in her grip. She shivered.

Time to go. She pushed open the door and tiptoed down the hall, past her mother's room where she slept with Rachel. She would have liked to hug her baby sister and tell her not to worry, but she could not take the chance of waking the house. At the foot of the stairs, she paused.

A stirring of pride prevented her from sneaking out the back door. Bad enough to steal away in the night, she would not leave like a servant. Careless of the clicking of her heels, she marched up to the front door and turned the skeleton key always left in the lock.

As the door swung open, cold air struck her cheeks. She closed the door behind her and marched down the steps. A fine mist off Lake Michigan wet her eyelashes. The gate creaked behind her.

Here she stopped. Which direction? The light at the corner beckoned, then the street curved. Where would she go? Not to a friend's. She had only a few friends and their parents would just send her back to her mother immediately. No. She must get completely away.

The theater. The playbill had said that the acting troupe was traveling on at the end of the week to an engagement in St. Louis. They were leaving tonight. If they had not already left, perhaps they could take her with them? Perhaps they would have a job for her? She could imagine that all those costumes must take a lot of work to keep clean. Perhaps she could wash and sew? That was about all she had learned to do in her grandmother's house.

The actor's face had never been far from her mind. Now she saw him again, smiling, laughing, winking at her. Romeo in maroon velvet. She hurried.

Two large wagons like Gypsy's caravans were pulled up at the back of the theater. Heavy horses stood stolidly in harness. Pressing her back to the wall, Miranda slipped by the huge animals. From the light of the single lamp, she could read the side of the first wagon. In red and gold it proclaimed, SONS OF THESPIS, ROYAL SHAKESPEAREAN COMPANY BY APPOINTMENT TO HER ROYAL MAJESTY QUEEN VICTORIA.

Miranda heaved a sigh of relief. Cautiously, she approached the rear of the wagon, then darted back into the shadows as the door to the theater opened. An enormous man with powerful hairy arms shoved a slighter figure down the steps.

A third man in shirtsleeves stepped into the doorway behind them. "You've got all you're entitled to!" he growled. "You and Sheila were supposed to do a special performance for those cattlemen."

The slighter figure recovered his balance and whirled. The deep magical voice of Romeo answered angrily. "I never promised any such thing."

"The hell you didn't."

"Damn you, Shorer. We're actors. Get someone else to pimp and whore for you."

"If you're so great, why ain't you playin' down on State Street?" The man gestured with a hammy arm. The bouncer lumbered back up the steps and into the theater. Shorer stepped back in the doorway. "You've got all you're gonna get. So get." He slammed the door.

"Come on, Shreve," a woman's voice called throatily from the shadow of the caravan.

Miranda shrank closer to the wall.

"No. Damn him. He owes us another fifty dollars. He can't treat us like that."

"He just did." The woman seemed unconcerned by the whole scene.

"That louse. That son-of-a—"

The door swung open. The man stuck his head out. "If I don't see them wagons rollin' down the street in five minutes, I'm sendin' Jobe for the sheriff."

"You bastard." Romeo leaped up the steps toward him. The door slammed again, this time in his face. He pounded on it cursing.

Two men jumped down from the second wagon and ran to him, pulling him back down into the alley. The actress called again. "Shreve, for God's sake, let's go."

"He owes us fifty dollars."

"Let it go, Mr. Catherwood." One of the men tried to soothe him. "We're getting out of here awful late."

Miranda frowned anxiously. They were leaving immediately, and no one was in any mood to hire anybody. Swifter than thought, she scuttled across the alley and slipped down the side of the wagon. The tailgate was partially open. Several large pieces of scenery had been hastily levered inside. She slid her grip into the space and pulled herself up by the chain.

The wagon creaked and swayed, but no one noticed, so intent were they on placating Romeo. "That damned pimp," he raged on. "We'll never play his theater again. No matter how much he offers."

"Sure, Shreve. That's the spirit," the actress called wearily.

"This has always been beneath us, Bessie," he continued.

"Sure, I know. Climb back on, boys. Everybody's

probably asleep but us."

"—but damnation! That fifty dollars makes me mad."

Miranda squeezed in between two flats. Fortunately, one had an open archway making a nook for her to fit into. The wagon tilted to the left as the actor climbed onto the seat. The second flat shifted, pinching Miranda's hip brutally. She had to stifle her cry of anguish.

"I ought to go back in there and punch his face in."

"He might punch yours in," the woman observed.

"Him. Ha! That shrimp. That louse. That whore-monger. He—"

"He wouldn't do it himself. He'd get Jobe to do it."

"Damn him." Catherwood must have taken up the reins, because Miranda heard the slap of leather against the backs of the horses. The wagon began to roll. Behind it the two men climbed back on the box and whipped up their horses.

The Sons of Thespis rumbled out into the windy night.

Lightning flashed so brightly that it filled the inside of the caravan. Miranda jerked upright, startled out of her uncomfortable doze. Without intermission, thunder crashed almost directly overhead. Fortunately, it drowned Miranda's panicky scream.

The caravan creaked to a halt.

"Come on, Mike," Romeo's voice shouted to the man in the other wagon. "We've got to close the tailgate."

Lightning flashed again, immediately followed by another cataclysmic boom. Miranda screamed again and covered her ears. The heavens opened up and rain mixed with hail slashed into the open wagon.

With a rattle of chain the tailgate came down; and suddenly flats were shifted, pulled out, and rammed in again with great force. The archway dragged her body with it as the men grunted with the unaccustomed weight. With extra force they slammed her back farther than before. She groaned in pain, but another clap of thunder drowned out everything.

Shreve cursed rhythmically as the stinging pellets of ice turned to pebbles and then to full-size rocks. One spattered on his cheek, drawing blood. Another minute and he and Mike were able to slam the tailgate closed and slide the bar into place.

By that time hail was striking the tops of the caravans with a steady drumroll that completely drowned out Miranda's screams and sobs. Lightning and thunder crashed together overhead. The teams neighed and fought their harness in panic. The big dray horses thrust their shoulders against their collars and lumbered away, dragging the wagon despite the brake.

Shreve Catherwood sprinted after it and leaped to the box. Instead of bringing them to a halt, he whipped them up, heading for a stand of trees. The other wagon followed. Into the woods they crashed, branches crunching and scraping against the sides of the caravan. Finally, the horses could drag the wagon no farther. The thick evergreens protecting them from the worst of the storm, the exhausted team hung their heads.

Shreve looped the reins over the brake handle and turned to his leading lady. All he could make out in the infernal darkness was a white oval of her face. He groped for her, found her shivering body, and gathered her into his arms. She looped her arms around his waist under his coat and they huddled together while the lightning zigzagged in the sky and thunder boomed.

In the pitch-black interior of the wagon, Miranda curled into a tight ball and sobbed for her mother. If she could have found a way—any way—to return to her home at that moment, she would have. If Benjamin

Westfall had suddenly appeared and told her he was taking her to the worst girl's school in the East, she would have gone willingly and thankfully.

But no one came. She was caught, trapped, locked in a miserable, cold, damp prison, squeezed between slabs of wood and canvas too heavy for her to think of moving. She had no one to blame for her plight but herself.

"I swear I heard someone screaming last night." Sheila rubbed her hands around the back of her neck to try to work the stiffness out.

"You must have been dreaming."

"I wasn't dreaming during that thunderstorm. I heard cries. They sounded like they came from the back of the wagon."

"Couldn't be. You heard the wind." Shreve ruefully surveyed the damage to the side of the caravan. Running the horses in under the trees had splintered a corner of the roof over the box and scraped the sides badly.

Sheila Tyrone, the Irish nightingale and worthy successor to Charlotte Cushman, shook her head. "I know what I heard. If they didn't come from the back of the wagon, then we must have passed someone on the road."

"Most likely it was your imagination," he insisted. "The thunder probably scared you."

Sheila gave him a disgusted look. "I'm not scared of thunder and I lost my imagination a long time ago."

"Along with a lot of other stuff."

"What?"

"Nothing." He knocked his knuckles against the scarred wood. "Come out, come out, whoever you are."

Sheila flounced around on the seat. "All right for you."

He grinned and held up his arms. "Come down, Bessie. Mike's got a fire built. Smell the coffee."

She switched back around and put her hands on his shoulders. "Call me Sheila. Otherwise, you'll make a slip in front of someone."

He swung her down with a smile. "I don't slip up and call you Juliet. I won't slip up when I need to call you Sheila."

"See that you don't." Lifting her skirts, she picked her way through the wet grasses and weeds. He followed her, knocking absently along the painted side as he went.

Mike Lonigan had built a small fire with the wood he always carried under the box of his wagon. Ada Cocks, the wardrobe mistress, had a pot of coffee heating and a skillet of bacon frying. All six of the Sons of Thespis, daughters included, stood around the campfire, warming their hands and drying the dampness out of their clothes.

Smoke blew on the strong wind in the direction of the first wagon.

Miranda awoke by fits and starts. She opened her eyes in the relative darkness, then blinked them several times to clear them. They burned more with each blink. The floor was desperately hard and cold beneath her side, but she was so wedged into the odd-shaped space that she could not stretch.

Distinctly, she smelled the tantalizing scents of coffee and bacon. Her mouth began to water. Acute pangs shot through her stomach. She drew in a breath and coughed. Her throat was sore from the cold, but the taste in it was acrid. Along with the bacon and coffee, she smelled smoke. Someone was cooking food nearby.

She opened her eyes. The space between the flats where she was wedged was swiftly filling with gray haze.

91

Smoke was drifting up through the floorboards. She sucked in a full lungful, and her coughs became spasms. Suddenly, terrible fears assailed her, unreasoning, beyond her control.

She was trapped, wedged in tight between heavy flats of lumber and canvas, boxed in a locked wagon. She would suffocate. If the wagon caught on fire, she would burn. In her terror she began to breathe in great gasps. Her coughs became louder. Tears streamed down her cheeks. She pulled her wool skirt up over her face and drew her legs up to her chest. Head on her knees, she coughed and wept.

Suddenly, light flooded into her face. The tailgate of the wagon fell with a clanking thud.

"I knew I heard somebody crying," the woman called Sheila declared. A face peered between the flats.

"What in hell!" It was Romeo's voice. "We've got a stowaway."

Miranda covered her head with her hands.

"Pull this out, boys." The flat that provided her crawl space moved pulling her with it over the bare splintery floor.

Miranda came tumbling within the space, head over heels. One foot rammed through the canvas of the flat at her back. Her leg was caught and twisted before the scenery tore. She screamed again. Remorselessly, the men kept pulling until finally she was on the tailgate on her back, her legs doubled in the air, her arms wrapped around her upper body to protect her face and head.

"Hey, it's a woman."

"She was the one I heard screaming last night."

"I'll make her scream."

The anger in Romeo's voice terrified her. Desperate to get herself out of her undignified position where she had ended up all but straddling the archway, she gave a frantic twist. Her body flopped off the tailgate and

92

landed with a sodden thunk on the muddy ground.

Shreve Catherwood dragged her to her feet. Her legs, cramped so long, could not bear her weight. She sagged against him, her head tilted back on her shoulders. His long black hair was tousled, his chin unshaven. The gold earring glinted in the strong morning light. His black eyes blazed down into her frightened face. "Who the hell are you?"

Six

No enemy
But winter and rough weather.

Miranda's entire world shrank to his angry face, wildly tossed black hair, and the purplish gray sky above it. He shook her again, his fingers digging into her arms. Her head jolted on her shoulders. Her teeth clicked together.

When she did not answer, he thrust her away and flung up his hands in angry disgust. "Another damned stowaway!"

Miranda reeled away, half bent over, coughing out the last of the smoke. When she could straighten, she swiped at the tears that were still spouting from her eyes.

Mike Lonigan pulled his body back out of the caravan and dropped Miranda's grip on the ground beneath the tailgate. "Looks like she tore the hell out of Padua."

"Damn you!" Shreve Catherwood caught her by the arm and shook her again. Her head bounced on her shoulders. "Did you hear that? That's part of one of our most expensive sets. Do you know how much that much canvas costs?" He pointed to the flat they had pulled from the wagon.

She shook her head. More tears were running down her face. She tried to speak, but her throat was so irritated by the smoke that no intelligible words came out.

"Of course, you don't. You don't know much of anything. You just love the theater," he snarled sarcastically. "And you'd do anything to be an actress."

Her teeth slammed together on her tongue. She squeaked in pain. "N-no."

"No?!" He released her abruptly. His expressive face managed to convey both disgust and disbelief as well as dark anger.

"No. I c-can't be an actress. I could never be anything so wonderful. I thought I might sew costumes or something like that." The feeling was coming back into her legs. She tried to straighten up, to stand at attention, the way her father had taught her. Unfortunately, her heels sank into the muddy grass tipping her drunkenly backward.

"A likely story."

"No, really. I did. I'm a good seamstress. I was going to ask you for a job."

His handsome mouth curled in a sneer. "And of course the best way to get one is to steal a ride and destroy an expensive piece of scenery."

"I'm so sorry about that. I would never have done it myself. It wouldn't have happened if you hadn't dragged me out so fast. I couldn't help tearing it. My foot—that is—my heel just went right through. I'm sorry." She peered intently into the caravan, twisting sideways to get the best view. "I'll bet I can fix it," she reported with more confidence than she truly felt. The rip was almost five feet long. She swung around, hands outstretched in appeal. "I can make a patch. Believe me, I know how to patch cloth. I can set it on the back and nobody—"

"If you wanted a job so badly, why didn't you ask for one?"

She took heart from that question. "I was going to. Last night. But I got to the back of the theater just as you were leaving. And you were mad."

The actress Sheila Tyrone snickered at that. "He's still mad, sweetie. Looks like you're out of luck."

Miranda searched the dark face above her. "Are you still mad?"

"I'm madder now than ever," came the grim reply.

"Please don't be." She smelled the bacon frying, smelled the coffee. Her mouth watered so badly that she had to swallow twice. The other members of the troupe had drifted back to the fire where the older woman was lifting the strips of meat out onto slices of bread arranged on a tin plate.

Catherwood's nose twitched. "Get on out of here." He gave her a push. "I'm missing my breakfast."

Panic joined hunger in her stomach. Fierce pangs made her clutch at her middle. She did not move. "Please," she whispered. "Please let me stay with you."

"No." He brushed past her and reached for the coffeepot. Pouring himself a steaming cup, he took a helping of bread and bacon. His beautiful white teeth tore into it.

Miranda could not suppress a tiny moan.

He heard her. One black eyebrow rose. Turning his head, he surveyed her as he took a swallow of coffee from a steaming cup. The woman at the fire looked up, too. "Have a bite if you'd like, dearie," she invited, pushing the plate closer to the edge of the little grill. "We've enough."

Miranda looked at the man hesitantly.

He glowered first at her and then at the woman. "Ada."

The woman frowned. "Don't be such a sorehead, Shreve, laddie. We've enough to share, and she can't have had anything to eat since yesterday. Come on, dearie. He's just in a temper."

Still, Miranda hesitated, until Romeo nodded shortly. Only two pieces remained on the plate. She chose the smaller. The woman poured coffee into a cup. "Hope you don't mind usin' my cup. We've only just got enough to go around once." She raised an eyebrow in Shreve's direction. "We ought to buy a few more."

"We don't need anymore."

"Sure we do. When we have guests."

"We don't have guests." He held out his cup again. She poured the last of the coffee. A drop of rain fell into the cup. More fell into the fire, making it hiss.

"It's coming again," Sheila observed unnecessarily. She swallowed the last of her coffee and set the cup down on the edge of the grill. Then scooping her skirts up, she tossed them over her arm and hurried back to climb into the box of the first caravan.

Still chewing, Mike Lonigan pushed the piece of scenery back into place and closed the tailgate. The woman called Ada collected the rest of the troupe's cups, wiped them out, and put them back into a small chest. Another actor picked up the iron grill

97

by its handles and carried it around to the back of the second caravan. The third pushed the bits back into the horses' mouths and fastened the cheek straps.

"Drink up." Ada urged as she climbed awkwardly to her feet and closed the camp stool.

Obediently, Miranda lifted the cup to her mouth to find she could hardly swallow past the painful lump in her throat. Terror made her cold all over. Another roll of thunder sounded closer. More rain peppered her head. With a tremulous smile, she handed the cup to Ada, who tossed the remaining liquid out and thrust it into the chest. Romeo stuffed the last bite into his mouth and strode away, ignoring the hard look that the older woman shot at him.

With a philosophical shrug she, too, climbed into the back of the second caravan. The tailgate slammed shut.

They were leaving. They were going to abandon her in the rain beside the road. She had no idea how far they had traveled during the night, but she knew she must be miles from Chicago. She looked around desperately.

A bolt of lightning streaked across the sky. Thunder rolled. The trees thrashed in the wind. The lead caravan began to back. She dived to save her grip, but Catherwood reined the horses to the left. The wagon began to swing in a semicircle.

Miranda clasped her arms across her body as she began to shiver. The rain was soaking through her clothing. Already her back and shoulders were wet to the skin. She slitted her eyes against the pelting drops. They washed her tears away as fast as they fell.

The horses plodded by her dragging the heavy caravan. The woman called Sheila had already taken shelter through a door behind the wagon box. Only Shreve Catherwood sat on the seat protected by the roof and a big yellow slicker covering him to his boot tops. Their eyes met.

Hastily, she broke the contact. She would not beg. She had stowed away, but he had torn his own scenery. All he had needed to do was ask her to come out. She studied the road to her left through the sheets of rain. She would wait here under the trees until they had gotten out of sight, then she would walk on. She would not return to Chicago.

The second team of horses came by and the second wagon box.

Mike Lonigan looked down at her, his face grim. "There's a town 'bout two miles back," he offered. "You can make it. Just follow the road."

She nodded. Her jaw clenched tightly to keep it from shivering. The rain was icy cold. She very much doubted that she could walk two miles in it.

"Hey!"

She looked drearily in the direction of the call.

Romeo had stuck his face around the front of the first caravan. He motioned to her. "Hey you. I've called you twice. Come on."

"I can— You don't have to—" Miranda's teeth were chattering so hard she could barely get the words out.

"Better take the ride," Lonigan advised. "I lied. The town's more like five miles."

"Come on up here!" came the command.

She wasted no more time in sprinting to the caravan. The actor's handsome face scowled down at her. Rain lashed her cheeks and stung her eyes.

99

Lightning crackled. The scent of ozone filled the air. Thunder boomed so close overhead that she ducked instinctively.

With a fervent curse Shreve Catherwood put down his hand and hauled her up onto the box. "Don't brush against me and get me wet, too."

"Yes, sir. I won't." She tucked her leaden skirts around her legs. Her hands were so cold that she had to look to see them touching the material.

He watched the line of her jaw tighten and turn white with the effort of holding her teeth still. He shook his head disgusted with himself. "Knock on that door and ask Sheila for the other slicker. You'll have to ride up here. We can't have you getting everything all wet back there."

"No, sir."

He peered gloomily out at the rain. "What's your name?"

"Miranda."

His mouth curled upward in a mirthless smile. "Of course. I should have known. It had to be."

"Why?"

"Miranda of *The Tempest*."

"I don't understand."

He looked at her as if he pitied her ignorance. "Shakespeare's play *The Tempest*. The heroine's name is Miranda. I hope it's not going to rain on us all the time you're with us."

The brown water rushed past, tearing sod away from the bank. A good-sized tree leaned precariously over it, half of its roots washed clean.

"Hell and damnation! We can't cross that." Shreve strode back to the wagons where the troupe

100

waited, exhausted and miserable.

"We can't go much farther," Lonigan commented morosely. "The horses are going to drop in the traces."

"Well, this is a fine how-de-doo. All this way on a shortcut and we can't cross. My toes are growing moss between them," complained the man whom Miranda had heard called Frederic. "I'm about to rot."

"He's always been rotten," Sheila muttered behind Miranda's shoulder. "It just might show for a change."

Shreve Catherwood ignored both Frederic and Sheila's comments. "Can they make it back to that farm we passed a couple of miles back?"

Mike shrugged. "I guess they'll have to."

"Poor things," Miranda murmured.

Sheila made a rude noise. "Don't feel sorry for them. More than half the time we work like slaves while they stand with their noses in the feedbags. They were getting fat as pigs."

The leading lady of the troupe retired to the small pallet compartment behind the driver's box and closed the door firmly behind her. Miranda's teeth set up a fresh chattering as Shreve swung the heads of the team away from the rushing water and into the wind.

"Will you kindly lock your jaw?"

She clamped it as best she could until the tendons strutted in her neck.

"When we finally do get to Saint Louis," he growled, "I want you to telegraph your folks as fast as possible." He grabbled up a handful of small stones from a box beneath his feet and cast them at the haunches of the team. The big horses threw

101

their shoulders into their collars and the heavy wagon swayed gently up the slope.

"No." Miranda clutched the edges of the seat and buried her nose deep in her muffler. The wet wind in her face was making her eyes water.

He shot her a sharp glance. "Suit yourself, but you can't stay with us."

"I'll stay at least until I get Padua fixed."

"Don't even try," he growled. "Just get on along with you. Go back to your family."

"Don't have a family," she declared saucily.

He shook his head mockingly. "Try another lie." As the animals strained over the incline and onto more or less level ground, he took his eyes off the road to appraise her. "Your clothes aren't anything to brag about, but clothes don't mean much. Your face and hair are the ones that tell the story. Clear skin. Good teeth. Bright eyes. Hair heavy and thick. Someone's fed you well and given you a lot of care."

She flushed and bit her lip. Training her eyes on the drenched landscape ahead, she lifted her chin.

"That look," he mocked. "Ah, what a look! Pride! Consequence! A lady *to the manner born*. How old are you?"

His question startled her. Beyond her first name he had really betrayed no interest in her at all. "Seventeen," she lied, wishing she was. "I'll be eighteen soon."

His eyes dropped to her chest, well hidden beneath her coat and layers of damp clothing. "I would have said younger. But it's difficult to tell at your age. At any age. Women lie so much."

She shifted and tugged at her coat collar. Embarrassed color heated her cheeks. "I'm seventeen."

He slapped the reins against the backs of the horses. "Suit yourself. It doesn't matter. The minute we get to Saint Louis, you'll be somebody else's problem."

"The girl was always a problem. Always. Dragged from pillar to post, raised on outlandish army posts most of the time among heathens, never associating with the right kinds of people." Erasmus Taylor was warming to his thesis when he observed the displeasure in his future son-in-law's face and remembered that Westfall was a career army man. Grumpily, he cleared his throat and addressed his daughter. "She'll turn up soon enough. The thing for you to do, Ruth, is to go right ahead with your wedding plans to Benjamin."

"Father." Ruth could barely control the sickness rising in her throat. "Miranda is missing. Your own granddaughter is missing. She could be injured, lying in a hospital bed somewhere needing us, crying for us. She could be dead. Oh!" Ruth covered her mouth to smother her sobs.

Westfall put his arm around her shoulders. "Ruth, I'm sure this is just a childish way to attempt to forestall our wedding. Undoubtedly, she's hiding somewhere."

"Just so," Taylor agreed heartily. "The little wretch will come home when she gets hungry enough."

Ruth shook her head. "This is not like Miranda. She's never spent a night apart from me in her life. I know something's happened. We have to report her disappearance to the police."

"Great Scott, no!"

"No, my dear." Westfall turned her into his arms,

so that she was leaning her forehead against his shoulder. "That's just what we mustn't do. She would be ruined. Think of the unfortunate publicity that would attach itself to her name."

"Just so," Taylor enjoined. "Just so. No man would ever take her knowing what she's done. Couldn't be sure—" He cleared his throat noisily. "Couldn't trust that—well, you see, I'm sure."

Ruth pushed herself away from Westfall and turned on her father. "None of that is important if she's hurt or lost or dying. Father, for mercy's sake, Miranda is your own flesh and blood."

Westfall put his hands on her arms. Over her shoulder he threw Taylor a warning look. "Exactly, my dear. For that reason we need to get married immediately. Publish the news abroad so that it can be seen and heard everywhere. This was undoubtedly a protest to keep you from marrying me. When she learns that we've married, she'll come home."

"And accept her punishment," Taylor added.

"Father!"

"She'll be welcomed as a beloved daughter," Westfall declared.

"Thank you for that." Ruth fumbled in her pocket for a handkerchief to dab at her eyes. "But don't you think the police should be called. Just suppose—"

Mentally damning his future stepdaughter to eternal perdition, he patted Ruth's shoulder. "I'll tell you what, my dear. While you and your mother work on your wedding things, I'll hire a private detective to seek her out. There must be some very good agencies here in Chicago."

"Indeed. Several. And all very discreet." Taylor brightened at the suggestion which would cost him nothing. He rubbed his hands together. With any luck his daughter would be out and gone with her problems by the end of the week. He loved her, of course, but she had caused him no end of inconvenience over these last three years. "That's a very good idea, Benjamin."

"Thank you, Erasmus."

"Now, Ruth—" Her father took her out of her intended's arms and guided her toward the door. "Go right upstairs to your mother, and you and she get right to work putting together that wedding outfit. And go through the family jewels. Pick out something extra special for yourself. I have it. Your grandmother's garnets. I always meant for you to have them. But when you married that Drummond—"

Ruth pulled back out of his arms and glared at him.

"Sorry. I didn't mean to imply that you did anything wrong. Just that there wasn't time to properly present them to you. But I'll make a point to give them to you tonight at dinner." He looked at Westfall for support. "You'll be dining with us, won't you?"

"Kind of you to ask me. I had planned an evening out for Ruth and me, but under these unfortunate circumstances, we'd better stay close. She might come home at any moment."

"Do you really think so?" Ruth asked unhappily.

"I think it's a very good bet."

When Ruth had left the room, Westfall and Taylor did not look one another in the eye. Instead, Westfall excused himself immediately to go out and hire a private detective to investigate Miranda's disappearance.

Taylor clapped him on the shoulder and offered another cigar as the colonel left. With any luck he should be rid of his daughter and her unfortunate family by the end of the month.

"Hell's fire! I can't see a thing. We could be within fifty feet of that barn or half a mile." Shreve wiped his sodden sleeve across his eyes and blinked through the water.

So cold and miserable that she had ceased to shiver, Miranda sat with eyes closed, shrunk back against the wall, her arms wrapped around her grip. At her companion's curse, she opened her eyes.

Sheets of rain fell before the caravan, striking the backs of the plodding horses and splashing the yellow slickers from the waist down. Their feet were six inches deep in the flood.

"I can't see anything either," she offered.

He nodded glumly. "Keep a lookout. We've got to come to something soon."

"What if we don't?"

He shrugged. "Then we don't. We'll survive somehow, but the horses are just about done." He slapped the reins along the backs of the team. "Poor brutes. They can't feel a thing."

Miranda pushed herself up. "They're good horses," she agreed solemnly. "They've given all you've asked."

He looked sideways at her. "You know about horses?"

"Of course." She was staring through the sheeting rain. "There's a shape over there." She pointed to the right. "It's big."

Shreve leaned across her. "I don't see it."

106

She put her cold cheek next to his and pointed through the driving rain. "Right over there."

"I can't see what you're talking about."

She drew back and looked at him. Then put her cheek against his again. She stabbed with her finger. "Right there."

He straightened up. "If you say so. If you're wrong, you get blamed for where we have to camp."

She shuddered as the wagon angled away from the flooded roadbed.

"Can you still see it?"

She waited to answer. The horses plodded on, the wheels sinking deeper into softer ground. She could remember hearing artillery men discussing rain like this. They had to keep moving. "Don't stop," she urged. "Keep them rolling."

He blinked owlishly, then looked at her again. "What if there's nothing there?"

"Look!" She grabbed his arm and pointed.

A largish square structure with a peaked roof took shape through the downpour.

"I'll be damned. You were right. Hi-up there." He slapped the reins across the team. Their speed did not increase.

"I'll jump out and run ahead and open the door," Miranda offered.

"That's not necessary. We'll open it when we get there."

"If you stop the wagon, it'll stick. Keep it rolling." She thrust her legs over the side and pushed off. Muddy water splashed to her knees, but she ignored it. Everything she wore was ruined beyond redemption. Running past the exhausted horses, she came first to a gate invisible from any distance in the heavy downpour. Swinging it open, she motioned the caravans through. Closing it, she raced past them again, making the barn just before the horses.

She struggled with the heavy bar, finally, dragged it back and swung the heavy door outward. The horses plodded into the dark interior.

"The wagon won't go in!" she yelled. "The top's too tall."

Shreve was already pulling back on the reins. "One more time, boys," he called to the team in a voice guaranteed to be heard in the farthest corner of any theater. "Back! Back!"

The tired horses responded, backing the heavy caravan out. When the wagon tongue had cleared the door, he let off on the lines. Behind him the second caravan circled and halted.

The rain began to change to sleet. Pellets stung Miranda's cheeks driving her back into the dimness. Shivering, she wrapped her arms around her and danced up and down on her numbed feet. Shreve jumped down from the box and began to unharness the horses as Sheila crawled down from her hidey-hole and scurried into the barn.

The other members of the troupe likewise were vacating their caravan. Last, Shreve and Mike led the teams into the barn. Miranda dashed out to drag the door closed.

"It's Noah's Flood for sure," Ada groaned. "I expected we'd see animals lined up two by two any minute."

"I hate rain," Sheila growled. "There's not a single thing good about it. Not one."

"Makes the flowers grow," Frederic commented. "Shouldn't like to be in a world without flowers."

"Spare me." Sheila rolled her eyes. "Any flowers

108

alive before this downpour are flattened and drowned."

"Do we dare build a fire?" Ada asked. "I'm freezin'."

Shreve looked around him. A couple of horses stuck their heads inquiringly out of their stalls. Mangers in the other stalls were filled with hay. A look overhead revealed that hay was stored in the loft. "Best not," he said. "Too much danger of setting the place on fire."

"You said the magic word," Sheila moaned. She of all the troupe had brought a quilt in with her. She clutched it across her bosom as she looked distastefully around. "What a dump! And now you tell us we can't build a fire."

"I can start a little one in the charcoal stove, if someone'll bring it in from the wagon," Ada offered. "Just a little one, inside the iron stove couldn't cause a fire."

Shreve looked doubtfully at the swathes of hay stringing down from the loft like Spanish moss. Behind his shoulder he could hear Miranda's teeth chattering. Sheila pulled the quilt up around her ears. The men stood on one foot and then the other, hands thrust deep into their pockets. A fire would improve everything. "Get it, Mike."

"Right you are."

"What about some coffee?" Frederic begged. "A spot of warmth for the inner man wouldn't go amiss right now."

Shreve shrugged. "If you'll get it."

"*I go and it is done.*" Frederic sketched a mocking bow before slipping through the door after Mike.

Wind and rain sheeted in through the opening.

Miranda thought of only one other time in her life when she had been so cold. Then she had looked out through the back of the wagon to see huge buffalo rolling in the snow. The memory made her teeth chatter more. Shooting pains lanced up from her toes to her knees. She tottered to the brace of one of the stalls and slid down the rough board. Her arms went around her knees hugging them up against her chest.

Catherwood strolled over to her. "Loving the life?" he jeered. "Quite a thrill, isn't it?"

"Back off, Shrevey." Ada set her fists on her hips. "Leave her alone. No sense adding to the misery." Mike Lonigan ducked back into the door with the stove. "Now we'll get something going here in a minute and we'll all cheer up." She turned her back and bent over, lifting her skirts. "Always carry my matches in the driest place," she informed them. "Never know when I'll need to start a fire."

Frederic returned with the coffeepot and basket of supplies. He looked around him worriedly. "What shall we do about water?"

Sheila snorted. "Just hold it out the door, Freddy. God! Nobody's dumber than an actor."

He made a rude gesture in her direction before following her suggestion.

By the time the coffeepot was full of rainwater, the charcoal and kindling were smoking.

Miranda crept closer. The Sons of Thespis huddled miserably around the tiny stove, welcoming its warmth, rubbing their hands above it, while Ada performed the ancient rituals of women with fire and sustenance. When the coffee began to boil, they inhaled deeply. Its very essence was precious encouragement.

110

"First cup goes to Mike," Ada said as she poured it and thrust it into his hands. "Second cup goes to Frederic."

"Thank you, ma'am."

Suddenly the barn door flew back. They all swung around.

A bearded man stood in it, water dripping off his hat and garments. His eyes flashed angrily around the circle, then lit on the stove where Ada knelt. His scowl deepened. He pushed a shotgun out from under the slicker. "Damned squatters! Put that fire out!"

Seven

And, most dear actors, eat no onions nor garlic,
for we are to utter sweet breath.

A tear slipped down the weathered cheek of the
farmer's wife. She hugged her tallest daughter tight
against her side.

"I'm sad and I'm lonely, my heart it will break."
Sheila Tyrone's husky contralto filled the barn. The
wind had dropped. The storm had abated. The
farmer's wife and seven children sat arranged like
stair steps on a board bridging two nail kegs.
The farmer stood, a scowling sentinel, at the entrance to one of the stalls. His shotgun was
propped beside him.

His two oldest sons hung over the top of another
stall. One's mouth gaped. Neither took their eyes
from Sheila's face.

"My true love loves another." She held the top
note. Her reproachful smile swept over them, sad,
forgiving, and warm with promise. The one closed
his mouth; the other blushed red as fire. *"I wisht I
was dead."*

The last note vibrated in the stillness. The

farmer's family sat transfixed. For perhaps twenty seconds no one moved.

Mike winked at Miranda, who shook herself, scarcely less mesmerized than the audience. He grinned and pulled the sides out on the squeeze box.

Sheila struck a saucy pose.

> *"When the farmer comes to town*
> *With his wagon broken down,*
> *Oh, the farmer is the man who*
> *feeds them all."*

Miranda clapped her hand over her mouth to stop the laugh as the farmer quickly looked around him. His face lightened, his scowl disappeared as the grange ballad continued.

> *"And the preacher and the cook*
> *Go a-strolling by the brook,"*

Sheila held out her arms and the players joined in.

> *"Oh, the farmer is the man*
> *who feeds them all."*

The wife threw a proud smile over her shoulder as her husband shoved his hands in his pockets and looked around to see how everybody was responding to the song. He caught her eye and grinned back. His teeth were dark and crooked in the tangle of his beard.

When Sheila finished her song with all joining in on the chorus, the farmer's wife was fairly glowing with pride and whispering to her daughter.

"Thank you, Miss Tyrone. Thank you. We are all the richer for your glorious voice." Shreve led the applause before he stepped forward, raised her hand, and kissed it reverently. The little girls tittered as Sheila winked at them and curtsied deeply. "And, now, for your further pleasure, all the way from London, England, where he has appeared before Queen Victoria, Mr. Frederic Franklin."

Miranda had to rub her eyes. The slight man who had complained bitterly about the cold seemed to grow six inches before her eyes. The way he walked, the way he carried his head, the set of his shoulders, became heroic. Again the speech was difficult to follow, but the longer she listened, the more she began to understand. The children she noted had the same problems, but gradually they, too, stopped fidgeting and listened.

The woman evidently knew the circumstances of the speech because she whispered to her daughter who passed the information down the line.

When Frederic came to the last words, *"My heart is in the coffin there with Caesar, and I must pause till it come back to me,"* she began the applause. Her husband put his hand on her shoulder and she looked up at him with shining eyes and said something in a language, Miranda had never heard before.

Her husband answered by placing his fingertips on his wife's cheek.

Shreve next introduced George Windom, who came forward with a long box and ceremoniously presented it to Frederic. Shreve opened the box and Frederic threw the audience a look of disdain. So effective was that look that one of the younger children popped his thumb into his mouth and shrank back against the older boy sitting next to him.

Both men drew foils and faced off. The two oldest boys looked at each other with excited grins. The blades flashed and clashed noisily as their hilts came together. The two men lunged and parried, passing each other and changing places, dancing and stamping back and forth on the hard-packed earth. At last Frederic executed a long series of brilliant slashes. They ended when the foil passed in under George's arm and seemed to emerge from his back.

George cried out piercingly. His body arched and twisted.

The younger children squealed. The thumbsucker hid his face completely. Then George slid backward off the blade, slumping gracefully to the floor, lifting his hand in farewell, before he died with a plea for God's mercy and a ghastly shudder.

Frederic made an appearance of wiping the blade and knelt beside his fallen foe. For a moment the tableau held, then he sprang to his feet, extended his hand, and pulled George to his feet also. The two bowed as the audience applauded and the younger children wiped their eyes.

At last Shreve Catherwood stepped forward. His beautiful eyes swept the audience, his smile caressed every woman equally from the wife, old before her time, to the daughter just in the blush of her youth, to the youngest girl, who turned up her face like a flower and smiled blindingly. He spun, stalked to the back of the stage, spun again, and began Petruchio's speech, *"I've come to wive it wealthily in Padua."*

The other actors fell into an abbreviated version

115

of *The Taming of the Shrew.* George stepped forward as Hortensio to explain that Katherine was curst and shrewd, but Petruchio vowed to wed her anyway. Katherine, played by Sheila Tyrone, appeared and the battle was on. Frederic made an admirable Grumio and Mike made a brief appearance as Lucentio.

The farmer and his family laughed and applauded.

All the older males hung in breathless suspense when Petruchio sent for Katherine in the middle of the night to tell her they were ready to depart for her father's house. When she agreed with him that the sun was shining brightly, they all grinned at each other in agreement.

At that moment another burst of thunder interrupted the actors. Shreve made a motion to the heavens. "Katherine," he called. *"I say it is the blessed sun."*

Sheila made a joke of running to the barn door and pretending to look out. When she came back, she replied lovingly, *"I know it is the blessed sun."*

The little ones fell off the bench laughing.

In the end when she delivered her last speech and he hauled her up into his arms, Miranda felt her own heart beat faster.

"Why there's a wench. Come on and kiss me, Kate."

Again the black eyes found her as they had from the stage the night he had played Romeo. She could feel them, feel their power, feel them pulling her toward him. In self-defense she wrapped her arm around a four by four that supported the ladder into the loft.

Shreve grinned at her at the same time that his

eyes swept the audience, stroking every woman. At the same time, Sheila Tyrone, bent back over his arm, turned her face to the same audience and winked saucily. Every woman sighed and every man swelled with pride.

The performance over, the farmer wrung Shreve's hand. The wife sent her the two oldest boys to bring a huge pot of stew and a basket of bread and cakes from the house. A tablecloth was spread over quilts and blankets in the hay, and the actors settled down to their food and lodgings for the night.

"You were wonderful," Miranda proclaimed enthusiastically around a mouthful of dark homemade bread. She had been so long without food that she had forgotten that she had not eaten all day. Now she could not seem to get full.

Sheila Tyrone huddled deeper in her quilt and looked around her morosely. "Wonderful. Wonderful."

"Cheer up, Sheila," Ada advised. "You never sang better. I was impressed myself."

"I had a reason to sing," came the sarcastic reply. "I was singing for my supper."

"I thought it was—all things considered—an above-average performance." Shreve pointed with his spoon at Frederic. "You were mixing Antony and Brutus again, Freddy. The farmer's wife spoke Latin. She might have understood."

"Sorry, old boy. But I had them eating out of the palm of my hand and didn't see any reason to quit."

"Such a tough audience," Sheila murmured sarcastically.

"The songs," Miranda gushed. "They were so beautiful. And the farmer was so pleased when you

117

sang the one about farmers. That was lucky."

They all looked at her astonished. Sheila snorted. Shreve shook his head and heaved a deep sigh. "I thought we picked you up in Chicago."

She looked at him puzzled. "I climbed into your wagon in Chicago."

"You sound like you're fresh off the farm."

"I don't understand."

Ada leaned forward kindly. "We have songs for every group, dearie. If she'd been singing to soldier boys, we'd have sung 'Johnny Has Gone for a Soldier.'"

"If we have a high-toned audience," Frederic said in a lofty voice, "she sings 'Barbara Allen' or 'The House Carpenter.'"

"Oh."

"Don't worry about it," Shreve advised. "Tomorrow we'll be on our way. One of the farmer's sons is going to guide us up the 'road a piece' as they so quaintly put it, so that we can cross at the ferry. Another week and we'll be in Saint Louis. And you, my girl, can find another troupe to tag along with. Or better still, go back to your family."

"No. I don't have any family to go back to."

Ada climbed to her feet. "Your mother must be frantic with grief, dearie. She'll be thinking you've been kidnapped or murdered."

Miranda closed her eyes. She missed her mother dreadfully, but she could not help remembering Westfall. Chills stood out on her arms. A sick feeling rose in her stomach. She had done the right thing. The only thing she regretted was not being able to tell her mother that she was safe. Perhaps in a few days, she could send a letter. When she opened her eyes, they were all staring at her. She bit

118

her lip. "I tell you I don't have any home to go back to."

Ada shrugged as she draped a quilt around her. "Stubborn. Stubborn." She settled down in an empty stall on a pile of hay. "Come over here, then, dearie, and keep me warm. I don't have any mother nor home neither."

"I've written a letter to Adolf Lindhauer," Ruth told Westfall. She appeared pale and distracted beneath the fashionable navy blue velvet hat her mother had bought for her.

Her husband of three hours shot her an angry look. "Who?"

"Adolf Lindhauer. His son was her best friend for so many years. They were practically inseparable at Fort Gallatin."

The fort completed the connection in Westfall's mind. "My God. You can't mean to tell me you've written to that immigrant squaw man. What could he possibly have to do with your daughter's disappearance?"

Ruth drew back at little in the face of his voiced disapproval. "I thought I would alert him. If she's run away, she has to go somewhere. Where better than back to Fort Gallatin, where she has friends."

"However would she get there?" Westfall scoffed. "There's no money missing, at least no more than a few paltry housekeeping dollars. You've told me that yourself. No jewelry. No silver. She doesn't have any way to get to Saint Louis, much less Wyoming. Train tickets and stage tickets cost money." At the sight of her white face, he put his arm around her and smiled down into her face. "Now don't be

119

upset. But really, Ruth, you should have asked me before you did such a thing. You've wasted your time. I'm sure she's here in Chicago."

"But why haven't we found her?" She clenched her fists in her lap.

"Because she doesn't want to be found." He covered her hands with his own and drew her to him. His thin drooping mustache tickled the corner of her mouth.

She stiffened, drawing in a sharp breath. "I can't help but worry."

He sighed briefly and slid his arm from around her shoulder. "I know, my dear. I quite understand."

"Do you, Benjamin? Do you really?" She turned to him with hopeful eyes.

"Yes, my dear. And I'm not a monster. We don't have to form an intimacy just yet." He touched the tip of his finger to the point of her chin.

"Oh, Benjamin." She smiled shakily. "I'm so nervous and upset. I want to be a good wife to you, but all I can think about is Miranda."

"Of course, my dear." He gathered her into his arms and cradled her head against his shoulder. "Of course." His eyes closed at the feel of her against him. He had wanted this woman for years. His thwarted flesh swelled and throbbed, but he smiled as he held her away from him. "We'll wait until you're ready."

She smiled, her relief poorly concealed.

"Let's go down to the dining room and have our supper." He opened the door for her. "But please be guided by me, Ruth. Don't write letters all over the country. Some of them might come back to haunt Miranda when she comes home." As she preceded him down the stairs together, her perfume wafted

120

up to him. He gritted his teeth and damned his stepdaughter to fiery hell.

"He's booked another act," Shreve announced angrily. "I can't believe the nerve of the bastard. Here we are only three days late and we've lost our place. He'll never get our act here again. And that's a promise." He shook his fist at the stage door of the Clarke Street Theater.

"I should have checked that axle," Mike groaned by way of apology.

"It's not your fault. The damn thing wasn't broken and then it was. You couldn't have told it was going by looking at it."

"No use crying over spilt milk," Ada said heartily. "The question is what are we going to do now."

"Walk the streets," Sheila sneered.

"With your experience, you'd probably do all right, old girl." Frederic regarded her lush figure.

Sheila Tyrone threw him a look guaranteed to set him ablaze. "Oh, I don't know Freddy, old thing. Put a little more rouge on and a certain element will fall all over themselves."

"Bitch!"

She shrugged. "This town has a waterfront, Shreve. With showboats. We should be able to find something down there."

"We're legitimate actors," Shreve objected. "They won't want us to play Shakespeare."

"So. We'll play what they want." She pointed back down the way they had come. "That's where we'll find work. You can bet on that."

In the end they did find work, just barely on the stage in the dining hall of the *Queen of Diamonds*.

The area was ten by eight with one exit to a tiny room where they all crowded together between entrances.

Capt. Connal O'Toole had a florid face and a fringe of graying pinky-orange hair. His nose was snubbed, his eyes watery blue. He was not really interested in hiring the troupe, but the name of Sheila Tyrone caught his attention. He looked over the rail of the floating casino. She smiled up at him and twirled her parasol. He slipped once on the stairs getting down to welcome her aboard.

"The Sons of Thespis are just what you'd be needing, sir, to entertain your customers while they're consuming the delicious repasts you provide." Sheila's bright red hair, freshly touched to cover the dark roots, hung in a crimped fringe above her glowing dark eyes. The yellow feathers on the saucy green bonnet nodded gently as she talked.

"Oh, aye, I do provide delicious repasts."

"I'll bet you do. And excellent wines."

"True, but ye see I've never had —" He started to shake his head, his regret obvious.

"This is the time to have a troupe, sir. Think how refined it'll all sound. A real troupe of actresses and actors for the pleasure and edification of your guests. Captain Connal O'Toole presents Sheila Tyrone." She gave him her hand, laughing throatily, and swept a deep curtsy. "And the Sons of Thespis."

Connal's eyes fairly glowed. He surveyed the lush figure, letting his stare dip into the deep cleavage between the grosgrain revers. Her skin was white, fine-grained, with delicious mounds rising on either side of the valley. He rocked forward on his toes. "It's doubtful I am that I could pay —"

"Oh, don't be talking to me about payment." Sheila waved him away, her brogue thickening by the minute. "A lady shouldn't be discussing money with a gentleman. May I be the one to present Mr. Shreve Catherwood, the manager of our little troupe? He'll be the one you'll be making the arrangements with."

Shreve stepped forward, his face carefully blank, though the back of his neck was red. "We're a royal troupe, Mr. — ah — Captain O'Toole. Mr. Michael Lonigan is —"

O'Toole locked his hands behind his back. His lower lip thrust out obstinately. "I can pay twenty a week for the little lady and twenty a week for the lot of ye."

"Forty-five a week for the troupe. Sheila gets ten and if you want to give her an extra ten for songs she'll be more than grateful. I get ten, Michael gets ten, the others get five. The little one works for nothing."

O'Toole shot a glance at the little one Miranda where she sat in the chair. "And what would I be getting for free?"

Shreve shrugged. "It's useful to have someone around to run errands and the like."

The captain looked at his small stage. His lower lip curled up over the top of his upper one making him look for all the world like a disgruntled bulldog. He began to shake his head, when Mike Lonigan pulled open his squeeze box.

Sheila smiled sweetly and began to sing, *"Oh! then tell me, Sean O'Farrell, tell me why you hurry so?"*

O'Toole froze. His stocky body swayed with the song, as gently as a baby rocked in a cradle. His eyes became moist.

" 'Hush, *ma bouchal*, hush and listen,' and his *cheeks were all aglow*." Slowly, gracefully, Sheila mounted the little stage and turned to face the rapt captain. Her ruffled parasol framed her lovely face. Mike Lonigan followed and seated himself on the apron, one leg crossed over the other. His own face serious, he fingered the notes and moved the box in and out.

> *"By the rising of the moon,*
> *By the rising of the moon,*
> *For the pikes must be together*
> *by the rising of the moon."*

Turning sideways she gave him the full profile of her magnificent bosom and tiny waist. Then she smiled at him.

Shreve Catherwood nudged his elbow. "Do we have a contract, Captain O'Toole? We like to book six weeks. We have quite an extensive repertoire. Audiences come back over and over to eat and drink and be entertained."

As Sheila began the second verse, O'Toole nodded irritably.

"We'd like the first week in advance, so we can pay for lodgings."

O'Toole blinked. "Miss Tyrone can stay here on the *Queen of Diamonds*. I've got nice cabins furnished on the top deck for special parties and the like."

Shreve cocked a black eyebrow. "For special parties, of course. In that case, Mrs. Cocks will have to stay with her as her chaperone."

"What?"

124

"Murmurs passed along the valley like the banshee's lonely croon."

Shreve aimed his voice at the man's ear. "I can't allow Miss Tyrone to remain here without a chaperone."

"What? But— Oh, of course, of course. Wouldn't be thinking about it. A lady like herself. Never." O'Toole blinked as Sheila finished and allowed the last note to die away in a tremulous silence. "Never," O'Toole whispered. "Never."

With thirty-five dollars' advance wages in his pocket, Shreve led the men into the boardinghouse. Renting a couple of rooms, he left them to move in and order baths.

Back out on the caravan, he crooked a finger at Miranda. "Climb down from there. I want to talk to you."

Slowly, she did so. When she stood in front of him, he took her arm and led her to a wicker sofa on the side veranda of the boardinghouse. From the small store of money, he pulled a couple of dollar bills. "I want you to take this and catch the first train back to Chicago."

She looked at it, then looked away to the traffic that moved by in the street. "No."

"Don't be foolish. Think of your family. You have one. I know you do. This is a hard life."

She smiled a little. "It certainly is. You told Captain O'Toole that I was going to work for nothing."

"You weren't part of the deal because you're going home."

"I'm not."

"Why not? And don't lie to me. I'll know if you're lying."

She swallowed. "My stepfather. That is, the man my mother is going to marry. He doesn't like me."

He made a rude sound. "Please. Just give me something a little more original than the evil stepmother. Or stepfather in this case."

"It's true." She shrugged. "You don't have to believe me. You don't have to know anything about me at all. Just let me work for you."

"For how long?"

His question stopped her. The idea of what she would do with her life after the troupe had not occurred to her.

He read her doubt in her face. "Hadn't thought about that, had you?"

"I-I can learn to do what Ada does. And when she's old, I can take over for her."

He shook his head. "You won't last that long. Hell, the troupe may not last that long. These things come and go. We formed only a year and a half ago. At any time we could split apart and go our separate ways."

She stared at the two dollars. "I can't go back," she whispered at last. "I really don't have anything to go back to. He was going to send me away from my mother and sister."

"I'll bet if you talked to your mother—"

"No, she would agree. He was going to send me to school."

Shreve put back his head and laughed. "Good Lord," he mocked, throwing his hand to his forehead. "Not school. Surely not school."

Miranda sprang to her feet. "I'm not going back and that's final."

He let his hard black eyes slide over her figure. His assessing gaze made her uncomfortable. She

126

plucked at the wrinkled skirt. "I need a bath. I know. And I need to change my clothes. I've other things in my bag."

Slowly, he rose to his feet, to his full impressive height of six foot three. The black hat with the flat crown was tipped back on his head. He removed it and smoothed his hair before setting it back in place, low on his forehead. "Miranda," he said softly. "I think you'd better go back to your stepfather, if you know what's good for you."

"No, I—"

His long arms reached out and swept around her waist. His mouth came down hard on her own as he hauled her in against him. Miranda pushed against his shoulders. Unintelligible sounds rose from her throat to be trapped against his hard lips.

His arms crossed behind her back and suddenly, she felt both hands clutch her buttocks. Her lungs sought to push a scream past his mouth, but again she could produce only the faintest of sounds. She doubled her hands into fists and beat at his head and shoulders, but her blows lacked power delivered off balance and from such a short distance.

He lifted her body tight against the hard muscled length of his. Her feet off the ground, she was helpless to prevent his walking with her to the wall of the boardinghouse and squeezing her between him and it. The position freed his hand so he could clasp her breast and squeeze it.

Desperately, she opened her mouth as wide as she could and brought her teeth champing down on his mouth.

He leaped back, letting go of her so abruptly that she fell to the porch. "Damn!" He clapped his hand to his mouth and drew it away stained with blood.

"Lord. How hard did you bite?"

She scrambled away to the edge of the porch and threw one leg over the banister. Poised to jump, she looked back at him. "Hard as I could."

"I guess so." He ran his tongue over his upper lip. "Damn! I think the skin's broken in two places."

"Good!"

He threw her an angry look. "That's the last time I ever try to do anybody a favor."

"Some favor."

He touched his lip again. "It's going to swell, too. I can feel it. Wonderful. Sheila's going to love that." He glared at her. "You didn't have to bite so hard."

"I wanted you to let me go."

"I would have in just a minute. I was trying to teach you a lesson."

She shook her head. "You're no schoolteacher."

He came around the back of the sofa and dropped into it, fingering his lip. "The bleeding's stopped. Maybe I'll be all right by tonight." He motioned to her. "Come on back and sit down."

"I'll stay where I am."

"Great. Stay where you are. Better yet. Go on over that railing and run away. Don't come near me or any of us again. After all, I'm a terrible villain eager to have my way with a fair maiden." He looked at her critically. "I think you're a fair maiden even though your hair hasn't been combed since I've known you. Your face is filthy, not to speak of your hands. Your skirts are black to the knees with mud and God knows what else."

Her eyes dropped to her hands. They were as he said. Filthy. Every knuckle was deeply cratered with

128

black. Her jagged nails showed black half moons. She balled them into fists and rammed them into the pockets of her skirt. Carefully, she took her leg down off the rail and stood.

"Come here," he coaxed, patting the sofa beside him.

She shook her head.

"All right. Don't come here, but listen. I kissed you to scare you. I grabbed you and put my hands on you and pushed you up against the wall to show you that you didn't stand a chance against any man bent on having his wicked way with you."

"I bit you and got away."

He shook his head. "You didn't get away. I let you get away. I didn't want you messing up my mouth, for God's sake. And I didn't want to hurt you. That's what you've got to get through your hard little head. I didn't want to hurt you. So I didn't hit you with my open hand or — worse — with my closed fist. I didn't grab you by the hair of the head and throw you down. I didn't grab your arms and twist them up behind your back."

His voice had grown deeper and more menacing with each sentence. His eyes gleamed beneath the black brows. Miranda felt the hairs on her scalp lift. She backed away from him. "I would have gotten away."

He leaned back, a mirthless grin twisting his mouth. "Maybe so. But what condition would you have been in? Hurt. Scared to death. And where would you get to?"

She stared at him wordlessly. Tears prickled at the back of her eyes. She could feel a lump in her throat.

"How old are you?"

"S-Seventeen."

He waved an admonishing finger at her, then shrugged. "If you say so. I would have said fourteen tops, but I'm no judge of young females. You need your mother. You need someone to guide you through the next few years. To help you find someone to marry. You don't need to be racketing around the country with a bunch like us."

She shook her head stubbornly. "I can't go back."

He threw up his hands. "Well, find somebody else. Don't pick us to be your second family. We're professionals in a tough business. We don't run a charitable organization." His eyes narrowed. "Why'd you pick us anyway?"

"I saw you and you were the only one I could think of."

"Saw me?"

"In *Romeo and Juliet*. It was the most wonderful thing I've ever seen. You smiled and winked at me when the performance was over and the audience was applauding."

"My dear girl, I smile and wink at the audience. My eye wasn't focused on you. It's part of an actor's skill to be able to make each person in the audience feel I'm looking at her alone. You're no one special."

Suddenly, she could stand it no longer. No one wanted her. The tears welled in her eyes. She could not stop them. Instantly, she spun around.

He jumped to his feet. "Don't cry," he begged. "I can't stand real tears."

"I'm not crying. I'm not." She swiped her filthy hands across her cheeks and turned back with a wide false smile. "I'm not going to cry, either. I'm going to work for nothing and get Padua sewn back together and then maybe you'll feed me. I'll just stay with you until I can think what my next move will be. I don't mean to be a burden."

"You'd better take the two dollars and go home."

She bit her lip. "I can't. I can't ever go home again."

Eight

This may prove worse than hanging.

Miranda had almost died of curiosity while Mike and Ada set up the narrow bed frame onstage. She had watched with interest while they put blocks under the upstage legs to tilt the whole toward the audience. A board with a thin quilt had gone down in place of a mattress. Then the whole had been covered with a red velvet throw, carefully turned to hide the rent in the hem.

Red damask draperies had been nailed to a central point in the ceiling and tied back with gold cords to the upstage bedposts. At the head of the bed Ada had placed several cushions of varying shades of red and pink with a gold one in the center. The effect was sensually barbaric. Miranda could not imagine sleeping on anything like that.

Evidently, neither could any member of the almost all-male audience of the *Queen of Diamonds*. When the stage curtain swished back, the applause sounded loud and long. Above the clapping of their hands, rose the whistles and jeers of the audience. Their lewd suggestions made Miranda's ears burn.

One man sitting at a table close to the front

grabbed the hand of his dinner partner and pulled her toward the stage. The woman with hair so gold it glittered pulled back giggling and halfheartedly protesting. Again the audience cheered and clapped.

Firmly, Connal O'Toole barred the couple's way and guided them back to the table. Behind him Shreve stepped out onto the apron. He wore a full-sleeved white shirt and tight black trousers stuffed into the tops of high black boots. A short cape swung from his shoulders.

"Gentlemen. And ladies." He smiled blindingly at the blonde whose partner was in the process of re-seating her. "We bring you for your pleasure and delight, a variety of songs and scenes from the lives of gallant gentlemen and the fair ladies they loved."

With a sweeping bow and a flourish of his cape, he moved into the scene and gestured. Frederic came out similarly attired. The conversation between them was brief, then both left the stage, Shreve to hover at the edge, Frederic to disappear entirely.

He had no sooner left than Sheila Tyrone entered carrying a mirror. She posed down stage, to stare at herself in it. Languorously, ignoring many rudely approving comments from the audience, she arranged her skein of long red hair over the shoulder of a rose pink satin nightgown with a deep décolletage. Over it she had drawn a sheer robe trimmed with yards of wide lace dripping from the sleeves and down the opening of the skirt.

The audience applauded, then as she bowed to them, they cheered. Several rose in their seats to get a better view.

She saw Shreve. Anger, alarm, and then fear played across her features. *What will you do to me?*

133

Shreve looked at her contemptuously. *"A bloody deed—almost as bad, As kill a king and marry with his brother."*

His words shocked Miranda. *Kill a king and marry with his brother.* Then they were shoved to the back of her mind by the spectacle on stage.

Shreve caught Sheila by her arms and shook her. She cried out, but he forced her to the bed and flung her down upon it.

She managed to fall so that her robe fell back and her gown opened to reveal a slit in the side. Her white knee and thigh presented a voluptuous contrast to the shades of red.

The audience went wild.

Miranda covered her face with her fingers as Shreve followed Sheila down and pulled her gown off one shoulder. Though her cheeks blazed and her whole body burned with embarrassment, she could not keep from peeking out from between her fingers.

Shreve glared at Sheila, then his expressive features changed. He looked away from her toward the audience, his pain, his temptation real, then he lowered his mouth to Sheila's shoulder. She pushed at him, pummeled his shoulders, but then she relaxed. His mouth moved lower as he pulled the gown farther down. The froth of lace fell back from her shapely white arms as she put them around his neck. Her hands threaded through his hair.

Miranda was no longer peeking through her fingers. Her hands had dropped. Mesmerized, she stared as the couple on the bed continued to run their hands over each other's bodies.

Both Sheila's legs were bare and Shreve's shirt was off his shoulders before the curtains finally swished together.

134

The audience booed, then clapped enthusiastically. Frederic bounced out in front of the curtain to sing a song about a man who loved several women at once. Though the words were not in Shakespeare's artificial English, Miranda still could not understand several of them. The audience, however, seemed to have no trouble at all understanding. They cheered and whistled, jostling and jabbing each other and laughing uproariously.

"Enjoying the show, dearie?" Ada whispered to Miranda.

The girl jumped guiltily. "I don't know."

Ada eyed her wisely. "Just as well you don't. Stay as innocent as you can as long as you can."

"The audience seems to like it well enough."

"Oh, them. And why wouldn't they like it? Drunk as they are. We could save ourselves the trouble and let Sheila stand on the stage and take off her clothes. But that would cause a riot, and we don't want to bring the police."

"T-take off her clothes!"

"Just you wait."

Frederic skipped off the stage as the curtain swished open. The bed had been removed and George and Mike tossed knives and swords back and forth to each other. And then Miranda thought she would die at the sight of Shreve, so handsome in a black velvet frock coat with black satin lapels. As he had told her, his smile touched every woman in the audience. Now that she knew what he was doing, she was ashamed of herself for thinking that he could possibly be smiling at her.

In a beautiful baritone voice, he began a soldier's song that she had heard over and over at various posts when she was a child. Homesickness smote her, burning loneliness for her father and the windswept ridges of Wyoming. The words burned in her heart. She did not try to stop the tears that trickled down her cheeks. Then he switched to a love song.

Just as the audience began to get restive, Sheila appeared again, to thunderous applause. This time her dress was green, forest green velvet that clung lovingly to her waist and enshrined the porcelain-white skin between her breasts. She and Shreve sang a duet and then she sang alone.

When the curtain closed for the final time, Connal O'Toole came backstage to kiss her hand and invite her to a supper.

"Tomorrow, boys, we go out and find another place," Shreve announced grimly when the two had left.

"Right you are," Mike agreed.

Miranda stared from one to the other. "But — but the audience applauded."

"They applauded Sheila with her dress open down to her waist and up to her arse," Frederic told her coarsely. "They didn't want to see or hear anything else."

"But the ladies in the audience—" Miranda began.

"Ladies! Ha!" George's interruption came as a surprise. He had been studying a nick on his hand made by one of Frederic's knives. Abruptly, he rose. "Ladies! Not them! God! What a night! I'm heading back to the boardinghouse."

Miranda blushed. "I enjoyed it."

"You'd enjoy anything," Shreve groaned. "We were lousy. They didn't even know that the scene was from *Hamlet*. If they'd figured out that Sheila was supposed to be acting my mother, they'd have booed us off the stage."

"A man is supposed to be in love with his—mother." Miranda's voice rose in a scandalized squeal.

"It's a tragedy," Shreve said sarcastically. "Bad things happen. A man kills his brother to marry his brother's wife."

"That's it." Miranda leaned forward excitedly. "That's what you said that I couldn't remember. A man kills another man to marry his wife. Tell me about that."

"Later." He waved her away. He looked at his departing colleagues. "I think I'll go down and mingle with the guests," he said with elaborate casualness. "Might sit in on a hand or two."

Heads swung toward him. Halfway out the door, George halted and came back into the room. "Then give me my money now. When you lose your shirt, don't lose mine, too."

Reluctantly, with many a complaint about lack of faith, Shreve divided it and went out. George, Mike, and Frederic tucked their portions into their pockets and strolled out. Only Miranda remained, sitting cross-legged in the corner, her eyes slitted, her chin in her hand. What had he meant—to kill a man to marry his wife? Suddenly, she had a burning desire to read this tragedy. A much battered and thumbed book lay among the actors' things.

She picked it up and looked at it. The names of the plays were at the top of the pages. With little trouble she found the one she sought. *Hamlet*. She curled up and began to read.

Shreve heard the knife sing through the air. He flung himself sideways into a companionway even as

137

it buried itself in the muscle in the back of his right arm. The burning, ripping pain took his breath away. But his survival instincts drove him to twist the knob of the first door he encountered. It gave beneath his shoulder, and he catapulted into the darkness.

He righted himself, shut the door, and locked it. Then he swayed back against it, clutching his arm, feeling the blade where it stuck deep in his flesh, feeling the hot blood coursing over his hand.

He was going to be sick. He took two steps forward, then staggered back and propped his shoulder against the wall. With a groan he curled his shaking fingers around the knife hilt. Just the slight pressure introduced by that simple touch made the pain lance into his fingertips. In the darkness he rolled bitter eyes heavenward. *God! But this was going to hurt! A hero would have had it out in a minute and turned it on his enemies.*

Footsteps, at least two pairs, thudded in the companionway. "I know I got him."

"So where is the bastard?"

"Probably heading downstairs."

"Just so's he don't pitch overboard with our money."

"You always were too quick with that knife, Taliaferro."

"You wanted him. Can I help it if he moved?"

The second speaker grunted. "You go down that way and I'll circle back. He can't go far. Just be sure he don't get off the boat."

They moved off. Shreve could feel the cold sweat beading on his forehead. The pain was making him faint. Losing the fight against his weak legs, he slid down the wall. The wound was throbbing around the knife. The blade felt as if it were cutting more deeply. He had to pull it out. Had to!

"Pretend it's someone else's arm," he counseled himself. He found the hilt again. "Talk yourself out of it. Think of it as a part. You're a hero. A wounded hero. Got to—" He hung his head, then jerked it up and sucked in air between his clenched teeth. "Got to pull the blade out and go save the heroine."

He was panting as if he had fought the duel scene in *Hamlet* twice. Sweat had soaked his clothing. His hand was shaking badly. *Do it.* He closed his eyes tight, grasped the hilt.

Do it!

He pulled.

The slashing pain drove a scream from his open mouth, but the knife did not slide out easily like a false sword. The very wound seemed to close around it and hold it tight. He cursed vividly and tried again.

He might have lost consciousness. He might merely have slumped over on his face. His mind, when he knew his mind, screamed at him to tear the alien thing from his body. Frantically, he grasped the slippery hilt again. His hand was shaking so badly by that time and the pain was so bad that he became convinced that it would ease when he pulled the knife from the wound.

Desperate to rid himself of the awful thing, he began to shake and twist it. Only after he was utterly mindless with pain and weakness, did it come free. Hot blood gushed out over his fingers, down his arm, down his side. His hand had no strength left to grip. The knife clattered from his nerveless fingers.

Face against the cold hard floor, he lay immobile, feeling his muscles jump and twitch beyond his control. "Vary the performance," he whispered to himself, his lips barely moving. "Audience gets restless if you don't move."

The blood was running down his elbow, soaking into his clothes, pooling under him. "Costume. Costume's going to be hell to get clean."

Such a little thing, but he was going to look as if he had been slaughtered. He imagined that he heard footsteps in the corridor, or was the noise only the pounding of his heart in his ears? No. He heard voices, muffled, distant. He pushed with his good hand, but it slipped in his own blood. With a groan he flopped back like a landed fish.

He would lie still a minute, gather strength, then make another effort. With that thought, he closed his eyes and slumped into unconsciousness.

"No sign of him in here."

"That bastard. When I find him, he's dead. Nobody takes Harry Taliaferro's money and blows."

"What about the little room?"

The door opened. Light flashed in Miranda's face. Owl-eyed, she bobbed up. "Hey, Kid, seen anybody?"

She stared into the silhouette, only half awake, the words not making sense.

"Nobody in here but a half-wit kid." He closed the door. The conversation continued outside it. Miranda rubbed her eyes and listened.

"Damn! Why'd you just pink him? If he fell over the side—"

"He didn't fall over the side." One man's voice adopted a soothing tone. "We'd have heard the splash. He's holed up in one of the rooms, probably bleeding like a stuck pig."

140

"He's got a hundred dollars of my money in his pockets."

"Don't worry about it. We'll get him tomorrow. He's got to go on stage. We'll get him then."

The word "stage" caught Miranda in the middle of a yawn. Instantly, she clamped her mouth closed. They could only be talking about one person— Shreve. He had gone to gamble. The others had wanted their money first. Evidently he had won. Now he was bleeding. He was hurt.

She scrambled to her feet and tiptoed to the door. Ear pressed to the panel, she could hear their footsteps fading away. Cautiously, she opened the door. The stage was dark. The supper tables with their chairs stacked atop them were skeletal shadows in the moon and lantern light that filtered in from the deck.

Still on tiptoe, she sprinted to the door. Curious, she had explored the ship in the afternoon before the performance. Now she wracked her memory for a place where Shreve might have hidden. The dining room was in the bow of the vessel on the main deck, but it was only a single huge room with a stage and a tiny dressing room at one end. It offered no place to hide except where she had hidden herself.

In the stern was the galley, the engine room, and various compartments. The crew worked and lived there. He could not have hidden there.

On the upper deck was the gambling in one big room with roulette wheel and blackjack tables. It, too, was only one big room with several semiprivate alcoves for poker. From the noise and laughter, she guessed that the gaming must be in full swing.

The only place that a wounded man might hide with any success would be on the upper deck in one of eight very private cabins that could be rented for an hour or two for very private parties. Sheila Tyrone occupied one of those cabins as did Ada Cocks. Shreve must have been trying to get to one of their cabins. But suppose he had not made it. Suppose he even now was lying bleeding in an empty cabin, helpless if the men caught up with him.

Miranda vaulted up the stairs.

Turning away from the bright lights streaming from the windows of the casino, she hurried back toward the stern. The moon had risen bright enough for her to see her way. She began to try doors. The first two were open, their interiors dark.

The next was locked. No light shone under it. She tapped softly. No answer. She would remember it for later. A fourth was open and occupied. She closed it, blushing deeply. Fortunately, the couple in the bed had not noticed her coming or going.

Finally, she turned into the companionway. She found the first door locked although none of the others were. Only two doors so far had been locked, one very close to the gambling hall, the other very far away.

She knocked softly. "Shreve."

No sound.

"Shreve." Had she heard a faint rustle? "Shreve?"

A groan.

Fearfully, she looked around. The companionway was empty. Sinking to her knees, she knocked as loudly as she dared near the bottom of the door. "Shreve."

Another groan, a muffled exclamation, a gasping breath.

"Shreve," she whispered. "Open the door. It's Miranda. I've come to help you."

She could hear the heavy breathing through the door. It seemed to go on interminably. Then before her eyes the lock turned. She pushed at the door. Again came a terrible groan of protest. He must be leaning against it. Suddenly, she became aware of cigar smoke. Someone must be strolling on the deck. Ruthlessly, she threw her shoulder against the door just managing to open it wide enough so she could squeeze inside.

"Shreve. Oh, Shreve, where are you hurt?"

He licked his dry lips. His voice was only a whisper. "Arm."

"Where? Oh. O-o-o-h." Her fingers were suddenly wet with blood. At the same time she became aware that dampness was soaking through her skirt. Her stomach heaved. She swallowed. "You're bleeding."

"Bad."

"I'll light—"

"*No.*"

"But I can't see."

He caught hold of her shoulder and dragged himself up to a sitting position. "Got—to get—away."

"But you're bleeding," she wailed.

Anger made his voice stronger. "Of course, I'm bleeding. Idiot. I've been stuck. With a knife."

Bright lights swirled before her eyes. The roaring in her ears blocked out the sound of his voice. Her strength went out of her, and his weight pulled her over.

"Damn! Don't you faint on me." He slumped across her. His arm hit the floor sending a sharper pang through him. It steadied him. "For God's sake! Pull yourself together."

She moaned at the sticky feel of the floor beneath her hand.

143

"Damn it!" he snarled. "Get on your feet." He pushed weakly at her shoulder. "Do it. Damn cowardly female."

The word "coward" smote her. She was not a coward. She was Francis Drummond's daughter. Pride propped her up, gave strength to her limbs. She swallowed heavily and forced herself to her feet. Bending over to lift him helped. Her blood carried oxygen to her starved brain.

He put his hand on her shoulder. She slipped her hands under his armpits without flinching at the squishy, sticky feel on the right side. "Together," she gasped. "Now."

She pulled with all her might, but he could not get his legs under him.

He swore softly. "Have to climb up the wall."

She wiped the sweat from her forehead while he maneuvered around until his back was against the door. Then she put her hands under him again. "Ready?"

"Yes."

He went up with surprising swiftness. Then almost toppled over. She had to push her head into his chest and brace herself. She could feel his heart pounding. His chest heaved. The odor of his blood and sweat filled her nostrils. She hung on to him until he felt steady. Finally, she stepped away. "Where to?"

"The boardinghouse."

"You can't make it."

"I can." He took a deep breath. His voice strengthened. Every syllable was perfectly enunciated. "It's over now. I am in control."

"You're not. Let me find Sheila and Ada."

"No. No need to bother them. I can make it," he

insisted doggedly. He reached back and turned the doorknob.

He actually walked as regally as a king, his right hand thrust into his pocket. His head was high. His face showed calm in the lights on the upper deck. Down he came, each foot carefully placed on the stairs. Several men passed them, but no one seemed to notice anything unusual. Probably the most unusual thing was Miranda's white face and hollow eyes in company with Shreve's imperturbability.

Down the gangway they walked. She followed a couple of paces behind. When they turned toward the boardinghouse, she caught up with him and slipped her hands around his good arm. "Are you doing all right?"

He did not answer. Sweat stood out on his forehead. The tendons in the side of his neck strutted out with effort, but his face was still serene. When they met a stranger, Shreve's mouth twitched in a faint smile. The steps up to the veranda were almost his undoing. He negotiated the first one, then stopped, rocking slightly as he tried to find strength to lift his leg.

"Wait here," she whispered. "I'll go get Mike and George."

"No." He took another step. And then another. Seven steps seemed like seventy, but at last he was up.

"You'll never make the stairs," she whispered. "Let me go get them."

"No." He had become set on this. Somehow he knew this experience would make him a better actor. A part of his mind, the artistic part, had begun to function as an observer. The pain—how did one handle it best? The effort—what muscles did he call upon to maintain his body? The endurance—what mind games did he have to play to retain consciousness?

The lobby was empty. He stood at the foot of the stairs, automatically counting them. Fifteen. Twice as many as the veranda. Head up, he began them.

"Why are you doing this?" the pesky voice at his side wanted to know.

He shook his head doggedly. "Must."

"I'm going to get help."

"No." But she was gone. He could hear her above the roaring in his ears knocking on a door. The sound of her knuckles sounded like gunshots. He took another step.

Then George was beside him, nightshirt flapping around his bare calves.

"Watch his right arm."

Her warning came too late. George grasped him around the upper arm and sent him headlong into darkness.

When he regained consciousness, Miranda was sitting beside him. Strong morning light streamed through his window. George and Mike lounged across the room. He licked his lips. "Good morning."

They all regarded him bleakly. Mike shrugged. "It's almost noon."

The expression on their faces alarmed him. He sat up gingerly. His arm throbbed with a constant drumbeat, but it was bearable. "How bad am I hurt?"

"The doctor took ten stitches."

"Ten. It must have been worse than I thought."

"You tore it up when you pulled the knife out,"

146

George supplied. A faint green tinge dyed his skin around his mouth. "If you're going to discuss it, I'm leaving."

Miranda held a glass of water to Shreve's mouth. He guided it with his left hand and drank deeply. "Then we won't discuss it." He eased back onto the rough muslin pillows. Suspiciously, he looked at the three of them. "What's going on?"

Mike shrugged. "We've been told not to come back."

"Himself Connal O'Toole" — George imitated the Irishman's brogue to perfection — "is dispensing with our services. He don't need 'no' troublemakers on the *Queen of Diamonds.*"

"I didn't make trouble," Shreve replied belligerently.

"You took a hundred dollars off one of his best customers," Mike accused. "Jehoshaphat, Shreve! When the idiot started losing like that, why didn't you fold? You might have known he was one of their regulars."

Shreve looked away, rubbing his arm. "I won from some others, too."

"Hope it's enough to last us a long time," George said. "We might be a long time unemployed."

Shreve shook his head. "We'll pick up something quick. Sheila can—"

Mike and George exchanged glances. Mike spoke. "Sheila's not going to do anything, Shreve. She's quit."

"What?"

"Connal O'Toole was so delighted with Miss Sheila Tyrone — and what she could do for him, including singing — that he has asked her to stay on as *the* Queen of Diamonds." Mike made the announcement with appropriate theatrical gestures. "I believe he presented her with a bracelet with an even dozen of the sparklers so everyone would know who she is."

"She's got a contract—"

"Connal said to tell you that he considers the money you took off his customers ample compensation for Miss Tyrone's contract."

Shreve cursed bitterly. "Ungrateful bitch." Then he grinned. "What would happen if we told him she's really Bessie Smith?"

"Probably wouldn't make any difference," Frederic said with a smirk. "Sheila never could act, but with her other talents most men didn't care."

Miranda was following the conversation with growing alarm. "Does this mean that the troupe is breaking up?"

The three men looked at her as if remembering her for the first time.

"Might." Mike heaved a sigh.

"Without a leading lady, we can't make much," George agreed.

Shreve's brow wrinkled. He reached out with his good hand and pulled Miranda down on the bed beside him. "What about her?"

Mike jerked his head back on his shoulders. "Her!"

"She's mighty young," George said critically.

"Oh, no." Miranda tried to pull away, but Shreve held her firmly by the wrist. "I don't want to act. You remember, you asked me about it and I said I didn't."

"Sit back down here." He shifted his grip. "Look at that face. Picture it cleaned up, hair done. Will you sit still?"

"But—"

"Sit still!" He thundered.

She subsided.

"Now look at the color. Natural blonde." He pulled her hat off and began to tug the pins out. "Ada can do wonders with it."

"She's awfully small."

"Yes, I am. I'm awfully small."

"We can always pad her in the right places."

"What places?"

"What if she can't learn the lines?"

"I can't. I can't learn the lines."

He caught her by the chin. His black stare bore down on her. "You can learn the lines."

"It might work." George grinned. "She's certainly the right age for our best shows. Ophelia, Juliet, Rosalind."

"She won't even have to change her name. She can be Miranda."

"Miranda what?"

"Just Miranda. We can add *Tempest* to our repertoire."

"She's too young for Lady Macbeth and Cleopatra."

"I'm too young."

"I don't know whether she could get enough fire going to play Katherine."

"I couldn't. I couldn't."

Shreve leaned back against the pillows, his face pale and set. "It's settled. Go collect our stuff from that tub and let's start teaching her the lines immediately."

"No— Oh, no. No. No."

His hand shot out recapturing her chin and toppling her over against him. "Yes," he murmured. "Oh, yes. Yes. Yes."

He kissed her triumphantly, sinking his tongue into the interior of her mouth, caressing every corner, kissing her, until her shocked struggle ceased and she relaxed soft and helpless. When he drew away, her eyes were closed and her hands lay limply on the bedcovers.

"Why there's a wench," he murmured with a wink at the other two.

Nine

*She has a good face, speaks well,
and has excellent good clothes.*

"She's not in Chicago. Or if she is, she's damn well hidden. She's not at the homes of friends or acquaintances or friends of friends. I've checked them all. She's not in the places that take in strays—charity homes and churches. She hasn't been in a hospital. She's not in jail. And she's not in the morgue." Parker Bledsoe, Pinkerton detective, closed his notebook with a snap and tucked it into his breast pocket. "I'll send you a detailed report of all our efforts along with the bill."

Benjamin Westfall smiled thinly. This effort to satisfy his new wife was costing a pretty penny. *Damn fool girl! Who would have thought she would have run?* "Then what's your next move?"

Bledsoe shrugged. "House to house with photographs. But that's mighty expensive. And my best guess is that she's not in Chicago at all. Probably if she ran away, she got picked up. She's most likely been kidnapped."

Westfall kept his face carefully still. "And if she has—"

151

The detective tugged at his earlobe. His eyes appraised the man who had hired him. He rocked back on his heels. "Then most folks don't want their girls back."

A pregnant silence fell between them. Bledsoe squinted at his client. He was an old duffer. Probably was a little slow on the uptake. "Yuh see," he continued with a show of diffidence, "there's a certain element of our fair society that like a night with a fresh one, so to speak. They don't care much whether she's willing. In fact—"

"Thank you, Mr. Bledsoe," Westfall interrupted. "There's no need to clarify your remarks. I quite understood what you were saying. And frankly I concur with what I can only guess was a suggestion on your part."

"Yes, sir."

"I was only considering." Westfall smoothed his mustache at the corners. "There is one possibility that I haven't asked you to pursue."

Bledsoe waited.

"She had a friend with whom she's carried on a correspondence. A boy. My wife, her mother, has given me letters with an address. She might have gone to him, or tried to. At any rate my wife wrote them letters early on. The family sent word back immediately that they had not seen nor heard from Miranda." Westfall hesitated. How much did he have to tell this man? "But perhaps, they might be lying."

The detective's eyes widened, then narrowed again. "Why?"

Westfall started slightly at the man's lightning question. "Er—she might have told them—er—that she didn't want to be found. She might have convinced them that she had a reason for running away. They might be hiding her."

Westfall waited for the probing questions, but none were forthcoming. Bledsoe merely nodded as he pulled the notebook from his pocket. "What's the name?"

"Lindhauer." Letting his breath out slowly, Westfall spelled the name. "Adolf Lindhauer, Sheridan, Wyoming."

"That all?"

"He owns a big trading post."

"And the boy?"

Westfall ground his teeth. "A half-Indian brat. Lindhauer's a squawman." He spat the words out, finding them bitter as gall. "If she's staying with that crowd, you hit the nail right on the head. We don't want her back. But her mother will be easier in her mind knowing she's all right."

Bledsoe made the notation. "Anything else you might want to tell me about her? I've got a couple more things to try."

"Such as?"

"Sometimes girls get funny ideas about going to different towns and working. I'll send posters around to our branch offices. We'll see what turns up."

"How much is that going to cost?"

"Not a lot. They usually just keep an eye out. If they see her or get wind of her, then it costs money."

"Do you usually have any success with this?"

Bledsoe shrugged. "Once in a while."

"It doesn't sound promising," Westfall observed

with careful neutrality.

Bledsoe nodded. "It's a matter of coincidence. An agent will be working on another case checking the same places I have, but in another case. One girl is pretty much like the next. In trouble. And trying to come home. What's happened is that she's run off with some boy. Then he deserts her, or she gets lonesome for her mammy. Back she comes. Sometimes she's married and pregnant. Sometimes just pregnant. Anyway, she's trying to get home." He looked at Westfall significantly. "And that's another case of by that time nobody's really glad to see her."

Westfall could feel the blood rising in his cheeks. He truly did not want to find the girl. If she should be found, she would be a thorn in his side so long as she stayed in his household and an expense when he sent her away to school.

On the other hand, her mother was almost prostrate with grief and anxiety. He could not understand the bond that seemed to exist between the two. If she could be found alive, but in unsavory circumstances, he was sure he could direct his wife's grief into righteous anger and indignation.

Bledsoe cleared his throat. "You want me to send a poster out on her?"

"That sounds like a capital idea."

One corner of Bledsoe's mouth turned up in an unpleasant grin as if he knew what Westfall had been thinking. He tipped his hat. "Then I'll be about it. I'll let myself out."

"You've got a lot of natural advantages." Shreve looked up at her critically. She stood uncom-

154

fortably some four feet above the ground on the lowered tailgate of a caravan.

"I really can't—"

He raised his speech to drown out her objection. "Educated speech. That's the first and most important thing. I don't have to teach you how to pronounce the words. You do them fairly well. A bit flat on the *a's* and you tend to make double syllables out of all your *i's,* but everything else is pronounced very well."

She flushed. "Thank you, but—"

"You stand straight. Neither shoulder's canted." He was reclining on a pallet in the shade of the livery stable. His right arm rested in a sling, his back was supported by a rolled-up blanket. She had carried a pitcher of lemonade out for him. He helped himself to a glass. "And you don't spring a hip."

At the mention of her hip, she blushed. "I was taught—"

He took a tentative sip, then a deeper swallow. "You've got a good pair of lungs on you. So many females don't speak up. But you can be heard in the back of the auditorium." He nodded as if he had made a decision to buy. "Yes, you'll do very well."

"And my price is right," she muttered.

He cocked a disapproving eye in her direction. "You can't expect to be paid when you're just an apprentice. And remember"—he gestured extravagantly with his left hand—"you're studying with the very best. I myself—who have trod the boards now for over a decade and acted before the crowned heads of Europe—will teach you."

"I want to sew the costumes and paint scenery."

"Nonsense." He settled himself more comfortably. "Now we begin. You are standing in the sun to get yourself accustomed to the lights. First lesson. Don't squint."

She frowned, then tried to relax her forehead. Perspiration trickled down the middle of her back.

He watched her critically. "Good. Now. Second lesson. You can't even start to act until you get the book out of your hands."

"I don't want to act." Miranda clutched her script and squinted again. The sun beaming hotly down into the corral was giving her a headache. Or perhaps the height of the tiny stage was causing it. She faltered and listed to the left.

Shreve reached up and motioned for the script. "Pitch that to me."

"I don't think—"

"Pitch it to me. That's a girl. Now of course, you don't want to act. But that's to your advantage. You'll go about it with no romantic delusions. And you've got to earn your keep. You can't stay with us if you don't work." He lifted his hand like a conductor directing an orchestra. *"O speak again, bright angel!"*

Miranda shuddered.

"Come on! I know you know this." He nodded to her encouragingly. *"O speak again bright angel!"*

"O-O Romeo, Romeo! Wherefore art thou, Romeo?" She held out her arms as he had taught her, then looked down at him for inspiration. He nodded again. *"Deny thine father—"*

"Thy father. Thy father."

"T-thy father and refuse thy name! Or, if thou

156

will not, be but sworn my love, And I'll no longer be a—a—" She stumbled to a halt.

"*Capulet.* Her name is Capulet. Juliet Capulet. Good you've got the most famous speech."

"I've got it?! I've got it?!" Miranda wrung her hands. Frantic tears poured down her cheeks. "I don't even know what it means."

He stared at her exasperated. "You don't have to know what it means. All you have to do is say it."

"But—"

"Opera singers just sing the syllables. They don't know what the words mean. You don't have to know what they mean." He jerked his thumb toward his chest. "I'll tell you what to say and how to look and when to move. Otherwise just stand there and look sad and try not to get your costume dirty."

"I don't want to do this." She shaded her face against the beaming sun, to get a glimpse of a script lying open on his lap. "Oh, Lord. The next speech is ten lines long."

He flipped it over on his leg. "Just get the part in about the rose. That's the famous part."

"Oh, there you are. Shreve. I say, Shreve."

When her tormentor shifted his attention to the interruption, Miranda dropped to her knees and leaned over the tailgate to make a grab for the script.

Over his shoulder, he passed it to her. "That's a good girl. Study."

Frederic waved his arms excitedly. "The show at the Clarke Street didn't work out. They're drunk every night and offending his customers. He's firing them and he wants us back."

Shreve thrust his fists to the skies in a gesture of triumph, then hastily crossed his arms over his chest. "He'll have to pay us more."

"I told him the price had gone up, but he's heard about what happened aboard the *Queen of Diamonds*. He knows we don't have Sheila anymore. He says he won't pay for her." Frederic nodded his head at Miranda.

"The hell he won't." Shreve flung up an arm in her direction. "The greatest discovery of the theatrical world. He'll put a plaque on his damn building someday commemorating her performance. The internationally famous Miranda made her first stage appearance in *Romeo and Juliet*. Go tell him that."

Miranda clutched the script to her breast and swayed forward. "Oh, don't tell him that, Shreve. Please don't. You all just go on without me."

Frederic read the terror in her white face. "Sorry, love, but we've got to have an actress, or at least someone to read the female speeches and Ada's too long in the tooth."

"But—"

Shreve hoisted himself to his feet with Frederic's help. Grimacing, he straightened his clothing, pulled the script from her hand, and shoved it into Frederic's. He pointed a long finger at her. "Come on now. Get up and say the next speech. Freddy, you keep her at it until she's letter perfect. I'll go down to the theater and get the contracts taken care of."

"Shreve!" Miranda could feel her throat close with terror. He was actually going to put her on stage in front of hundreds of people to make a fool of herself.

"O, speak again, bright angel!" Frederic began.

"Shreve!" She went down on her knees in supplication.

He turned back to her, his face only slightly below hers. "You're going to be the greatest actress, Miranda," he promised. "I myself will teach you. Kings will pay tribute to your talent and beauty. Princes will vie for a night with you. You'll be the toast of two continents."

"No. O-o-oh."

He extricated his arm from the sling and placed his palms on either side of her face. His face set against the pain, he nevertheless kissed her softly on her open mouth. Her breath sighed out of her lung. Her lips trembled beneath his. Then he was kissing her harder. His closely clipped mustache abraded her upper lip. His hot lips moved, sucked at her. The kiss was demanding that she do his will, commanding her to study, to recite her lines.

As quickly as he had begun, he ceased. Pulling his head back, he looked deeply into her eyes. His own were black, so dark that she could barely distinguish the pupils from the irises. They pierced her, looked into her soul, saw the girl's fright and beyond that, stirring, breathing, uncertain, the woman's passion.

And when he saw that, he smiled. It was a calculating lift of his mouth. It exposed his white teeth, it twinkled with assurance and practiced charm. "Study, Miranda," he told her. "Work hard with Frederic until I come back. Then I'll see for myself what you can do. All right?"

His right hand fumbled for the sling, his arm

slid into it. Only his left hand cupped her cheek. She nodded against the palms. "Y-yes. All right."

"Good." As if she were precious stuff, he carefully lowered her back on her heels. Then he took her hand and guided her to her feet. "I'll be back." He smiled blindingly again.

She could feel unfamiliar heat and weakness curling in her belly. Dazed, she watched his gray-clad figure as he strode around the corner of the stable and out of sight.

Frederic cleared his throat. *"O, speak again, bright angel!"*

Her eyes remained fixed on the spot where Shreve had disappeared. *"O Romeo, Romeo! Wherefore art thou Romeo?"*

Frederic did not bother to hide his knowing grin.

"I don't know whether she ought to eat." Ada stood with one hand on her hip, the other holding the plate of food in her hand.

Shreve looked at the pork chop, the baked apple, and the English peas. "Better feed her. Can't have her passing out on stage."

"It might make her sick. Some can't eat before they go on."

He shrugged. "I've never had any trouble."

"Oh, you," Ada scoffed. "You're the one's made of iron. You don't have no nerves at all."

"Can't afford them, Ada. Nerves get in a man's way." He looked at the plate again, a little hungrily although he had just finished. "Give it to her."

Miranda was almost catatonic when Ada came into the tiny cell that served as a dressing room. Blue eyes glassy, skin white and cold, she clutched the edges of the dressing table and stared at her mirrored image. Her blond hair hung in long curls held back from her face by a wreath of pink silk flowers. A low-necked nightgown of pale pink muslin showed beneath a darker pink velvet robe clasped at the waist.

Clicking her tongue at the sight of such beautiful misery, the wardrobe mistress bustled in and set down the plate. "Now, eat up, my girl. Less than an hour till curtain time."

Miranda moaned softly. Her eyes glanced at the plate, then slid hastily away.

"Don't care for it," Ada said sympathetically. "That's all right. I told himself—"

A knock sounded at the same time that the door swung open. "Ready, Miranda."

She looked up, panic pinching her face and draining her lips.

Shreve came across the room to put his hands on her shoulders. He held his cheek to hers, smiling at her reflection in the mirror. "Beautiful," he pronounced. "Of course, for Juliet we should have dyed your hair black."

"Hush up about that. What do these yahoos know about Italians or English for that matter. 'Twould have been a crime and a shame," Ada declared. She lifted a lock of hair from Miranda's shoulder. "Guinea gold, I've heard my grandmother call it. And so much of it. Didn't have to add a piece at all."

"Makes a nice contrast to mine," he agreed, looking at them both. "She's too short for me, but I'll work around it." He straightened up. "Come on, Miranda, eat. Can't have you passing out on

161

the stage."

She managed a weak shake of her head.

"Nonsense." He dragged up the only other chair in the dressing room and proceeded to cut a bite of meat from the pork chop. "Now here."

She drew back, her eyes closed.

"Miranda." He drew the syllables out. "Come now. Open your eyes and take a bite."

"I don't want anything." All she could manage was a husky whisper.

"Of course, you don't. But you have to eat it anyway." He poked it under her nose. "I refuse to have your debut spoiled by a faint. What an embarrassment for your biographer to record. No. That won't do at all. Besides, I refuse to carry you off stage unconscious. Now, open up."

Unwillingly, she opened her mouth and he popped the bite in.

"Now chew it thoroughly." He cut himself a bite and ate it with gusto, demonstrating how she must chew, all the while smiling.

It tasted like sawdust and stuck in her throat. When she choked, Ada put a glass of water into her hand and guided it to her mouth. "Maybe we shouldn't press her?"

"Nonsense." Shreve forked up a bite of baked apple. "I know you'll like this, Miranda. I had a second helping myself."

She turned a look of absolute hatred on him.

He laughed. "You see, Ada, she's already getting color back into her cheeks. Good girl, passion. Passion makes for great drama. Eat."

Through the thin walls wafted the sounds of the piano. She started as if she had been shot. A whimper slipped between her tightly compressed lips.

He poked the bite of apple into her mouth and stood up. "Time for me to go. Ada, I leave her in your capable hands. See she eats several bites of everything. Then check her makeup and trot her out."

Miranda caught at his wrist, her eyes pleading. He dropped a kiss on her forehead. "We're all counting on you."

The variety program of the Sons of Thespis had announced Miranda's debut in Scenes from *Romeo and Juliet*. The curtain swished open to reveal her standing on the balcony, lighted at right and left and inside by gaslights. For a few minutes the brightness kept the rest of the theater black.

When Romeo's disembodied voice came from below her, she jumped. *"O speak again, bright angel."*

She looked out into the blackness. *"O Romeo, Romeo? Wherefore art thou Romeo?"* Suddenly, she was aware that white ovals had appeared in the blackness. *The audience.* Her breath caught in her throat. Her heart impossibly stepped up its rate until it fairly knocked against her ribs. Her throat closed on the next words. She could not speak them.

Below her she could hear a whisper, but the roaring in her ears made it impossible for her to understand it. Instead, a restless murmur seemed to roll toward her.

The balcony shook beneath her feet, it tilted her

163

forward and into his strong, warm arms.

Shreve threw one arm around her shoulders. "I am here." He turned her toward him. "Now!" His voice brooked no argument. Each word was separated and directed at her. "Tell me thy name."

"Er—Juliet."

"I cannot love thee unless thee deny—deny—" He nodded encouragingly.

"Deny thy father and refuse thy name!"

"Or—" he prodded inexorably.

"Or, if thou wilt not, be but sworn my love, and I'll no longer be a Capulet."

One side of his face smiled, the other blazed threats at her. "Tell me about thy name."

She had come to the long ten-line speech, but she had control of herself now. She took a deep breath that cleared her head. " *'Tis but thy name that is my enemy—* "

With her eyes never leaving his face except when he had specifically directed her to turn to face the white blobs that were the audience, she became Juliet. The story suddenly made sense in an odd kind of way. They had fallen in love at a masked ball. Juliet loved Romeo. Only fourteen years old and she loved him. A girl two years younger than Miranda loved without thinking. Juliet loved Romeo. Miranda loved Shreve.

The words so laboriously learned came from her lips easily, passionately. The threatening look faded from Romeo's face to be replaced by an easy smile and then a faintly incredulous expression.

"Good night, good night! Parting is such sweet sorrow, that I shall say good night till it be morrow."

He kissed her hands and then lowered himself from the balcony. She caught at the railing to steady herself. The movement dipped the low-necked gown revealing the mounds of her breasts.

Someone in the audience whistled approvingly. The sound broke the trance. She raised startled eyes, suddenly frightened.

Romeo backed away from the balcony to the center downstage. *"Sleep dwell upon thine eyes, peace in thy breast! Would I were sleep and peace, so sweet to rest!"*

The wag whistled again and Shreve signaled to the wings. The curtain swished closed.

Miranda clasped her hand to her bosom and stumbled down the ladder, her stomach heaving. Frederic caught her arm. "This way, love. Time for the curtain call, and be sure to dip low. Let 'em get another glimpse of that cleavage."

With a groan, she twisted out of his arm and bolted for the stage door. Outside in the alley, she doubled over a box of excelsior and paper, giving up all she had. Never would she put herself through such torment again. Never.

The door opened behind her. Music welled out, then stopped abruptly. "Miranda?"

She straightened against the wall and looked in his direction through a haze of tears. "Here."

Shreve could smell the disaster. "Hope you were able to keep your costume out of the way."

"Monster," she croaked.

"Me?" He spread his arms wide. His voice rose incredulously. "Why am I a monster?"

"You made me eat."

"You don't have to eat anymore. In fact, I forbid it."

"You made me get on stage in front of all those people."

"And you were pretty good. You'll get better."

She carefully shook her head, afraid that the movement would set off another bout of nausea. "I swear to you, I will never, never—"

He held out a folded towel. "Wipe your mouth."

She took it, surprised to find it wet and cold; but when she would have wiped her face and throat, he took it away from her and replaced it with a glass of water. "Rinse your mouth and don't smear your makeup. We've got to be back on in just a few minutes. Mike and George are extending their duel so you can get yourself under control."

He was a monster. He expected her to go on for the last scene. She would not. She tried to edge around the packing case.

"Don't," he warned. "I don't have time to chase you down the street. Just wash your mouth." He looked her up and down in the dim street lamp, then asked again, "Did you get any on the costume?"

Horrible embarrassment swept her. The color rose in her cheeks. Valiantly, she pulled herself up straight. "I did not get *any* on your precious costume, Mr. Catherwood. No thanks to you, I might add. You were the one who insisted that I eat."

"You've already told me that and I've admitted my mistake. Let's not play that scene again. I can see you're in control again." He pulled her toward the door.

"No."

"Yes. It'll be easier this time. I promise. You

166

don't have to do the long speech at the end. We'll cut it. But only for tonight," he added. "Next time I'll expect you to do every line. Letter perfect."

"There won't be a next time."

"Of course there will. Everyone gets stage fright the first two or three times, but you'll get over it. Come on."

"I can't. I can't do it."

He put his arm around her to help her up the three steep steps. The heavy door swung open in his hand. "Actually, you were very good. When you forgot the audience and looked at me, you began to be believable. With a lot of work and training, you just might be a passable actress."

Before the stage door had closed, Ada hurried forward and gathered Miranda in. "Poor baby. I told him you shouldn't eat."

"He wants me to go on anyway," Miranda told her wearily. "Tell him, I can't. Tell him—"

"Now, poor little thing—"

"Don't start coddling her until she does her part." Shreve pulled them both on into the wings where Mike caught sight of them. With a grin more for their benefit than for the audience's, he pulled back, then leaped at George, knocking aside the other's blade and sending his own home between George's upstage armpit and rib cage.

George died with much thrashing and cursing, his hands clawing theatrically at the blade and then reaching out to Mike, who dropped and caught them to exchange forgiveness with his valiant enemy. The audience clapped and cheered. Both men rose and bowed acknowledging each other. The curtains closed.

"I can't," Miranda protested. "I really can't."

Shreve motioned to a man on the catwalk. Above their heads a scenic drop creaked slowly down. George and Mike sprang to their feet and rolled out a piece of scenery. Miranda gaped. It was a bed, the same bed on which Sheila and Shreve had performed aboard the *Queen of Diamonds*. Behind her, Ada began to divest her of the deep pink velvet robe.

"No!" Miranda clutched at her shoulders. "No. I'm supposed to wear it in this scene. We rehearsed it that way. Oh, no."

Her voice rose alarmingly, but Shreve swept her up in his arms and kissed her. His mouth still on hers, he carried her to the center of the stage.

She pounded his head with her fists, kicked her legs. "You lied to me," she accused, her voice muffled. "You lied. Liar."

He lifted his head. "Hit me again and I'll drop you." To demonstrate he let her fall a couple of inches. Afraid of falling, she grabbed for his neck as the curtains opened. The audience cheered and applauded.

"Ah, wife, Juliet." He carried her to the bed, deposited her upon it, and knelt beside her. The bed was hard as any plank covered with velvet could be. But she was most aware that her futile struggles had caused her gown to ride up to her knee. She bolted up, trying to reach it to pull it down.

Shreve forced her back down against the pillows. Somehow they had been arranged incorrectly because they arched her back and threw her bosom into prominence. "Say your line," he whispered. "Say it."

Hating him with every fiber of her being, she drew a deep breath. "No."

"Say it." He bent and kissed her, hard, passionately, demandingly. His tongue driving into her mouth. His hands at her waist. The audience cheered. "Say it," he whispered, "or I'll pull your gown off."

She stared up into his face, reading cruel determination.

"Say it." His hand bunched the material at her waist and tugged it fractionally. She could hear the stitches break.

"Wilt thou be gone?" Her voice gathered strength. *"It is not yet day. It was the nightingale, and not the lark—"*

Ten

—not all so much for love
As for another secret close intent.

Grip in hand, Miranda flung open the door of the room she shared with Ada. The sight of Shreve Catherwood lounging against the wall opposite stopped her short. She felt the quiver in her belly as the black eyes surveyed her quizzically. Defiantly, she lifted her chin and strode across the threshold. "I'm leaving. I won't go through another night like this."

"Why not? You were good. Really good." Shreve pushed himself upright with an encouraging smile.

"Good! What difference did it make to the audience whether I was good or not? All they could see were my—my— Oooh!" She hurried down the hall.

He kept pace with her to the top of the stairs where he blocked her way. "I know you're upset about that."

"Upset! I'm so mad I could just about kill somebody." She glared at him, her eyes like daggers, promising him that he was her intended victim. "And so embarrassed, I could die. I just want to get out of here."

"It's the middle of the night, Miranda. You can't go out into the streets."

Her determined expression never faltered. "I can't stay here. You all pretended to be my friends, but not one of you told me how it was really going to be. Not one of you told me the truth."

"Would you stay if I promised it wouldn't happen again?"

"No!"

She tried to duck under his arm, but he caught her by the upper arm and turned her to face him. She twisted in his grasp, but he would not let her go. Instead, he transferred his hands to cup her shoulders. While they did not bruise, they were tight enough that she could not escape. "I admit to being guilty of arranging for George and Mike to set up that bed. But I did it to protect you."

"Protect me!" Her blue eyes flashed with righteous scorn. "Oh, of course. How stupid of me not to realize. You were protecting me by throwing me down on a bed and threatening to tear my clothes off. You made me feel so much safer. Let me go!"

He ducked his head and appeared to study the floor. When he looked up, his forehead was creased, the corners of his mouth downturned. His voice dropped so that its timber had deepened into a rumbling purr. "Miranda, please. You must believe me. I was really regretting that I had forced you to play Juliet."

She looked up at him trying to read the truth in his face.

He stared back intently, then broke the contact. Instead, he let his eyes skim over her determined chin, her smooth cheek flushed with angry color, her temple where a faint tracing of blue vein throbbed. "So young," he murmured. "So very, very young and so inexperienced. And you'd worked so hard. I thought I'd thrown you in over your head. I wanted above all and everything to protect you. I thought—" He cast his eyes heavenward. "I thought you'd be terrible and the audience would be booing and laughing. Sometimes they get really violent and yell and curse. Sometimes they throw rotten vegetables. Sometimes it's rocks."

"Rocks!"

With a heavy sigh he hung his head. "You've noticed that scar on Mike's cheek."

Her eyes grew enormous. She shook her head solemnly. Her free hand rose to her own cheek. "Was that where someone hit him?"

Shreve nodded, watching her carefully. "He's been an actor all his life, but when that happened, he almost quit the theater. He almost gave up his career. Now wouldn't that have been a terrible mistake?"

"Oh, yes."

"You must see that I couldn't take the chance of something like that happening to you. Especially not on your first performance."

"But—"

172

"Your beautiful skin torn and bruised." He trailed his fingers down her cheek. "I just couldn't take the chance."

She shivered, then stiffened. "Thank you for caring about—"

"As it turned out, your natural talent shone through." He released her shoulder at the same time he slid his arm around her waist. Hugging her to his side, he led her slowly, step by step back down the hall, talking to her softly, his dark gaze studying her solicitously. "You were young but you showed flashes of real brilliance."

Her eyes glowed like stars at the fulsome compliments. He felt a momentary twinge of guilt, the veriest hint of embarrassment. But business was business. "Miranda, your talent kept you from any danger. And as for tearing your clothes off. Why I would have cut off my hand before I would have done anything so barbaric!"

"You threatened."

"That's right. But it was an empty threat. And you gave the performance of your life when you were angry. All that passion poured out of you and rolled over the audience. And the audience loved you."

The words "loved you" uttered in Romeo's liquid tones sent more shivers through her. Hypnotized by his beautiful face, the sound of his deep voice, so full, so resonating, filling her ears with its beauty, she did not notice when he led her past her own room and opened the door to his own.

"That's all acting is," he murmured. He took the grip from her unresisting fingers and closed the door. "It's projecting passion."

"P-passion?"

"Passion." He loomed above her.

"I-I—"

"Passion," he insisted softly. His fingertips caressed her temple as they tucked aside a wisp of hair. He kissed her cheek, the corner of her mouth, her lower lip with feathery kisses. "Not pretending passion, but real passion. Acting is bringing your experiences into play."

She set her teeth as his warm breath played over the side of her throat. Her skin felt hot and prickly. He stroked her arms, cupping her elbows, pulling her closer, guiding her hands around his waist. Without her being aware of what he was doing, he turned her and urged her back toward the bed. His mouth slid down the side of her face to nibble at her earlobe.

The backs of her knees came in contact with the mattress. "Shreve," she whispered. "Shreve, I don't think—"

"Ssh," he cautioned. "Experience. All you lack to make you a great actress is experience."

"But—"

He kissed her deeply, sliding his tongue into her mouth, caressing its interior. One arm lifted her at her waist, holding her tight against him. The fingers of the other insinuated themselves between their bodies. With practiced efficiency they began to undo the buttons of her blouse.

"Shreve—"

He kissed her again and drew back, looking down into her eyes. "You're a sweet girl, Miranda.

174

Your mouth, your eyes, your sweet face." He began to kiss her again, kissing a catalogue of her features, naming them as he went. Every other one, he would draw back to look into her face and smile at her with Romeo's mouth.

She sighed, drowning in his eyes, so black with long black lashes. They were Romeo's eyes. Romeo's voice warmed her ears. The hands stroking her body were Romeo's hands.

"Miranda?" He put one hand on the bed and lowered her with infinite care. She floated backward held by his strong arm around her waist. "You're a beautiful girl. You'll be a great actress. All you have to do is put yourself in my hands. I'll take care of you."

Her head was on the pillow and she was looking up at him with luminous eyes. Somehow her blouse was unbuttoned to the waist and his hand was warm on the swell of her breast.

"In my hands you'll be safe." He kissed her neck beneath her ear and then the hollow at the base of her throat. The ribbon on her camisole came free as if by magic and his hand was on her bare flesh. His index finger touched her nipple.

She moaned in pained embarrassment. "You mustn't."

He chuckled softly against the swell of her breast. "You see. You don't understand what you need."

"What I—need?"

"That's right." He bared the other breast and stroked it. The nipple prickled and hardened beneath his touch.

She gasped and stirred reflexively. "I don't think—that is, I don't—"

"Wait. If you don't like it, you can ask me to stop." He kissed her breast, rolling the nipple with his tongue, his mouth shaping itself to the aureole.

Every nerve in her body leaped. She clutched at his shoulders. "Please."

"Yes, sweetheart. Whatever you please." He transferred his mouth to her other nipple, laving it with his tongue while his index finger took up the rhythm on the first. His free hand pulled her skirt and petticoats up until his palm clasped her knee.

"Shreve!" His name came out on a shudder from between set teeth.

One hand closed over her breast, squeezing it gently. The other slid past her stocking to the bare inner flesh of her thigh.

She began to whimper. Small frightened sounds slipped out of her throat while a painful tension began in her lower belly. "Shreve!"

"You're beautiful, glorious," he told her. "No wonder you're such a natural actress. You're made for passion. It's your nature."

She was drowning in his praise. Through a mist she saw his face, Romeo's face smiling. "I can't—I don't know—"

He put his finger to her lips. Then replaced it with his lips. As she shivered beneath his kisses, he shifted his weight, stretching out beside her, pulling her skirts up to her waist. She made a protesting sound deep in her throat when he touched the mound at the top of her thighs. He drove his tongue into her mouth. He leaned more of his

176

weight against her breasts. She could feel him draw a deep breath.

He raised his head. "Let me show you, sweet Miranda. Let me show you a brave new world. *A brave new world, that has such people in 't.*"

"I don't understand." Tears welled out from the corners of her eyelids. "I don't under—"

He kissed them away. "Miranda? Let me—" He slid his fingers through the curls at the bottom of her belly and found the moist, hot silk they covered.

She arched up on the bed, shocked at the sensation, but too confused to utter a coherent protest.

"Sssh. You're hurting now because you want me," the deep voice told her. "You're hot and wet with a sweet itch between your legs. You want me to scratch it." He drew the word out and out as his finger moved in sensual rhythm across a spot she had not known existed on her body until that minute. His breath was hot in her ear. "You want me to scratch it so you'll feel good." His voice was no longer Romeo's, but she was too entranced to care. Romeo had faded before the reality of this all-encompassing heated desire.

She twisted and bucked her hips. His finger dipped lower still into the tiny opening between her legs. She was impossibly small, he thought regretfully. This was going to be difficult. He pushed his finger inside her to the first knuckle. While she writhed and whimpered, he considered leaving her altogether, or at least allowing her a little taste of pleasure and then letting her off. The effect would probably be the same for him.

177

She turned her head and buried her face in his shoulder. In her mindless ecstasy she caught his shirt between her teeth.

She was a wild little thing. He realized he had told her the truth about her passion. It called to his own. He loved a demonstrative lover, loved a woman who moved under him, who lost control and bit and scratched, loved—

Damn! He wanted her. His theatrical training had allowed him to play the part of the rake seducing the innocent maid with a sort of amused detachment. He had watched himself manipulate her body and her emotions. Now he felt himself harden. The silken female flesh enclosing his finger became inexpressibly tantalizing to him.

He could smell her, fresh, womanly, powerfully erotic. She twisted her hips again. He moved his finger, pressing down with the palm of his hand. She cried out, then brought her teeth together.

He lunged up over her, tearing himself away, her teeth grazing his skin. Straddling her, he opened his pants at the same time he twisted his finger inside her.

She moaned helplessly tossing her head from side to side on the pillow. She clawed at the bedclothes and lifted her hips reflexively. He parted her thighs and moved between them. Slipping his hands under her buttocks, he lifted her to his lips, breathing hotly, kissing her sex. She cried out shivering, as he laved her, his tongue driving her into a frenzy. Her thighs stiffened. Her climax was very close.

He positioned himself at her opening now wet

178

and ready. Still she was so small. He closed his mind to the pain he would have to inflict and entered the portal of her body. She shivered again. Her head arched back, teeth bared to the ceiling.

He leaned forward, gathering her into his arms. His teeth closed over her earlobe. He bit down and at the same time he pushed forward. He felt her tear, then he was inside her. Hot moisture, silken folds of flesh caressed him, squeezed him.

She screamed at the pain, but which pain she could not tell. Both were sharp. Both severe. Both quick. They drove her wilder still. She struck at him, clawed at his shoulders, writhed and twisted, dug her heels into the bed and arched up.

"God, Miranda!" He found himself embracing a tiger. Her clawing, writhing violence literally wrung his climax from him without his will. Arms at full stretch, he braced himself above her, shuddering as helplessly as she had been a moment before.

For Miranda the pain eased miraculously, but the need for another kind of ease did not. She still writhed and twisted. Little mewing sounds poured from her throat as she tried to find she knew not what.

Shreve raised his head. Through slitted eyes he recognized the need in the impassioned face, the fair skin flushed and damp with perspiration, the tendons strutted in the slender neck. "Not satisfied, Miranda. Not yet. Not yet." He thrust his hand between their bodies and found the spot.

She froze. Her heels pushed into the bed, lifting herself toward him. She screamed as light and sound exploded in her brain directed by the sensations of her body. He threw back his head and howled at the convulsion when her muscles gripped him.

Together they collapsed, their bodies falling away, breaking the joining that had brought them such unbelievable pleasure. Side by side, they lay on the rumpled sheets, unconscious of anything except the pounding of their hearts.

"Been cherry-picking, old man?"

Frederic's sarcasm froze Shreve in the act of sitting down at the table. His eyes narrowed, his face darkened. "Keep your filthy mouth shut!"

"Sure, he's right." Ada jabbed her fork into the British comedian's face. "What business is it of yours, I'd like to know?"

Frederic drew back from the sharp tines, but his humorless grin remained firmly in place. "Just thought I'd pass the time of day."

"Bad time, Fred," Ada scolded. "If she were to overhear you, she'd be crushed."

Mike and George kept their eyes fixed on their plates though the rhythm of their eating had been disrupted.

Shreve lowered himself into his chair and put his forearms on either side of his plate. "I'm going to say this just once, Franklin, and you'd better heed it if you know what's good for you. In fact, all of us had better pay strict attention. It's to our advantage to keep Miranda happy. She's just about the only draw we've got. She's young and not bad looking. She's got a strong clear voice."

"And no talent."

Shreve shrugged. "I admit she can't act, but we can act around her. With the right clothes—"

"Or lack of them."

"We can make her look good while she learns."

"She'll never learn."

Ada raised her fork again. "You were young yourself once and a beginner, Freddy, m'boy."

"I was never that young. And I never whored for the parts."

Shreve slammed his fist down. "That'll be enough of that talk. If you want her to run away again, just let her hear you say stuff like that. And you'll be out of a job before she gets to the river. Now you will all"—he sent a warning stare down the table—"all tell her how wonderful she was last night."

"She really wasn't that bad," George inserted grudgingly.

"Exactly. She was so nervous she threw up, but she still managed to say most of her lines where the audience could hear them."

"And climbed into your bed after the performance," Frederic sneered.

"The important word being 'after,'" Ada admonished him.

Shreve could feel his ears turning hot. He was furiously angry that they were saying these things about Miranda. He had set out to seduce an innocent for the benefit of them all, and they were blaming her for her own downfall. "Goddamn it!" he snarled. "You will act like you don't have any idea at all what it took to keep her with us—"

"Great-hearted Shreve," Frederic scoffed. "Giving his all for the theater. What a sacrifice! I may be sick."

Catherwood sprang to his feet. His right hand lashed out and gathered in the little man's shirtfront. Ignoring the sharp pains in his arm, he dragged Frederic over the table. "Do you want to keep those rotten teeth a little longer?"

"Boys," Ada warned. "She'll be coming down any minute."

"Do you?" Shreve pushed his fist hard against the point of Freddy's chin.

"Let go." He twisted and clawed at Shreve's wrist. "Let go! You don't need to worry. I won't queer the deal. She's not my type anyway."

"Good morning, dearie," Ada trilled. "I was just about to come and wake you up. You were just about to miss breakfast, and it's flapjacks."

Miranda stared at the two men who grinned pleasantly. Frederic smoothed his shirtfront and moved to pull out a chair. "Sit down, m'dear. Sit down. Wouldn't want you to miss a bit of breakfast. After that stirring performance you must be starved."

She looked at him nervously, then up at Shreve who smiled pleasantly. "I— Did you think I was all right?"

"All right!" Ada exclaimed. "Why you were just wonderful? Didn't you hear them clapping, dearie?"

Mike smiled warmly at her as he passed her syrup. "Good show, Miranda."

"Did you really think so?" Her eyes scanned

their faces, nervous, half frightened, dreading their censure. To her relief they seemed intent on her performance. But did they know what she had done with Shreve? Surely, they would despise her if they knew, in spite of what she was coming to believe was not at all a bad performance.

Shreve smiled reassuringly as he lifted his coffee cup. "To the new rising star, Miranda."

When the others raised their cups and toasted her, she slowly let out the breath she had been holding. *They did not know.* At least they would not throw her out.

Ada nudged her. "Eat your flapjacks, dearie. We've got to do two shows today."

"Right," Shreve agreed. "And we need to go over your lines again before curtain time."

At the mention of two shows, her stomach clenched. In despair she looked at the plate of steaming cakes. They would sit like lead in her stomach. She pushed them back. The four of them looked at her in some surprise. "I'd better not," was all she said as she looked around the table at them.

One by one they dropped their eyes before the haunted, frightened eyes peering out from above purple smudges.

"You can have a big supper tonight after the theater." Shreve patted her hand.

"I think we might have found her."

Westfall's eyebrows drew together in a frown. "Really."

Parker Bledsoe drew his notebook from his

183

pocket. "A young actress going by the name of Miranda—no last name—of approximately the correct age and resembling the sketch on the poster is acting with a theater troupe at the Majestic Theater in Saint Louis, Missouri."

"Acting?" Westfall looked incredulous. "On the stage?"

"That's right. According to this information, she's been playing every night in one show or another for three months."

Westfall shook his head. "I doubt that she could be my wife's Miranda. Why she's just a child. Barely sixteen. Barely passable looks. No training."

"The troupe's last engagement was Chicago. They announced that on their posters. Likewise, she's making her debut. That's on the posters, too."

Westfall's frown deepened into a scowl. "What kind of theater is this?"

"Now that I don't know. I can find out. In fact, if you give the word, I can take the train down to Saint Louis tomorrow. If she's your girl, I can have her back here in a few days." He waited while Westfall plucked at his lower lip. "I won't know until I get there, of course, but this sounds right. The name's the giveaway. It ain't Mary or Betty, you know. Miranda. Not many of them around."

Westfall hesitated. Through the closed door, Bledsoe could hear people talking in the hall. A young girl's voice asked a question. A woman answered her. A cry of delight, the sound of the front door opening and closing, then silence. The

184

shelf clock ticked noisily.

"Go to Saint Louis," Westfall said at last. "Find out if it's her. Get all the information. What kind of acting is she doing? How did she get the job? How is she living? But don't let her know you're doing it. When you have all the information, I'll make a decision based upon what would be best for my family." He nodded his head toward the door, indicating that he, too, had heard the sounds.

"Could be expensive just to get information," Bledsoe reminded him.

Westfall shrugged. "A good military tactician lives or dies by his information. Surprises can be costly."

"Would you be Miranda Drummond?"

Skin prickling, smile slipping from her mouth along with the color from her face, Miranda stared up at the tall man in the uniform of a colonel in the U.S. Cavalry.

As he took the hand she had already extended, he inclined his head above it. Yet his eyes never left off the study of her face. "I swear you are. You're Francis Drummond's own daughter."

A sinking feeling in her stomach, she nevertheless managed to lift her lips in a smile. "You have the advantage of me, sir."

"Forgive me. I'm Reed Phillips. I served with your father at Fort Gallatin."

She looked around her nervously. Shreve and the rest of the Sons of Thespis knew her by her first

185

name only. Although she had given her heart and body to Shreve Catherwood, she had never trusted him with her name. Sometimes, she thought she would like to tell him, to tell her whole story, but then she would have to tell her age. And he might be very angry over that.

Of course, he would get over his anger, she was sure. The troupe was enjoying one of the best engagements of its career, so Ada told her. It had moved up from the Clarke Street Theater to the more prestigious Majestic. She had received a very good review from the critic who had seen her performance as the fiery Beatrice in *Much Ado About Nothing*. They would not easily find another actress to replace her. And now she found that she liked acting more than she had ever thought possible. She did not want to leave. She would never leave—

—unless somehow her mother found out where she was and came and took her away.

"I—"

"You have the look of him." The man in the uniform straightened with a satisfied smile. "Those blue eyes. There's not another pair of blue eyes like those on the planet. I know I'm not mistaken. I'll never forget them as long as I live."

Uncertain whom he might betray her to, Miranda interrupted. "Major Phillips, I beg you not to continue this conversation."

He looked at her shrewdly. His eyes shifted to Frederic and to Shreve on either side of her. He shrugged. "Certainly not, dear girl, if you wish. I merely came back to pay my respects."

186

He bowed and would have moved on. Suddenly, she wanted desperately to talk to someone from home or at least from the home where she had been happiest.

The night after her debut as Juliet, she had turned seventeen. Alone, far from her mother and sister, she had told no one, least of all Shreve, who had made love to her again that night with memorable thoroughness. No members of the troupe had celebrated her birthday, for she dared not tell them her true age. She caught his sleeve. "Perhaps later?"

He looked down at her small hand. "With pleasure."

"After the show I always eat a supper."

"The hotel near here is open at all hours. May I escort you?"

She smiled. "I should be delighted."

"What's this?" Shreve stood at her shoulder his teeth bared in what might have been a smile.

She threw him a startled look. "May I present Major Reed Phillips. Mr. Shreve Catherwood, whom you saw tonight as Benedict."

With a pleased smile Phillips extended his hand to Shreve. "I've just invited Miss Miranda to a late supper at the hotel."

She made her expression animated. "Isn't that wonderful of Major Phillips? I won't have to eat alone in my room."

Shreve scowled. His grip tightened on Phillips's. "I'm afraid that won't be possible. Miss Miranda must rest after her performance. She should eat and go right to bed."

"But I'm really not tired," Miranda protested.

"I'm sure you understand." He increased the pressure.

Phillips winced, but he was no limp-wristed dandy. Hands that had saddled horses, cleaned and assembled rifles, performed the myriad tasks required of a cavalry officer did not falter. He tightened his own grip in retaliation. "I think the lady should make up her own mind."

Shreve winced in his turn and bore down to the limit of his strength. "She's a lady and a valuable member of this troupe. She can't be going out with strangers."

A muscle leaped in Phillips's jaw as he hunched his shoulder. "I'm an old friend of the family."

They were jaw to jaw now, the blood squeezed from their hands, their elbows driven back by the force.

"Stop this," Miranda hissed. "Stop this, both of you."

Conscious that they were causing a scene, both men eased off and dropped their hands. Beside his thigh each flexed his fingers.

"Shreve, I have to eat anyway. I should think I would be perfectly safe with an old family friend. I'd be delighted to accompany you, Major Phillips, but Shreve is right. You'll have to bring me right back after dinner." She smiled at both men in turn.

Before she could say more, Shreve caught her arm and hustled her out of the reception line. "You are not going to eat dinner with a perfect

188

stranger in a hotel."

"He's not a perfect stranger. He's a friend of the family."

He looked beyond her shoulder at the uniform. "He's too old for you. And just who is your family anyway?"

She stopped. An admission that an army major was an old friend of her father's might cause problems. "That's not important. They don't want me anymore, but I guess he hasn't heard. He wasn't even sure he recognized me."

Shreve's black eyes bored into her. His mouth curled beneath the close-clipped mustache. "So he's not a very close friend."

"No. Not very close."

"Then you'd better not go with him. You don't really know him."

What was he so angry about? She started to agree with him, then changed her mind. She lifted her chin defiantly. "I haven't seen him in a long time, but I could get to know him again. I can have dinner with a friend once in a while."

"You need your rest."

"You don't rest every night," she countered. "You go out and gamble. Sometimes you don't come in before sunup. I know you do. Why do I always have to eat in my room and then go right to bed?"

His expression changed. His shrugged his shoulders. He was barely controlling his rage. "Because an actress has to take care of her beauty."

"Then I see why Sheila Tyrone didn't want to act anymore. Why would anyone want to be an

189

actress? I can't go anywhere or do anything. All I do is work. I haven't even been out for a walk since I played Juliet. Miranda, study your script. Miranda, rehearse your lines. Miranda, don't get that costume dirty. Can't I have any fun at all?"

His mouth curled in a nasty sort of way. "I thought I was providing you with all the fun you wanted."

"For heaven's sake—" She cast a frightened glance over her shoulder at Phillips, who had done his best to move out of earshot. In that instant, Shreve closed the distance between them. His mouth came down on hers.

She was kissed by Shreve Catherwood every day on stage. Eight shows a week, six nights, and two matinees. At first, they had been practiced seductive kisses, calculated to take her mind off her nervousness and turn her inward. Sometimes they had been so effective that she had forgotten her cue and he had had to prompt her. Later, they had been perfunctory. She had known he was thinking of the reaction of the audience, judging how long to make it last, how close to hold her. At night he held her in bed beside him with passionate kisses calculated to drive her wild with wanting and longing.

If he had kissed her like that, she would have surrendered the argument and told Major Phillips she could not go.

But this kiss was different. Punishing her, demanding that she obey his orders, his tongue drove into her mouth. His hands moved over her body, sliding down her back, shaping her waist, fastening on her buttocks. A silence fell over the entire room as he pulled her in against him, possessing her before the entire room.

"Shreve!" Her protest was uttered against his mouth. He eased the pressure although he did not cease the kiss. It became importuning. His lips caressed her own. They offering little velvet kisses, sucking her upper and then her lower lip between his.

A curling flame began between her thighs. She shifted her weight from one foot to the other. Her costume for Beatrice was suddenly too sheer, too flimsy to contain or conceal her heat. He was doing it to her on purpose. He did not care about her, only that she obey him.

"Monster," she hissed against his teeth.

He finished and stepped back with a sardonic smile. "Go on," he murmured, turning her gently toward the door. His breath stirred the silky hair behind her earlobe. She shuddered, rolling her shoulders reflexively. Beneath his hands he felt the vibration and smiled. "Go have your fun. But when you come back, you come back to me."

She looked up over her shoulder. "Shreve—"

"Go on." He gave her a little push.

When the door closed behind her, he frowned. He should have kept her with him and to hell with the army officer who had asked her to dinner. She belonged to him. She was his actress, his bed partner, his creature. She belonged to him body and soul.

Eleven

But here I am to speak what I do know.

"He sent them out, ordered them out when he knew— Hell! He planned for them to die!" Reed Phillips tossed the rest of his wine into his mouth uncaring that he drank the bitter, purplish dregs. Without setting the glass down, he reached for the bottle, found it empty, and looked around impatiently for the waiter.

Across the table Miranda sat stunned, images whirling in her mind. Foremost was her father's dead face, his scalp taken, his throat cut in a blow so vicious it had almost severed his head from his body. She closed her fingers around the wine stem, lifted it, then set it back down hastily. The wine was the color of blood. She swallowed convulsively. "I— You must be wrong. You've got to be."

A waiter appeared, uncorked another bottle, and filled Phillips's glass. The major took another drink and shook his head. Despite the amount he had consumed, he did not seem unsteady. "I'm not wrong. And so I told them at the court-martial."

"Court-martial?"

"His lawyers were good. Too good. Bastards." He shot her a look that dared her to be offended by his language. "Got him off. Defamed Bob's good name. And Francis's, too."

Miranda clung to the edge of the table. "Then Colonel Westfall didn't actually do anything wrong?" she pleaded hopefully.

"Wrong! Wrong! Hell, yes! He was wrong." Phillips leaned forward, his pale eyes intent, the blackness of their pupils stabbing her. "They're calling it the Clarendon Massacre. As if Bob Clarendon did it on purpose. He was a good soldier. Good friend. Good man."

"B-but he led them into an ambush." Frantically she dredged snips from a memory long suppressed. "He was a glory-hunter. I heard someone say that. Several people said it."

Phillips ignored her protests, ignored her very speech. He took another drink. "It ought to be the Westfall Massacre. He's the one who caused it."

This time she waited to be sure his spate was finished. Lips stiff, hands turned to ice, she asked the inevitable question. "Why?"

The monosyllable hung in the air between them. For a full minute she did not believe he was going to answer her. Then he shook himself. His eyes scanned her as he leaned back leaving off his wine. "What are you doing up there on stage? You can't be eighteen. You were just a little girl when I saw you last."

She blinked at his shift in conversation, then drew herself up haughtily. "I'm an actress. I'm making my way."

"Where's your mother? What was her name?"

"Ruth."

"Ah, yes. The beautiful Ruth Drummond. With the coils of beautiful golden hair. And the beautiful blue eyes. So beautiful that Ben Westfall couldn't keep his eyes or his hands off her."

"My mother—" she began angrily.

"Stayed over at the general's quarters more than she stayed at home," he sneered. "Night after night."

"She was nursing Mrs. Westfall."

"Sure she was, sitting right by the bedside."

"You're not making any sense."

His lip curled. "Think about it. You're not that stupid. That man you introduced me to didn't exactly like the idea of you having dinner with me. Are you sitting by his bedside? Holding his hand? On stage and off?"

Hot color flooded her cheeks. She raised a trembling hand to her mouth. "I don't—"

Phillips interrupted her protests with a wave of his hand. "Everybody knows about actresses. You parade around on stage showing off your legs and your bosoms."

Miranda crushed her napkin and threw it down beside her plate.

His hand flashed out to close over her wrist. "Don't leave. Finish your dinner. You probably don't get good meals like this every night."

She flushed again because he was right. She had

194

hardly had time to taste the excellent roast beef.

"Please," he coaxed.

She subsided though her chin remained high as she took up her napkin.

He leaned forward; his whisper carrying only to her ears. "Listen, Miranda Drummond. I don't care what you do. That's your business. Francis Drummond's not here to protect you. Lord, but he'd have raised a stink about this."

When she tried to twist her wrist away from him, he held up his hand. "But if you're paying for your keep, then you're to be commended. The fact that you have to should be laid at Westfall's door, too. I just wonder if he loses sleep over what he did."

Her cheeks felt on fire. "He married my mother," she whispered.

"No! That bastard." Phillips set his glass down. "There's no justice. None in this life. He kills eighty-one men and does he pay for it? Not much. He gets what he wanted. He's still a colonel, and he's got Francis Drummond's wife."

"He came to pay his respects," Miranda protested faintly. "He just came for a visit to see if she was all right."

Phillips laughed bitterly.

"Really. He did. He just wanted to see if she were all right," she repeated. "He was concerned about us because of F-Father's death." Her words trailed away.

"I take it his invalid wife finally had the good sense to die."

Miranda was silent.

"Probably he didn't wait until the clods stopped falling on her grave to take himself off to your mother. A very single-minded person is Ben Westfall."

"I d-don't know."

His expression became glazed; his voice, as solemn as if he were pronouncing a eulogy. "Bob Clarendon was my friend. We went through the Point together. He was a fine soldier. He and I planned to soldier together, rise in the army, and eventually we'd have commands. He wanted to clear those damned Indians out of the way. Vermin. Nothing but vermin."

Miranda stiffened at that. White Wolf's Brother was an Indian as was his mother. The fact was that Sioux and Cheyenne had destroyed Fort Gallatin, burned it within hours after the Second Cavalry had rode away. Indians were great fighters.

Phillips's voice lost the funereal tone and became martial. "We should have marched out. We could have saved Bob." He looked at Miranda. "You yelled at us. Told us to do it. We should have gone. When that horse came back—"

"Wellington."

"Your father's horse."

Miranda nodded.

"Westfall wouldn't move. Bastard. He sent them out to die. Eighty-one men died because he wanted your mother."

She shook her head. "You're mistaken. It couldn't be that way. He couldn't. No one would."

He shot her a look of pity mixed with contempt. "Westfall would."

In the silence that grew between them, she hugged herself tight against the awful pain. Her father, whom she had loved beyond everyone else in the world, had died because another man wanted her mother. And now this man had married her mother. She could feel the helpless anger and the pain rising in her. Her teeth began to chatter. She clamped her jaw against the sound.

The silence grew between them. The roast beef congealed on their plates. Phillips drank the wine in his glass and started to pour more, when Miranda put her hands on the edge of the table. "I would like to go now. I can't eat anymore."

"I'll take you back to your hotel." The major pulled a sheaf of bills from his pocket and peeled off two. The waiter darted forward to hold Miranda's chair. She stumbled getting to her feet; her crumpled napkin fell to the floor. When Phillips offered his arm, he had to guide her hand into it. She could see nothing but fuzzy shapes through her tears.

From the porch of the boardinghouse, Shreve saw them coming. His jaw tightened as he saw the way she was leaning against her escort. Only when he stepped out to confront them, did he hear her sobs.

His anger exploded. He shouldered his way between them, pushing her against the wall of the building, and caught Phillips by his coat collar. "What the hell did you do to her?"

Phillips's hand closed over the actor's wrist. He twisted viciously. "I merely told her some truths she would rather not have heard."

"What did you say, you damned—" Shreve's left landed on Phillips's jaw.

"Shreve!"

Phillips staggered. His lapel ripped and then he was free. "You'll be sorry for that."

"Shreve, stop!" Miranda screamed.

Shreve whirled back to her. "What did he say to you that made you cry? He didn't—"

The actor's breath exploded in a whoosh as Phillips drove his left fist into Shreve's midriff. The pain almost paralyzed him. He doubled over, sinking to the sidewalk. Before his knees touched, Phillips's right fist crashed into his temple.

"Major Phillips!"

The major turned to Miranda contemptuously ignoring his opponent's fall into the muddy street. He made a courtly bow. "Believe me when I say how sorry I am for upsetting you, Miss Drummond. I would never have spoken to you had I known I would cause you such pain. You were, after all, one of the many innocent parties in this."

Horrified, she wrenched her eyes away from Shreve's body, lying on its side, half unconscious, limbs twitching like a wounded animal. "For heaven's sake, Major Phillips, please go away. What you've told me has been too much to take in. I don't know what I believe. And even worse, you've hurt Mr. Catherwood, who has been a great friend in need."

"I merely told you what happened, ma'am. If you would have preferred to remain in ignorance—" Phillips rubbed at his smarting knuckles.

"Shreve. Shreve, can you move?" No longer caring what Phillips did or said, heedless of the muddy street and the gathering onlookers, Miranda dropped to her knees beside Shreve's shoulder. She slipped her arm under his neck and tried to lift him. Through glazed eyes he looked up into the major's grinning face. He tried to push himself up on one elbow, but the vision swam and he slumped back.

Phillips bowed ceremoniously, executed a perfect military about-face, and marched off down the street.

Miranda sank back on her heels staring after him. Her tears still wet her cheeks, but she had all but forgotten why she had shed them.

"M-Miranda." Shreve plucked at her sleeve. "He didn't insult you, did he?"

She looked down into his face illuminated by the light spill from the boardinghouse windows. A huge knot was rising above his left eye. He would look terrible tomorrow. "No," she whispered. "He didn't insult me."

"Then why were you crying?" As he watched, two more tears slipped down her cheeks. "You're still crying."

She gave her head a quick shake. "Don't worry about that. Come on, we need to go inside and get you taken care of."

"What did he say to you?" Shreve insisted.

She pulled his arm over her shoulder. "Can you stand?"

"Of course, I can stand." With a groan and a

mild curse, he got his feet under him and climbed up, supported by her. "That bastard really packed a wallop."

"That bastard is an army major," she informed him. "He's served on the Western frontier. He's tough as they come."

Together they made their way up the stairs. "How did you know him?"

She hesitated. Then capitulated. She could do herself no harm by telling him. "My father was a soldier."

"Was that man his commanding officer?"

She lowered Shreve to the bed. "No. They served under the same commanding officer at the same post."

"And he remembered you?"

"Yes." She lifted the pitcher and shook it. "This is empty. I'll just go get some fresh water to bathe your face." She took several minutes to return. When she did her face was calm, all traces of tears washed away.

Though Shreve questioned, she would not say any more. After she had helped him get undressed and settled for the night, she let herself out of the room they had come to share and went down the hall to sleep with Ada.

"We've got an offer for a return engagement in Chicago," Shreve announced with a flourish of the letter.

"On State Street?" Frederic asked hopefully.

"Well, no. At the Meridian."

"That dump."

Miranda felt a chill run down her spine. "The Meridian." Where Westfall had taken her and her mother the night she had first seen Shreve as Romeo.

"What do they want us back for? They didn't like us worth a damn," Mike wanted to know.

Shreve directed a lazy-lidded smile in Miranda's direction. "Evidently the fame of our new leading lady has spread. Her name is written into the contract."

"My name!"

Frederic bared his teeth. "It's those coker-nuts. They'll get 'em every time, love."

Instantly her hands flew to her bosom. A rosy blush tinged her cheeks.

"Pay him no mind, dearie." Ada put her arm around Miranda's shoulders. "They've heard what a fine actress you are, I'm sure."

"Fine actress, like hell. Whenever she bends over, the whole crowd sees the kind of show she puts on."

To Miranda's surprise George interrupted the slender man's tirade. "Lay off, Freddy. She's not that bad. Anyways, what do you care why we're going, just so we're going? You need to give this town a rest. You've spent too many nights down on the docks."

The cryptic comment had the effect of energizing the little Englishman. He spun around to face George, his face red and teeth bared. The older man's eyes narrowed, but he did not otherwise react. Frederic drew himself up smartly and ran a slender hand over his carefully combed hair. "Chicago has its pleasures, too."

"When do we leave?" Mike asked.

Shreve folded the paper carefully and stuck it back into his breast pocket. "At the end of the month."

"Are they paying more than we're getting here?"

"A bit more, which is surprising, since they paid us quite a bit less last time." He caught up Miranda's hand and kissed it with a show of gallantry. "You've brought us luck as well as fortune."

She tugged her fingers out of his hand. "I can't go."

They all stared at her as if she were crazy.

"What?"

"That tears it!"

"Leave it to a female."

"Of course, you can."

She backed away from them shaking her head. "I can't go back to Chicago."

"Poor dearie," Ada reminded everyone. "That's the town she was running away from."

Shreve came to her side. "You don't have to worry. It'll be all right. Believe me. You don't have to see your folks if you don't want to." He threw the others a worried look. "In fact, it would probably be better if you didn't. Sometimes families get—er—envious when they see what a success their daughter's made. Of course, you'll be beautiful in your costume as Juliet. You always are. If they could see you, they'd probably just about burst with pride."

"We're just using your first name," Mike reminded her. "Likely, they won't even know you're

202

n town if you don't contact them." He exchanged a worried glance with George.

Frederic's sneer deepened into a malicious chuckle. "On the other hand, they might. Oh, yes, indeed, they just might. Her family will just burst with pride when they see her 'tread the boards' in a low-necked nightgown with her coker-nuts hanging out."

Shreve spun around and made a grab for the little comedian, but Frederic skipped out of his reach jostling against George. Ada put a protective arm around Miranda, who continued to shake her head adamantly.

With a growl Shreve strode to the door and held it open. "Get out, all of you. I need to talk to Miranda alone."

When they had all filed out, he took her by the elbows. "Now, sweetheart—"

"I can't go back to Chicago." She tried to back out of his embrace, but he pulled her tight against him letting her feel the heat and hardness of him.

"I won't let anything happen to you." His voice had mellowed, deepened. He loomed over her, his lips only inches from her forehead. "You don't need to worry. Haven't I taken care of you?"

When she did not answer immediately but turned her head away, he kissed her temple. "Haven't I?"

"I can't go back," she repeated. *Especially not after what Major Phillips told me.*

"We're your family now," Shreve went on softly. "We care what happens to you and you have to care what happens to us."

"Please. You don't understand." She might have to face Westfall. She was not sure she could. Still uncertain about what she believed about him, she could not face him.

"You'll be perfectly all right with us," Shreve continued persuasively. "You can believe we wouldn't let anything happen to our rising star."

A look of horror spread across her features as new terrors assailed her. A din in her ears were Phillips words, *I know about actresses, parading around the stage, showing off their legs.*

What if her mother found out? What if she actually were seated in the audience and looked up on the stage and saw her daughter? What if her mother found out that she shared Shreve Catherwood's bed on occasion? She shivered violently and backed away, pushing him away with her hands, repeating, "You don't understand."

He caught at her. "Then tell me."

"I can't go back."

"We'll be right beside you. Besides, your parents probably won't even know you're in town. They'll never connect the little waif who crawled into the back of our wagon with the celebrated, the beautiful, the Magnificent Miranda." His voice rose majestically as he uttered the heroic epithets.

She shook her head. "You don't know what you're asking."

"Miranda." Suddenly, he became deadly serious. "You have to go with us. We kept you with us, gave you a job, fed you, clothed you, sheltered you. We trained you. We gave you your break. Because of us your fame has spread. How could you be so ungrateful. Poor old Ada and George and Mike, your friends. What about me?"

"I can't go back to Chicago."

He heaved a theatrical sigh. "Where will you go?"

The question was like a slap in the face. "Go?"

He shrugged. "Of course. We'll have to keep the engagement. I don't know where we'll get an actress to replace you on such short notice. I wonder—"

She pressed her hands to her cheeks, at the same time conscious that he was watching her through the screen of his eyelashes. She could feel herself begin to tremble. She had been foolish and incredibly lucky when she joined this troupe. The past few months had convinced her of that. She had seen the garishly painted girls in front of the theater, some looking younger than she, trying to attract the attention of single men. She knew her own fate. If she left Shreve Catherwood, where would she go? Whom would she go to?

"I really hate to lose you," he said, turning away.

She shivered, then with a trembling hand she plucked at his sleeve. "What will we play?"

He laughed as he gathered her into his arms and kissed her forehead. "I've a mind to do something a bit different. Your Juliet's developing nicely; you're getting some depth of character. Time to try you with something that'll give you more range."

"Do I have to wear a nightgown on stage?"

He kissed the tip of her nose. "You get to wear

flowers in your hair and sing."

"Me? Sing?"

"You're crazy so it doesn't matter if you sing off-key. You'll have new lines to study on the road back."

"What's my part?"

"You'll play Ophelia, to my Hamlet." Before she could say more, his mouth claimed hers in a triumphant kiss.

"He told me this was *not* another nightgown part."

"Hold still," Ada commanded around a mouthful of pins. "I can't take this up to match your measurements if you keep twisting."

"This is Sheila's nightgown, that she wore to play the queen. I'm not playing the queen. I'm playing Ophelia. I asked him specifically if I had to wear a nightgown, and he said I wear flowers in my hair and sing." Miranda lifted the muslin skirt and spread her fingers under it to test its sheerness.

"Don't worry about it, love." Ada stuck another pin in the shoulder, hiking the low neckline up a good inch. "You're a poor crazy girl while you're wearing it, so the audience will be looking at you differently. And any way, you're no Jezebel, but a good girl, you are." She knelt down to give her attention to turning up the hem. "Do you see much different in Chicago? It looks and feels exactly the same to me. Cold and windy even in the spring. Not my favorite place."

Miranda dropped the skirt and stared down at

the wardrobe mistress and sometime actress. "He promised me that I wouldn't have to be on stage in a nightgown again. He promised me I could wear a robe."

"We'll have your hair down in long curls to cover up your whole front. It'll be just like wearing a robe. Have you had a chance to get out and walk around, sort of get your bearings?"

Miranda ignored Ada's efforts to change the subject. "My hair's not that long."

"Then I'll fix you a wig."

Miranda groaned. "No wonder actresses have bad reputations. We parade around in our underwear."

Ada finished the pinning and lifted the skirt, to help Miranda slip the garment over her head. "You're a good girl, dearie. Anyone can see that at a glance."

Miranda plucked her dress from the back of the chair, where the older woman had draped it. Head down, concentrating fiercely on turning it right side out, she muttered, "You know that's not true, Ada."

The seamstress stabbed her fists into her ample hips. "I know nothing of the sort. You're a good girl. You're working for honest wages."

Miranda slipped the dress over her head and turned away to button the front of the waist. "I'm not earning wages."

"Well, of course, you are, dearie. You get a salary—"

Miranda's voice trembled. "No. Shreve's never paid me."

"Never paid you. My stars."

Miranda managed a false unhappy smile. Like a parrot she recited, "I'm just lucky to have some place clean and safe to live and work. I don't need any money." Her voice turned rueful. "I don't go anywhere anyway. People would recognize me—and know—what I did—what I do."

Ada clapped her hands to her cheeks. "Well, forever more. Miss Miranda, people aren't going to think bad about you."

"People throw rotten vegetables and rocks at actors. Shreve told me so."

The wardrobe mistress rolled her eyes heavenward. "Well, maybe on stage at a very bad performance. But you're a good little actress. Is that why you're always hanging around here in the boardinghouse or backstage, helping me?"

A snubbing sound was her response and a quick nod of the head.

Ada put her hands around the drooping shoulders. "Oh, my stars. Listen, dearie. You really should get out in the sunshine more. It's not good for you to stay cooped up here backstage. And don't worry about what people think. They don't know—"

"You heard Freddy."

"Frederic Franklin! Tush. Don't pay any attention to the likes of him. If people were going to throw rocks at actors, they'd throw 'em at him. Why he's—he's—" She paused at the curious expression on Miranda's face. The girl didn't even know about Freddy. "You just don't need to worry about yourself. You're a good girl. Anybody can see that at a glance."

"Don't." Miranda shrugged away and reached for the doorknob. "I know what I am. You don't have to whitewash it."

"Oh, dearie—"

Unable to listen to more, Miranda ran out and down the hall.

"Damn it, Ada, you must have some idea where she went."

The seamstress threaded a needle with practiced ease and tied a knot in the end of the thread before she answered. Her eyes, when she deigned to look at Shreve Catherwood, were baleful. "All I know is that she was upset because she'd found out she was going to have to wear this nightgown on stage when you'd promised her she wouldn't."

He ducked his head. "Her hair will cover her up."

"Her hair's not that long."

"Then you can fix her a wig."

"That's what I was trying to tell her. She said it was no wonder that actresses had bad reputations having to wear nightgowns on stage."

He threw up his hands. "She's got a head full of crazy ideas."

"Not so crazy, Shreve, laddie. After all, you are sleeping with her."

He shrugged his shoulders and shifted uncomfortably. "Ada, it was just something that happened."

Arms akimbo, she directed a furious frown at him. "It was not just something that happened,

209

Shrevie, me-boyo. That girl hadn't been out of her mother's sight when she ran away and came with us, and you know it. You took her sweetness like taking candy from a baby."

His ears burning, he hung his head.

"And you don't even pay her a salary," Ada went on inexorably.

"I give her everything she needs."

The seamstress shook her finger at him. "Here I've been thinking you were a better man than that. Shows how even the best of us can be wrong."

He scowled at her. "Where did she go?"

"How should I know? I suggested she get out for a while. The poor thing won't leave the boardinghouse except after dark and then she slips backstage and stays. She's that upset because she thinks she's a bad girl."

"She's not a bad girl."

"Then what is she?"

"She's not a bad girl," he repeated doggedly.

"I'll tell you what she is. She's what you've made her. Seems like the poor little thing was running from a bad life at home trying to find something better for herself and now she could be in worse trouble. If she's run away again, that's your fault, too. Making her wear this nightgown when you promised her—"

"Get rid of the damned nightgown then!" Shreve yelled at Ada. "She can wear a ball gown, a sack, a nun's habit. I don't care. Just let's not have any more about this."

"I'll fix her a habit." Ada's smile indicated her

deep satisfaction. "The audience can think that's where she's been. After all, *Get thee to a nunnery.*"

"But where is she now?"

Finding no answer to his question with Ada, he hurried to the theater expecting to find Miranda there. A worried frown knitting his brow, he made a thorough search through all the dressing rooms, all the nooks and crannies where a small girl might curl up and study her script—or cry. The thought of her crying somewhere irritated him mightily. She had absolutely nothing to cry about. She was an actress. The profession required a certain daring. So he would tell her when he found her.

He stomped into his dressing room and bent to unlock his trunk. The sight of the lock froze his blood. Someone had pried it open. Someone had broken into his trunk where the company cashbox was kept. With a heartfelt oath he flung the lid back. Sure enough, the cashbox had been moved. A cold weight in the pit of his stomach, he lifted it out and opened it.

The money was still there, though the bills were disarranged. Rifling through it, he could almost swear that someone had taken four or five one-dollar bills. He could not be sure of the silver and gold coins.

Such a petty thief. Miranda!

He cursed fluently. But where had she gone and why?

Twelve

*For look you how cheerfully
my mother looks.*

Miranda tapped on the roof of the hansom. The cabbie pulled to a halt and waited for his passenger to descend. When she did not move, he leaned far out over the side to peer in through the window glass. She sat pressed back against the cushions, staring intently at the house across the street.

"What's y'r pleasure, missus?"

She started, looking at him as if she had no idea who he was. Then she smiled slightly. "I'm not sure. That is, I'm—er—not sure this is the place. If you'll just wait a few minutes."

"Long as y' want, missus. It's y'r money." So saying he straightened and settled himself more comfortably on the seat.

Inside the cab Miranda tried to stem the rising tide of emotions. Inquiry at the post office upon the troupe's arrival in town had provided Benjamin Westfall's new address. She had purposefully chosen a time of day when the man would unlikely be at home. Now, carefully dressed in the most lady-like costume Ada had ever created, her face bare of makeup, she waited outside the house, waited for a glimpse of her mother and sister, waited for her nerve to come back to her.

Her mother! A lump formed in her throat and grew, choking her. Salty tears unshed stung her eyes. Blinking rapidly, she bowed her head. In so doing she caught sight of her hands, knotted into tight fists in her lap. She managed a rueful smile. As if she were about to go on stage, she put back her head, took several deep breaths, and flexed her fingers.

For the first time Shreve's tension-relieving tricks did no good. Once started, she could not stop crying for her mother, whom she missed with all her young heart. Yet she was so afraid.

Ruth would be glad to see her. But after the first hugs and kisses were over, she would want to know where her daughter had been over the past six months. She would look at Miranda with hurt, loving eyes and a sweet mouth. And Miranda did not dare to tell her.

Ruth would be dismayed to learn her daughter had been traveling and living with a troupe of actors. She would be horrified to learn that Miranda had been acting on the stage in her nightgown. She would be prostrated if she learned of the awful shameful relationship with Shreve Catherwood.

Miranda shifted uncomfortably in her seat. Her cheeks reddened and burned. If her mother knew about Shreve Catherwood, she would probably not want to see her daughter again.

Miranda closed her eyes against the pain. Her

mother had been the dearest person in the world to her in the three years after her father's death. They had been more than mother and daughter, closer than sisters. Together they had reared Baby Rachel into a chubby darling who toddled from one to another. Miranda's sister had loved nothing better than to put her arms around both their necks and hug and kiss them each in turn.

Miranda tilted her head back, but still the tears oozed out beneath her eyelids. Oh, the feel of those loving arms around her!

Why had her mother turned against her? As if Benjamin Westfall were some sort of savior, Ruth Drummond had welcomed him eagerly. She had left her own mother and father who had given her shelter, albeit with a certain grudging air. If she were perfectly honest with herself, Miranda could understand Ruth's feelings for her parents. The parallel between her own flight to Shreve Catherwood and her mother's to Benjamin Westfall did not escape her.

What she could not understand was why her mother had also turned against her own daughter. Why had she agreed with Westfall's decision to send Miranda away? No doubt, if Miranda appeared again, Ruth would again defer to her husband? Would Miranda be bundled off to a girl's school in—where had he said?—New Orleans?

If the thought of such an existence had been abhorrent when Westfall had told her of his plans, it was so much more so now. Despite the hard work, the nightly stage fright, the constant stream of criticism from Shreve, the embarrassment before the audience — despite everything, she thrived on the excitement of it. She could not say why. Perhaps her army life had bred a strain of toughness in her. No, she could not go back to being what she had been. She did not want to return to live with Westfall. She only wanted so desperately to see her mother.

The coach horse switched its tail and shifted its weight. The movement jiggled the cab.

Miranda opened her eyes in time to see the door open in the fine white house across the street. Her little sister skipped out clad in a buttercup yellow dress, with a yellow bow in her pale cornsilk hair. White stockings covered her pudgy little legs, and her little feet were clad in white patent leather shoes. On the edge of the porch she danced up and down in the sunlight, swinging a tiny reticule of the same yellow material. She was so beautiful and so dear that Miranda could almost feel the chubby arms around her neck and hear the precious words, *"Wuv oo, 'randa."*

On tiptoes the little girl ran to the edge of the wide white porch to peer around the corner of the house. Jumping up and down with excitement, she ran back to the open door where she called out something Miranda could not understand.

Hardly a moment passed before Ruth Drummond Westfall joined her daughter on the porch. Leaning forward in the cab, Miranda gasped at the picture her mother made. A small voice told her she would have had great difficulty in recognizing the older woman on the street.

Gone was the saddened and defeated soldier's

widow who had been eager to leave her father's house. No longer did her posture droop. No longer did her face reflect her hurt and loss. The new Mrs. Westfall looked much younger than the old Widow Drummond. Moreover, the smile she bestowed on her excited daughter was one of such love and pleasure that Miranda felt a twinge of jealousy. Just such a smile had Ruth Drummond been wont to lavish on her older daughter before Benjamin Westfall entered their lives.

Ruth's hair was swept up under a brown crush hat with a cream plume that curved flatteringly over one ear. Her dress was brown also, but cut in the very latest style. She had draped an exquisite lace canezou over her shoulders and tucked it into the belt. More lace trimmed the cuffs of the three-quarter-length sleeves and the apron effect on the draped and gathered-back skirt.

Miranda had spent enough time with Ada Cocks to know the worth of a gown like that. Benjamin Westfall had taken her mother up into the lap of luxury. No wonder the recipient of a captain's meager pension was happy. A flash of resentment heated the blood in Miranda's veins. She hesitated, drew in a deep breath, and leaned forward to open the carriage door.

A pair of high-stepping bay horses came around the corner of the house. They were hitched to a spanking new coal-box buggy painted dark blue with maroon stripes. The driver was Benjamin Westfall

Smiling, he pulled the horses to a halt and stepped down. Curls bouncing, Rachel held up her little arms and was swung up onto the seat. In a burst of childish happiness, she hugged him tightly and planted a swift kiss on his cheek. An indulgent smile lighted his dark, thin face as he handed his wife up beside her.

The very sight of the man had driven Miranda back against the cushions of the cab. With burning eyes she watched the colonel climb up himself and settle Rachel between him and his wife on the leather seat in the bright autumn sunlight. Where were they going so elegantly dressed at this time in the morning? Then she remembered. Of course. The hypocrite was taking his family to church.

Miranda was swept by anger so fierce that her nails drew blood from the palms of her hands. Only the bones of her father remained. His young life had been snatched from him by piercing agony. Not for him the handsome carriage, the prancing horses, the beautiful blond child in buttercup yellow, and the exquisite wife with love in her eyes. This man had taken all that love away from him.

Miranda ground her teeth as the red tide of vengeance ripped through her. What would Ruth say, if Miranda told her the horrible story Maj. Reed Phillips had told? *As kill a king and marry with his brother.* The lines blazed in her mind.

What if she instructed the cabdriver to catch the buggy? What if she confronted them and denounced him in her mother's presence? She raised her parasol to tap on the roof, then brought it down.

Other lines floated in her memory. *Nor let thy*

soul contrive against thy mother aught. Ruth would not want to live with her new husband when Miranda told the story. Westfall had sent Francis Drummond and a whole troop of men into an ambush. His selfish purpose was the destruction of one man, Miranda's father, so he could court Ruth Drummond. But Miranda could not lay blame for her father's death upon Ruth. She was the innocent victim in all this. Only Westfall was guilty.

The carriage turned the corner at the end of the tree-lined street and disappeared. Miranda's anger subsided to a gnawing pain. They were going to church together, and she was so far from them, from the life she had once known that she had lost track of Sundays. In her world people did not rest and worship together. They worked eight shows in six days and rehearsed on the day they did not perform.

They gambled and drank. They prostituted themselves and their specious talents. They slept with each other without benefit of wedlock. Fierce anger turned to shame. Suddenly, she felt exhausted, wrung by destructive emotions she could not begin to control.

In a hoarse voice she called to the cabbie. "Drive along Lake Shore Drive. Drive down Michigan Avenue. Drive around until I tell you to stop."

Shreve Catherwood caught her by the arm as she came through the stage door a couple of hours before curtain time. His face like a thundercloud, he dragged her back into his dressing room.

"I want to know where you've been," he blazed. "And you'd better make the story good."

She accepted his maltreatment numbly, allowing him to shove her down in a chair and unwind the reticule from her wrist.

Opening it, he poured the money out into his hand. He stared puzzled at a crumpled dollar bill and a small handful of coins. "How much did you take?"

"Just five dollars," she replied dully.

"Five dollars!" He looked at her in disbelief. "Is that all?" He caught himself. Even though she had taken very little, she must not be allowed to get away with this. She could not just help herself anytime she felt like it. "Do you realize that's a whole week's wages?"

"Is it?"

He slammed the money down on the dressing table. A couple of coins shot away and rolled across the floor. "Damn you, you know it is. And you've spent more than half of it."

"I hired a cab."

His mouth twisted. "A cab. What for?"

She did not answer. Somewhere within her a tiny flame of rebellion ignited. He had no right to be angry. She was back in plenty of time to get dressed and run through her lines.

"Answer me, Miranda," he insisted, angry at the way she sat with her head bowed, so he could not see her face. "Where did you go?"

"I went for a drive."

He could feel his anger rising. Damn her! She would tell him the truth. He would have the truth from her and then he would make damn certain she never did anything like this again. After all he was responsible for the discipline of the company. "Oh, you did. Without a word. Without permission. You took money that didn't belong to you and just drove around. Doing what? You latched on to us here. Don't tell me you were out sightseeing."

She hunched her shoulders as his sarcasm assailed her. Her hands which had been lying limp suddenly clenched. "What if I were?"

His long fingers seized her chin and tilted up her face. She tried to twist away, but he tightened his grip. "Have you been crying?"

She made no answer, merely stared at him.

Suddenly, he became aware that she wore the gown of the leading character in *Much Ado about Nothing*. The costume was a walking dress with a plaid taffeta skirt and a dark green jacket. Her hair was tucked up under a dark green toque. She might have been any young woman of good family.

He slowly spread his fingers releasing her chin. When he spoke again, his voice was gentle, coaxing. "What have you been up to?"

She took a deep breath. *"I wonder that you will still be talking.* That's certainly my business."

He recognized the line, recognized Beatrice's line uttered with the voice and intonation he had taught Miranda to use. The pronunciation and enunciation of all syllables was precise.

He straightened instantly. "Don't you use that tone with me. I taught you that. You're acting.

You may be able to fool whatever idiot you've been with, but you can't fool me."

His accusation startled her. "What makes you think I've been with anyone?"

He folded his arms across his chest. "Because—unlike him—I am not a fool. Couldn't you get enough with me? Did you have to go out into the street?"

She gaped at him. "I don't know what you're talking about."

"I'm talking about going out and finding some-one—some man to have a little fun with."

Suddenly, she realized what he was suggesting. Her cheeks turned bright red with shame. She sprang to her feet and backed away. "Is that what you think of me?"

He hesitated. "What else am I to think? Tell me what I should think."

Backing away from him, she shook her head. One hand rose to cover her mouth to hide the hurt as his words sank into her brain. The lesson was cruel and salutary. He had no respect for her at all. And she could not blame him. Her de-fiance instantly deflated. "You're a fool," she countered softly. "And I'm a worse one for what I've let you do to me. It's Sunday, for heaven's sake."

"So you've been to church? Make it better than that."

"No, not to church. But I didn't go out and find a man to satisfy my *passion* with, as you seem to think. You're the only man who's ever touched me. But what should you care if I did go out and—and do what you think I did? I thought *passion* was what you wanted me to discover. Isn't that what you said? Wouldn't you want me to find out what I'm capable of now that my *passion* is aroused?"

"You—you—" The devil flamed in his black eyes. Enraged, he started toward her. His hands knotted into fists.

She backed away from him. "No! Damn you! You're not going to strike me! Not again." The corner of the trunk caught her behind the knee, upsetting her. Though Shreve lunged for her, she tipped sideways and ended up on the floor.

"Miranda—"

"Stay away from me." She rolled over and staggered to her feet evading his reaching hands. Humiliation flowed out of her in a storm of tears. "Stay away. Just stay away."

"Now, Miranda." He drew back aghast. "Take it easy." Terrible sobs tore out of her throat. All this emotion could not have been because he had frightened her. He had only been angry. She had seen him angry before when rehearsals had not gone well. She had hardly reacted at all then.

She spun away, presenting her back, her shoulders shuddering with sobs. "You just stay away. You won't strike me. No one is ever going to strike me again."

He shook his head in bewilderment. What was she thinking of? "Miranda," he said soothingly. "Miranda, don't cry." The tips of his fingers touched her shoulders.

"No." She tried to shrug him off.

222

"Miranda." He lowered his voice, taking on a chiding tone. "I'm not going to strike you. I'd never hurt you." He slid his palms onto her shoulders; his fingers splayed across her chest.

She snatched at them, throwing them off and stepping away. "Let me go. Don't come near me. I know what you think of me. I know!"

"Miranda." He tried a stern approach. "Get hold of yourself."

"Oh, yes. I must get hold of myself." She laughed shakily, her voice still thick with tears. "I guess I let a little too much *passion* overflow then, didn't I?" She turned to face him. "I just want you to know that I didn't do what you seem to think I did. But, of course, once a girl is 'ruined'—"

"You're not ruined."

"—then everyone, even the man who 'ruined' her thinks she's going to go out and start whoring for a living."

He caught the hysterical girl by the shoulders. "Miranda! As God is my witness, I swear to you, I never thought you were whoring."

"Why would I go out and find someone to have fun with when you're—I'm—?" She choked on the words, unwilling to reveal her true feelings for fear he would somehow laugh.

"I didn't believe you did," he soothed. "Really I didn't."

"Didn't you?" She looked up at him wildly. "You thought I stole money from the company. Well, maybe I did that, but I had never been paid a cent."

223

"I've been meaning to pay you," he muttered.

"And what difference does it make if I took a few dollars and went driving, I'd like to know? You've never paid me at all. I should think I'm entitled to some money. To something."

Her words stopped him. Guilt washed over him in a chilling flood. She was right. He had never paid her anything. He had gotten used to thinking of her as his property. She was reminding him that she did not belong to him. She was her own person.

"You're mistaken," he improvised quickly. "All you had to do was come to me and ask. I've been saving your money for you. I—er—I do the same with everybody. I'm sort of the banker. I keep it all in the trunk. When they need something or want something, they just come to me."

"Do Mike and George come to you?"

"Yes."

"Does Freddy come to you?"

"Well, not Freddy. He likes to keep his own. But Ada comes to me."

"Oh."

She was calmer now. Her chest no longer rose and fell with the turbulence of her breathing. The lifelessness was returning. Her defiant stare faltered.

Gently, he removed the dark green toque. Her hair tumbled down, a long swathe of gold divided at the shoulder, spilling over her breast and down her back. She made to gather it up with hands that had begun to tremble. He stopped her, smoothing it himself into one skein which he

draped over her shoulder.

He smiled his most practiced smile. "I'm sorry I said what I did. But I was worried. Chicago is such a tough town. And to tell you the truth, I didn't remember this was Sunday."

She smiled back wanly. "I didn't, either."

"When I found you gone, I got worried. Don't you know I worry about you, Miranda?" His fingers touched her temples, trailed down her jaws, slid beneath her ears. His lips caressed her forehead in a kiss that was like a benediction. "I didn't know where you'd gone. You'd never gone off before. And when you didn't come back, I was afraid for you."

She closed her eyes beneath his ministrations. Chills played down her spine at the delicacy of his touch. She shivered. "I went to see where my mother was living."

He nodded. He should have thought of that. What a lot of trouble he would have saved himself. His thumbs ran along the underside of her jaw. He kissed her again. "And did you see her?"

She went very still. "No."

"No?"

"No. The cab was a waste of money. I'm sorry I took it."

She was a dreadful liar. Her face flushed. Her breathing quickened. Her fingers twitched. Still, he was infinitely relieved. If she had been welcomed like the prodigal returning, he might be out an actress and the biggest draw the Sons of Thespis had ever had. He pulled her against his chest and rested his cheek on top of her head. "I'm sorry."

"I'm not."

"But you didn't get to see her." He slipped his arm around her waist and led her to the hard wicker chaise. It was not very comfortable, and it creaked, but it would have to do. "Did you go to the wrong house?"

"I didn't go to the wrong house."

He wracked his brain, trying to remember what, if anything, she had said about her former life. "Did you see your father?"

They sat down together, his arm latching her warmly to his side. She shook her head. "My father is dead."

With his free hand he smoothed the tumbled locks. "What did you see?"

She lifted her head sharply and shook back her hair. "I don't want to talk about it. I'm sorry if you thought you'd been robbed, but I didn't know that I had to ask you for money. I didn't know—I thought perhaps I hadn't really earned any."

"You can have money when you want it. All you have to do is ask." His arm slid up across the back of her shoulders.

"I'll pay it back."

"You don't have to do that." He reached across her body, resting his free hand on her thigh. "Just keep it."

The heat sank through the layers of material to her flesh. She caught her breath; her stomach muscles clenched. She could not believe that the touch of his hand pulled such a swift response from her. She could feel the blush rising out of her throat. Hastily, she ducked her head to hide its effects.

"It's yours." His voice throbbed scant inches from her ear. "You've earned it. And more."

His warm breath fanned her cheek. The heat grew at the bottom of her belly. She shifted nervously. "Thank you."

He put his finger under her chin. "Miranda, you don't have any reason to thank me. It's your money. You've worked hard to earn it. Each performance is better than the one before."

"You didn't seem to think so last night," she reminded him, alluding to the late rehearsal when she had gotten her blocking reversed and he had cursed her for an inept amateur.

His arm tightened around her shoulders as he touched his lips to her cheek. "Who cares about a rehearsal? We were all tired. We'd been through that scene too many times. Besides, you know me now. My bark is much, much worse than my bite."

He punctuated the last sentence with tiny kisses down her jaw to her earlobe. On the word "bite," his teeth inflicted a tiny pain that was really no pain at all. His breath tickled her ear.

She squirmed, making the wicker creak. "Shreve—"

"You've had an unhappy day, Miranda. You've been crying. It takes a lot to make you cry. Come to think of it, I've never seen you cry."

"I'm ashamed of myself," she whispered, arching her back. "Crying doesn't do any good."

"Sometimes it makes you feel better." Every

word was a breath in her ear, tickling her, drawing tiny whimpering noises from her. Efficiently, he opened her gown and slid his fingers inside to tease and shape her nipple. "But something else makes you feel a whole lot better." He bit her earlobe again. "Mi-ran-da. Let me make love to you. I want to make you feel good."

She opened her mouth to draw breath only to have him instantly cover it with his own. His kiss was deep, his tongue playing over hers.

He was right. The need for reassurance, for love rose within her. At that moment she wanted him more than she ever had. Her body was on fire and still she shivered.

He felt the vibration. His hands and tongue felt her quaking. "Miranda?"

She sucked in a steadying breath. "I'm sorry."

He pulled her tight against him, holding her against his chest. "Do you want me to make love to you? You've had a bad day. You're too unhappy. I can make you happy."

"Yes, please, Shreve," she whispered. Her arms wrapped tight around his waist. "Make love to me."

He kissed her again. "That's my sweet Miranda. Just put yourself in my hands. You need to know that someone cares for you."

She wanted to believe him. "You care for me?"

The pleading tone in her voice made him hesitate. Then he smiled his beautiful practiced smile. "How can you doubt it? When I've been out of my mind with worry." He shifted his position and tugged her skirts up.

She had bathed and dressed with care. Hose with fancy garters, petticoats, and pantalets. The sight of all that underwear was oddly erotic to him. He was used to finding her in crude plain coverings. His nostrils caught the scent of lilac-scented soap. For the first time, he felt a wave of real desire. "Miranda."

Her eyelashes flew up. His voice was hoarse, unlike itself. His gaze was not on her face, but turned downward to her lap. Suddenly shy, she caught at his wrists when he placed his hands on the insides of her thighs and parted them.

The slit in her pantalets gaped, revealing the curly blond hair. He could not resist. "Stand up."

"What — ?"

"Hold your skirts."

"Shreve."

He pressed his mouth through the opening in the warm linen.

She cried out in surprise and embarrassment. Her fists clutching the bundles of her skirts, pushed halfheartedly at him, but he ran his hands up the backs of her thighs under her drawers and clasped her buttocks. The scent of her was in his head, the taste of her in his mouth. His tongue demanded more, burrowed deep, touched the throbbing nub protected by soft lips in the nest of golden hair.

She moaned with pleasure. Despite the nervousness, the fear that somehow he had lost his mind, that what he was doing to her was wrong, the ecstasy of her body overrode her mind. With legs spread, she pushed her hips forward and arched

229

her back. The heat from her belly rose to her stiffening breasts; her nipples began to ache.

Abandoning her skirts, she clutched at her own breasts. They felt heavy and hard, the nipples prickling. The feeling was unbearable. She caught first one nipple and then the other with her thumbs, crushing them against the side of her index finger.

Heat and painful tensions radiated from the spot where Shreve's mouth tormented her flesh. She moaned again. Her heels pushed against the floor, tensing every muscle unbearably. It was enough. It was more than enough. She convulsed, crying out in pleasure, twisting in his hands, slumping, falling. He managed to guide her body across the chaise. Her head found no pillow, but empty air on the other side. Her long hair fanned around her and spilled to the floor.

Jaw set, eyes blazing, he rose. With the hot honeyed taste of her still in his mouth, he unbuttoned his trousers. Setting his knee onto the cushion beside her, he drove into her body in one swift stroke. She gasped, opening her eyes to see the ceiling and the wall behind the chaise.

An unintelligible sound escaped his lips, as he pulled himself back and drove in again, sheathing himself, feeling her hot clasp around him. For the first time in their lovemaking, he lost control. No longer was he acting. And in that moment he was not gentle, not civilized. A male creature moving by instinct to find the pleasure for which his powerful body was designed.

His strength did not frighten her. She welcomed

it, wrapped her legs around him, and drew him deeper. She arched her back, the wicker protesting beneath her, offered him her breasts.

He bent to them, suckled them, grazed them with his teeth, while she pushed against him whimpering in pleasure-pain. Their bodies were slick with perspiration. Their disarranged clothing binding them.

She could feel him thickening inside her. Her hands clasped his shoulders, pulled herself up. Her ankles locked one over the other. She drew him in, forcing his body against her mound, grinding herself against the iron-hard bone that cradled his pelvis. She would have the pleasure again. And the release. She would. She would!

They came together in a burst of passion, of incandescent heat, of light and color and darkness, of rushing sound, of hoarse voices crying, urging one another, in a paean to forces unknown who had fitted them for this supreme moment of pleasure.

Thirteen

Call you me daughter!

"Oh, what a noble mind is here o'erthrown! The courtier's, scholar's, soldier's eye, tongue—"

"No doubt about it, George." Freddy lounged in the wings, his arms folded forbiddingly across his chest. "Our lovely Miranda is giving the performance of her life."

George peered over his shoulder with a smile. "Aye, she's got 'em in the palm of her hand."

"She doesn't even have to act," Frederic continued nastily. "Ophelia's in love with Hamlet and that's plain for all to see."

George stifled a yawn. The late nights were getting to him. "She'll get over it. Shreve won't hurt the girl. Ada'll see to that."

Freddy placed his eye to the peephole in the scrim. "Not too soon, I hope. She's got them sitting openmouthed. Four weeks of that and we'll be able to open in New York. Maybe even London."

On stage Ophelia huddled sobbing in a pathetic ball, her long blond hair spread wildly about her. Hamlet knelt beside her to catch up a lock and press it to his lips. His face toward Freddy and George was tormented. He rubbed the silken stuff between his thumb and fingers before letting it go.

Freddy suddenly gave a snort of disbelief. "Perhaps she's not the only one feeling a bit of emotion." He grinned. "What a joke! The lady-killer finds himself dead through the heart."

Hamlet backed away off stage left and Freddy as Claudius entered left followed by George as Polonius. *"Love? his affections do not that way tend—"*

The cast stood in the green room accepting the accolades of the Chicago theatergoers. This *Hamlet* was by far the purest rendition of Shakespeare that they had ever done. The swordplay between Hamlet and Laertes with Mike playing Laertes had been practically their only holdover from their previous types of performances.

The audience they had attracted thanks to the attention being paid to Miranda's acting were people who either appreciated Shakespeare or believed that they should. Consequently, the room was full of flowers, bouquets given to Miranda at the end of the performance or sent backstage in tribute.

Out of the corner of his eye, Shreve watched her sparkle as young men, under the watchful eyes of their mothers and fathers, complimented her extravagantly and tried to engage her for dinner.

Suddenly, he heard the swift intake of her breath. Frowning, he looked into the dark face of the man who had taken hold of her hand with uncommon tightness. "Miranda."

She tried to wrench her hand away. When that failed, she cast a frantic look at Shreve, who frowned pointedly at the handclasp. "Is this someone you know?"

"Indeed I am someone she knows. Though I would rather not know her." His dark eyes never left Miranda's white face.

He was not a prepossessing man at all. Slightly under medium height with a thin dark beard, going to gray. His face was set in the harsh stern lines of moral outrage.

Alarmed, Shreve stepped between them closing his hand tightly over the man's scrawny wrist. "Let her go."

The cold, dark eyes glared upward into the actor's face. A larger man standing directly behind put his hand on the small man's arm. "This is probably a bad time, Westfall."

The conversation in the green room stilled, then took up again on a new tone as patrons of the theater began to stare and whisper.

Slowly, Westfall loosened his grip on Miranda's hand. Instantly, she jerked it out of his reach and stepped back. With a twist, he released himself from Shreve's grasp. He bowed formally. "I'll wait until the crowd has left to speak to you."

"We have nothing to say." Her voice shook.

"Oh, I very much think we have. Your mother has been most upset over your absence."

She shook her head. "Not so much that she refused to marry you."

He smiled tightly. "No, not so much as that."

"Then go away. I'm not bothering you. I'm out of your hair and you don't have to pay for my schooling."

"Ah, if only it were that simple," he replied ob-

234

scurely. Nodding briefly, he passed on to Freddy and then to Mike.

"What was that all about?" Shreve spoke out of the side of his mouth. "Is he your stepfather?"

She nodded slowly, then smiled blindly at the statuesque lady who complimented her performance. "I've not seen anyone do Ophelia so well since dear young Agnes Ethel."

Westfall retired to a settee in one corner, crossed one leg over the other, and lighted a cigar. His companion took up a post in back of it. The last well-wisher at last departed. Shreve squared his shoulders and stalked across the room. "Perhaps you'd like to tell me what this is all about."

Westfall rose to his feet. "Gladly. I've come to claim my daughter."

"I'm not his daughter," Miranda cried. "I'm his stepdaughter. He doesn't have any right to claim me."

"On the contrary, my dear. I am your mother's husband. You are my responsibility. You are also sixteen years old—"

A collective gasp from the Sons of Thespis interrupted him. Ada Cocks clapped her hand to her cheek and stared at Miranda.

"I'm not sixteen," Miranda denied hotly. "I'm—er—seventeen."

Westfall's lip curled. "Nevertheless, you are a minor child. And you will come with me."

Shreve stepped forward. His face was red, his eyes angry. "Are you really seventeen?"

"Y-Yes."

A sharp bark of laughter from Frederic Franklin caused them all to start. He slapped Shreve on the

235

shoulder. "Bad luck, old man."

Shreve shot him a furious look before turning to Miranda with a look only slightly less so. "Is this really your stepfather?"

"I assure you I am," Westfall interposed. "And you, sir, if you have harmed one hair on this precious head, you will be arrested forthwith. Mr. Bledsoe here is prepared."

By way of illustration, Bledsoe pulled a folded legal document from his pocket.

Shreve held up his hands. "Now, just a minute. Of course, I haven't harmed one hair on her precious head. Why would you think I would have?"

Westfall's mouth quirked again. "I am not a fool, sir. You are a man, I suppose. Although some in your company may leave cause for doubt." He looked pointedly at Freddy, who bristled. "But be that as it may, you have been traveling around the country with this young woman. Tonight she was dressed in clothing that showed off her youthful charms."

"Oooooh!" Miranda covered her face with her hands.

Ada came forward and gathered her in. "There, there, now, dearie. You're quite wrong, you know, Mr. —"

"Westfall."

"Westfall. We've taken this poor waif in and given her food and shelter. We've taught her a trade. I've treated her like me own daughter. No one's laid a finger on her."

"Of course not." Shreve leaped into the conversation, smiling his most charming smile. "As a matter of fact, we've shouldered expenses for her for several months. I offered her money, offered to pay for her to go back to her family, didn't I, Miranda?"

She nodded drearily as she turned away from Ada's shoulder. Hopefully, she looked around the circle. Her friends. She had thought they were, had worked hard for them. Now they looked at her with stern faces, the faces of strangers. "Shreve—"

He set his jaw. "She wanted to be an actress. Of course, we wouldn't have taken her on at all, but our leading lady had just quit. We needed someone to fill an engagement. She was awful, of course, but we acted around her, covered up for her mistakes. Actually, you've saved us the trouble of dismissing her."

The words were like blows to her pride. Tears started in her eyes, but she tilted her head back and blinked them away. His half-truths made her into a pitiful creature. She would not confirm that conception by crying. But she was not a poor actress, at least not now. Unless they had been lying to her all the time?

She looked from face to face. Freddy was grinning his malicious grin. George looked pityingly at her. Mike dropped his eyes before her pleading stare. Shreve was looking directly at Westfall. She turned to the one who had always been on her side. "Ada—"

The wardrobe mistress gave her a gentle pat. "Now your mother wants you, dearie. You're a lucky girl, you are. Better you go with your stepfather than hang around here with a troupe of actors."

Westfall stared from one face to the other unconvinced but unwilling to argue. "Get your things,

Miranda. We'll be going."

Shreve watched as she trailed toward the door with Ada following close behind. He cleared his throat. "I know how glad you must be to be taking her back to her mother."

"To her mother. Yes. I'm glad."

The actor moved to block Westfall's exit. His expression was carefully calculated. "Well, that's good. That's good. The fact of the matter is that we've been out quite a bit on her. Food, of course. Room and board at hotels and boardinghouses. Clothing. Lessons. She had to earn her keep, but she was shocking at first. A wooden Indian had more life."

Westfall chuckled humorlessly at the emergence of the profit motive. His dark eyes swept Shreve's tall, elegant figure with contempt.

Miranda shot her lover a fierce glance. How could he say those things? How could he?

He ignored her. "The troupe's going to be out some more money to find and train a new actress. There should be some sort of reward for finding and protecting a runaway until she can be returned to the bosom of her family."

"Ah, yes. A reward. You want money, do you?"

"It seems fair."

Westfall grinned. "You, my scoundrelly friend, may count yourself lucky that I don't have the law on you. You probably kidnapped her. If not that, then surely you lured her away. Be glad I don't have you locked up for statutory rape."

"Not me." Shreve stepped back hastily, raising his hands in protest. "Never laid a finger on her. She was just a child after all. What do you take me

238

for?"

Westfall did not deign to answer as he strode out the door.

Bledsoe started to follow him, but Shreve caught the detective's arm. "Say," he whined, "he won't cause me no trouble, will he? I never touched her. Wha' does he take me for?"

The detective looked at the actor's hand, then moved it carefully off his sleeve. "An idiot."

"Where are we going?"

Westfall did not answer. The horses' hooves echoed in the dark, nearly deserted streets.

"This isn't the way to your house."

He looked at her. "So you've been spying."

"Not spying. I planned to pay my mother and sister a visit. Sometime when you weren't around."

"I rather thought you would. That's why I didn't let that charade continue. Someone might have recognized you up there half dressed. And then my reputation would have been damaged."

"And we couldn't have that, could we?"

He glared at her. "No, we could not."

"Especially not when you killed my father to marry my mother."

He shuddered as if an arrow had struck him. "What did you say?"

"I met Reed Phillips in Saint Louis. He told me what you did."

"Phillips is a liar. A disappointed and frustrated man will say anything to justify his ineptitude."

"You killed my father. You sent him out to die and wouldn't ride out after him when he was ambushed. I saw him after they brought him in. His

239

head was almost cut off. He was scalped. We all heard the shots, but you wouldn't go rescue him. Because you wanted him dead."

Westfall's face was a stark white oval in the darkness of the coach. "I had to defend the fort."

"You wanted him dead, so you could marry my mother. But you had a wife. Did you kill her, too?"

"Shut up!" His hand flashed out and cracked her hard on the cheek. The blow drove her back against the squabs in the carriage.

She screamed.

On the box of the rented hansom, Parker Bledsoe winced and hunched his shoulders up around his ears.

Westfall hit her again not quite so hard the second time, but the blow knocked her off the seat and onto her knees. "Keep your mouth shut."

"Murderer," she accused, lunging for the door handle.

He caught her by the hair and dragged her back against his knee. "Do you know what I plan to do with you, my vicious, promiscuous little stepdaughter?"

The pain in her scalp made the tears start from her eyes. She could not twist free.

"My lying, corrupt, delinquent little stepdaughter."

"No," she gritted between clenched teeth.

"I intend to take you to a house of correction. For wayward girls. There is one here in the city."

"I'm not wayward."

"You are if I say you are, and I'm going to give them enough money so they won't ask questions. And believe me, Miranda, the price I'll have to pay will be cheap."

"They won't keep me there very long."

"Long enough. By the time you get out, your mother and sister and I will be in Washington, D.C., I'll be a brigadier general, and whatever stories you may try to tell, whatever charges you may try to bring, will be dismissed because you are a lying reform-school girl."

She swung her doubled fist from the floor of the coach. It landed on the side of his cheek and knocked his head back. The cab rocked on its springs with their struggles.

"Why you miserable brat!"

She never saw the blow that drove her into unconsciousness.

The matron pinched Miranda's nose together. When the girl opened her mouth to breathe, the woman rammed a wide wooden spoon in between her teeth. "A good dose of salts usually takes the viciousness right out of a girl, Mr. Westfall."

"I'm glad to hear it."

"These girls come to us, their bodies just full of poisons and offal. We don't hold with beating or hurting a girl the way some places do. We just clear their systems of all that and set them on the road to clean lives."

Westfall nodded in agreement with the matron's sanctimonious speech.

Miranda squirmed in the grip of the two husky women who held her between them. "You can take my mother to Washington or to the moon, but I'll find you and tell her the truth. I swear."

"Perhaps another dose of—er—salts, Mrs. Mortimer."

"Well, I generally don't like to give 'em more'n one dose." Her eyes rolled heavenward as if seeking guidance. "Sometimes it's hard on the system. Gets their bowels in a dreadful uproar."

Westfall reached into his breast pocket and withdrew his wallet.

The matron eyed the thickness of the object and shrugged. "But in her case, it probably can't do no harm." She poured another dose of the foul-tasting purgative into the wooden spoon. "Open up there, you. It's for your own good."

"No!"

The wooden spoon clicked against tightly clamped teeth. One of the orderlies pinched Miranda's nostrils together and tugged her head back. Still fighting, Miranda held her breath until she felt her senses failed. Then the spoon stretched her mouth wide again. The evil concoction slid over her tongue. She gagged, coughed. The second woman forestalled her when she tried to spit it out. Added to the grip on her nose was a hard hand covering her mouth. She had no choice but to swallow. White-faced, tears starting from her eyes, her knees buckled, but she was held upright by her captors.

Westfall watched the process with a marked degree of satisfaction. "I can see I've brought her to the right place."

The bill Westfall passed the matron disappeared instantly into the deep pocket in her apron. "You sure have. She'll learn proper manners and an honest Christian trade. Some of my girls even get married."

His eyes met Miranda's through her haze of tears. His smile was unctuous. "Good. Good."

"Now, Phoebe, you and Hettie shut her up in the first-night room. She'll have plenty of time to think about why she's in here while that tonic works on her."

Miranda tugged and braced her feet, but the two powerful women turned her and dragged her away. She swiveled her head, throwing Westfall one last malevolent glare. "I won't forget my father," she yelled. "I'll never forget. Don't think I will. Never! And someday I'll make sure everybody else believes that you killed him."

The door closed behind the struggling figures. Westfall pulled an envelope from his breast pocket. "Here is the agreed-upon price, Mrs. Mortimer. And a bit extra for you to continue your good works."

"Thank you kindly, Mr. Westfall. Bless you. You're providing for a whole slew of people with your gift."

"I'm sure I am."

"Get in there. And keep yer mouf shut." The woman's heavy hand in the middle of Miranda's back sent her staggering into darkness. A couple of steps only, then she regained her footing and stopped dead.

As her eyes adjusted she stared around her. The first-night room was small with a tiny window about six inches square near the ceiling. Light from an outside lamp cast a box on the wall to the right of the door. Its reflection was enough to allow Miranda to make out her surroundings. Behind her the lock turned and a heavy bolt thudded into place.

Straw ankle-deep covered the floor. A fetid odor rose from it as she shuffled a couple of steps into the center of the space and turned slowly surveying her prison. It was so small that it might at one time have been a dressing room or even a broom closet. Curiously, it was empty except for two white enamel slop jars set together beside the door.

Still shuddering from the taste in her mouth, Miranda clasped her arms tight around her. For a time she dared not move, fearful of what might lurk in the straw at her feet. She swallowed convulsively and gagged as the foul taste lingered on her teeth and tongue.

A rustling in the straw along the wall swung her around. She stared with burning eyes in that direction. Did the straw quiver? A dark head reared from the pale mass. Beady eyes stared balefully.

She screamed. The head disappeared. The straw rustled again toward the corner. She backed against the door, but she did not pound on it. No doubt the matron knew what lurked in the room.

She leaned her head back against the panels and allowed the tears to trickle down her cheeks. Alone. She was alone, and no one to help her but herself. Somehow she must get through the next days until she could escape. And escape she would. They might be able to lock others away, but not Francis Drummond's daughter. She did not belong here. And she would not stay.

"Oh, Daddy," she whispered. "Oh, Daddy."

Gradually, she became aware of nausea. Her legs began to tremble and she let herself slide down the door. There she wrapped her arms around her knees and bowed her head. Perhaps soon she would vomit up the foul stuff and then she would feel better. She cast a look at the pale slop jars. No doubt other inmates of the first-night cell vomited. She supposed she should slide herself closer to them, but her limbs were trembling.

The first griping in her belly came as a shock. Under the nausea, yet in some terrible way a part of it, it was a sharp pain that seemed to burrow through her. In its wake, it left weakness. The matron's words, now dimly recalled, were suddenly real. The awful stuff they had given her worked swiftly. She had to get rid of it. Had to.

Rolling over on to her hands and knees she crawled through the straw to the jars. Conjuring up sights as horrible as she could, she tried to force herself to vomit. Nothing would come. She tried again. Before she could manage, a sharp spasm gripped her bowels.

Frantically, she tugged up her skirts and pulled off her pantalets. Just in time. Hovering over the slop jar, the sound and stench of her bowels rising in her head, she shuddered with pain, with embarrassment, with disgust. Unfortunately, she knew the purpose of the "salts" she had been given.

Westfall had watched her with a smile. He had asked that she be given a second dose even though the matron had expressed a doubt. She shuddered again as another spasm racked her.

She had nothing to lean against except the bare wall. The jars were low with a narrow rim. They offered no place to sit. Her legs were already trembling with weakness.

The straw. Now she knew. The straw was to catch the mess when she could no longer use the jars.

Tears ran down her cheeks. She moaned with pain. The light from the tiny upper window flickered, dimmed, then steadied. At least she was not in total darkness.

"Time fer ol' Hettie t' get y' cleaned up." The larger one of the two orderlies stood in the doorway. "Phewee-e-e. Don't you smell ripe."

Miranda opened her eyes at the sound of the voice but could not find the speaker. Her single effort to raise her head was a dismal failure. She could only roll it in weak negation.

"Come on, girl. We gotta burn them duds and get y' washed off." Rough hands slid under Miranda's armpits and dragged her to her feet.

"Can't—"

"Now, just walk ahead of me."

"No, I c-can't."

A hand between her shoulder blades propelled her forward. "Sure y' can."

"Much of a mess, Hettie?"

" 'Bout like usual. Get one o' them big girls to shovel it out."

Miranda moaned in shame. Her stomach clenched, then revolted. She dropped to her knees and retched. Tears spouted from her eyes, but she had nothing in her to give up. Hettie stood over her unconcerned.

When the spasms finally ceased, the big woman hauled Miranda up again and pointed her down the hall. A line of perhaps six young girls marched past her. All of them kept their eyes carefully averted.

Through a back door, down a flight of steps, and across a narrow brick courtyard, Hettie pushed her. "In here."

Here was a long narrow building with stalls. Hettie swung back the single yard square of wood that served for a door to the first one. "Get in there and take y'r duds off."

"M-my clothes."

"Don't waste m' time. Peel outta them things. They're filthy. Y' don't want to stay in 'em, do yuh?"

"No — but —"

"Then strip."

The floor was cold and dark with spaces between the boards through which a dank fetid odor rose. Miranda leaned against the unstable side of the stall, while she pulled off her befouled pantalets, her petticoat, her skirt. Her hose and shoes were also filthy. She had not been able to control herself once the worst of the cathartic had struck her. She was sick all over again at the sight of her legs and inner thighs.

When she was finally naked except for the thin camisole that covered her breasts and reached to the top of her hipbones, Hettie looked over the top of the stall. "That, too."

"W-what will I wear?"

"We've got a uniform for you. Just gimme the rest of it."

Trembling, Miranda tugged off her last garment. Hettie passed her a thin bar of lye soap. "Now, listen, y' get jis' a bucket o' water to wash y'rself with. If y' don't get clean that's your lookout. I tell the girls to soap theirselves all over and then pull that chain. The water'll come down and rinse 'em off."

"What about my hair?"

"It's not real dirty. Yuh didn't get yer face in it, did yuh?"

"No." Miranda grimaced. "No. I don't think so."

"Lucky." Hettie was staring at her over the stall door.

Miranda could feel her body blushing. "Please. You can go away. I'll wash myself. I really will."

"Oh, that's all right. I like to watch. Sometimes I see something I like right off."

Miranda froze dumbfounded, horror written on her face.

"Get on with it."

Numbly she shook her head.

"Oh, all right. I'll back off. But it ain't gonna do y' no good to be no shrinkin' flower. You could use a friend in here. And I might be persuaded t' be that friend."

The orderly backed away and stood at the door of the wash house, grinning.

Miranda realized that Hettie could see her legs from midthigh down. With hands trembling so hard that she dropped the bar twice, she managed to pass the soap over her body.

" 'Bout done, ain't yuh," Hettie observed. She stomped over to the shower stall and caught hold of the chain. "Here it comes."

Water so cold it shocked her, fell in a torrent over her head. She screamed at the shock and jumped back, but Hettie's big hand pushed her back. "Get back under there and wash. Or do y' want me to do it fer yuh?"

Fortunately, the water ran out in less than a minute. Miranda pushed her hands down her body, rubbing off the soap that was already beginning to scum in the cold. With it came a large part of the filth, but not the discomfort nor the outrage. Teeth chattering painfully, she turned at the creak of the shower stall.

Big Hettie stood there grinning, her little eyes roving over Miranda's body. "Here's yer dress." She held out a dark blue serge. "Jis' pull it on over yer head."

"Don't I get any underwear."

"Not fer a while. Y' might start spoutin' again. Some do."

Again Miranda gagged but managed to hide the sound and the sight behind the folds of the dress.

"What about shoes?"

"Y' get some when y' get used t' bein' here. We don't want any of the girls runnin' off. Y' can't run too far without shoes."

The wind off Lake Michigan for which Chicago was famous was blowing when Hettie guided Miranda back across the yard. She was freezing from her bath and from the lack of underwear. The wind whirled up under the shapeless blue dress and chilled her body.

"Now," Hettie said, "Just climb up those stairs. I'll come right behind yuh."

Miranda realized that Hettie had lagged far behind so she could see up under the blue dress. The big woman snarled when Miranda reached between her legs and pulled the back of her skirt through to the front. "Y'll be sorry fer that. I could let y' have some dinner and a blanket."

Neither spoke as Hettie escorted her along the

hall to the back of the house. Unlocking the door, she pushed Miranda in. "Last chance, little girl. Want a blanket and some nice hot dinner? Something to soothe them innards?"

Miranda turned her back and stalked into the room.

"Just holler real loud if y' change yer mind. Course I won't hear yuh. I'll be down where it's warm in the kitchen. Where the food is." Hettie slammed the door.

Again the rattle of the bolt and turn of the lock. Miranda tottered to the bare cot and sank down upon it. She pulled her legs up to her chest and tucked the hem of the serge dress over her bare feet. Through the dismal barred window, she fell asleep. She did not see the day brighten and fade. Her chilled body wakened her as the second night began.

Fourteen

The best actors in the world.

The new inspector from the Board of Health surveyed the girls with a disapproving eye. "Mrs.—um—Mortimer, these girls sure do look malnourished. They gettin' enough to eat?"

Mrs. Mortimer's face flushed a deep puce. As if to block them from his sight, she marched between him and the line of silent females and shook her finger in the man's face. "Now, just a minute, you! Old Doc Harrison knew these girls were getting plenty to eat. You just check with him."

Unintimidated by her virulence, the health inspector merely raised his bushy gray eyebrows. Although her face was no more than a few inches from his own, it was considerably below his. Like a rock he stood, coldly glowering down upon her, until she backed away a couple of steps. Before that hard officious gaze, she retracted her offending digit and clasped her hands together in front of her.

He cleared his throat. "Harrison don't have a thing to say about this. Not a thing."

"Well, why not, I'd like to know? He's been handling everything for years. Where'd you come from?"

He managed to look official and bored at the same time by peering beyond her at her charges. "I'm a public health official with the City of Chicago. We're trying to trace a—um—dangerous and highly contagious disease. It's bad. Real bad. Like a combination of smallpox and TB. Anything like that around here?" He moved on past Mrs. Mortimer and selected a particularly emaciated young female. Placing a hand in the center of her back he instructed, "Cough for me, girl."

"Now you leave that girl alone."

"Begins with a deep chest cough. That's the first sign."

"That's the first sign of a lot of things."

"That's why it's so dangerous. This stuff turns into a 'massive pulmonary infection.'" He rolled the words off his tongue in a clear imitation of a higher authority.

The woman shook her head. "We don't have anything like that here."

He patted the girl's shoulder encouragingly, then continued inexorably to the next, his black eyes glinting. "The advanced stages get worse and worse. They get a high fever and suppuratin' lesions the size of silver dollars all over the body."

"Sup-pur-ating what?" Mrs. Mortimer stammered.

"Boils," he supplied. "Open up and say 'Ah.' Running sores."

"B-boils. If it's so awful, how come I haven't heard about it?"

He heaved a deep exhausted sigh. " 'Cause we've been real careful that you shouldn't. Don't want to get a lot of citizens all worried and runnin' around doin' crazy stuff. This stuff's worse than smallpox. Liable to get a lot of people scared."

The woman faltered, then quickly regained her belligerent attitude. "Well, I'm sure no one here has the disease. Nobody's allowed to get sick in my house. The girls have plain, healthy diets. I don't hold with fancy food. They get plenty of exercise working in the house and gardens. And once a week I give 'em a physick. Not a one has so much as a cold, Dr. —"

"Not a doctor. I'm an inspector. M' name's Taliaferro." He produced a card.

She squinted at it. "What?"

"Taliaferro."

Unable to read it without her glasses, she handed it back to him at the same time indicating the door with a dismissing gesture. "Well, Mr. Tolliver, there ain't no sickness here. You can take my word for that. So you might as well get on with your business."

"Ma'am, I'm about my business. If you'll just kindly take yourself off to the side." The inspector walked slowly down the line of young girls scrutinizing their pale faces. None of them raised their eyes to him. He could not guess their ages. A couple supported gravid bellies, but by and large they were thin to the point of emaciation. One and all, their cheeks and temples were hollow; their lips thin and almost colorless. Shadowy smudges under-scored every eye. He frowned heavily. "These all look pretty bad. Better get a look at your records. When did these girls come in here?"

Mrs. Mortimer set her mouth in a tight line. "My records. What good would my records do? What do you want to look at them for?"

At the end of the line he swung around with a lithe grace unusual for a man his age. His hand rested on the shoulder of the last girl. "I thought you'd got that clear. This stuff is fairly new to the city. You just might be right about none of them in this—um—institution having it. Specially if you haven't brought in any new girls in the last few weeks—"

A distracted look settled on Mrs. Mortimer's face. She shifted nervously. "We ain't admitted no one."

"Then you may be safe. Just the same, I've got to have a look at your records. It's for *my* records."

"You don't need to look at my records," she snarled.

The health inspector patted the thin shoulder of the girl on the end. Then he came back up the line. The closer he came, the more nervous the ma-tron became. Finally, he stopped in front of her, as close to her, as she had come to him at the begin-ning of the interview. The difference was that his face hung over her from the top of his imposing height.

His eyes were very black and very angry. His shoulders squared and blocked the light. "I'm gonna see those records. One way or another. We can do this easy, or we can go at it hard."

She shrugged angrily. "If you'll come this way—"

She hung over his shoulder while he ran a thumbnail down the entries in the ledger. "I told you we didn't have nobody new."

"That's right, you did," he agreed.

"Then you don't have any reason to think that we've got that—whatchamacallit."

"Infectious pulmonary tuberoses."

She drew in a sharp breath. Her lips moved as she tried to repeat it.

He closed the book. "Yep, everything looks pretty good in here. Now just one more thing. I'll inspect the rooms, and then I'll be off."

"The rooms!" Her voice rose incredulously. "You don't want to inspect the rooms."

He rose and picked up his black top hat. "For my records, don't y' know? It's part of my job."

"Listen, Dr. Tolliver. I've got work to do. I don't have time to take you on a tour of this place."

"You don't have to bother with that," he agreed in a gentle voice. "Why don't you just hand over them keys, and I'll make my own tour?"

He held out his hand as she clasped hers over the ring of keys and spluttered angrily, "You can't walk around here by yourself."

"I've already seen all the girls," he pointed out. "I'm just gonna poke my head in empty rooms."

"You're a man." She looked at him closely. Her eyes narrowed suspiciously.

"I'm an inspector."

"But it ain't fit for you to walk around in a home for girls."

"I ain't interested in the girls. I'm supposed to see if you got any rats and such."

"Rats!"

"Stuff breeds where they breed. Just like that oldtime plague."

"You sure this is the last thing you have to do?"

He held up his hand solemnly. "Swear to God."

"All right. All right. You come with me. It's a waste of time, but if it'll get you out of my hair, I'll do it." She led him through the first floor with poor grace, swinging doors open and allowing him only a brief look inside before she slammed them.

"What's in this room?"

"That's a — um — "

"Open it."

"I don't know if I can find the key."

He waited patiently. Finally, after several tries she managed to find the key that fit the lock.

The odor almost drove his breath away. He looked at the stained floor, the pile of discolored straw. "What in the name of God's gone on in here?"

Her mouth was set in granite. "One of the girls was sick."

Struggling to control his heaving stomach, he squatted beside the largest stain a couple of feet from the door. "You're sure right about that. Throwin' up blood was she."

Mrs. Mortimer hunched her shoulders uncomfortably. "Sometimes the — er — physick don't set too well in one of the girl's bowels."

He shot to his feet so fast that she retreated. His bushy brows drew together in a malignant glare as he kicked at the pile of straw. It bore the same unmistakable red stains. "That's pretty rank stuff. You'd better watch it, lady. You're gonna have somebody dyin' in here. I'm gonna have to put that in my report."

"My mother held with physicking," Mrs. Mortimer whined. "A body gets overloaded with waste. It needs to be cleaned out regularly. That sort of accident only happens once in a great while. And there's no harm done. Least not any that lasts for very long."

The inspector, his face pale and slightly green, backed from the room. "You give this to them big-bellied girls, too?"

"It's good for everybody," Mrs. Mortimer insisted doggedly. "My mother always held that a 'physicking' was good for nearly everything. You're pretty weak-stomached for your line of work, aren't you?" she remarked, as the inspector pulled out his handkerchief and wiped the perspiration from his forehead and mouth.

He thrust the cloth back into his pocket. "I'm just supposed to check empty rooms. Most of the time I don't have to put my nose into messes like that." He motioned her on. "Now. Let's get on with this. I've got another place to go this afternoon."

"You've seen most of it."

"I'm gonna see it all. So keep them keys handy. Otherwise, I might just have to call a couple of my men in here to break some of 'em down."

Less than half an hour later at the top of the house, Mrs. Mortimer unlocked a narrow door. The doctor thrust his head inside. It was empty save for a narrow cot. A still figure lay on it, a huddled shape of dark blue with yellow hair. "Who's this?" he asked, his voice unnaturally loud and deep.

Mrs. Mortimer shrugged. "Just one of the girls. She's—er—resting."

"In a locked room?" A couple of strides brought him to the narrow cot. He bent over the figure. "I didn't see her downstairs. Where'd she come from?"

The girl was huddled so tightly that the inspector could not see her face. He laid his hand on her head. Her bright yellow hair was damp. In ropy cattails it spread across her shoulders and trailed onto the dusty floor. Instead of a blanket, her covering proved to be the skirt of her dress, drawn down over her legs. Small bare feet peeked out whitely from beneath the dark material.

With gentle fingers he drew the hair back from her cheek. A spot of fever glowed on the sculptured bone. For an instant his control almost broke. Then he swallowed. He rose again. "How long's this girl been sick?"

"She ain't sick." Mrs. Mortimer came into the room. "She's just resting." Jostling him aside, she bent over and shook the girl's shoulder. "Here you. Get up."

Miranda moaned but did not open her eyes.

" 'Get up,' I said." Mrs. Mortimer pulled her over onto her back. The cot tilted dangerously.

Only the inspector's quick grab for the rail kept it from tumbling its burden to the floor.

Miranda opened her eyes. Faces hung above her, but her vision was too hazy for her to see their features clearly. " 'm thirsty," she managed to groan. Then, "Water."

"Get up," the matron commanded.

Miranda blinked twice. Her eyes focused on her tormentor. She flailed her arm weakly hitting the woman across the cheek.

"Here now, you." Mrs. Mortimer grabbed the arm and pulled the girl off the cot. Miranda fell hard on her hip and Mrs. Mortimer wrestled her across the floor. "If you're strong enough to hit out, you need to be downstairs working. You've rested long enough. Get on your feet, I say."

"Now, just a minute there, Mrs. Mortimer."

Glaring, the woman threw her arm around Miranda's shoulders and tried to block the inspector's access to her. "She ain't sick."

"I'll be the judge of that."

The deep voice sent a shock through Miranda's body. She froze, driving a grunt from Mrs. Mortimer, who shoved hard against the elbow she had hold of.

"I reckon I'd better examine this girl immediately."

"This girl's just fine," Mrs. Mortimer argued, shoving Miranda harder.

"She's burning up. Just feel her skin. If she's got a fever and a deep chest cough, then she might be in the early stages. When'd she come in?"

"Er—I don't know for sure."

The inspector took Miranda's other arm. "Look at that face. Red spots on the cheeks. They're gonna turn into boils. Yep! She's sure got 'infectious pulmonary tuberoses.' "

Miranda raised her aching head and looked up into Shreve Catherwood's black eyes. She blinked, swayed, then began to cry.

He gave her a sharp shake. "Here, now, don't take on. You might not have it. Have you got a cough?"

Her head snapped up. She looked into his eyes again and read the silent command as if he had shouted it aloud. It was her cue. Her cue. She swallowed her tears and desperately cast aside the weakness that made her knees tremble. The pain gnawing her belly, the ringing in her head, all would have to be ignored. Her cue.

"Is your throat sore, girl?"

She took a shallow breath. "Yes, sir," came out in a weak sigh.

"She just got too tired. She'll be fine now that she's rested." The matron tried to drag Miranda out of the room.

He shot a furious glance at Mrs. Mortimer. "If this girl's got infectious pulmonary tuberoses, you're gonna give it to everybody. You might be infected yourself."

Mrs. Mortimer dropped Miranda's arm and stepped back. "Well, she looks all right to me. I told you we let her rest. The physick made her a little sick."

Without the woman's support, Miranda swayed helplessly. Pain and nausea emanating from her belly threatened to overwhelm her. *Her cue.* She coughed long and wrackingly.

Mrs. Mortimer put her hand over her mouth.

Miranda coughed again. Her eyes flickered briefly on the stern, gray face. Months with the Sons of Thespis had taught her to judge the audience. Evidently, her performance was believable. She coughed again, a deep hacking sound, dragging it out of her throat, ignoring the pain.

Shreve put his arm around her shoulders. "This girl's burning up with fever." He turned her carefully. "Now open up for me and say 'Ah.'"

Obediently, she tipped her head back. "Aaaaah."

He frowned. "More lesions."

"L-Lesions."

"Sure looks bad. Lesions way down in her throat. They're gonna break out real fast. I've got to get her out of here. The faster the better."

Mrs. Mortimer backed to the door. "You mean she's got that pulmary thing?"

The inspector looked sadly down into Miranda's face. "I sure do hope I'm wrong. She's a pretty little thing. But I better take her downtown and let the doctors look at her."

Mrs. Mortimer wrung her hands. "She can't have that stuff."

"I sure hope I'm wrong. This place could be shut down so fast. The mayor's thinkin' about havin' places where it turns up burned."

"Burned!"

Miranda coughed wrenchingly. Spurred by fear of detection, she expended too much of her small store of energy. Her head spun; black spots whirled in front of her eyes.

"Look here." The inspector's voice echoed hollowly in her ear. "She's about t' pass out."

"She's just had too much physick," Mrs. Mortimer protested weakly.

Miranda felt his hand tighten on her shoulder. His arm bound her protectively against his side. "I better get her out of here," he insisted.

Brushing by Mrs. Mortimer, he half guided, half carried her out into the hall.

"Here, what's goin' on here?"

Miranda uttered a small agonized cry.

The inspector threw a look over his shoulder. Coming down the hall toward them was a massive woman, with forearms and calves like huge hams.

"Who the hell are yuh, and what're y' doin' with that girl?"

"She's sick. I'm taking her out of here."

"She ain't got anything that anybody needs to cure," the large one objected.

"It's all right, Hettie."

Hettie stared incredulously at Mrs. Mortimer standing in the doorway.

"But she jus' got here."

"Ah," the inspector interrupted. "So she's new. And you sure weren't anxious to tell me about her. That's got to go in my report, too."

"She's not a regular girl," the woman protested bleakly. "I must of forgotten about her."

The bushy eyebrows drew almost together in a furious scowl. "You mean to tell me you've got girls here that you just take in? The courts are supposed to send 'em. You're violating your charter.

What hell kind of place are you runnin' anyway."

"Mr. Tolliver—"

As he pounded away at the woman's confidence, he helped the fainting Miranda down the stairs. "Where're this girl's shoes?"

"She just got here. She hasn't been issued any."

"Well, get her some."

"No," Miranda protested faintly. Her voice was so low that it reached his ears only. "Take me away."

His answer was a tighter hug. She groaned loudly. He was holding her so tightly by this time that she could hardly breathe. "On second thought, never mind. I think the best thing would be for me to take her on off before she spreads it around."

They came down the hall past the terrible room where Miranda had been physicked. The stench from it lay heavy in the air.

"The best thing you could do would be to burn that room," the inspector told the two women. "If that's her blood and stuff on the floor in there, it'd be somebody's life to go in there."

"Sweet Jesus," Hettie growled. "Y' mean to tell me she's really sick?"

"Sure looks like it." The party reached the front door. The inspector turned. His busy eyebrows drew down. "That's a real bad report for this place," he remarked casually, opening the front door a crack. "How many black marks was that? Four? Maybe five?"

"Mr. Tolliver." Mrs. Mortimer gave a cloying sickly smile. "Why don't you just step into my of-fice? You can leave the girl here in the hall. She'll be all right. Hettie'll look after her. I'm sure there's something that I can say—or do—that would convince you to change your mind. Your job can't be a highly paid one."

The strong wind off the lake belled the loose blue dress around Miranda's naked body. She was shivering violently. Her head drooped on the inspector's chest. She began to cough again. She threw up her arm and caught his shoulder to keep herself from falling. "Get me out of here," she muttered. "I can't stand much more."

He clutched her tighter. "Some other time, Mrs. Mortimer, I might consider takin' you up on some sort of a deal like that, but this is real serious stuff. Be sure and let the board know if any more of the girls turn up sick."

He stepped out on the street and whistled sharply through his teeth. A hansom rounded the corner, the horses trotting. Dimly, Miranda recognized Mike Lonigan on the box.

"So long, ladies," Shreve Catherwood said. "Be sure to burn out that room. Mighty nasty business."

As they watched the cab drive out of sight, Hettie turned to Mrs. Mortimer. "What y' gonna do about that gal?"

"Well, I'm not going to give back the money they've paid. You can bet your boots on that score," the matron declared stoutly. "After all, it's not my fault if she ups and dies. I can put that money to good use."

Hettie nodded, a smirk twisting her thick lips. "S'pose they come and want t' see 'er?"

Mrs. Mortimer did not hesitate. "When did we ever have anybody come back? They're too glad to forget they ever had any of these bitches. If we do, well, we'll cross that bridge when we come to it. For now we'll just pretend she's right in the next room."

As the carriage slowly made its way through Chicago's noisy crowded streets, Shreve cradled Miranda's body across his lap. Every so often a wheel would drop into a rut or pothole. The jar would cause her to shudder. Likewise, the heat and the sick odor emanating from her told him he had not lied to Mrs. Mortimer. The girl was ill.

And she was just a girl. How had he failed to recognize her youth! He hugged her tighter, pressing his cheek against the top of her head. In his mind he damned himself for letting her stepfather take her for even twenty-four hours. He had sent George to follow them thinking to contact her before their engagement was over. Then when he learned that she had been taken to a bleak house with bars on the windows, he had set out at first light to discover what sort of home she had been taken to.

He had been shocked speechless, to learn she had been placed in a home for wayward girls, one with a black reputation for maltreatment and suspected abortions. Her stepfather must have somehow discovered that she was his mistress. He flushed at the thought, clasping her a bit tighter.

She murmured something and clutched at the front of his shirt.

"What?"

"Shreve, you came."

"Of course. I need you for the performance to-night." His voice sounded hoarse and shaky to his ears.

"I don't know," she whispered. "I don't know whether I can go on or not. I don't feel so well."

"A good meal and a bath and you'll feel right as rain," he said with false heartiness.

She was silent for a minute. "I didn't think you would. Come, you know. I got you into trouble."

"No trouble we haven't been in before. Some-one's always taking exception to some performance or other. Actors are used to stuff like that. It's part of the trade. Just rest. Ada's waiting to take care of you."

"Is she?"

"And worried sick. You know Ada. You were never alone. George was right behind you. He saw them take you into that place. He came back to the theater with the word."

She was silent against him. He thought she might have drifted off again, but she sniffed. "It was awful."

He could feel the hot tears soaking through his shirt. "Stop thinking about it. It's over. You won't be going back there."

"I don't know what they gave me, but it made me sick." She moved convulsively, squeezing her legs together and clutching at his lapel. "I—I was—awfully sick."

"Yes, I know."

"You couldn't."

"I saw where you were. I saw —"

"Oh, no." She began to cry in earnest. "I'm so embarrassed. That you should see —"

He pulled a handkerchief from his pocket and pressed it into her hands. "Hush. I'm a grown man. I know how you're made. And I know what they did to you and why."

"She said it was to take the poisons out of me. But I didn't have any poisons. I didn't."

He dried her tears and rubbed her back between her shoulder blades. "Of course, you didn't." *Nor did you have a baby that those bastards wanted to get rid of.*

"He told her to give me two tablespoons full."

"I should have knocked that bastard down and taken you away." Shreve could barely contain his anger. If she had been pregnant, she would have lost their child. He felt some amazement at the height of his rage.

"I don't blame you because you didn't," she whispered. "I had lied to you."

"I didn't realize what he was going to do. And you're saying he was your stepfather?"

The tears started again. "Yes."

"No wonder you ran away from home."

"He killed my father."

"God! And your mother married him anyway?"

"Oh, she didn't know. She still doesn't know. She's a good mother. A wonderful mother. I have a little sister Rachel. He came and offered her marriage. She was so lonely and unhappy. We were living on the charity of my grandparents."

"Sounds sad."

"It was."

He did not seem curious beyond that. They rode in silence. At last they drew up at the hotel. Despite her protests, he would not let her out of his arms. "I'm going to carry you up to Ada's room."

"Not" — she swallowed hard — "ours?"

"There is no 'ours,' Miranda. Not until you come of age."

His face was so forbidding that she made no protest. Keeping her face hidden, he stomped through the lobby in his best performance of Macbeth, King of Scotland.

At the top of the stair, he paused to look down at her. "What's your real name?"

"Miranda," she said.

"Miranda what?"

"Just Miranda. I don't intend to be anything else until I do what I have to do."

He frowned thunderously. "And that is?"

"I don't know yet." Her face was bleak. The blue eyes drooped with weariness. She turned her head into his shoulder. "I really don't know."

Fifteen

The play's the thing.

"My poor dearie." Ada bent over the tub to scrub Miranda's hair. "What a terrible time you've had of it."

Miranda did not answer. She had been unable to eat more than a few bites of the steak and potatoes George had brought up from the dining room with his own hands. Even now her abused stomach threatened to throw it up. Her body felt alternately cold and hot. Bells jangled in her ears and a drum pounded in her temples.

She closed her eyes and tried to concentrate. Shreve expected her to go on tonight. He had said so. Several times. They were going to shave her eyebrows and paint them on at a new slant, paint her mouth in a different way, use more makeup, and pad her breasts and hips. If anyone came backstage to inquire, they had hired a girl with long blond hair and a mild facial resemblance to stand in the wings. She would wait in a costume like Miranda's and be introduced as Miranda to patrons who came backstage.

269

Ada had told her all these plans while Miranda had been unable to rest for fretting.

Now she had to get better. She simply had to. She could not disappoint them. They had been so wonderful to her. They had rescued her. She did not doubt she owed them her life.

"—lucky girl to be working for Shrevey-boy. Ye may not think so because he's so selfish. A screamin' demon he is and demandin' as a prince about his shows, but self-interest is a mighty comfortable and predictable thing. He'll fight like a tiger that boy will for—"

Miranda drifted away again. Later she stood like an exhausted child while Ada dried her body and slipped a nightgown over her head. "Now just climb in between the covers and let sleep mend you, dearie."

"But the matinee—"

"Ye're not up to it."

Miranda took a deep protesting breath shaking her head. The pain made her sway and clutch at her temples.

"See. Now what did I tell you?"

"I have to go on. Shreve—"

"Himself told me to put you to bed. I'll wake you in time for tonight. You and Shreve can talk about it then." Gentle hands guided her to the bed. She sank down upon the soft mattress, and Ada pulled the covers up to her chin. She was unconscious before the woman had gotten back to the tub to begin to empty it and haul it away.

"Here's your money, Bledsoe. And a letter of

recommendation should you ever need it. I've had excellent service from you." Westfall extended the envelope.

Parker Bledsoe eyed it calmly, then shook his head. "Well, now, I can't take that money."

The colonel looked at him in astonishment. "Not take it?"

"No, sir. According to company policy, I can't take money for investigations that lead to criminal acts."

Westfall's frown drew his brows together. He withdrew the envelope. "What do you mean by that statement?"

Bledsoe lifted the lid of the humidor on Westfall's desk and selected a cigar. With it carefully poised between his index and third fingers, he looked at his client appraisingly. "Colonel Westfall, you know what I mean as well as I do. You took that girl and locked her up without a hearing. She didn't get the first sign of a trial. That's illegal."

A muscle in Westfall's jaw twitched. "You're wrong, Mr. Bledsoe. I'm her legal guardian. She was leading a life of prostitution. You saw her on the stage yourself. The press might have gotten wind of a hearing. It could have been an embarrassment to her family."

He looked at Bledsoe, trying to read the effect his words were having. The detective's expression remained calculating. "I merely arranged to have her put in a correctional institution for her own good." He extended the envelope again. "There was absolutely nothing illegal about it. Take this and be on your way."

Still Parker Bledsoe did not move. "Yes, sir, there is. That wasn't a private sanatorium. If it had been, then you'd have been within your legal rights, but it wasn't. It was a city-owned and city-operated institution. It requires a judicial hearing to commit someone to it."

"Those girls that were in there hadn't been—"

"I don't know that, sir. I only know what the law is. And you broke it."

"Now see here—"

"If I have to report what was done to my superiors, I'd have to tell the truth. Company policy not only requires me to refuse the fee, but I'd be obligated by it and my superiors to report you to the law. We'd have to cooperate in an investigation."

"An investigation?" Westfall's face did not betray his panic, but he felt the clench of pain in his belly. *When would this ever end?*

"That's right. Those are the rules."

Westfall leaned back in his chair, eyes slitted. His mind twisted and turned like a rat in a maze. Feverishly it sought a tunnel to safety. The clock ticked loudly.

"On the other hand," Bledsoe suggested, with just a hint of nervousness in his voice, "perhaps with some extra hours' work, I could turn in a report that would satisfy my superiors."

Westfall relaxed slightly. The pain eased. *A damned blackmailer.* He might have known. "How many extra hours?"

"A couple of hundred ought to be sufficient."

"I see."

272

"Of course, they'd be overtime. So naturally, they'd cost double."

"Of course." Westfall laid the envelope carefully on his desk. "Suppose I give you this check to give to your superiors. And write another one, in advance for services that you will render. Will that be satisfactory?"

Bledsoe smiled. The eye contact between the two men broke as he discovered the cigar in his hand was still unlighted. "Should just about cover everything."

While Westfall wrote, Parker Bledsoe scraped a match against the flint on the side of the container. He puffed away at the cigar until it was well lighted. He blew the smoke toward the ceiling.

"Here you are," Westfall said quietly.

With a grin, Bledsoe accepted both envelopes. Stowing them in the inside pocket of his coat, he tapped his hat into place on his head. "It's been a pleasure doing business with you, sir. If you should be needing my services again, please let me know."

"Never fear." Westfall closed the door behind him. "I'll be in touch."

Bledsoe left the office late that night. His pay envelope plus the envelope containing the second check made a comfortable pad in his pocket. He felt good about himself, good about the day's work. Benjamin Westfall had certainly taken the whole thing like a gentleman. An army man like that with a penchant for authority might have been angered into doing something foolhardy.

Bledsoe had taken a calculated risk and had been more than relieved when the old man had passed the check right over to him.

Good manners made everything so much neater and tidier. When a man was caught, he was caught. The best ones admitted their blunders, took the consequences, and went on to better things. Bledsoe's conscience did not remotely touch the plight of the girl locked away under Mrs. Mortimer's tender care. She was undoubtedly no better than she should be. A few years and she'd come out a sadder but wiser woman.

He passed under the streetlight, turned the corner, and moved down a dark side street. His boardinghouse was less than two blocks away. He was looking forward to a whiskey before the last call for meals.

Behind him he heard the hoofbeats of a single horse. He cast a look over his shoulder. A rider trotted his mount around the corner. A broadbrimmed hat cast the rider's face in a dark shadow.

Bledsoe paid him no more than a passing glance. He was hungry and the night air was chill. He turned up his coat collar and walked faster.

The rider spurred the horse into a gallop. Down the street he swept, iron-shod hooves pounding. Bledsoe stopped to watch him go by. Just as he turned, he saw the rider raise a cavalry saber high above his head. The blade flashed in the lamplight. Its whistling course ended in a sodden thunk as it separated Parker Bledsoe's head from his body.

The horse galloped on down the street. The rider turned it and cantered back. He paused beside the body, whose blood still spouted across the stones. Assuring himself that the street was still deserted, the rider dismounted and knelt beside the corpse. From the right breast pocket he extracted both envelopes and from the left the little book where Parker Bledsoe had made all his case notes. He wiped the saber carefully on his victim's trouser leg.

Mounting again, the rider galloped back the way he had come.

"Lady, shall I lie in your lap?"

Miranda could scarcely hear Shreve's line, so harshly were the bells jangling in her ears. He caught her wrist guiding her firmly to the chair stage right. Her mouth moved stiffly. *"No, my lord."*

He shoved her down into it and dropped down before her, crossing his hands over her knees and leaning his chin on them. From there he spoke the next line. *"I mean, my head on your lap?"*

She was supposed to draw back in shocked horror, but she could manage no more than a weak shake of her head. The movement cleared it somewhat but made the pounding ache worse. She lifted a white face, strained beyond belief, and looked distractedly around. The audience saw her torment. Her voice echoed hollowly in her head. *"Ay, my lord."*

Shreve raised his head and twisted away to look in the direction of Freddy and Ada as King

Claudius and Queen Gertrude stage left. One arm slipped down between her legs, his hand curved over her thigh. The audience gasped. *"Do you think I meant country manners?"*

The king and queen looked suitably shocked. The audience tittered, some with a bit of secret embarrassment, some with appreciation for the jest.

"I think nothing, my lord."

His hand slipped out of sight between her thighs. *"That's a fair thought to lie between maids' legs."*

She was losing consciousness. She could feel herself slipping away. Then he pinched her, sharply, shockingly. His thumb and third finger caught pieces of flesh covered by the thin material of her costume and drove her instantly upright in her seat.

"What is, my lord?" Her line was practically squealed. The audience laughed.

Shreve gave them a conspiratorial wink. *"Nothing."*

They did not believe him. Another laugh.

"You are merry, my lord." She said the line with more force than it really called for.

"Who I?" He cut her next line and went directly into his long speech after which the play within a play began.

She sank back in her chair. Her limbs were trembling and she was perspiring. Surreptitiously she wiped the moisture from her upper lip with the trailing sleeve of her costume.

He had not removed his hand from between her

legs. Now he rubbed the portion of her he had abused a minute before. Even as ill as she was his fingers stirred her. She shifted uncomfortably. "Good girl." His back was to the audience as a watcher of the play and then the king.

"I'm not sure I can go on," she whispered.

"Don't worry." The time came to say her line, but he said it instead, weaving it into his own and answering himself. It might not have been as Shakespeare had written it, but the audience was pleased.

The action built. The players, Mike and George, performed their scene. Shreve as Hamlet announced the reason for the murder. Miranda managed to call out her line. Ada as the queen screamed. Freddy ran down center, thundered his line to the uppermost balcony, and fled with a flourish of his ermine-trimmed cape.

Miranda staggered to her feet, took two steps, and collapsed. Shreve dashed across the stage, gathered her up, and held her across his arms while he spoke his next speech as a soliloquy. Her long blond hair trailed almost to the floor as he declared he would take the ghost's word for a thousand pounds. Maroon velvet curtains swept up before them.

The audience burst into delighted applause with a few cheers thrown in for good measure. The performance had not been so much Shakespeare as exciting theater.

Shreve carried Miranda to a cot set up in the wings. Ada hurried off to fetch a cup of cold tea.

"I don't want anything," Miranda whispered.

He laid her down and touched his finger to her lips. "You're doing a fine job. The audience is loving you. A real trouper."

She smiled weakly. "You saved my life twice now."

"Twice?" He bent to kiss her forehead, finding it bedewed with perspiration and salty to his taste.

"You kept me with the troupe in Saint Louis. You didn't send me back to him. He would have killed me. I know he would have if I hadn't run away with you."

"Don't worry about him."

"I'd be dead or worse if you hadn't been so brave."

He raised a quizzical black eyebrow. "I wasn't brave. I was acting. Actors just do what it takes to make people believe they're brave."

She shook her head. "You were brave."

Ada came around to the other side of the cot. "Here, now, dearie. Drink this. A body can usually keep it down better than anything and you've got to keep drinking. You're just starved for water."

Shreve held her hand while she drank. "Just one more scene," he reminded her softly. "Think you can do it?"

She pushed herself up on her elbow and finished off the tea. Her sides ached from strain, she had an agonizing burning in her belly, but she managed to keep the tea down. "I'll do it," she whispered, then smiled. "After all, it's my best scene."

He kissed her forehead. "You're learning."

* * *

At the boardinghouse Ada put her to bed in a separate room. She lay staring into the cold darkness, her body too racked by the residue of her ordeal to drift off into sleep. Adrenaline inspired by anger and fear had pumped too long through her veins. Her muscles jumped and twitched. A slight fever made her painfully aware of her overstrained nerves.

Westfall had tried to kill her. She could not doubt that. Imprisoned in that house with those women under those conditions, she would not have lasted long. She had heard him with his own words double the vile potion that had left her without strength, almost without the will to resist.

Closing her eyes, she lay shuddering as her memory turned the experience over and over in her mind. It was like some drama played on the stage, and she, the captive, sat in the audience forced to watch her own humiliation and torture. Tears seeped from the corners of her eyes and slid down her cheeks, dampening her hair and the pillow beneath her head.

Chills wracked her. She was so cold. She had not slept alone in many weeks. Shreve had been there for her to cuddle against. A touch of her hand, a coaxing tug at his hip, and he obligingly rolled over and enfolded her in his arms. Cradled spoon fashion, she had been lulled to sleep in warmth and security.

Shreve!

Her eyes flew open. Why was she here alone? Why had he not carried her into his room, their room? The room they had shared together. He had not even bothered to take a room for her in Chicago. They had both assumed that they would be together.

The thought made her angry. How dare he leave her alone? She had turned in the performance of her life for him. Almost too sick to stand, in danger of losing consciousness on stage, she had not forgotten a single of Ophelia's lines. Not one muff. Not one false move. And her reward for that effort was a cold and lonely bed away from him.

She did not even know which direction his room lay in, but she was damned if she was going to lie here and freeze alone. Sliding her feet out from under the covers, she pushed herself upright. The tail of the nightgown caught and hiked up to midthigh. Weak as she was, it hampered her while cold air bathed her ankles and slid up her legs.

Her teeth began to chatter and her stomach to shudder. She hauled the quilt from the bed and it dragged over her shoulders. On tiptoe she made her way across the room and opened the door.

The hall looked familiar. Shreve's room was the first one at the top of the stairs. Quick as light before she could lose her nerve, she dashed down the dark hall, the ends of the quilt billowing behind her like a cape.

She had a moment of fear that he might have locked the door, but the doorknob turned in her hand. She slid through the smallest opening and closed it behind her.

"Who's there?"

Silent as she was, she had awakened him. Or perhaps he had been lying there as sleepless as she? "It's all right. It's me. Miranda."

"Miranda?"

The springs creaked as he sat up in bed. She could see the oval of his face and the whiteness of his nightshirt. "My God! What are you doing here?"

She came to the foot of the bed. "I was c-cold."

"Cold?"

Before he could object, she put her knee on the foot of the bed and tumbled over into his arms.

"Miranda." He caught her by the shoulders and held her at arm's length. "You shouldn't be here."

She was too cold, too excited. The scent of him, the warmth emanating from his body. She realized that her hips were between his knees. Deliberately, she pushed herself toward him, pushing him back onto the pillow, clambering over his belly and chest, throwing up her arms. Her cold hands framed his face. She kissed him hard.

"Miranda!" He tried to twist his mouth away. His next words were muffled as she turned his face back to her and kissed him again.

He caught her wrists and pushed her back. "Umph! Let go! Quit that! You shouldn't be here."

"I couldn't sleep alone. I was too cold."

"Get out of here. Go back to your own bed. I'll send for a hot water bottle." He could feel her shivering. Her clothing, the quilt she had wrapped around her, her hands and wrists, her very lips were cold. In spite of his command, he wrestled the covers from between them and pulled them back up over her.

She groaned in pleasure as he began to chafe her arms and shoulders. Her cold little breasts nestled against his ribs. Belly to belly they lay, his hardening manhood a rod between them. She twisted sensuously.

"Stop that!"

Instantly, she was still. "I'm just trying to get warm."

"Don't lie to me. You know what you were doing."

She was silent for a minute. The heat grew between them. In another minute she would be perspiring. Involuntarily, his thighs clenched, locking about her hips. She rested her head against his chest. "Why didn't you bring me back to your bed?"

His voice was husky. "You're a child."

"I'm seventeen."

He cursed softly. "And I'm twenty-seven, way too old for you."

"I don't care about that."

"I repeat. I'm too old for you," he groaned. His thinking moved him in directions he did not want to travel. "I'm closer to your father's age than yours."

"My father is dead."

"Well, you can't have me for a father."

She raised her head, trying to look into his face in the darkness. "I don't want you for a father."

He threw back his head, striking the headboard a solid thunk. "Damn!" Then, "God help me!"

She could feel him hardening to metal beneath her belly. Despite her will to be still, she moved her hips, wiggled them from side to side, as though trying to find a way to lie on top of him. Her mound rubbed against him.

He groaned again. His hands tightened. "You can't do this. I can't do this to you. You're too young to know what you want. I seduced you."

"I know."

"Well, then you know that you shouldn't be here. You're a girl. You ought to be in school."

She dropped her head onto her chest. "I know that, too, but I'm not, and I never will be again."

He smoothed her hair on the back of her head. His eyes were open to the ceiling, fire raged in his belly. Despite his will, his erection throbbed. He knew she could feel it prodding her. He shook his head angrily. "This is wrong."

She inched upward, her soft parts sliding over him in a total caress. "No, it isn't. I couldn't sleep without you. You've taught me to want you."

"No! God, no!"

Her mouth touched his chin. Her lips caressed it, shaped it. Her teeth nipped it. Unable to resist her, he bent his head to take her mouth.

Her hands slid down his rib cage to his hipbones. She pulled their clothing from between their bodies.

"Miranda, don't do this."

For answer, she reached down to grasp his rod and guide it to the opening in her body. Her thighs pressed hard together, her ankles locking, forming a tunnel of sensation, a welcoming sheath scarcely less moist than the tight wetness inside her.

He groaned as if he were being tortured. She nipped his chin again. Her palms slid up his ribs to his nipples, pinching them, her fingernails scratching at the turgid nubs. He bucked upward. "When did I teach you that?"

She giggled. "Must be three or four months now." The tip of him entered her body. She pushed herself downward.

"Miranda, I'll be damned for this." His voice was husky with pleasure. Where it had been chiding, trying to drive her away, now it was coaxing, approving.

She took him into her body. Hands flat on the bed beside his waist, she pushed herself up, pressing her hips down at the same time. He moved within her, lifting her, glorying in the unceasing pressure that only his movements could relieve.

"Miranda!" His shout of pleasure came as he drove himself into her deeper, higher than ever before. His hands clapped over her buttocks, holding her and forcing her to the pinnacle of pleasure. Swirls of excitement began in her belly and rippled outward. She could not move, could not twist away, could not in any way avoid the force building in her. Her loins were melded to his, her body filled and stretched to agonizing tautness by him.

When it crested, she could only take it. Wave on wave of pleasure crashed over her. She cried out, wordlessly. Her fingers clenched in the sheet, her nails like cat's claws ripping it. He held her, bucking beneath her, finding his own pleasure, when suddenly she cried out again as a second explosion tore through her.

Her teeth grazed his collarbone. Her hot forehead pressed against his neck. "Please," she begged mindlessly. "Please don't please don't please don't —"

Again! Darkness and roaring sound. The pounding of his heart beneath her ear. The bellows of his lungs rocking her to dizzying heights. The hardness of him inside her.

"—stop stop stop."

The words trailed away into a whisper.

She was asleep before he went soft within her. He slid her off him, arranged her limbs and pulled down her clothing. Tenderly as a father with his child, he fluffed the pillow and slipped it under her head. Then he laid himself down beside her and drew the covers up around them.

With a sigh, she snuggled her buttocks into the curve of his hips. He groaned like a man being crucified as he rested his hand on her waist.

"I haven't been a young girl for a long time."

"You were green and innocent." He sat on the edge of the bed, his back to her, the morning light streaming over his shoulders.

She lay on her side, snuggled beneath the welter of covers and clothing. The scent of their lovemaking was a warm fume in her nostrils. "I was a virgin. Physically. Mentally, I was a hundred years old."

He snorted contemptuously. "You were a babe in the woods. I seduced you. I knew exactly what

I was doing, every line, every move. I'd played the scene a hundred times."

"A hundred times?"

"Well, perhaps not a hundred times," he acknowledged with a grin.

"You were very good."

He twisted around on the bed. His arms came down on either side of her head. "Why aren't you angry, damn you?"

She looked up into his dark face, Romeo's face, the morning after the seduction of Juliet. The midnight black hair was tousled, errant fishhooks plastered to his forehead. A blue-black shadow covered the sculptured jaw. The beautiful mouth was angry and swollen from their kisses given and received with passionate abandon.

"Because I fell in love with you. The very first time I saw you." She smiled at the memory. "You winked at me."

"No! Goddamnit! No! That was Romeo. I'm not him."

"No. You're Shreve. And as Ada says, self-interest is very comforting. You're very dependable."

"I don't understand you."

"You need me. You want me to be your actress. You'll do anything to keep me. You'll kiss me. You'll teach me to act. You'll seduce me. You'll rescue me from the clutches of my wicked stepfather. All I have to do is act."

"God!" He sprang to his feet and strode across the room. She watched him, the beauty of his body making her feel hot and moist between her legs. Pivoting, his body perfectly controlled, he

286

stared at her, black eyes accusing. "Don't say things like that to me."

"Why not? I'm only telling the truth."

He shook his head doggedly. A comma of blue-black hair fell over his left eyebrow. "It's more than that. We have more than that."

She slid her tongue along her lower lip. "Do we?"

His gaze turned poisonous, but his heavy organ swelled and lengthened.

Her eyes slumberous, she held out her hand. "Come here, Shreve. Lie down beside me."

Slowly, he returned, his expression mutinous. His body readied itself against his will. He slid into bed and took her in his arms. "Goddamnit," he groaned. "You're seducing me."

She put her hand over his mouth when he would have kissed her. "That's right. And I had the best teacher in the world?"

He tried to pull away, but she held him with her hands lightly resting on his shoulders. "Listen." The word was just a puff of air in his ear. "Just listen. And then we'll make love."

He groaned as he shifted away, putting space between their bodies. She lay on her back. Her hands clasped on her chest. Her attitude reminded him powerfully of Juliet on her bier.

She hesitated, swallowing hard. Her chin thrust upward with some defiance. "My father was a captain in the U.S. Cavalry. He was scalped and mutilated by the Sioux. I walked through a blinding snowstorm to the base hospital to see his body."

He looked at her with horror in his eyes.

"Alone?!"

She turned her face to look him in the eyes. "You don't understand. I wasn't curious to see a dead body. I wasn't some silly child looking at her father for the last time. I knew my father's spirit was gone. But what the Sioux did to his body was a testimony to his bravery. They didn't want their worst enemy to experience pleasure in Heaven. Of course, I don't believe that. But they do. And they must have r-respected him greatly." Blinking rapidly, she shifted her stare back to the ceiling.

His warm hand closed over her shoulder. "Miranda, I had no idea—"

"My mother and I left Fort Gallatin in the dead of winter. I couldn't understand why we left so fast. But now I do. My mother must have been afraid of Colonel Westfall. But when he came offering marriage, she married him. She should have spat in his face." Her fists clenched into the covers.

"Miranda. A soldier's paid to fight Indians. When men fight, they get killed."

She ignored him. Her voice gained strength as she heaped calumny upon herself. "I shouldn't have run away. I should have stayed and kept him away from her. She shouldn't have married the man who killed her husband."

His hand tightened. He shook her gently, trying to rescue her from the hell she burned in. "You don't know that. That man who told you all that stuff could have been crazy. Don't forget. It was his word against Westfall's. And the court-martial believed Westfall."

288

She looked at him again. Her jaw clenched. "Well, I don't. And someday I'll find a way to get him to admit it."

Shreve shook his head. "Give it up. Don't waste your time. He'll never admit to anything like that. He's no fool."

"He may not be a fool, but he'll admit it. I'll force him. And thanks to you, I know how." A flicker of a smile played across her face.

He looked at her curiously.

"He's like Claudius. And she's Gertrude. And I'm Hamlet. Not Ophelia. I'll play her—silly, stupid thing that she is. And weak. How I loathe her." Her adamant declaration made him draw back a little. "No. I'm not Ophelia. I'm Hamlet. And *'The play's the thing, wherein I'll catch the conscience of the king.'* "

Act Three
Scene 1
Chicago, 1883

Sixteen

Our very loving sister, well bemet.

"We fail? But screw your courage to the sticking place, and we'll not fail." Miranda insinuated herself into Shreve's arms. His face, darkened by stage makeup, loomed above her. She dropped her head back against his shoulder.

The audience held its breath.

Her hands, starkly white against the blackness of his cape, moved up behind his head, fastening in his long tousled locks, pulling him down to meet her mouth. The kiss was long, the simulated passion so convincing that a faint murmur rose from the audience.

When she heard it, she pulled away, tore herself out of his grasping arms and strode across the stage. There she turned with a swirl of her own cape, giving the audience a flash of scarlet lining like flame in darkness. Pointing a long finger, the nail tipped bloodred, she told him how they would destroy the unguarded King of Scotland.

Her voice was terrible in its intensity, its determination.

Shreve reacted to her, his face reflecting equal parts horror and admiration. *"Bring forth men children only."* He strode down center stage to deliver his vow to murder his cousin.

She gravitated behind him, burning blue eyes watching him, smiling like a great cat, with sharp teeth framed by her lips painted the same bloodred as her fingernails. Three steps up on the dais upstage, she stopped. Her hand possessively caressed the elaborate carving of the throne chair.

He turned to her, mounted the same steps to the other side of the chair. They stared into each other's eyes. Heat lightning seemed to crackle between them. The audience held its breath. Then he jerked her roughly against his chest. He delivered another kiss, brutal, overpowering. She responded with fervor that matched his own. Like great predatory beasts they wrestled in each other's arms. Then he stepped away. They faced the audience together. Her face was a portrait of sensual excitement and desire. His face was a study in ruthless ambition and lust.

"Away and mock the time with fairest show." He swept her up in his arms. *"False face must hide what the false heart doth know."*

The curtains swished together on the first act. The audience sat stunned for an instant before bursting into sustained applause.

In the wings Shreve lowered Miranda to her feet. "You were slow. Your timing was off. I thought I was going to have to throw you your line."

"Don't worry about my line. You came in too fast. Give them a minute to digest what I'm saying. They don't know the play the way we do."

He scowled thunderously. "You gave them too much time. They had already started fidgeting."

"You're impossible. They were not fidgeting." She spun away striding to the dressing room.

He followed her, continuing the argument. "You didn't hold the kiss long enough. We could have gotten another five seconds out of it."

Ada Cocks heaved a deep sigh as she removed Lady Macbeth's heavy cape from Miranda's shoulders.

"Another five seconds!" Miranda presented her side of the argument to her dresser, wardrobe mistress, and confidant. "Another five seconds and we would have been closed down for indecency. I could hear the Puritans in the audience drawing in a deep breath to set up the hue and cry."

Ada removed the leather gauntlets and collar from the basic underdress. "She's probably right, Shrevey, me boyo."

He turned in exasperation. "Nonsense. You didn't see it? We could have held it another five seconds. The applause would have been deafening."

"You got a wonderful lot of applause as it was." Ada unfastened the dress for Miranda to step out of as she slipped the long white nightgown over her head.

"He's never satisfied. Another five seconds! Impossible. Someone would have tittered. His clock is slower than everybody else's." Miranda plopped down before the dressing table and removed the heavy black wig with rhinestone tiara attached.

"We could have gotten more applause," Shreve grumbled.

Ada gave his shoulder a playful push. "Go on with you. They clapped for more'n a couple of minutes. He's greedy to a fault. Always was, always will be." She reached up to unfasten Macbeth's heavy cape.

Another two minutes and they were dressed for

Act Two. Miranda drank a glass of water. Shreve held out his hand. She slipped her own into it. "Don't cut my entrance," he said. "Let them get the full effect."

"Don't wait too long. It'll slow down the scene."

"I taught you everything you know about acting. Why don't you do it the way I tell you?"

"Because I'm not a puppet."

His glare was already in place when he entered stage right to confront Banquo.

"I have all the information you requested, Miss— um—Miranda." The Pinkerton detective, Henry Keller, passed her an envelope.

"Miranda please. Just Miranda." She opened it and unfolded a neatly typed report. Her eyes scanned it, her stomach clenching as she scanned the record of sixteen years. It was very short, only a few lines. Rachel Drummond, Place of birth, Chicago, Illinois. School records, church confirmation, an injured hand, the index finger broken. It had healed perfectly. Now she was being sent to boarding school here in Chicago while Brigadier General and Mrs. Benjamin Westfall were moving to Washington, D.C. The dates of the general's reinstatement to active duty and promotion to his new rank were also included.

(*Thou hast it now,* she thought bitterly, *King, Cawdor, Glamis, all.*)

With an effort she pulled her attention back to the page. Her little sister Rachel was to remain here alone in Chicago. "When are the general and his wife leaving?"

"Actually, they've already left. At the beginning of

296

the month when the school term began. They've sold his house and closed up Mrs. Westfall's home that she inherited from her parents."

Long eyelashes drifted down over striking blue eyes. So her grandparents were dead. She thought a moment of the parsimonious man and the cold, strict woman. She supposed they had no choice but to leave their house to their only daughter. "The report seems awfully brief."

Keller shrugged. "Nothing more to report. Rachel Drummond is just a well brought up young woman. Very ordinary. People like her haven't had time to do anything to report."

"I see." A tiny smile played around her mouth. What a report he would have had of her at age sixteen! Reared on a frontier fort with a half-wild Indian boy for a playmate, educated catch-as-catch-can, hardly ever attended a church service. At sixteen, a runaway turned actress, the mistress of Shreve Catherwood, "Romantic Star of Three Continents."

His interest piqued, Keller stared at the incredible beauty before him. Her smile complete with dimple in her left cheek fairly blinded him, yet it gave nothing away. What was she thinking behind that perfect face? "I suppose I could dig a little deeper," he offered.

"Why don't you?" she said after a moment's thought. "Investigate her stepfather. His profile might help me to understand more about Rachel's life. From the time he became her father. George Windom, our business manager, will take care of your fee."

Keller nodded. "Pinkerton's is always glad to be of service to you, Miss—that is—Miranda— And may I say, it will be a real pleasure to continue to help a beautiful lady like yourself."

"Thank you, Mr. Keller." Her smile dazzled. Her teeth were perfect and pearly white. She escorted him to the door of the dressing room. "I'll ask George to leave two tickets at the box office for you to pick up tonight."

He smiled in turn. "Why thank you, ma'am. I'll really appreciate that. Course I don't know who I might bring with me."

"I'm sure you'll find someone, a clever man like yourself."

He went away with a broad grin on his face.

Shreve held her against his broad chest. "Did you get the information you wanted?"

Beneath her ear she could hear the steady thrumming of his heart. The heavy muscles of his chest and diaphragm expanded and contracted his lungs with a reassuring rhythm. They had lain together like this for thirteen years. He had held her against the terrors of her youth. She had held him against the follies of his age. Through good times and bad, in sickness and health. They were more than married. She held him a little tighter. "I got it."

His chest expanded in a sigh. "Leave it, Miranda."

"I can't. You know that. Besides, she's my sister."

He gave a negative shake. "She's not. Miranda Drummond had a sister. But you're not that Miranda anymore. You don't have a sister. You don't have a mother, except Ada. You don't have a father, except me."

"You're not my father." She chuckled. She slipped her hand down over his flat belly to cover the limp,

298

satisfied organ that lay nestled in the black curling hair. A film of residue from their lovemaking clung to it. She covered it possessively. "Thank God. That was so good."

She turned her lips to his chest and suckled his nipple. It hardened in instant response.

"Stop that."

"Sorry. Are you all tired out?"

"Don't change the subject."

She laid her cheek back against his chest but kept her hand where it was, clasping his sex, letting her gentle warmth arouse him. "I want to see my sister."

"You'll only end up hurting her and yourself," he predicted direly.

She snuggled closer to his side. Her knee slipped between his legs, spreading them. Her hand slid down between them, caressing the ultrasensitive satiny skin hidden there in the most private spot of his body. "You sound like a Greek Chorus. All gloom and doom."

"I'm just concerned that you'll be sorry, and then your acting will be worse than it is."

"Worse," she murmured lazily. "How can it be worse? According to you, it's unbelievable."

"It could be worse." He deepened his voice to its Mephistophelian base. "Much worse."

She pulled her hands away and flounced over on her side clasping the pillow instead of his torso. "Don't talk anymore. I need my sleep. I want to look my best tomorrow."

He lay staring into the darkness, listening to her feign even, quiet breathing. She could never get it quite right.

"Ordinarily, I don't allow the girls to have visitors except on visiting days. Visitors interfere with the routine, don't you know?" The headmistress looked like somebody's grandmother, white hair drawn back in a bun, glasses on her nose.

"I'm sure that's a very good rule."

"Ordinarily, I'd have to turn you away, but since you're—who you are, I wouldn't want to deprive Rachel of the chance to see and talk to you. Of course, if you were an ordinary actress, that would be different. But you're playing Lady Macbeth." The woman's tones became reverential.

Miranda smiled graciously. "Have you seen the play?"

"Not in years."

"Please bring a friend to the theater tonight. I'll have tickets waiting in your name at the box office."

"Really!" The woman's smile was angelical. "Oh, thank you. I'll ask my sister to go with me. She'll be so thrilled."

"I hope you both enjoy the performance. And, of course, I'd want my friend's daughter Rachel to go, and perhaps one of her best friends."

The headmistress frowned faintly, then capitulated, her eyes like stars. "I don't suppose there would be any objection. We could act as chaperones. It'll be a real theater party."

"I promise to be at my very best. You'll be educating the girls at the same time you entertain them."

"That's very true." The woman rose. "If you'll come this way, you can visit with Rachel in the best parlor."

She was so beautiful and so much like Francis

Drummond, that tears started from Miranda's eyes. "I think I would have known you anywhere, Rachel."

"You would?"

Rachel's expression was one of dazzled bewilderment. She stared openmouthed at the beautiful lady with the exquisitely coiffed blond hair. Miranda had dressed with special care, choosing to wear the taffeta suit from Harrod's in London. Of a deep sapphire blue, it had a pale blue lining that showed in the swept-back effect to the bustle. From beneath the bustle, the paler ruffles cascaded down the back of the dress. She rustled as she came to Rachel and took her hands.

"You look just like your father."

The remark drew a quick frown. "No, I don't. My father has brown hair and hazel eyes—and a big mustache."

"Not your real father, Francis Drummond."

"How do you know my father's name?"

Too soon, her mind warned her. *Too soon.* "I knew him."

Rachel tilted her head to one side. Her eyes narrowed as she frankly stared at the beautiful lady. "He's been dead a long time."

"Nevertheless, I knew him."

"Then you must know my mother, too."

"Yes." Miranda flashed her famous smile. "She was once my best friend."

Rachel extricated her hands from Miranda's grasp and stepped back. "Mrs. Wilcox said you're a famous actress."

"I'm an actress."

"She said your name was Miranda," Rachel continued, curiosity making her voice a little shrill.

301

"That's my stage name."

"Oh."

Miranda hesitated, trying to decide what to say to the girl who seemed to be capable of waiting forever if need be. She stood with her feet together in her thick blue hose and black lace-up shoes. Her hands were now clasped tightly in front of her. Spots of high color stained her soft cheeks. She looked nervous, uncertain of —

Rachel broke into Miranda's thoughts. "I didn't know my mother knew an actress."

"I haven't been an actress all my life. Just the last fourteen years of it."

Rachel's smooth brow knitted between the fine blue eyes. She studied Miranda carefully. "Fourteen years."

"That's right." Miranda looked away. "I wanted to come and see you since I'm playing here in Chicago. I thought you might enjoy going to the theater. It's *Macbeth*. I've reserved tickets for you and your headmistress."

"Is she going?"

"She said she would be delighted. She's going to take her sister. I thought you could go, too, and perhaps take one of your friends from school."

Rachel looked stern. "I've never been to the theater before. Father doesn't approve of it. He says it's morally depraved."

Miranda felt a desire to laugh. Westfall had certainly become virtuous since he had courted Ruth. Or perhaps Miranda's escape had made him leery of the theater in general. "How silly! It's just a form of entertainment. Like reading. Just like there are good books and bad books, there are good plays and bad plays. *Macbeth* happens to be one of the very best."

Rachel shrugged. Her answer was decidedly unenthusiastic. "It might be fun."

"Do you have a lot of fun with your mother?"

"She doesn't have much time to spend with me."

"Oh."

"She's been part of Father's career for a long time now. That's why they've gone to Washington, D.C." She lifted her chin with the merest hint of defiance. "They begged me to go with them, of course, but I didn't want to go. Father's career is at a crucial stage. They were going to be really busy."

Recognizing a long-rehearsed lines when she heard them, Miranda met Rachel's eyes. Her own revealed her sympathy.

"They were," Rachel insisted. "I really didn't want to go."

"I'm sure you didn't. Why don't we sit down?" Miranda indicated the uncomfortable-looking settee. Her mind moved swiftly, with an actress's skill improvising, trying to decide what to tell Rachel and what not to.

"Anyway, I'm almost grown up," Rachel continued. "I'm just here at Mrs. Wilcox's for the finishing touches. Then I'll join them in Washington."

"It sounds ideal."

Again the silence, then Rachel spoke. "My sister's name was Miranda."

Miranda smiled encouragingly. Her heart was beating fast.

"She disappeared nearly fourteen years ago. Father said she ran away, and then she died before he could find her."

The girls stared at each other. Miranda felt a knife

303

twist deep within her. Of course, she had known they thought her dead, but hearing it was surprisingly painful.

"My sister would have been thirty years old if she had lived," Rachel continued.

"I'm thirty. But, of course, in the theater we never admit to more than twenty-four."

"Am I supposed to suddenly realize that you're my sister?" The question came after a pregnant pause during which time Rachel stared rudely at Miranda's face.

Miranda lowered her head, her heart thrumming powerfully in her chest. "Would you like me to be?"

"Not really."

Miranda was shocked to the core. Rachel had not reacted in any way as she had expected. She schooled her face into a cool mask. "I'm an actress. I can be anything you want me to be."

"It wouldn't be hard to fool me, if I were a fool," Rachel continued. "I was just a baby when she disappeared. I hardly remember her. Of course, I've seen pictures of her."

"I'm sure people change."

Rachel's jaw tightened pugnaciously. Her voice quivered with angry emotion. "My sister ran away because she didn't love my mother and me anymore."

"No," Miranda denied instantly. "That's not true. She hated to leave you and Mother, but she had to."

Rachel's expression never changed. "Why did she have to?" she scoffed. "I'll bet she didn't. She was just in a fit of bad temper. I've heard the story so many times. Mother and Father used to fight about it. Anyway, she's dead. My sister's dead. Father said so."

"So you call him Father."

"He is my father. In every way but one. Mama says so. My real father was killed before I was born. But my sister knew him. The one who died."

"Yes. She did."

"After my sister ran away from home, Father searched and searched. He even hired a private detective. And then, finally, the private detective found out that she had died."

"How did she die?" Miranda asked softly.

"She did something very bad." Rachel's eyes were defiant. "She was put in a home for wayward girls. And she died there."

"She didn't die. She almost did, but a wonderful man rescued her."

Rachel snorted skeptically. "Sounds like a fairy tale to me. A prince rescues Rapunzel from her prison. I can't imagine why you've come here today. I can't imagine why you'd take the trouble to lie to me."

"Perhaps I'm not lying. Why would I lie?" Miranda was beginning to feel desperate.

Rachel lifted her chin to look down her nose. "My father is a very important man. And he's going to be more important. The more important you are, the more strange people you attract. People want you to do them favors. They appear at odd times. He's always warned me that people do all sorts of strange things."

"I'm sure Benjamin Westfall would like to be very important. That's why he married your mother," Miranda acknowledged. "Why don't you ask me something that only Miranda Drummond would

305

know?"

Rachel stared at the beautiful woman. Then she smiled. A dimple appeared in her cheek and tugged the corner of her mouth up. "What was my dog's name?"

"If you got a dog, it was after I left. Grandfather wouldn't allow me to have a pet."

Obviously the answer shocked her. The superior smile was wiped from her face. She hesitated before asking, "How did my daddy die?"

"He was killed by the Sioux on the ridge beyond Fort Gallatin in the Wyoming Territory," Miranda informed her bitterly. "He died with his troop trying to make it back to the fort."

"You could have read all that in a newspaper or a history book."

Miranda shrugged. "I don't know what to tell you that I couldn't have read."

Suddenly, Rachel's smile was back. One eyebrow rose as if to say *I've got you now.* "Who was Wellington?"

Miranda smiled in turn. "Our father's horse. A mahogany bay stallion. Wellington made it back to Fort Gallatin, but—the commanding officer of the fort said it was too late to ride to the rescue."

Suddenly, the sixteen-year-old eyes looked immeasurably older. "I've read that in the account. But he had to say that. He had to protect all the rest of the people in the fort. He did say that."

"I know. I was there. He said it to me."

"Maybe you really are my sister."

"I swear that I am."

"My sister." Angry tears welled in the girl's eyes, blue like Francis Drummond's. She sprang up and

306

began to pace. "You can't be. You can't be. You're dead. You're not Miranda."

"I'm sorry that upsets you." Tears trickled down Miranda's cheeks. She held out her hands. "Oh, Rachel, I've wanted to hug you for so long."

The younger girl whirled. "Keep away from me. I thought you were dead. Mother believes you're dead. She's wept and grieved herself sick. I don't think she's ever gotten over what you did."

"I had to leave. Benjamin Westfall would have sent me away. I wanted to go on my own."

"Where would he have sent you? To school?" Bitterness dripped from Rachel's voice.

"Well, yes—"

"And so you ran away," Rachel scoffed. "Sounds like a good idea to me. You didn't like the idea of school, so you just ran away. I might try that. Then my mother could just crawl into a hole and die. You were spoiled. That's what you were. You couldn't take not being the apple of her eye any longer."

"It wasn't like that."

"You don't know what it was like," Rachel accused. "You weren't there. I was. Mother blamed herself. She couldn't eat, couldn't sleep. She almost lost her mind. Grandfather raved and ranted. Grandmother wouldn't let me come in the same room with Mother for more than a few minutes. I was little, but I remember. I—"

"Rachel!" Miranda interrupted the tirade. "Please. I didn't know."

"No. And you didn't think, either. Father insisted that she marry him. She cried and cried. She said she didn't want to, but between Grandfather and him, they forced her to. They forced her to marry him.

307

And then slowly, she began to get well. We worked together, he and I. We healed her."

Dimly, Miranda could remember Shreve saying something about her family being frantic with worry. He had been trying to get her to leave the troupe and return to Chicago. He had even offered her some money to get home, but she had refused.

"And where were you while she was crying? Roaming around the countryside. Dressing up in pretty clothes." Rachel eyed the exquisite taffeta dress. "Were you having a good time? Well, let me tell you. Your family wasn't having a good time. We weren't having a good time at all."

Suddenly, Miranda felt cold as ice. Her hands were shaking. The anticipated joy of the day had turned to ashes. The blue taffeta dress she had donned with such care to present the very best picture seemed affectation. She should have come to her sister in sackcloth and ashes, begging forgiveness.

"I'm sorry," she whispered.

Rachel stalked to the door. Miranda could see the ugly heavy shoes, the trim ankles clad in the navy blue stockings beneath the hem of the scratchy wool skirt. "I don't want to go to the theater to see your play. I don't want to see you again. I'm going to tell Mrs. Wilcox if you come here again that I don't want to see you."

One ugly shoe pivoted. The heels clomped to the door. It opened and closed. The footsteps broke into a run before they died away completely.

Miranda put her hands to her face and wept.

Seventeen

Do you call me fool?

"What did you expect? The prodigal sister returns?"

"Yes," she sobbed. "Yes. Yes! *Yes!*"

Shreve threw up his hands. "I never realized how much you're out of touch with the world."

She looked at him from an unlovely face, her eyelids swollen and bruised, red mottling on her cheekbones. "I am not. I've lived and worked right along side you in the theater. If I'm out of touch, then what are you?"

He regarded her sadly, then shook his head. "I've got a lot to answer for in you."

She made a visible effort to pull herself together, swiping the tears from her cheeks with the edges of her fingers, setting her mouth in its customary shape. Her denial was made in a modulated voice. "You don't have anything to answer for in me."

Again he shook his head. "You don't understand. You've never known anything except what I've told you. I've made damned sure you didn't. You've lived in my shadow."

She lifted her head proudly. "How can you say that? I'm on stage every night, and I meet the public every day."

"That's it. You meet the public. You don't mingle with them. I stand at your side while they adore you and congratulate you. George handles your business and Ada puts on your clothes. We all insulate you from anything unpleasant."

"You make me sound like a backward child," she complained. "You make it all sound like a bed of roses. I work hard for—"

He put a soothing hand on her shoulder. "I know you do. But you're an actress. Actors and actresses don't live like everyone else. They live in a world of make-believe, a world of heroic gestures and happy endings, of reconciliations, and triumphant returns. A world of long sentences and artificial language."

"A world of long hours and hard work, rude audiences, and foul theater managers," she interrupted angrily.

"That's true, but in the end everything turns out happily. Lost children are found and restored to their ecstatic parents. Lost lovers are reunited after twenty years. Life's not like that. The parents, the children, the lovers continue with their lives. They become different people. Come on, tell me. What did you expect your sister to do?"

Miranda hesitated. She had tightened her mouth in a sullen line, but now it began to quiver. "I thought that she might not believe me. I thought that I might have trouble getting her to believe who I was."

"But she didn't have a bit of trouble with that, did she?"

"No. She recognized me."

"She'd have to have been half-witted not to. She's seen pictures of you, I'm sure. You haven't changed that much. Your poor mother probably has a shrine in her home dedicated to her dear dead daughter. What did she do after she recognized you?"

His words were like blows adding to her distress. "She acted as if she h-hated me. You should have seen her. She accused me of awful things. She said I deserted her and Mama."

"Didn't you? What's running away if it's not desertion? You never went back to find out what happened to her. Your mother's probably had a hard time of it, never knowing whether you were alive or dead. Always hoping. Crying on your birthday. Mourning during the Christmas festivities. Weeping—"

She clenched her fists. "Stop it!"

"The happy ending?" he asked somberly. "Did it happen?"

"No. She told me she never wanted to see me again. My own sister. When she was a baby, I loved her so much. She used to hug and kiss me." Miranda struggled to stem the fresh tears. "I don't mean to cry again. I really don't."

Shreve regarded her bowed head with bleak dark eyes. "Put it behind you as soon as you can. We've got to think what to do next."

"Why we?"

"Because *we* may have a big problem. How do we get the lid back on this kettle of rotten fish?"

Miranda abruptly swallowed her tears and took several deep controlling breaths, her favorite trick—one he had taught her—to alleviate stage fright. She

311

dabbed at her eyes with her sodden handkerchief. "I don't want it closed."

"The hell you don't."

She turned back to him, her chin lifted defiantly (Beatrice in *Much Ado about Nothing*). "I mean it."

He looked at her, allowing his disgust to show in the curve of his lips. "Miranda, what you want is for her to have the discretion to keep your unwelcome visit to herself."

"How can you say that? I had hoped that we could be friends." She leaned forward, hands outstretched like the supplicant Isabella.

He quoted *Measure for Measure* to her. *"Most dangerous is that temptation that doth goad us on to sin in loving virtue."*

She whipped her hands behind her, glaring. "What does that mean? You should have been there. My little sister is living in that terrible school, wearing uniforms and ugly shoes."

"Did the headmistress have a whip coiled around her shoulder?"

"No."

"Did your sister look malnourished? Was her face bruised?"

"No."

"Did she beg you to take her out of there?"

"No."

His shrug was a masterpiece of theatricality. "Condemned by your own words."

"Damn you. This is not a play."

"No. It's not. But you can't stop acting. It's your sister's life. She deserves to live it the way she wants to. You don't see her running away, do you?"

She shook her head reluctantly.

312

"Just forget about her. And pray that she won't want to write a letter to Westfall. Or worse yet, to your mother."

"I was just trying to help her. He's pushed her out. The way he pushed me. And my mother let him, just like she did before."

He raised his voice to overwhelm hers. "He's sent her to one of the most exclusive schools in Chicago. Probably a lot of her friends go there. She'll get a very expensive and socially correct education. When she finishes, she can go to Washington, D.C., and be introduced into society."

"He's separated her from her mother. They've gone away and left her."

"She's old enough to be separated from her mother. She's older than you were, for heaven's sake. I'll bet she wanted to stay." He looked at Miranda closely. "Did she say something like that?"

She ducked her head. "She was obviously putting on the best face."

"You don't know that." He flung up his arms. "The main problem is to get this forgotten. Your mother thinks you're dead. But if she finds out otherwise, she'll want to see you again. Your profession would be an embarrassment to her. And when she finds out about our relationship—"

She had almost forgotten how she felt when she blushed, but she remembered now. "I never thought Rachel would tell. I thought she'd be angry with him, the way I was."

"You were wrong the first. You're probably wrong about the second. We'll just have to hope that she doesn't want to hurt her mother. We surely don't need him showing up here. He could make

313

a lot of trouble for us."

She sprang to her feet, pointing her finger at him. "Now I understand why you're objecting so strongly. I should have known. You're worried about business."

He did not flinch from the truth. "Somebody's got to worry about business. Our careers could be hurt by this."

"Don't be ridiculous. We're famous now. You're Shreve Catherwood, 'Romantic Star of Three Continents.' I'm the 'Mysterious and Lovely Miranda.' I'm a grown woman. He can't come around with a detective and put me in a home for wayward girls. He can't do anything."

Shreve turned away with a dismissing wave of his hand. He dropped down wearily into the first comfortable chair and lifted his feet up onto a stool. "He could make trouble for us. He's not without influence here in Chicago and now in Washington. My guess is that he's completely reinstated himself in the army."

"He doesn't even believe in going to the theater," she scoffed. "Rachel told me so."

"That's not surprising, considering where he found you."

"He thinks I'm dead."

"Not if she tells him you're alive. Maybe he never did believe you were dead. Maybe he just meant to break you and scare you half to death, so you wouldn't ever try to see your mother again. More than likely he knew within hours that you'd escaped from that place."

"I tell you—"

"No." He held up his hand. "No. Let me tell you,

Miranda. Once and for all. Listen to me. No theater manager wants trouble. A word here, a word there, and our run will suddenly be shortened. A booking will be canceled. Another. The word goes out and we're not working."

"We have a tour contracted."

"And you know how much that's worth if someone puts the word out."

She stared into his implacable face and blasted him with the deadliest look that she was capable of.

He raised one black eyebrow. "Lady Macbeth to the life. How I wish you could generate that much fire on stage!"

Anger, grief, disappointment, frustration, all the most bitter emotions boiled over in a scream. She flung herself at him, her fingers curved like claws, her teeth bared. He caught her by the wrists, twisted her arms behind her, and brought her down against him, her body slanted across his lap, her bosom pressed painfully against his chest. Their faces were inches apart. His was smiling.

"Don't you dare," she warned. "Don't you dare kiss me."

"Why not? It's exactly as we've rehearsed it. Perfect timing. It seems a shame to waste the scene."

"This is not a scene," she hissed.

He rubbed the tip of his nose back and forth against hers. "Perfect distance."

"Stop it." She struggled and twisted, trying to pull her wrists free.

He sighed. "I'll let you go only if you promise not to scratch my face. Makeup over scratches never looks quite right. And it's such a bother."

She sucked at the insides of her cheeks.

Tightening his grasp on her wrists, he reared up so his face was above hers. "And don't spit! You never get it right. And you're so close to me you'll probably get it all over yourself."

"May God Himself damn you to hell!"

His beautiful mouth spread mirthlessly. "Very good. Very good. Excellent enunciation. Nice crescendo. Started low enough so that you didn't get shrill at the end."

She stopped struggling and held herself stiff across his lap.

Slowly, warily, he took his hands away from her wrists. Judging her by the look in her eyes, he returned his arms formally to the arms of his chair.

She pushed herself up, clumsily, catching her foot in her skirt, staggering sideways, righting herself with effort. Rage and mortification had turned her skin lily-white. Never had she hated him as much as she hated him at that moment. For fourteen years he had dominated her life. He had controlled every act waking and sleeping from the most public appearance to the most intimate detail.

He had taught her to breathe, to move. He had taken her barely educated dialect and turned it into perfect enunciation.

He had taken the child Miranda and had made her his creature, the actress 'The Mysterious and Lovely Miranda.' The little girl who had played in the hills with White Wolf's Brother was a story of someone else. Not a gesture, not an intonation, not a drawing of breath, but he had taught her how to do it. To save her soul, she could not stop acting. The very passion that he had awakened in her body had been for his delectation.

316

And now he mocked her like a laughing god.

Suddenly, she saw herself as he must see her. She was his thing with no feelings, no will except his.

The laughter was like a knife in the gut. It twisted and wrenched at her until she thought she would be ill. With all the skill she was capable of, she put on a calm face. "I have to go and get ready for the performance tonight."

"Miranda." His voice called to her as she put out her hand to open the door. "Don't take this so much to heart. Let it go."

Giving no sign that she had heard, she turned the knob.

"Miranda. Don't bother your sister and mother again. You've chosen to live your life away from them. Don't try to—"

The door thudded shut behind her.

"Mrs. Wilcox, I've changed my mind. If it's not too late, I'd like to see the play tonight."

The headmistress smiled at Rachel. With more familiarity than was her usual custom, she put a reassuring hand on the girl's shoulder. "My dear, I truly believe you've made a wise choice. Your earlier decision to eschew this outing because of your father's sometime disapproval does you credit. Indeed, I don't know of another girl who would have given up the opportunity."

"No, ma'am."

"But I'm sure you may be guided by me in this affair. Your father, like many concerned men, is fully aware that the theater is frequently a place of great depravity. Choices must be scrutinized very

317

carefully. Many conclude that the entertainment and education are not worth the time and trouble required to find them. I'm sure that was the case with your father." She looked hopefully at Rachel's set face.

"I'm sure you're right."

"The seats are free. And your mother's friend, Miranda, would have only your best interests at heart. What a wonderful opportunity for you to see *Macbeth!*"

"Yes."

"In any case, to be perfectly correct and to absolve you of any blame, I have written a letter to your father explaining that I was the one who insisted that you attend. Because of the uplifting cultural experience."

Rachel stiffened. "You wrote to my father! Oh, Mrs. Wilcox, I don't think that's a good idea."

"Nonsense, my dear. You should be able to see the play with a quiet mind. Shakespeare's immortal verse should flow over you and—"

"Have you already mailed the letter?" Urgency made her voice high.

"It left by this morning's post." The headmistress put her arm around her charge's shoulders. "Now I want you to put your fears to rest. If your father disapproves, he will cast no blame on you. Go along with you now and get dressed."

"Mrs. Wilcox, I wish you hadn't done that."

"My dear, you'll have a wonderful time. An experience that many of our young ladies will never have. Box seats. Just imagine."

"Did you send the letter to my father and mother, or just my father?"

318

"Oh, both, my dear. After all, Miranda said she was your mother's friend."

Rachel's stomach clenched. She could imagine her mother's state of mind when she read the letter.

Mrs. Wilcox smoothed a strand of silvery blond hair back into Rachel's braid. "Now run along and inform Dorinda that she should wear her Sunday best rather than her uniform." She allowed herself a bright smile. "We will all wear our Sunday best tonight."

Henry Keller was surprised to discover that Benjamin Westfall had been a client of Pinkerton's. Parker Bledsoe, the detective assigned to the case, had located a runaway stepdaughter, Miranda Drummond.

At the name Miranda, Keller sat up straight. Were the actress, the incredibly beautiful Miranda, and Miranda Drummond the same person? Was she investigating her sister Rachel's life?

A quick reading of the old file confirmed his suspicion. A photograph in the file was clearly one of Miranda at a very young age. Likewise, she had been found with a troupe of actors, The Sons of Thespis. The detective had accompanied his client to the theater where he had talked with his stepdaughter. The manager of the troupe, Shreve Catherwood, had denied that he had known the girl was a minor.

Here the record ended with puzzling abruptness. The outcome of the conversation as well as the resolution to the case was absent.

Keller turned the paper over. Nothing. He

shrugged. Probably Westfall had decided to leave her where she was. Certainly, his decision had been a wise one. The exquisite face, the beautiful voice, the elegant carriage were becoming famous all over the world.

A totaling of expenses followed. Westfall had paid the company in full, and the amount of his payment and date of the draft, the day following the conversation in the theater had been entered.

Keller's eyes opened wide as he read the last line in the file.

"Detective Parker Bledsoe, murdered. Assailant unknown."

A set of initials followed, probably belonging to a clerk, possibly to another detective, perhaps the one assigned to investigate the Bledsoe case. (The department took care of its own.)

Keller set aside the report. Curiosity aroused, he searched the files again. In a separate filing cabinet, he found Bledsoe's.

The detective had been struck down in the street the same night he had closed the Drummond case. Keller's eyebrows drew together in a frown. The word "bizarre" did not often occur to him, but "bizarre" described the description of the death. Parker Bledsoe had been decapitated.

He had returned to the office, turned in the Westfall check, evidently done the paperwork necessary to close the case, and started to walk to his boardinghouse. His body had been found the next morning on the sidewalk within sight of his boardinghouse.

He read the investigator's report. The head had been struck from his body. The murder weapon was

320

thought to have been a long knife or saber. The angle suggested that the assailant had been on horseback. No other signs of violence marked the body. "Killed with a single stroke."

No motive for the murder had ever been discovered. Bledsoe had specialized in missing persons cases with a better than sixty percent success rate. He was unmarried, had no known enemies. The detective in charge of the case had speculated that it had been a case of mistaken identity.

The murder had never been solved.

Henry Keller sat back in the chair staring at the file. *Coincidence,* his mind said. *Too much of a coincidence. A saber. Who used sabers? Cavalry officers.* He made a note of the name of the investigator. If the man still worked for Pinkerton's, Keller wanted to talk to him.

Brig.-Gen. Benjamin Westfall, due to receive his second appointment to the Mountain District, Department of the Platte, crushed the sheet of letter paper in his hand. The lumpy blue veins and liver spots strutted on the white skin.

With his other hand he fumbled the cigar from the ashtray and sucked on it furiously. Blue-gray smoke laden with nicotine rushed into his lungs. He held it there, eyes slitted against its sting. A tremor shot through him. Cold began in his stomach and spread upward and downward until he thought his whole body would be consumed with it.

He wallowed the cigar to the corner of his mouth, clamped his teeth tight on the end, and spread open the letter again.

". . . Mrs. Westfall's friend . . . Miranda . . . tickets to the theater."

His anger, unsuccessfully vented on the letter, flamed impotently. He had been forced to depend upon incompetents. Somehow, the stupid woman, Morrison— no, that had not been her name—Mortimer, had not kept the rude, headstrong girl in her charge long enough to break her spirit.

Miranda had gone right back to her troupe of actors and now was an outstanding success in Mrs. Wilcox's judgment.

With shaking hands Westfall fumbled a second piece of paper from the envelope. He enfolded a playbill listing Shreve Catherwood, "Romantic Star of Three Continents," and the Mysterious and Lovely Miranda.

Catherwood! He would bet his last dollar that she had not stayed at Mrs. Mortimer's long at all. And he had paid a sizable sum to the matron, good money he could ill afford to part with at the time.

In his anger he champed right through his cigar. The lighted stump fell into his lap. Cursing, he lunged up brushing at the lighted ash clinging to his thigh. The cigar rolled onto the floor. He had to squat down, arthritic joints protesting, and duck his head inside the kneehole to retrieve it before it burned a hole in the carpet. When he pulled himself up and reseated himself at the desk, he was shaking and sweating.

Bedamned to Francis Drummond! The man had haunted him for nearly twenty years. First, he had been married to the woman Westfall had wanted. Then he survived skirmish after skirmish with a tenacity that was as astonishing as it was frustrating.

Finally, his retreat toward the safety of Fort Gallatin along with his colorful scout Hickory Joe Magruder had become the leading subject of articles in several pulp magazines. The outlandish and oft-retold tale had been purported to be a "true" account of the most valiant part of the Clarendon Massacre. Westfall had seen himself portrayed as a coward on every occasion and a villain in at least two.

Now Miranda Drummond was becoming more of a thorn in his side than her father had ever been.

The entire affair of her runaway had been bungled. The girl had been a troublemaker; the detective, a blackmailer. In retrospect, he realized that he should have killed them both. He doubted that Bledsoe had even seen the stroke coming. Sharp, painless, efficient. Both bodies could have been dumped in Lake Michigan with no one the wiser.

He stabbed the cigar into the ashtray. Mercy was for fools.

He read the letter again. The idiot headmistress Wilcox had opened the doors of the school and allowed Miranda to meet her sister. He must be home for the next few days to catch the mail before his wife saw it. Above all, Rachel must not write to Ruth that Miranda had been found.

Equally bothersome was the task of keeping Rachel from speaking to her mother about Miranda. He could censor Rachel's letters until he could himself write to her forbidding her to tell her mother about Miranda. But he could not be certain that womanlike, she would not let the information slip out in conversation. He had almost despaired of Ruth's ever getting over the loss of Miranda.

The two must have had a most unhealthy relationship. Ruth had mourned her daughter for years. He shuddered to think of the repercussions if Miranda and Ruth should meet and Ruth should learn that he had found Miranda and had not brought her back home.

Once the appointment was announced, he would take his wife to the Wyoming Territory with all haste. She would be occupied with the business of the post as all good army wives were. He would throw himself into rebuilding Fort Gallatin and making the Sioux pay dearly for the disgrace he had lived with all these years.

Custer's defeat in 1876 had been the chance for him to turn his career around. He had sent letter after letter, detailing his experience at Fort Gallatin, reminding them that he had been acquitted of charges brought against him, describing his exemplary style of life, including the fact that he had married Francis Drummond's widow, and begging them to reinstate him to command.

Finally, the humiliating self-abnegation had paid off. The War Office with the intercession of his first wife's father had agreed that the army needed him and his knowledge of frontier fighting to defeat the Sioux.

Once back on the frontier with a sizable troop to command, his plans would come to triumphant fruition. Fame, promotion, a seat in Congress, even the presidency would not be beyond him.

He leaned his head on his hand and closed his eyes. Again he damned Francis Drummond and all his get. Rachel must be kept from forming an attachment to her sister. He could not go himself. The timing of his career was crucial. He must hire something done to drive Miranda Drummond out of Chicago. Something violent, something frightening.

He opened his eyes. The letter and playbill lay open on the desk. With a steady hand, he held the playbill's corner to the much abused cigar. Instantly, it blackened, withered. A tiny wave of flame rose from it. He turned it deftly controlling the fire, allowing his stare to be drawn into its golden heart. When the heat touched his fingers, he dropped it into the ashtray and repeated the process with the letter.

When both were nothing but blackened curls, he took the cigar and crushed their ashes.

Shreve Catherwood opened the door slowly. The room was shrouded in the darkness of late afternoon. "Miranda," he called softly.

Silence.

He entered, closing the door behind him, and moving softly toward the bed. "Miranda."

"What?"

"We need to get going."

"I don't intend to go on."

He sat down on the side of the bed. Immediately, she turned over, presenting him with her back. "Of course, you do. You may be mad at me, but you're a professional through and through."

"Not according to you."

"Miranda, I—"

"Go away." She tugged the covers more tightly around her and turned so she was practically lying on her stomach.

"You can't disappoint your audience."

"According to you they don't come to see me. Anybody could stand on stage in my costume and you could do all the work."

"You never believed that for a minute."

"Didn't I? It hardly matters. I don't think I want to act ever again."

He rose and then stretched out beside her, his thighs tucked up under hers, his belly pressing against her buttocks. His hand slid over her waist, headed for her soft breasts, but she intercepted it and flung it back.

He smiled to himself, hunching closer to her until his mouth was only inches from the nape of her neck. "Miranda." He blew gently but directly toward her earlobe. "Miranda. It's time to go."

She hunched her shoulder higher and buried her cheek more deeply into the pillow.

"Miranda."

"Damn you. Leave me alone."

He put his hand on her shoulder. "You have to go on tonight."

"No."

"If you don't, you'll be sorry."

"You'll be the one who's sorry. The theater manager might make you give back a percentage of the gate."

"He'll never make me do that. There's a clause in the contract which allows for the illness of the leading lady or leading man."

"You're so clever."

"Yes, but I'm not a very sensitive man."

"I can't believe I'm hearing you say that."

"It's true." He moved still nearer to her until he

touched her at all points. His hand slid down from her shoulder to her elbow and back again, rubbing gently. "You're the one with all the passion, all the fire."

"I may be sick."

"It's true. You're the heart and soul. I'm the brains of this team."

"Oh, thank you very much."

"A brain is nothing without a heart and soul."

"You were doing fine without me, as you're so fond of telling me."

"That's why I need my heart and soul. To keep me from lying when the truth would do better." He kissed the tip of her ear.

She shivered and tried to edge away, but he held her. "Why do I let you do this to me?"

"Because I'm right. And you know I'm right. Because you've known it since you saw me from the audience as Romeo, and I've known it since I pulled you out of the back of the wagon."

"You're a damned liar." She said it without heat. The only heat was the warmth that his gentling hands were kindling in her body.

"But you already know that." He drew the covers from her. "So if you know it, how can my lies hurt you?" He slid his hand beneath the waistband of her petticoat.

"Shreve—"

"I don't want to make love to you now." He sucked her earlobe into his mouth caressing it with the silky lining of his lips. His fingers slid through the opening of her drawers. "I don't want to hurry and spoil what we'll have tonight."

"Shreve," she gasped.

"I just want you to remember what we have tonight. It'll be good. It'll be so good." He bit her earlobe.

She cried out in pain and pleasure as he parted her nether lips with his index finger.

"You have to get up and come to the theater," he urged. "Now."

"Now? Oh, Shreve." She clutched at the pillow with both hands.

"Now. Your sister doesn't hate you. She was just jealous." His finger continued to move. He blew hot breath into her ear.

"Oh, Shreve, I can't believe—"

"She was just punishing you for not being dead. When she's had time to think about it, she'll change her mind."

Miranda shuddered. "I don't think so."

He took his hands away and sat up, pushing her over onto her back and holding her down by the shoulders.

"Believe it. Even if she isn't used to the idea of her sister, she'll still come."

She looked at him, her blue eyes luminous, teary. "Why?"

He bent and kissed her swiftly. "Because you're Miranda. And you're the best actress this town has ever seen."

Eighteen

According to the fair play of the world,
Let me have audience.

"The seats are full. The seats are full." Miranda caught Shreve's arm and hugged it to her.

"I told you." He patted her hand, then lifted it carefully from his sleeve. "Now don't wrinkle the costume."

She clapped her hands to her cheeks. "I'll never be able to get through the last scene. I can't even remember what I'm supposed to say. I feel as if I've never spoken a line."

He rolled his black eyes expressively. "Dear Lord, deliver me."

She rubbed her hands down the side of her robe. "I'm not kidding. I can't remember what I'm supposed to say."

Patiently, he took her by the hand and led her up the stage stairs to her entrance. He stripped the robe from her shoulders and thrust a lighted candle into her hand.

"Shreve," she rasped. "No."

"Yet here's a spot." The words burned into her ear as he pushed her into view.

Clad in Lady Macbeth's long white night robe, she took another step out into the softened light and began to descend the stairs. The doctor and the gentlewoman stopped their speech and looked at her expectantly. Like the madwoman she was portraying she looked dazedly over the audience. Her gaze shifted to the box and sharpened as she found the face she sought among the four white ovals.

Her training moved her body, for without conscious thought she set the candle down on the stairs behind her and began to rub her hands furiously. *"Yet here's the spot. Out, damned spot! Out, I say!"*

Her furious rubbing shook her entire frame, terrors of the mind reflected themselves in her face. She could hear the bell. *"One; two. Why then 'tis time to do it."*

The character's guilt somehow became her own. Lady Macbeth had antagonized Macbeth until he murdered the king. Miranda Drummond had left her mother in the hour of Ruth's greatest need. The lady could not forgive herself. The girl sought forgiveness from her sister. The words were heavy with remorse. *"The Thane of Fife had a wife. Where is she now?"*

The audience watched spellbound. Not a few followed Lady Macbeth's stare to the dimness of the box. In the wings Shreve watched, eyes slitted, palms damp as the woman transcended the actress and the performance became real.

The doctor and the gentlewoman's lines penetrated Miranda's consciousness and brought her back to her part. She became the wretched queen again. *"Yet here's the smell of the blood still."*

When she had returned up the stairs, carrying her wavering candle, and the watchers had parted, the audience made no sound, thereby paying the greatest tribute possible to an actor or actress. So immersed were they in the performance that the play had become real. No one applauded the very stuff of tragedy.

"You were just marvelous, Miss Miranda." Mrs. Wilcox's eyes were starry, her cheeks quite pink.

"Yes, marvelous," her sister chimed.

"We want to thank you so much for the tickets. I've never before seen a play from a box. I couldn't quite take it all in. And then your performance. Wonderful."

Miranda's mouth ached from the smile she forced it to wear. The audience had filed through the green room in seemingly endless procession. She had not been sure that her sister would even come back to speak to her.

At last Mrs. Wilcox and her charges had appeared in the door. Rachel was actually in the same room with her. She held out her hand to a slender brunette who was Rachel's friend Dorinda. The girl congratulated the actress in an awestruck voice.

And then Rachel stood before her, expression blank, blue eyes not meeting Miranda's, but focused just to the left. "Thank you very much for the box seats," she said. "I enjoyed the play very much."

331

"You're very welcome." Miranda slowly withdrew the hand she had extended. The full, trained voice faltered, the pear-shaped tones croaked.

Hearing her distress, Shreve put his arm around her. "The Bard gives us the greatest lines to speak. We know the play is great. We're always pleased to hear that our audience enjoyed our performances."

Rachel's mouth curled faintly as she stared at the embrace.

Suddenly, Miranda was too tired to care. Eyes weary yet defiant, she faced her sister and leaned against him, letting him take a little of her weight. "Yes, we're very glad that you could come."

Before the party could move on, Shreve spoke affably to the headmistress. "And now we have a special favor to ask."

Mrs. Wilcox smiled sweetly. "You have only to ask it."

"Miranda and I would like to take her friend's daughter Rachel to lunch tomorrow."

"Why how wonderful!" Mrs. Wilcox turned to the girl. "You would enjoy that, wouldn't you, Rachel?"

The blond head dipped, then rose with just a hint of defiance. The tone was chilly. "I have quite a bit of studying to do."

"But you still have to eat," Shreve countered smoothly. "Good. Then we'll come for you at noon."

When they had left, Miranda looked at him with tears overflowing down her eyes. "Shreve Catherwood, I've thought time and again that you were the greatest bastard that ever walked the earth. Now for all my bad thoughts I apologize. I most humbly apologize."

He took her into his arms, cradling her head against his shoulder, rubbing her back between her shoulder blades. "Don't," he murmured, planting a tiny kiss on top of her head. "Don't cry."

"I couldn't think what to do, what to say. You said exactly the right thing. I'm so grateful."

"You may not be so grateful by the end of lunch tomorrow," he warned.

"Still, you gave me the chance to talk to her again with you there as a sort of chaperone. You're so good."

He grinned. "You don't believe that. Not at all. And don't change your opinion of me in the slightest. I'm exactly what you think I am. I just don't want to see you tearing yourself to pieces the way you did tonight. It's not good for your performance."

She bowed her head. "I'm not surprised that it was terrible. I couldn't seem to concentrate on Lady Macbeth at all. I was awful."

His grin twisted sardonically. "No. You were too good."

"Too good!" Her head snapped up.

"You gave everything you had. You lost yourself in the part. You weren't acting. You *were* Lady Macbeth. The guilt was real. Yours merged with hers and you lost yourself. That's bad."

"But I thought—"

He shook his head. "This is a job. It's something we do for a living. Then we separate ourselves from it and become entirely different

333

people. I'm not Romeo nor Macbeth nor Hamlet nor Benedict. I'm Shreve Catherwood playing those parts. When the play's over, I'm an entirely different man. And Miranda can't be Juliet or Ophelia or Beatrice. If she is, then she'll lose Miranda."

"You've said that before."

"And I'll say it again. You've got to learn to act." He kissed the tip of her nose. "And never, never lose yourself in your part. It'll kill you."

The restaurant looked out on Michigan Avenue, but the diners did not come to view the historic street. In a private corner screened by potted palms, Rachel and Miranda faced each other. The younger girl's face was sulky, her lower lip thrust out, her eyes angry.

When the waiter had taken their order, Shreve flashed the brilliant smile that had made women in the upper balcony turn warm and flustered. "So, Miss Drummond, I know you're anxious for your studies at Mrs. Wilcox's to be finished."

Rachel concentrated on aligning the handles of the silverware. "Not particularly, Mr. Catherwood."

He raised one eyebrow in Miranda's direction. Her eyes were bleak, her skin white around the mouth. "I thought all women your age were anxious to make their bow in society and find a handsome young man. From what Miranda's told me, your mother and stepfather have moved to Washington. That's a fine place to make a debut. Lots of wealth and power. Great opportunities there to meet the right person."

"I won't be going to Washington."

Miranda glanced at Shreve and then at her sister. "Do you have a young man that you're already engaged to?"

"No, of course not," came the irritable reply.

The waiter brought their soup and they began to eat it in silence.

"Father only went to Washington to accept the new assignment. He's to be reassigned to the Mountain District as the Agent for the Bureau of Indian Affairs." Rachel smiled maliciously at her sister. "He and Mother will be going there as soon as the official announcement is made."

"To the Mountain District," Miranda exclaimed. "You mean Montana."

"I suppose." Rachel put down her spoon. "I really don't care. I don't intend to go."

Miranda was no longer looking at her younger sister. She stared at Shreve. "He's going back to Fort Gallatin." The timbre was gone from her voice. "Why would he do that?"

"The Montana Territory's a big place," Shreve cautioned. "Nearly as big as Texas. He could be assigned anywhere."

"He's going to rebuild Fort Gallatin," Rachel said. "It's his great dream. He told us about it often enough. The night before they left for Washington, D.C., we had to hear it again. He's going to set it all right."

Miranda gripped the edge of the table. "Set it all right! Never. He wants revenge. He's going to take his shame and anger out on the whole Sioux nation."

"Easy, sweetheart, don't get so excited. Think about what you're saying. You don't have any reason to say that. It's ridiculous."

"It's not ridiculous. I know this man."

"How can you know him?" Rachel inquired nastily, speaking to Miranda for the first time that day. "You left the house before he even married Mother. You never lived with him."

"He never intended that I should live with him," Miranda snapped almost absently.

"That's not true."

"It is true." Miranda's response sounded distracted. Suddenly, she was no longer so vitally interested in making her peace with Rachel. Her mortal enemy, the man who had murdered her father, possessed her thoughts. "He never planned for me to live with him. He told me as much the night I ran away. I was to be sent to school. Probably one like Mrs. Wilcox's. He planned to separate me from my mother as he's done you."

"Why won't you believe me?" Rachel demanded. "I picked that school myself. I've wanted to go to Mrs. Wilcox's for a long time."

"Ladies," Shreve entoned.

Miranda looked at Rachel pityingly. "You've never been free. School sounded like freedom to you. It sounded like prison to me. Do you know when I heard that you had been sent to a boarding school, I actually thought that I would be rescuing you."

Rachel's mouth dropped open. For the first time the pouty defiant look disappeared. She frowned faintly.

Miranda turned her attention back to Shreve. "You see what he's doing, don't you? He's going back to the scene of his crime. When he killed my father, he ruined his own career. He's nursed this grudge for years."

"Miranda—" Shreve began, but she interrupted him.

"The Sioux were too fierce. Or perhaps not fierce enough." Her eyes lighted with blue fire. "If they'd killed them all in one fell swoop—my father, Hickory Joe, Clarendon, the whole troop—then he couldn't possibly have been blamed. The press could have been made a hero later for defending the fort."

"—you're dramatizing this whole thing. I've warned you about that. Life isn't like Shakespearean tragedy. There's no such thing as fate."

"Isn't there?"

Rachel stared from one to the other, her food forgotten on her plate.

"My father ruined his great heroic gesture for him. And Wellington got away."

"Wellington?" Rachel said the name softly.

"Yes, Wellington. You asked me about him. But did you know that when Wellington came back, the men at the fort wanted to ride out? We could hear the shooting. They could have rescued my father even then."

"Rescued my father?"

Shreve shook his head. "Rachel, this is your sister's fantasy."

"It's not a fantasy. They all knew Westfall was a

coward. Or worse. There was a court-martial."

"And he was acquitted."

"But he lost his rank and command. And the Sioux burned Fort Gallatin to the ground." Miranda's breath came short. Her magnificent eyes flashed. "Now he's going back to rebuild it, and start an Indian war so he can be a hero. And punish the Sioux in the bargain."

"You don't know that."

"I do know it. I do. Remember what he tried to do to me. You saw how I was treated. I would have been dead in a week."

"Dead?" Rachel whispered weakly.

"I've still got friends in the Sullivant Hills. I'm going to contact them. Adolf Lindhauer was an important trader seventeen years ago. If he's still alive, he's probably rich as Croesus. He wouldn't want to see the peace broken."

"You don't know this person anymore." Shreve tried to reason with her. "He's probably dead."

"Not him. He knew how to keep his scalp. He married a Cheyenne. He's got sons that are part-Indian." The dimple appeared at the corner of her mouth as she thought of White Wolf's Brother. She had not thought of her friend in years.

"They won't pay any attention to you. They know the situation. You don't."

"I know they probably don't have any idea that Westfall is about to be named the Indian agent. If they did, they might be able to use their influence to stop the appointment."

"Miranda." Shreve tried to catch her hand. "This is none of your affair."

338

"It's everybody's affair. You don't understand. You didn't see what was done to my father. To the other men. That can't be allowed to happen again. It's only been seven years since Custer. His troop was wiped out to the last man, too. The Sioux are very good fighters, maybe the best in the world. If Westfall has his way, there'll be another massacre."

She rose from her seat and threw down her napkin. "Excuse me. Shreve, will you entertain my sister and see her home safely? Rachel, I'm relieved to hear that you are happy at your school. I hope you will soon meet a nice young man to take care of you. I promise that I'll never bother you again."

Rachel's face went white. Her lower lip trembled.

"Miranda, for God's sake, think what you're doing." Shreve rose and caught her hand.

She squeezed his reassuringly. "I'll get a cab to drive me back to the hotel. I have some letters to write that cannot wait."

Someone knocked softly at Miranda's door. A dazed expression on her face, she looked up from her writing. "Who is it?"

"It's me, Rachel."

"Who?"

The door opened. "Your sister, Rachel. May I come in?"

Miranda smiled faintly. "Certainly, come in."

Rachel closed the door behind her and came to the center of the room. "Shreve and I finished our lunch."

"Good."

"Er—I wanted to compliment you on your performance last night."

"Thank you."

"It was really exciting, especially the last scene before you went off to kill yourself. You had me believing you were really guilty."

"If you believed that, I must have done well."

The two sisters faced each other, their roles reversed. Where Miranda had been nervous, uncertain, she was now distant, unconcerned.

Rachel twisted her hands behind her. Her eyes skittered to the table. "Are you really writing a letter to a man in Montana?"

Picking up the sheet she had been writing on, Miranda fanned it thoughtfully. "Actually, I'm writing two letters to two men in Wyoming."

"Would your letters actually ruin my father's career?"

Miranda shook her head, her expression disgusted. "I wish I had that much power, but I don't think so. My best hope is that he'll be appointed somewhere else. Where he can't do any harm."

"I think you're all wrong about him."

"You've lived with him a long time. Your loyalty commends you."

"He really wants this position."

Miranda's eyes were glacial. "My father wanted to live. Anyway, I should think you'd be pleased. I know our mother will be."

"Why?"

"Because the eastern slopes of the Sullivant Hills

can't have become very civilized in the past seventeen years. It's a terrible life for a young woman. Our mother must be close to fifty years old. She can't be looking forward to having to make a home there again."

Rachel's mouth formed an O. "I never thought about that."

"That's all right. No one can think of everything." Miranda smiled faintly, then went back to finish her sentence. She signed her name, blotted the ink. Rising from the desk, she came around it and stood facing her sister. Her arms were folded across her body.

Rachel fidgeted. "Are you going on stage tonight?"

"Of course, it's my job. Besides, Shreve wouldn't allow me not to go."

"Are you married to him?"

"No. We're not married."

Rachel's eyes widened. "But — but you — er — you're his — "

"I think the polite term is mistress."

Rachel blushed beetred. "He's very handsome."

"And very practical. We have an understanding that doesn't include marriage."

"Does that mean you see other men?"

"No." Miranda suddenly felt every one of her thirty years as she looked at her baby sister coming face to face with a different moral code. "But he used to see other women."

"Oh." Rachel's skin whitened. "Didn't that make you mad?"

"I didn't know he did it at the time. Other actors and actresses, my friends in the troupe, protected me. And after a while he stopped. Now it's just him and me."

Rachel shook her head, frankly shocked at such an admission. The silence grew in the small room. Finally, she cleared her throat. "I wrote to my stepfather and told him that you'd come to see me."

Miranda said nothing. There was nothing really to say.

"Mrs. Wilcox had already done it. I just wanted him to know that I hadn't been taken in by anything you said."

"Good for you."

"I was determined not to be," Rachel added with a touch of pride.

"And so you weren't."

"I didn't write a word about it to Mother." She stared at a spot on the worn carpet. Her voice was low. "I didn't want to hurt her or upset her. I thought if you wanted her to know you were alive, you'd tell her." She raised her eyes to catch the pain on Miranda's face. "You've never tried to see her in all this time."

"Once I did. I saw you and her together on the front porch in the sunshine. You were wearing beautiful clothes. He pulled around a carriage. You all looked so happy. So complete. I didn't want to spoil it for you. I probably wouldn't have ever bothered either one of you." She smiled sadly. "But, as I said, I thought he had pushed you out. I was rescuing you." She chuckled mirthlessly.

Rachel shivered. "Your play is about to close."

342

"That's right. At the end of the month. But we've been held over. The audiences have been good."

"Where will you go then?"

"Saint Louis. And then New Orleans. And then Buenos Aires, I believe. Shreve is very popular in Buenos Aires. We both are. He's so dark and I'm so fair. The Argentinians like the contrast."

"What if you don't hear from your friends in Wyoming before you leave?"

"I'm not sure what I'll do. I've been thinking about that, too. I've been thinking about Fort Gallatin. I've been thinking about my father." At this Miranda turned away. Arms wrapped tightly around herself, she stared down at the desk.

"What do you think about him?"

"I think about his spirit."

Rachel took a step closer. "His ghost."

"No." Miranda shook her head. "I don't believe in ghosts. I think about his spirit, roaming those hills. He's roaming with the spirits of the men who were killed with him and the men he killed."

"That's scary."

"Not really. The spirit has to go somewhere. Roaming the hills is a good clean place to go. But it makes me very sad. I haven't done what I vowed to do." She put out her hand unconsciously imitating Shreve's gesture in *Hamlet*. *"Rest, perturbéd spirit."*

Rachel shivered again at the sight. She realized that she did not understand her sister at all. Sometimes she seemed to be acting. "What if they

343

don't answer your letters?"

"I don't know. I haven't thought that far ahead."

"I'll bet they won't." Rachel came to the desk, bending slightly to see her sister's face. "And anyway, it's too late for your letters. Father already has the appointment."

Miranda's head snapped around. *"Has?"*

"Yes. He's already got it. I received a telegram. They're leaving at the end of the month for Wyoming. They're going directly to Saint Louis by train and then north. You can't stop them."

Miranda faced her. The beautiful face took on the look of Lady Macbeth. "Perhaps not. Perhaps I wasn't meant to stop them."

"I insist that we take the train to Chicago."

"Ruth, you've only just seen her a few weeks ago." Westfall bit his lip in perturbation. Even though he had received Rachel's letter, he could not believe that his stepdaughter would not betray him by some word.

"Months. Four months." Ruth twisted the handkerchief in her hand. "We could take the train from Washington to Chicago and then on to Saint Louis."

"It's days out of our way."

"My dear Mrs. Westfall, you surely must understand that Ben needs to get to his appointment as soon as possible. Things have been neglected there much too long."

Ruth looked up into the senator's deeply wrinkled face. Hugh Smith Butler, Maud Mary West-fall's father, loomed above her from his height of six feet three. "I want my husband to get to his job as soon as he possibly can, but—"

"Remember, my dear," Westfall interrupted. "The railroad only goes so far. After that—"

Ruth closed her eyes a moment. Any journey to a military outpost west of the Mississippi was difficult. Memory stirred of a journey so horrible that she had actually prayed that she would fall asleep in the wagon and freeze to death. She sighed. She was not a young person any longer. Still, she had married for better or for worse. "I am well aware of the problems of travel; that is why I want to see my daughter before we go. We might be separated for months, even a year."

"Nonsense, she can join us when the school term is over. I want you to be comfortable," Westfall assured her. "I've hired a private car to take us from Washington to Saint Louis. We'll be able to sit back and enjoy the sight of this great country as it stretches before us to the Mississippi."

"Excellent." Butler clapped his former son-in-law on the back. "Excellent idea. It's the only way to travel."

"I'll be able to work on the way, make plans for the celebration."

"Celebration?" Ruth directed her attention sharply to her husband. "What are you planning?"

Butler drew smoke from his cigar and then blew a cloud toward the ceiling. "Your husband has had an excellent idea, Ruth. He's presented it to the congressional committee and they all like it immensely. We'll have an Independence Day celebration. It will commemorate the gallant men who've lost their lives fighting the Indians on the Powder River and in Montana. At the same time it will rededicate our troops to civilizing the West."

"The Powder River?" Ruth's question was sharp. "Did you say the Powder River?"

Butler looked from wife to husband, who smiled nervously.

"I haven't told her all the news."

Ruth's face had gone dead white. "What is your news, Benjamin?"

"Simply the best, my dear." His own control appeared to be slipping. He rubbed his hands together nervously. "I've been commissioned to head a new Indian Agency office for the Mountain District. It will be a great deal like a frontier fort with trading post, infirmary, and a troop of soldiers to keep order. It'll be in the heart of what was once hostile territory. Now it can take care of the needs of the peaceful Indians on the reservations in northern Wyoming."

"Northern Wyoming." Ruth looked at him with a sick understanding in her eyes. Her throat dry, she asked the unnecessary question. "Where is it to be?"

He swallowed. His mouth worked under the heavy mustache. Finally, he got the words out. "Near Sheridan."

"Where?" she insisted.

"On the site of old Fort Gallatin."

"No!"

The senator's mouth dropped open. He caught

346

his cigar to keep it from falling. "My dear, of course, this is somewhat of a surprise—"

"How could you?" Ruth sucked in her breath sharply, her eyes accused her husband. One hand rose to her mouth, covering it as if to suppress a scream.

Westfall bent to her instantly. He slipped one hand under her arm and tried to lift her to her feet. "Ruth, perhaps we ought to—"

She pulled away from him, shoving at his hand. "I can't believe you would actually accept this."

"Ruth—"

"Is this what you've been planning all along? Is this why you married me? So you could get back to Fort Gallatin."

He looked for aid to his former father-in-law. "I'm afraid we're going to have to leave."

The senator nodded. "That would be best. Better learn to control her, Ben. This sort of thing looks bad."

"I can't go back there." Ruth shook her head. Her earrings jingled. "Don't you understand? I left my husband's body in that terrible country. I left Francis buried in that icy barren place. No. I can't go back there. I won't."

At the sound of her voice rising shrilly, several people turned to look in her direction. Color darkened General Westfall's sallow cheeks as he moved to shield her from their curious gaze. Unfortunately, his spare body was little more than a column of black around which they might peer, or move a step or two to the right or left to get a better angle.

"Why, Ruth," Westfall tried to say heartily, "you're a soldier's wife. You won't stick at a few discomforts. Let's go home and discuss this. You'll be glad of this when you think about it."

"I'm not a soldier's wife. I haven't been in twenty years," she almost screeched. Her hands clad in crocheted gloves, gestured frantically. "I'm a politician's wife." She sprang to her feet and caught at Westfall as he shot a distracted look over his shoulder.

"Of course. Of course. My dear, let's go home so we can discuss this in private."

"When you told me you were seeking an appointment from the Bureau of Indian Affairs, I never dreamed—never for one minute imagined—that you were going to be assigned to Wyoming. What about Texas? What about New Mexico? Arizona? Colorado? Oklahoma? Oklahoma is a lovely state. Beautiful trees, rivers, a delightful climate."

"Get her out of here, Ben," Butler grated through clenched teeth. "She's creating a damned spectacle."

"I'm sure you're right, Senator."

"May I help you, Mrs. Westfall?" The hostess put her arm around Ruth's shoulders.

Ruth turned into the woman's arms. "I can't go back there. I'm not a young woman anymore. I've buried one husband out there. I don't want to go through that again."

"Of course, you don't." The hostess patted her soothingly.

"Ruth, here's your cloak."

348

"I just can't go back there again. I won't."

Westfall draped the garment around her shaking shoulders. With Butler and the hostess shielding her from the majority of the guests, they led her from the room.

"I won't," she sobbed. "I won't."

Nineteen

The secret'st man of blood.

"You're crazy!" Shreve Catherwood thundered. As he swung around to face her, Macbeth's cape billowed out, disturbing the leg curtain that shielded him in the wings.

"Please." Miranda put her hand over his mouth. "The audience out front will hear you."

He tossed his head like a madman. "I don't care if they hear me in Wyoming. You can't go there. You can't just leave."

On stage the man playing the second witch raised his voice in his chant. The others, both women, also increased their volume. *"Double, double, toil and trouble."*

"I won't let you." Although he lowered his voice, he flung the words into her face with all his force. Expelled by his powerful diaphragm muscle, they felt like bullets hitting her face.

"I'll come back as soon as I've done what I have to do." She tried to turn him around.

"You don't know what you have to do. You don't have anything to do. This is just a piece of stupidity."

She pointed frantically to the stage. "The witches are almost through."

He did not so much as toss a glance behind him. "Damn them."

"Shreve." She pushed at his great shoulders, all the greater for Macbeth's costume with its heavy velvet and fur. "Shreve. You'll miss your entrance."

"By the pricking of my thumbs, Something wicked this way comes," called the second witch with more than usual nervousness.

"Get out there."

"You haven't heard the last of this." He spun on his heel and strode out. *"How now, you secret, black, and midnight hags?"*

The audience watched fascinated seeing nothing wrong. With thunderclaps and flickering lights, the apparitions appeared one after another from the bubbling cauldron. The show of kings paraded across the stage. Macbeth yelled for *"No more sights,"* and the stagehand stopped turning the crank for the flickering effects behind the scrim.

Except they did not cease. The flickering redness seemed if anything to leap higher. Shreve finished Macbeth's aside and turned, then halted in mid-stride. Fear slid up his spine. His scalp prickled. He drew in a deep breath and then he smelled the smoke as it curled up in fantastic spirals between the scrim and the lights behind it.

He turned Macbeth's exit into a leap for the wings.

At almost the same instant a scream tore through the audience.

"Fire!"

"Close the curtain!" he thundered, then executed

his own order as the frightened stagehand abandoned his post and ran. As he pulled the act curtain to, pandemonium erupted in the auditorium. Hundreds of people lunged to their feet, a concerted scream in their throats, panic in their hearts.

"Help me!" He caught the shoulder of the second witch as the actor hiked up his robe.

"Leggo!"

"We've got to get the fire curtain down."

"You ring down the damn curtain. This place'll go up like a tinderbox." The actor twisted away and ran for the theater entrance. At the same time some of the more athletic patrons in the front rows had climbed onto the stage and were batting aside the act curtain.

Shreve caught another stagehand. "Come on, man. Get ahold of yourself. Help me bring down the fire curtain."

The man shot a terrified look above him, then shook his head frantically. Without a backward glance, he ran for the stage door. Threads of flame trickled up the fly lines and disappeared in the smoke-filled loft.

"Get the hell out of the way!" A tall man in evening clothes, his hand locked around the upper arm of an elegantly dressed lady, threw his shoulder into Shreve's chest.

"Help me! We can keep the fire from spreading, if we can get the fire curtain down."

But the man was already gone, dragging his sobbing companion through the wings.

Behind the curtain, the screams grew in volume. Shreve could hear the crack and snap of splintering furniture as the seats were demolished under the stampeding herd. He struggled with the cable that would lower the iron fire curtain. It had probably not been lowered since it was hung. The knot was like granite. He spun in desperation with some vague memory of an ax on the wall, but the smoke was rapidly filling the backstage area. He began to cough. Tears streaked through the dark makeup on his cheeks.

"Shreve!" Miranda came running to him out of the thickening haze. Dimly, he was aware of Ada Cocks also hovering loyally in the background.

"Get out, Miranda! Take Ada and get out."

"You come, too," she begged before she began to cough.

"Come on, Shrevey-boy," Ada wheezed. Throwing a glance aloft, she cringed, then motioned frantically with her hand. "Come on, boyo."

"Got to get this down." He bent again. His fingers worried the iron-hard knot. People streamed by, screaming, cursing, weeping. He turned a deaf ear to their din.

Miranda caught Ada's arm and fled with the older woman. Together they threaded their way through the jumble of scenery and tangle of lines arriving at the single stage door by a swift circuitous route. At the back of the theater, the scenery in front of the fireproof scrim caught. Canvas, oil paint, and turpentine fueled a great whoosh of flame and black smoke.

Cringing beneath the blast of heat, Shreve drew Macbeth's sword and hacked at the cable. A single strand spanged apart.

"Let it go!" Miranda screamed at his shoulder.

"Where did you come from?" He shook his head in disbelief to find her beside him tugging at his arm. "We've got to get out of here."

The black smoke billowed out from under the valance at the top of the proscenium arch. The gaslights in their sconces dimmed. The shrieks and curses from the auditorium increased in volume. Fistfights had broken out. A man fell and was trampled. Another man tried to avoid the crush in the aisle by clambering across the backs of the seats. He screamed in agony as his ankle caught and snapped when his weight toppled forward.

In their rush downstairs people fell and piled up in the bottom of the narrow wells. Women screamed and wept hysterically as they were separated from their companions or were deserted by them. At the only two exits, the double doors at the back of the house, the jam was deadly. People clawed and punched and trampled their way to freedom.

"Get out of the way!" With both hands Shreve swung Macbeth's sword up above his head. With all his strength, he brought it down on the knot. The inferior metal snapped. The knot remained intact. "Damn! Oh, goddamn!"

"Shreve! You've done all you can! Come away!" Miranda caught his arm and threw her full weight against it. A couple of men careened through the curtain and ran full tilt into them. Shreve staggered and she was pitched to the floor. The fire snaked through the loft, leaping from batten to batten. The painted canvas backdrops burst into flames. Burning cinders began to sift down onto the stage.

"Miranda!" Shreve stooped to catch her wrists and pull her to her feet. "Get the hell out of here."

She went into his arms. "Not without you."

"In the name of God—" He could not decide whether he was furious or thrilled to the depths of his soul. He dropped his head and kissed her full on the lips, a hard kiss that she returned with equal fervor.

Then she twisted away. Above the pandemonium came the faint, distant clanging. "The fire trucks are coming. You've done all you can. Come outside and meet them."

He went with her, then jerked to a halt. "The trunk!"

She would have rolled her eyes had she not been coughing so hard. "Shreve, the money's not important."

"The hell it's not. There's over five hundred dollars in there." Before she could object, he pushed her in the direction of the stage door and vaulted for the circular iron staircase that led to the dressing rooms.

"Shreve! No! Shreve!" The fool. The greedy idiot. How could he? How could he? She watched him pause halfway up to throw Macbeth's cape over his head.

She would have followed him, but a man thrust her aside with a fist in her midriff that doubled her over. The stage was filling with smoke. She straightened up coughing.

"Lady, come on outta there. We're gonna turn the hose on."

She turned and staggered toward the voice.

355

"Turn it this way," she cried. "This way!"

"What?" A helmeted fireman stood in the doorway, the nozzle of a huge hose in his hand. "Where?"

"The stairs. There's somebody up there. He's got to get down."

"If there's anybody up there lady, he's dead. The temperature up there must be a thousand degrees."

"Aim for the top of the staircase!"

She thrust Lady Macbeth's cape in front of the hose, just as the water started to flow out. Soaking the heavy material, she threw it over her head and dashed for the stairs.

"Lady! Come back, lady!" The fireman made a grab for her too late.

Halfway up the stairs, the water pressure could follow her no farther. She took a breath from the smoky cooler air under the cape, then knew it was her last breath. *Shreve, where are you?*

He staggered into her at the top of the stairs. Like her, he was swathed in his costume. "Miranda!"

She did not answer but caught his arm. They fled down together. The stream of water hit them halfway and led them through the choking smoke to the door.

Out they burst into the relatively clear night air.

He caught her arm and together they fled past the firemen and their equipment to the back of the alley. There they leaned together coughing. "I could kill you," were his first words.

"I could kill you," she managed before she doubled over trying to get her breath.

"When I met you at the top of those stairs—"

He pulled the cloak off his head and ran a hand through his matted hair. Somewhere he had lost Macbeth's crown.

"When you started up those stairs after that handful of pennies—"

"Pennies!"

"Pennies! If you had died up there, what then?" She raised her fists and pounded his chest. "What then?"

"I wasn't going to die. I had plenty of time." He coughed, then caught her wrists and held them in one hand while he fished in the neck of his costume. He drew forth a wad of bills. "Over five hundred dollars."

"Pennies," she cried. "You couldn't have spent it if you were dead."

He grinned as he stuffed it back into his costume. Then his face changed. His look grew deadly serious. "Why did you follow me? If I'd passed out, you wouldn't have had a chance of dragging me out of that hell. You would have burned up, too."

"Oh, I wouldn't have tried to drag you down the stairs," she declared cheekily. "I'd have just given you a shove and you'd have rolled and bumped. Besides, the firemen had their hoses on me."

"Not all the way into the dressing room they didn't." He enfolded her in his smoky arms holding her as if he would never let her go. One hand tenderly smoothed her tangled hair. "How many times do I have to tell you? There aren't any happy endings. This is not a play."

"You're right," she agreed hoarsely. "I thought maybe you'd forgotten."

Their lips met in a kiss of peace and perfect understanding.

Water began to run across their feet as it poured out of the door of the theater. Black smoke continued to billow out the top of the door, but the firemen could pass in and out in relatively clear air.

Shreve looked back at the door regretfully. "I really wanted to get that fire curtain down. It probably would have saved a lot of damage."

She caught him around the neck and brought his forehead down to touch hers. "You wanted to be a hero," she accused. "After what you said to me about life not being heroic gestures."

He grinned. His teeth flashed in his smoke-blackened face. "I didn't want to be a hero. I just thought if we could bring down the curtain, the damage might not be so bad that we couldn't go on for our extended run."

"I might have known." She kissed him hard, sucking his tongue into her mouth, pressing her breasts against his chest. It was Lady Macbeth's kiss of triumph.

His scorched lungs strained to cough up more smoke. He pulled his head up. "Let's walk back to the hotel. I think we've done all we can do here tonight."

She dragged his arm around her shoulder and slipped her arm around his waist. They walked out of the alley together.

Ada came to them, her eyes wet with tears. "I thought for a minute there I'd lost the both of you. I might have known you'd come through the fires of hell together."

She came to Shreve's other side. He kissed her forehead and put his other arm around her. The three of them held each other close and did not let go until they reached the hotel.

"Miranda can't be seeing anyone. She's resting from her terrible experience. You can't be disturbing her." Ada's voice carried just the right note of sternness.

"Oh, I wouldn't think of disturbing her. I came because I wanted to be sure she got this report before she left town."

Miranda raised her head from the chaise. The voice sounded vaguely familiar. *What report?*

"Is she—is she all right?" the voice continued. "She wasn't burned?"

"No, the dear girl's not burned, thank the good Lord. But such a shock to her system. She's that exhausted from the ordeal."

"Who is it, Ada?"

"A gentleman."

"Henry Keller," he supplied.

"Oh, Mr. Keller." Miranda sat up. "I'll see him, Ada. Ask him to wait in the hall a moment."

Ada's lips compressed. "You heard her." She leaned forward to whisper, "Don't you be staying overlong nor making her talk. She's still got smoke in her lungs."

Miranda put on a blue silk wrapper trimmed with ecru lace. Ada brushed her blond hair until it shimmered and tied it back with a blue ribbon. Left unstyled, it hung down her back almost to her waist. Before she went to open the door, she looked at her charge in the mirror. "Now, don't spend too long with the man. Whatever he wants, it can't be worth your rest."

"No, Ada." Her blue eyes shone as she smiled and held out her hand to the detective. "I'm glad you've come, Mr. Keller. Although to tell you the truth, I had forgotten that I'd asked for this investigation."

He took her hand thinking that he had never seen a more beautiful woman. Her other hand, he noticed, lay in her lap, a gauze bandage wrapped around it. "My dear Miss Miranda, I can't tell you how happy I am to see you alive and well. I thought you were not burned."

"Just Miranda, please. I don't use the Miss." She lifted the hand. "I wasn't burned. Sometime during the riot, I knocked against something and lost some skin, but it's nothing serious. I'm happy to be here."

"I won't take but a minute of your time." He extended the file to her. "I don't know what you'll make of this. There's a lot that puzzles me."

She nodded as she laid the file open on the table beside her and turned to it. "I'm sure there would be many puzzling things in any report that has to do with General Benjamin Westfall."

"He actually engaged someone years ago to find you, but you know that."

"I had heard recently that he had, but I didn't know I was being investigated at the time. Now that I think about it, I remember he had a man with him." She skimmed over Parker Bledsoe's brief report. "This is incomplete."

"How so?" Keller leaned forward alertly.

"I'm assuming that the man who accompanied my stepfather to the theater that night was Parker Bledsoe. The three of us left together. They took me to an institution, a prison really, for wayward girls run by a woman named Mortimer."

Henry Keller looked appalled. "Good Lord, not that place. It's been closed down for a couple of years now. Some of the girls died. One got away. When she was picked up by the police, they discovered she had been beaten pretty badly. She told the most terrible stories."

"I'm sure nothing she told could have been more than the truth."

Keller shook his head. "If you were taken there, a warrant had to have been issued. An order for your detention there. It wasn't in the file, nor was there any record of it."

"Bledsoe doesn't mention the institution at all," Miranda pointed out. "Surely that would have been in the report."

Keller nodded his head. "He billed Westfall for that day, but not the night. Perhaps he wasn't with him after all."

"But he says that he accompanied Westfall to the theater. And they only came the one time."

"And took you to Mrs. Mortimer's." The detective plucked at his lower lip.

Miranda tapped the paper. "It sounds as though I was put in that house illegally."

Keller looked alarmed. "Pinkerton's would never countenance illegal action either in the course of or stemming from one of their investigations. Possibly, Westfall got some friend of his in legal circles to issue a warrant to detain.

But Bledsoe should have recorded it."

"Where is this Bledsoe?"

The detective stirred uneasily. His mind was adding up the items of information and the results did not look pleasant. "He's dead."

Miranda waited.

"He was killed the night he filed this report. He was murdered."

Miranda cleared her throat. "I'm an actress, Mr. Keller," she said distantly. "I deal in plays where all the strings of action and intrigue tie together neatly in a bow at the end. Things are destined to happen and they do. Destiny. My costar tells me that destiny isn't real. It doesn't happen in real life, but I persist in believing that it does. How did Mr. Bledsoe die?"

Keller pointed to the file. "There's a page describing his death. I included it since it seemed somehow relevant to the investigation."

"Did you now?" She met his eyes, then turned over the paper just below the Pinkerton report. " 'A saber' for a murder weapon."

"Only the possibility of a saber."

She closed the file. "Thank you, Mr. Keller. I'll study this at my leisure. Right now, I'm feeling very tired."

He rose instantly. "Of course. You must rest." Ada brought his hat and opened the door, but he hesitated turning it by the brim. "I've been a detective for ten years, Miss — er — Miranda. I've seen the most amazing coincidences prove themselves to be nothing but just that. Coincidences."

She nodded. "And on the other hand —"

362

"I've seen the most amazing events tie together in amazing ways."

"Almost like a play," she murmured.

"It's been a pleasure to work for you. If Pinkerton's can be of service to you again, don't hesitate to call us."

"I won't. Be sure to see Mr. Windom for your fee."

He bowed himself out. Ada came to stand at her side. "Did he tell you things to upset you, dearie?"

"Yes and no." She massaged her forehead. "I must think about what I must do. And I'm so tired."

"Of course, you are, dearie. You need to have a nice nap and then you'll be fine."

Backstage was a shambles of water and darkness and unrecognizable tumbledown shapes. Poking through the rubble were a couple of helmeted firemen, a couple of policemen, and a middle-aged man in a suit. He stared at Shreve over the tops of his glasses.

Shreve nodded and made for the staircase down which he had followed Miranda the night before. He still felt a rush of emotion at the thought of her climbing that stair after him. In all his years, he could never remember anyone caring for him enough to do what she had done. The girl was bravery and honor personified, the stuff of heroes. Undoubtedly, that father of hers had instilled it in her.

A brisk shaking assured him that the staircase

was still firmly anchored at both top and bottom. He mounted it, soot coating his hands and clothing wherever he touched. With care he put his foot on the floor of the platform that led to the dressing rooms. It, too, seemed untouched by flame, only badly smoked and scorched.

The dressing room assigned to Miranda and him had a thin layer of black soot. He looked around him in distaste, then acknowledged his luck with a sigh of relief. Everything was more or less intact. With the exceptions of the costumes they had been wearing, they had lost little.

He took a few minutes to sweep the makeup off the dressing table, pull the costumes from the pegs on the wall, and stuff them all in his trunk. A stagehand, if one were to be found, could carry their luggage downstairs. If the garments would clean, then they would have them cleaned. If they would not, then they would wear them smoky. The audience would never know.

As he closed his trunk and locked it, he patted it solemnly. He had not needed to make the death-defying run for their money, yet he knew given the same circumstances, he would have done so again. Miranda did not realize she had never known a moment's want because of his miserly ways.

He vowed now that from this day forward, she would never know a moment's insecurity. He would protect her with the full force of his love. When she had come climbing through that smoke and heat to meet him, his heart had stopped in his body. The pain of love that streaked through him had almost unmanned him.

He dragged the trunks one by one to the head

of the stairs and descended. From the manager's office he heard a voice screaming.

"That bastard! That sneaking son-of-a-bitch!"

"Who?" Shreve strolled to the doorway and looked in.

Nehemiah Horowitz tipped the contents of a charred desk drawer into a garbage can. "That stupid schmuck. Torch my theater. He'll swing for it. I've got influence. He'll swing."

"Somebody set the fire!?"

"Hell, yes! You didn't think my theater would just start to burn. Not my theater. I've got every safety measure. Every one."

Shreve shrugged. "The fire curtain wouldn't come down."

"We'll fix that. The son-of-a-bitch who's supposed to lower and raise it every week's lost his job. He'll go dig ditches. I've already hired a new man. From now on, not once a week, but twice. Twice!" He lifted two fingers and stabbed them in a vow toward heaven.

"Who set the fire?"

"That schmuck Archie Doight. May he roast in hell. Set my theater on fire—" Nehemiah pulled out another drawer and lifted out a bottle. "Hell, there's still some in it. First good thing I've seen today." He uncorked it and turned it up. "Man, that's good."

He offered it to Shreve, who took it and swallowed some. The whiskey burned his smoke-damaged throat all the way down to his stomach. "Who's he? Is he crazy?"

"Might be. One thing for sure, he's dumber than dirt." The manager took another draw from the bottle. "I myself caught the Mick bastard backstage, just a few minutes before the fire. 'What the hell you doin'?' I say. 'You don't hide out in my theater.' Booted him out the back door. Five minutes later"—he flung his arm up in an obscene gesture—"it all goes up."

"You actually saw him?"

"Yeah, I saw him, but I didn't see what he was doin.' Otherwise, I'd 'a roasted the dirty—" The string of obscenities that flowed off his tongue made Shreve raise his eyebrows.

"How'd you know—?"

"Sent the coppers around to his shack. The dumb schmuck had coal oil on his boots. May he rot in hell. Still had some rags soaked in the stuff. He's too stupid to get rid of 'em. Guess he thought he'd come back and try to finish the job." Nehemiah finished the bottle and dropped it into the center of the garbage can.

"Do they have any idea why?"

The manager shook his head. "Not a clue. It's not like he's a critic or somethin'. He's never been inside a theater in his life. Just a dumb ex-soldier."

"Ex-soldier." A premonitory chill raced down Shreve's spine.

"Most likely deserted."

"Most likely."

"Listen, I'm sorry about that extended run. I guess you see I can't do nothin' about that." He burrowed in his desk and dragged out another bottle, this one full. Pulling the cork, he passed it to Shreve. "Help yourself. Take it with you. That's good stuff. A friend of mine brings it in from Kentucky."

"Thanks." Shreve accepted the bottle with a grimace. He had already signed the contract with Horowitz, but, obviously, the man was unable to fulfill it. If he insisted on their adhering to its terms, the theater might close permanently. Neither would profit. However, he would be sure before he left that Horowitz understood that Shreve and Miranda were giving him the two weeks out of charity and cooperation for which they expected favors later.

"Was your stuff damaged upstairs? The stage's a mess, but what about the costumes up there in the dressin' rooms."

"Smoke damage."

"Have 'em cleaned. Have 'em cleaned." Horowitz strode to the door. "Manny! I'll have him get those trunks downstairs and down to the cleaners."

"That'll be a big help." Shreve put the cork back in the bottle of whiskey and tucked it away into his pocket.

"Don't think about it. Heard what you did last night, tryin' to drop that fire curtain when everybody else was turnin' tail. The rotten bastards. Nehemiah Horowitz never forgets. Count on it."

"I do."

The man dressed in the business suit appeared in the door of the office. "Mr. Horowitz."

"Yeah."

"I'm Detective Florio. We've questioned Mr. Doight. He's finally confessed. Says he was paid to set the fire."

"Paid! Who the hell paid him?"

"He doesn't know. Or at least he says he doesn't. Says he does jobs for all kinds of people

367

through his contacts, letters, messages, telegrams. He says some army officer sent him some money wire."

"Army officer. What the hell does he know army officers?" Horowitz thrust out his chin pugnaciously. "He's lyin'."

"Do you have any idea why an army man might have a grudge against you? Have you maybe thrown out some soldiers for misbehavior?"

"Naw! Naw! This is a legitimate theater. Troublemakers don't come in here. Only high-class types. Officers and such."

Shreve stood quietly, his scalp prickling. Miranda would be bolting to attention right now. Thank God, she could not hear this.

"Doight says he used to be a soldier. When he got out, he kept in contact with several of them. They use him to run errands. He says the fire was just a joke."

"Joke! *Joke!* Ten thousand dollars' worth of damage. No telling how many thousands in lawsuits. My theater closed down for probably a month. And he calls it a joke! Go back and beat hell out of that bastard! Find out the truth!" Horowitz's curly black fringe was practically standing on end. His anger was a potent thing in the small office.

The detective waited. When the theater manager finally fell silent, he continued. "We're inclined to believe that he was hired to play a joke. He had a fifty-dollar bill on him as well as a twenty, a ten, and some change. We found a receipt for the purchase of coal oil and some other purchases of food and necessities totaling another twenty. Very likely, he was paid a hundred dollars."

"Some joke. Some joke. We're lucky as hell people weren't killed. A hundred dollars. A hundred lousy dollars, and he burns down my theater. Hell, I'd 'a paid him a hundred not to burn it down." Horowitz fell to cursing.

Shreve slipped by with a nod at the detective and walked quickly out into the alley. His whole body was on fire. By telegram an army officer had contacted a former soldier, a man who, according to Horowitz, was not bright. He had paid the man to set fire to a theater as a joke. Shreve's body burned; his own anger seethed just below the surface with a peculiar cold dread.

According to Miranda, Westfall had been willing to sacrifice a whole troop of men to kill her father. Such a man would not hesitate to burn down a theater full of people if he could kill his stepdaughter.

Twenty

Good lover, let me go.

"Of course, I love you. How could you ever have doubted it? What have I done all these years except exactly what you told me to?"

Shreve ducked his head. "I thought you just wanted to be an actress."

"Oh, for heaven's sake. You know better than that. I fought against acting with every breath in my body until I realized that the only way to stay with you was to do that for you. And I never did that very well," Miranda finished humbly.

He tipped up her chin and kissed her long and lovingly. His lips whispered across her, touched the corner of her mouth, her cheek, her eyebrow, the tip of her nose. She shivered. "I never thought much about love," he murmured. "I thought it was just something that playwrights, like Shakespeare created great theater with. I didn't think anyone would be stu—er fool—"

She laughed a little. "Go on. Say it. 'Stupid.' 'Foolish.'"

"No. That's not what I meant. What you did was crazy. It endangered your life, and more than anything I didn't want your life endangered. That's why it was crazy to me. I would have done something just as stupid and foolish if you had been in danger. I just didn't think that anyone would do something like that for me." His black eyes roved over her face studying the play of expression. She was so beautiful. Her heart was in her eyes. Had it always been there and he had not been able to read it?

"Why should you be capable of the grand gesture and not me?"

"Because I'm not. Not really."

"Risking being burned alive for a fire curtain and a handful of pennies."

"Dollars. Dollars. They represented security. I'm the practical one. Remember!"

"Because your grand gestures are made with an eye to saving yourself as well as other people, doesn't make them any the less grand. It just makes them more honest. Ada says I can always count on you to be selfish. She's right. And that's my security." She rose up on tiptoe to kiss him. It was a good kiss—a thoroughly satisfying one—and when it was over they were both breathless, and his eyes were shining with suspicious moisture.

She took his hand and led him to the chaise. "Now, I've got something I must discuss with you."

He struggled to come out of the daze of pleasure and happiness.

"I've discovered that my stepfather probably tried to kill me."

Instantly, he was alert. "Who told you?"

"A detective."

"Damn! When did he come here? Did he question you?"

"No. He had just prepared a report."

"He should never have bothered you. You don't know anything about Archie Doight."

"Who?"

He flashed her a startled look. His mouth closed like a steel trap.

"Who?" She sat bolt upright. "Who is Archie Doight?"

Shreve tried to disengage himself from her arms and stand. "No one you know. I'm sorry I mentioned the name."

She tightened her hands on his shoulders. "I'll bet you are. Tell me."

"He's just a thug."

"And—"

"He set fire to the theater last night."

The silence in the room was terrible. Finally, she spoke in a flat voice. "Did my stepfather send him?"

"We don't know that."

"But you do." She shook him. "You know and you thought I did, so you let it slip. Otherwise, you wouldn't have told me." Suddenly, she clapped a hand to her mouth. Her eyes were big with horror. "My God. He paid somebody to set a whole theater full of people on fire to kill me."

"Miranda. This man Doight said it was supposed to be a joke."

"Then where is the person to jump out and laugh? Is someone stepping forward and admitting that he caused this? Benjamin Westfall paid that man for one reason and one reason only. My sister wrote him that I was alive and he didn't want me alive. He tried to kill me at that institution. Then he killed the detective who helped him put me there."

Shreve gaped. "How did you find that out?"

"Bledsoe was his name. His records were incomplete. He was killed the night that he filed them. His head was struck off with a saber."

Shreve shook his head. "That doesn't necessarily prove anything," he said lamely.

She put both hands to her cheeks. "You could be next. You could have your head cut off or—"

"Miranda!" He put his arms around her and dragged her in against him.

"I have to go to Fort Gallatin. He's a murderer who will kill again and again. Innocent people are nothing to him. A whole troop of soldiers. A theater full of people. He has to be stopped. He's utterly without mercy."

"Miranda. You can't do this. It's too dangerous and besides it's not your place."

"You can't change my mind about this," Miranda insisted. "I'll never be safe, nor will anyone around me. I've had to do this from the minute I heard those shots on Lodge Trail Ridge. I've put it off for more than half my life, but I can't, I won't do it anymore. If I have to cross the floor of Hell itself, I'll go to Fort Gallatin to face my father's killer."

The coldness of the words affected Shreve deeply. They were not the pear-shaped tones of the trained actress. A hoarse intensity underscored her voice. Nevertheless, he stooped to look her in the eyes. "You can't do that?"

"Why not?"

He gulped. His only card was a weak one, but he played it anyway. "You have an obligation to your public. You've a contract to fulfill."

"As you said to me just a few days ago, contracts are made to be broken."

"You have an obligation to yourself. You're a great actress."

373

"You've always told me I'm only barely adequate."

He shook his head, a winning grin pulling his mouth wide. "You've been improving recently."

She did not take the bait. "Still, I'm getting old. You can replace me with a younger woman. She'll be able to act circles around me."

"Miranda!" He threw up his hands and began to pace back and forth in front of her.

"Shreve!"

He stopped, hands spread wide. "I lied. You know I've lied about that, over and over."

Her eyes narrowed. "Yes, I've known you've lied. Over and over. It's good to hear you say it. Of course, you might not mean it this time. You might just be saying it to get me to stay."

"How can you say that?"

"Easily. You've always got what you wanted from me by lying."

He flushed. The dark blood suffused his cheeks. His beautiful Romeo eyes dropped then engaged hers again. "But I mean what I say now."

She put her hand on his arm. "Shreve, I have to go. I can't live with myself if I don't."

He caught her by her shoulders. "No. That's all drama. You've had this thing in your mind, this revenge vendetta right out of a bad Italian tragedy. You've refused to see that what happened twenty years ago has nothing to do with you."

"It has everything to do with me. My father was murdered. *Murder, most foul!* Now his murderer has tried twice to kill me. Another man has been murdered. A whole theater full of people was terrorized. My life and my mother's and my sister's lives were changed drastically, and we've all suffered for it."

His hands bruised her. He shook her. "You don't know the last three. You don't know them. You're just guessing. And as to the first, I can't see how you've suffered. You're a famous actress, beautiful, adored, living in luxury. Your sister's being educated in an exclusive girl's school. Your mother's lived a much better life in Chicago than she would have had 'following the drum.' "

"We would have had whatever we wanted with my father," Miranda retorted.

"Would you? Would you? If he hadn't died at Fort Gallatin, who's to say he wouldn't have died at the next fort? Your mother could have died trying to have Rachel on the frontier. You could have caught typhoid or cholera."

"I don't want to listen to this."

"Your father might have made it to Washington, but the chances are that he would never have been much more than he was. A captain on a frontier fort living in conditions that would make your mother old before her time. Westfall at least married your mother and—"

"He murdered my father to get her. My father never had a chance to do anything for her, or anything for me or Rachel. He died, along with eighty other men, and the man who killed them for the most selfish reason has gotten an appointment to the Bureau of Indian Affairs. My God! Where is justice? He'll ultimately decide the fate of thousands of people, whites and Indians alike. He'll cause another war all in the name of glory. I won't let him. I won't."

"Miranda." Frustrated beyond belief, Shreve

dragged her in against him and kissed her hard. His tongue drove into her mouth, silencing her protest. Ignoring the way she stood like a statue in his arms, he moved his hands over her body, down her rigid back, over her tightly clenched buttocks. He lifted her against him, letting her feel his hardness. "I want you," he growled. "I love you. Do you hear me? I love you."

Her arms closed around his neck. "Oh, Shreve. Please don't say that now. Not now. I've wanted to hear it for so long, and now it's coming too late."

"It's not too late." His mouth turned gentle, seeking the secret places on her neck, behind her ears. His hands caressed her breasts, cupped them, pulled at the nipples through the thin material of her blouse and shift. "Miranda."

"Don't, Shreve." She was all but crying. "Oh, please, don't."

"You don't mean that." He covered her mouth with his own, kissed her deeply, moving his tongue over and over the sensitive interior. He could feel her shudder. With a tiny grin, he pulled her skirt up.

Her protests were muffled as his palm slipped through the slit in her drawers and covered her mound. She was warm and moist, her body ready. His thumb found the nub of pleasure while his fingers caressed the opening of her body.

Suddenly, she wrenched herself away. Her bosom heaving, her whole body shuddering, she tore herself out of his arms. "I said, 'Don't.'"

He grinned, "Don't say don't. Just come here where you belong."

She put out a protesting hand. "Just keep away from me."

"Sweetheart, you don't mean that." He backed her toward the bed.

"I do mean it. Stay away."

He caught her, put his arms around her, bent to kiss her mouth, her throat. She shuddered as her body welcomed his hands while her mind rebelled. He freed one hand to open her blouse.

"Don't," she moaned. His fingertips caressed and shaped her nipple, then his mouth bent to take it. His lips laved it and then his teeth bent down gently.

Tears started down her cheeks. "Barbarian," she whispered. "You're an evil, spoiled, selfish man."

He lifted his head to smile into her face and kiss her mouth. "And you love me. Yes, I'm all those things, but I love you, and now you know it."

"Shreve, for pity's sake—"

He swept her high on his chest and carried her to the bed. She lay shuddering as he bared her body, part by part, and kissed each one in turn. By the time she was naked, she nearly was mindless in her desire. He parted her legs, and lifted her to his mouth, kissing her, sucking her, compelling her to shudder and writhe.

He played her as he played his greatest audience, his sense of timing flawless. At the moment just before her climax, he lifted his face. Darkened with passion, his mouth gleaming with the comingled essence of her body and his, he shuddered in his turn. "You'll never leave me," he vowed. "We belong together. We always have. We always will."

Her face was frozen, her eyes wild and glazed with passion.

He closed his mouth over her again, sucked hard at the pearl of pleasure.

She screamed and convulsed trying to twist away

from ecstasy too intense to be borne. He would not release her. He held his mouth against her, his breath coming hot, his tongue flicking back and forth.

She screamed again. "Shreve! Shreve! Stop!"

At last, his own body throbbing, he laid her down. She lay with half-slitted eyes, limbs sprawling. He pulled his own clothing aside. Rampant, his organ glistening, he positioned it. With deliberate slowness he slid into her welcoming heat.

He seemed bigger than he had ever been, jolting her awake, filling her, dominating her. She had never loved him so much. Nor had she ever thought he could hurt her as he did. This wonderful love-making was nothing but a ploy to distract her from her purpose.

He moved with deep, slow strokes and she moaned with the pain of her soul as well as the ecstasy of her body. The thought galvanized her.

With a wild cry that clenched her sheath tightly around him, she erupted. He had no time to avoid the weak blows she struck at his temple, at his ear, above his eyebrow. "Let me go. Stop this right now. You can't change my mind with sex."

"I can." He laughed. He pushed harder against her, harder and faster, faster and deeper. "If I have to keep you tied to the bed, you—will—not—go." His last four words were punctuated by his thrusts, rhythmic, deliberate, a calculated assault on her senses.

"Don't," she moaned. "Don't. Don't. Don't."

He pushed harder, pressing himself down on top of her, imprinting her with his body. "You belong here with me. We belong together. Shreve and Miranda. Miranda and Shreve."

She arched beneath him. Her hair swirled as she shook her head violently.

"Say it," he insisted, drawing back and pushing in again. His own passion roused to desperation sent tremors through his entire body, tremors that communicated themselves to the walls of her sheath. His breath, furnace hot, seared her cheek. His sweat slicked her breasts and belly.

"Don't." The word had no meaning. He drove her relentlessly over the threshold, drove her into the special world where only he had taken her for more than half her life.

"Sa-a-aaay it!"

But her legs tightened around his waist, the muscles of her sheath sucked at him with power that drove him, too. He tried to control himself, tried to hold back, but he could not. She pulled him deeper into her, and he exploded with a frustrated cry.

Miranda screamed, too. The power of him overwhelmed her, frightened her not a little, drove her to try to twist away from him even as she felt the ripples of painful pleasure begin for a third time.

His fierce black eyes closed. The scowl smoothed away to be replaced by the pleasure she recognized. His weight slumped against her, but she had no will to push him away. Instead, she took the weight on her body and clasped him as his head sank onto the pillow beside her own.

Eyes open staring at the ceiling, she waited, stilling her whirling thoughts while she caressed his damp curls. Gradually a flame of anger grew within her. He had come to her to sway her from her purpose. When she would not give in to persuasion, he had used what he had used so many times before—

seduction. Except this time she had not been seduced.

He had loved her within an inch of her life. She shivered and clasped him closer to her exhausted body. But he had not changed her mind.

Did she owe him the truth? If she let him believe she was seduced, he would suspect nothing. She would be able to leave before he could physically stop her. "Tie her to the bed," he had said. She knew him well enough to know he would do just that if he thought he must. She would not tell him.

This afternoon might be one of their last times together. She clasped him a little closer. She had always loved him. And hated him. And loved him.

At the added pressure of her arms, he murmured something unintelligible and rolled to the side, taking her with him. They remained joined together by long practice. One big hand caught her thigh and pulled her over his hip, so that she was completely open to him, her mound pressed to his belly, the hard pelvic bones cushioned by warm flesh.

His special pleasure was to wake in a half hour or less and tantalize her and himself. Sometimes he would love her again, sometimes not. She kissed his neck where the pulse throbbed strongly.

Tears filled in her eyes. Some trickled directly onto his shoulder; some pooled in the corner of her eye where they stung and burned. Let them burn. Let them hurt and remind her that she had chosen a bitter burning way.

Tipping her head back to forestall more tears, she faced the absolute and incontrovertible truth that one of the main reasons he had loved her with such passion was because he did not want to lose her as an actress. If she were killed, if Westfall managed to kill her, then Shreve would have to search days, perhaps weeks to find a replacement. He would have to spend hours in auditions, followed by more and more hours of rehearsal as the new actress learned all the lines and movement that she had taken years to learn.

The task would be arduous. And frustrating. And Shreve Catherwood, Romantic Star of Three Continents, did not like to be inconvenienced.

He had the actress and the lover he wanted. He did not want her to leave him. Her own plans, her quest meant nothing to him.

She sniffed and managed to free one hand to press it to her temple where a headache was beginning. She closed her eyes against it. In the darkness behind her eyelids, she conjured up Romeo's face. He was so beautiful. And so utterly selfish. But for his willfulness, his pursuit of her, Juliet would have lived to marry her cousin Paris.

Shreve, like Romeo, had used her ruthlessly all their lives together.

He was a fantastic lover. She did not know her own body so well as he knew it. She stretched under him, luxuriating in the feel of her skin, slick with sweat, sliding along his, the curling black hairs on his chest and thighs creating an exciting texture.

He patted her thigh, where he had drawn it over his hip. His hand slid upward along it, tracing the curve of her buttock, his fingers straying to the most private parts of her body, touching them with a freedom that made her sense quicken all over again.

Why had he waited until now to say he loved her? She would have given her soul to have heard it even a few short weeks ago. She could not doubt that it was said now to manipulate her, to have his way.

She lay still against him, feeling him touching her, feeling his fingers caressing the silken opening, finding himself filling that opening. She forced herself to lie motionless and breathe normally and evenly.

In a moment his fingers stilled and his own breathing evened. He had gone back to sleep.

She would not tell him. When they reached St. Louis, she would write a letter and take the train for Cheyenne. He would not follow her. He would never break a contract.

She closed her eyes as the headache attacked her with clawed hammers. The next week would be the greatest performance of her career, and she had never felt less like acting.

The following morning Rachel appeared at Miranda's door. "I heard about the fire at the theater," she said immediately. "I wanted to be sure you weren't hurt."

Miranda smiled tentatively. "No, I'm fine. I wasn't hurt. Thank you for caring about me."

"Of course, I care about you. You're my sister." She hesitated in the hall. "May I come in?"

"Of course, please do. I'll ring for coffee." She held the door wider.

"That would be nice." Rachel sat, then fumbled open her purse. "I've had a letter from Mother," she said when Miranda had ushered her into the sitting room of the suite and rung for coffee. "It's just as you said. How did you know?"

"What did I say?"

"You said she'd be upset. You said she wouldn't want to go back to Wyoming. How could you have known that?"

Miranda looked at her younger sister pityingly. "I know because I don't want to go back to Wyoming myself."

Rachel handed her sister the letter. Miranda read it through. Her mother's unhappiness, her distraction were evident in every sentence. Miranda felt the burden of her guilt increase. She had left her mother in Westfall's hands. She blinked rapidly as she handed it back. "Thank you for bringing it to me."

Rachel did not miss the tears as her sister folded the paper carefully and replaced it in the envelope. "Are you going to Wyoming?"

Miranda cast a hasty glance at the door to Shreve's room. He was usually a sound sleeper, but if he happened to be awake, his hearing was acute. "Why should you think that?"

Her sister followed the look. "I think you might. No, that's not true. I think you are. I think you're going because you're planning something really awful."

Miranda kept her face impassive. "I have a contract for a show in Saint Louis."

"But you're not—"

A knock sounded at the door. Miranda rose to usher in the hotel attendant pushing a cart with coffee, tea, and a collation of toast and cinnamon rolls. Miranda tipped him generously, and he departed with a bow.

"You're not going to stop in Saint Louis," Rachel insisted. "You're going to Wyoming. You're going to Fort Gallatin."

Miranda poured herself a cup of hot coffee. "Don't be ridiculous. What would I do at Fort Gallatin. They have no theaters there. Have one of these cinnamon buns. They're a specialty of the hotel. Shreve's exceptionally fond of them."

Rachel demurred. "I can't eat or drink anything, until I know what you're going to do."

Miranda took a long revivifying drink of her coffee. "Why do you want to know? None of this has anything to do with you."

Rachel rose angrily. Hands knotted into fists at her sides, she poised in front of her sister. "Don't. Don't patronize me. Don't try to put me off. This has everything to do with me. You're all my family." She choked, then went on. "You're going to try something. You've still got friends out there."

Miranda felt a surge of sympathy. "Yes, good friends."

Rachel gave a frustrated cry. "Do they hate my father, too?"

"They buried friends on the Lodge Trail Ridge," her sister acceded. "They don't like him."

"But they're not crazy like you."

Miranda rose, pulling the tie of her robe tight around her too-slim waist. She had been a prey to her shattered emotions for weeks now. The fire and the subsequent revelations had taken the last of her appetite. She felt weak and shaky. She had been wakened earlier than usual from a restless, troubled sleep, but a sleep nevertheless. Now she was being insulted.

"I'm not crazy," she told her sister icily. "But I am very tired. If you have anything important to say, say it. If not, please leave."

Rachel took a deep breath. "You're not going to get by with—"

"What in the hell is going on out here?"

Both women jumped as Shreve Catherwood

384

opened the door to his bedroom. His hair was tousled, his jaw blue-black with night stubble, his temper foul.

Out of long habit Miranda hastened to pour him a cup of black coffee and carry it to him.

Rachel's mouth curled as her eyes followed her sister's every movement. "Like a slave girl serving her master," she remarked nastily. "Do you prostrate yourself next?"

Miranda flushed miserably.

The cup rattled in the saucer as Shreve set it down. His temper, never even on the best of mornings, quick-fired. "Have you come here insulting your sister again? I suggest you leave if you don't want some very unpleasant truths aired yourself."

"I'm leaving. I wouldn't want to interrupt the two of you." Rachel closed the catch on her purse and looped the handle around her wrist. "I'm sure you have things that you usually do in the morning." The word "things" was turned into a nasty word.

Shreve set the coffee down and strode to the door. He wore only a robe loosely belted around his middle. As he walked, it swung open, revealing almost all of his hairy muscular leg.

Rachel's shocked eyes were drawn to it. Involuntarily, she raised her hand to cover her mouth.

Shreve grinned maliciously. "If you intrude upon people's privacy, you're going to get to see their most private parts."

"Ooooh!" Rachel whipped around and twisted the doorknob frantically. The door stuck. She could not get it open.

Shreve reached around her. "Madam, allow me to aid your departure. After all, you are keeping us from the 'things' that we usually do in the morning."

He swung the door wide for her. She all but tumbled through it, and ran down the hall.

He shut the door behind her and pretended to dust his hands. "Too bad she left so soon. I could have shown her several other things."

Ruth Westfall stared bleakly out the window as the train rumbled and clicked along the rails. *Francis,* she thought. *Francis.* Her dead husband's name echoed and reechoed in her mind. Twenty years had not dimmed her memories. He had remained forever young and handsome, gallant and heroic. *Francis.* Like a charm she called him up, repeated his name as the train rocked through towns and hamlets.

Her present husband had covered the table with an ordnance survey map. As she watched, he made a measurement on it, then another, and then noted the results in a notebook. He was humming through his teeth, his face set, his eyes intense.

She was just about to look back at the scenery, when he raised his eyes. His glazed look never focused on her. Instead, he pushed aside his glasses and rubbed his eyes. Without ever really catching her looking at him, he returned to his note-taking.

She dropped her eyes to her hands, lying limply, palms up in her lap. They were beautiful hands, especially for a woman her age. Unlined, soft, white. She curved her fingers, to study her nails. They were perfect ovals, buffed to a high gloss.

When she was younger, when she had lived with Francis, her hands had been rough and red from the housework. The nails had been cut very short with hangnails and chips. Sometimes in the icy winters the cuticles had peeled and bled.

After his death she had been forced to go to her parents. Even in their home she had done housework. While it had not been heavy, the amount of it had precluded her spending any length of time on her grooming. Now when she was free of any burdens and faultlessly groomed, why did she dream of the old leathery life.

Westfall cursed mildly as the train rounded a curve. His books and papers slid. A pencil rolled from the table and ended up on the carpet at her feet. He looked at it in annoyance, then looked at her.

Perhaps the sadness of her expression communicated itself to him. He rose, steadying himself on the table and swayed to the lounge chair opposite her. Dropping down into it, he swept a hand toward the papers. "I was just making some calculations. Just preliminary stuff. More to while away the time than anything. I'll need more men than Hugh originally thought. The territory's too vast for me to keep the hostiles properly subdued with just a small troop."

She looked at him with haunted eyes. "I didn't think you were supposed to subdue the Indians. I thought you were supposed to provide supplies, trade goods, education for their children, medicine for the sick."

His mouth tightened. A muscle twitched in his jaw. Questions of this type irritated him mightily. He had fielded not a few in Washington before the appropriations committee. "Not until they are properly under control. You can't start civilizing people without first knocking the barbarism out of them. They're like children. They need discipline."

"But they're on reservations. They're under control, more or less."

"Ruth." He stood up abruptly. The motion of the train threw him back into the chair. His eyes were blazing as he pushed himself up again. "I know what I'm doing. I expect you to be a helpmate. Not a hindrance."

He strode away down the car as fast as the swaying would allow him, and pushed open the door at the end. A gush of smoke-laden wind rushed into the car. Then he let the door slam to and moved to the side of the platform. Through the etched glass, she could see him fumbling for a cigar.

Her eyes returned to the blur of rocks and pebbles in the roadbed. She did not look at the scenery. The Appalachian Mountains, the green farmlands of Ohio, all had been the same, unobserved, unappreciated. The train carried her toward Wyoming. She could not get off, no matter how much she wanted to.

"Francis." This time her lips formed the word. She spoke it aloud to the empty car. Reaching into her sleeve, she pulled forth a linen handkerchief crumpled and damp. With it she dabbed at the tears. "First Francis, and then Miranda," she whispered again.

She looked at her hands. What a terrible price she had paid for that soft white skin.

She did not deceive herself. The western frontier was not much changed in the nearly twenty years since she had left. She was the one who had changed. The train bore her relentlessly back to the privation, the discomfort, the pain. She had faced them when they had all been young together and love surrounded and shielded them. But she could not face them now. She was no longer young, and

388

certainly she had little to love.

Out on the platform Westfall took a long time drawing fire into his cigar. The wretched wind, hot and searing, ripped it away, everytime he began to get it started.

If not for the creature sitting in there weeping like a watering pot, he would not be here in the first place. He would be sitting at his table, planning his campaign.

The wind whipped his thin gray-brown hair. He coughed deeply, as much from the smoke streaming back behind the train as from the smoke he was drawing into his lungs. His anger and sense of injury grew. She had been a mistake and an embarrassment.

The first years of their marriage, she had spent moaning and groaning. The beauty and life that had attracted him to Ruth in the days when she had belonged to Drummond, she had buried under an avalanche of totally unreasonable grief and depression. Although her grief had dimmed, he knew she still mourned that wretched brat.

(Was she still a problem? Or had his little plot succeeded? Probably it had not, since he had received no news reports of her death. The little monster possessed more lives than a cat.)

Most recently, Ruth had become an embarrassment. He clenched his hand around the iron rail of the platform. Neither he nor quite a few Washington dignitaries would soon forget the embarrassing scene she had created at a reception. He thought about Maud Mary. She would never have created such a scene. Now there was a helpmate.

He clamped down on his cigar in wild frustration.

"Put my traveling clothes in that small suitcase, Ada. I'll need them in case my trunks don't arrive."

"Now that's hardly likely, dearie," the wardrobe mistress replied. "It only happened once. And that was when you had to change trains twice. No change between Chicago and Saint Louis."

"But baggage is constantly put off and taken on. Who knows where the trunks might end up?"

"That's true enough. If it'll make you feel better, we'll do it." The older woman laid her hand on Miranda's shoulder. Their eyes met in the mirror. "You've got to put it all behind you, dearie. You tried and that's all a body can do. Best forget it."

Miranda's eyes dropped immediately. "You're probably right, Ada. I certainly can't make my sister like me."

"Probably, she's loved you and hated you all these years. She can't let go of either feeling. They're tearing her apart just like you're being torn. Let it rest. Maybe in a few years, she'll grow up enough to come around." Ada put her cheek against Miranda's and hugged her close. "You just be there for her when that happens."

Miranda closed her eyes against the loving embrace. "I hope I will be."

"Mrs. Wilcox, I've received a letter from my father. I suppose you've received one, too." Rachel's unhappy tone was mirrored by the expression on her face.

"Why, no, my dear. I haven't received anything." The headmistress's hand scrambled through the mail on her desk. She looked at the return addresses through her eyeglasses. "Whatever does your letter say?"

"It's an instruction to leave immediately for Cheyenne, Wyoming. Ugh!" The girl shuddered violently. "I don't even know where that is."

"West of the Mississippi River," Mrs. Wilcox replied drily. "The territory is quite unsettled. Are you sure you've read the letter correctly?"

For answer, Rachel passed it over. She held her breath. She had worked for hours to get Westfall's endlessly flowing script correct.

Mrs. Wilcox read it through twice shaking her head. "This is most unusual." She looked up at Rachel. "My dear, I don't see how I can possibly allow you to leave."

Rachel's head snapped up. "Why not? My father wants me to come. He even sent a train ticket." She pulled it from the envelope and handed it over. "I have to go."

Mrs. Wilcox did not even glance at the ticket. Instead, she shook her head. "You would be traveling alone without a chaperone in the first place, something that young ladies do not do. In the second place, you would be going to a wild outpost. You might arrive without a problem, but your parents might not. Then what would you do? I cannot believe that your father has made a wise decision."

"But I have to go. He's written to me. He's sent me a ticket." Rachel's voice rose.

Mrs. Wilcox stood behind the desk. "Calm yourself. Your behavior now convinces me that you are unfit to travel alone."

"I am fit. I am perfectly fit. And what's more I'm going. You can't keep me here." With that she snatched the ticket and letter from Mrs. Wilcox's hand and all but ran from the office.

Shreve took a deep breath that swelled his chest. He adjusted the cravat around his neck and flashed his practiced smile at the mirror. He should have been satisfied with his appearance. It was perfect. His hair was in perfect waves, his teeth were pearly white, his skin an even, clear tan.

Yet he knitted his forehead uncertainly. She had seen all this before. It was as familiar to her as breathing. She knew how every bit of it was acquired just as he knew how her beauty was enhanced, her best points emphasized, her weakest downplayed.

They knew each other better than husband and wife. They had worked and played together, dressed and undressed together, slept and bathed together for fourteen years. Together they had built a career that had taken him farther than his pragmatic soul had ever envisioned.

He should have married her years ago. He should have been faithful to her and perhaps gotten a child or two by her. Children constituted a problem for acting couples, but they could be dealt with. He knew of several couples who toured extensively with large families at home with relatives or nurses.

With children to occupy Miranda's attention, she probably would have lost track of her other family completely. He had thought she had. This harebrained visit to her little sister had come at him out of the blue. If he had only known what it would have presaged, he would have nipped it in the bud.

Still, better late than never. He patted the breast pocket of his immaculate suit and tugged gently at the lapels to adjust the coat an inch over his chest.

"Miranda." He used Romeo's voice, the one she loved best, the one she had fallen in love with. "Miranda." He opened the door to her room.

Ada found him sitting with his head in his hands. Pieces of paper were scattered on the floor around his feet. "Shreve. Shrevey-boy."

He raised his head. His voice was one she had never heard. "She's gone." He drove his long fingers into his hair and pressed the heels of his hands against his temples. "She's gone."

The wardrobe mistress got down on one knee reaching for the pieces of paper. One was Miranda's note, terse, to the point.

"Goodbye. Forgive me if you can. I have to do this. Please try to understand."

"Oh, Shrevey-boy." Ada put her hand on his shoulder.

"Yes," was all he said.

She reached for the other pieces of paper. Two pieces printed elaborately with English capitals and scrolled handwriting. They were two halves of the whole. It had been a marriage license.

Act Three
Scene 2
Wyoming, 1883

Twenty-one

*If the great gods be just, they shall assist
the deeds of justest men.*

The hawk soared on the air currents, broad pinions outstretched, eyes trained on the rough ground for the movements of tiny creatures. It uttered its hunting cry. Miranda tilted her face up to the sound. The wide-brimmed hat slipped from her head to her shoulders, where it swung by its leather thong.

The hawk screeched again.

In the rocks a ground squirrel's head shot up in panic. It barked once, then fled for its hole.

Like a thrown spear, the hawk dropped, wings reticulated, talons outstretched.

Eyes shaded by her hand, Miranda followed its stoop. A shudder raced through her as she heard the squirrel's tiny shriek. The hawk balanced over the spot, wings flapping. Then the mighty spread of flight feathers gathered the air underneath them and lifted both predator and prey aloft.

With twenty trenched gashes on his head, The least a death to nature. Miranda's mouth curved in a wry smile. Even here on the Montana Road, a world away from Shreve Catherwood, his education persisted. Was he really right? Did she see things in terms of drama rather than life? Had her father's death no more meaning than that tiny death? Was Benjamin Westfall no more a murderer than that hawk?

No. The raptor killed cleanly, intent upon one thing only—survival. It had no greed. Once it had eaten, it would not kill again until it needed to eat again. No useless slaughter of innocents littered its trail.

The Wyoming wind carried dust across the spot where the kill had been made. All traces of it were instantly erased.

She kicked her horse into a lope up the trail toward whatever remained of Fort Gallatin. As she topped a ridge, she halted the gelding again. A flagpole flew the Stars and Stripes proudly on what must have been the spot it flew on the old parade ground. A fifteen-foot tower of rough stone pointed a finger into the blue sky. Around it were stacks of raw lumber. Men were at work erecting skeletal structures.

Had she come to the wrong valley? Had her childhood memories led her so far afield. She pulled out her compass and checked for landmarks on the surrounding hills. No, this was the site of Fort Gallatin. And obviously the site of some new enterprise rising. Cold dread coursed down her spine.

Her eyes surveyed the ground beyond the construction. Twenty blistering summers and twenty winters with stone-breaking freezes and winds of upward of seventy miles an hour had swept the area clean. Probably the first to go had been the grave-markers. The fort's cemetery had disappeared and with it her father's grave. No dropping to her knees beside it and sobbing out her heart.

The actress in her, long tuned to the drama of the situation, turned her eyes away from the workmen with their hammering and sawing. Instead, she looked upward to the distant rise of the hill. Pain rose in her, filling her throat. *My father—methinks I see my father.*

No, her father's spirit would not lie here where they had interred his mutilated body. He was up there on Lodge Trail Ridge where he had died, among the spirits of slain warriors, both white and red. She knew it.

She headed the gelding up the ridgeback. Her eyes searched for and found more familiar landmarks.

The only passenger to remain after the stagecoach pulled out was the girl. Victor Wolf stared at her at first because she was strikingly pretty and incredibly young. Her blue eyes and butter yellow hair were uncommon in a world where the majority of women were dark-haired and dark-eyed Sioux and Cheyenne. Moreover, the soft mouth, with its faintly uneven look touched his memory. Although he was certain he had never seen her before, she had a vaguely familiar air about her.

"I'm looking for"—the girl consulted a scrap of paper in her gloved hand—"Adolf Lindhauer."

"I'm his son," Victor replied, smiling warmly. "Perhaps I can help you."

She did not return his smile. In fact, she looked distinctly annoyed. "I really need to see your father."

"He's at the store in Laramie this week."

"Oh, my, I just came from there." She scowled

first at the slip of paper as if it had somehow betrayed her, then up at well-stocked shelves behind his head. "I didn't even know he had a store in Laramie."

"Actually, he has several. Stores, I mean, throughout Wyoming. But they're all stocked with the same types of goods. If you'll just tell me what you need—" He paused. "Or maybe you don't need anything at all."

She sighed audibly. Keeping her head down, she pushed the paper into her glove. "I need to see him. I have to talk to him about a private matter."

Victor shook his head. "I'm sorry to tell you he isn't here. He'll be here next week."

"I can't wait a week." Distractedly, she looked around her as if by some effort of will, she could materialize the man she sought. Instead, she saw shelves heavily stocked with all kinds of goods to trade. Likewise, tables and counters were covered with bolts of cloth, blankets, furs, work shirts, overalls. Even the aisles were partially blocked with barrels of beans, flour, and rice.

While she looked, Victor looked at her. Her clothing was wrinkled and travel-stained. Her hair, stuffed up under her hat, had begun to scraggle down her neck and cheeks. She had a smudge of dirt along the side of her jaw. She licked her cracked lips.

"How about a sarsaparilla?" Victor suggested. "Wet your whistle, and things'll look better."

The girl clutched at her reticule. "How much?"

She was very young to be traveling alone, he decided. Too young. "On the house."

"Oh, but I would have to pay. I would expect to pay."

He came out from behind the huge silver metal cash register and walked to the back of the store. Opening a wide porcelain cabinet, he took out a brown bottle and expertly pushed up the metal spring with his thumb. The porcelain cap fell to one side and he pushed the drink bottle into her hand. "Ought to be cool. That cabinet's got a marble slab in it."

She looked at it longingly.

"Go ahead." He grinned disarmingly.

She took the bottle soberly and lifted it to her lips. "Thank you. You don't know how thirsty I am."

He watched her throat work as she swallowed greedily. She was certainly beautiful, her face delicate and fine-grained. Her voice was cultured, with no twang or dropping of letters. Her clothes, too, were fine material, but with a youngish look. Again he wondered how she came to be traveling alone. "You're welcome to wait here if you'd like. There's a back room here."

She jerked the bottle away from her mouth and stared at him. The blue eyes widened with alarm. "I couldn't do that."

"It's not used."

"I couldn't pay."

"It's not for rent. It's for anyone to use who needs it."

She pushed the bottle back into his hand and took a couple of backward steps. "Thank you very much for the drink. I have to be leaving now."

"Miss." Victor held out his hands from his sides. "I swear I don't mean any harm."

She stared at him, taking in his collarless linsey-woolsey shirt, his buckskin breeches, his soft deerhide boots that came up to the knee. His thick blond hair hung long and straight down his shoulders. His sapphire-blue eyes were kind.

"I'm just trying to help," he continued.

She heaved a deep sigh. "If I could just stay for the night—"

"You'd be welcome here. Nobody would bother you."

"—I'd be willing to work for a few hours. To pay for the lodging." She looked around. "I could sweep out the store. And dust."

He studied the proud face. Exhausted, but unwilling to put herself in debt. He liked that in her. "That'd be great. Things sure get dusty in a store like this." He held out the bottle to her. "Why don't you finish your drink and then I'll see what we can do about getting you started right to work?"

She looked startled.

"After all, you're going to want to pay for some supper, too."

At that she smiled. That smile stunned him. One side of the beautiful mouth turned up into a dimple. Suddenly a light flickered in his brain. He would never forget that smile.

"Where're you from?"

He made the question casual enough that she was not alarmed. "Chicago."

"Chicago. Of course, Chicago."

"That's right. Chicago, Illinois."

Victor stared at her so long that she stirred uncomfortably. He shook his head. "You can't be," he murmured. "You're too young."

She started in alarm and backed away. "I think perhaps I'd better go after all."

Suddenly, he clapped his hand to his forehead.

"Of course. Do you have a sister named Miranda?"

She stopped in her tracks. Her expression turned sullen. Her response came out as a groan. "Yes."

"My God. You're the baby."

She looked at him in real disgust. "I am not a baby."

He laughed. "Not anymore. But you were when I saw you last. You weren't even born yet. You were in your mother's stomach. Mirry told me about you, but she and her mother left before you were born."

"I was born in Chicago," Rachel confirmed stiffly.

"And your name is—?"

She hesitated. "Rachel."

"And you're here to see my father?"

"If Adolf Lindhauer is your father."

"He is. He was a good friend to your father. We all were friends together. You've come to the right place." Overwhelmed with enthusiasm, he reached for her hand and shook it vigorously. "Rachel Drummond. I'm sure glad to meet you. Mind if I ask why you want to see him?"

Frowning, she tried to free her hand. "Yes, I do."

He released her hand and backed away from her obvious hostility, but his smile never faltered. "Well, that's all right. I'm Victor Wolf."

She hesitated, uncertain how to proceed. The lean brown shopkeeper with the blond hair and startling blue eyes seemed to know a great deal about her and her family. On the other hand, knowledge did not guarantee trustworthiness, especially not here in this strange country.

She had bought a ticket to this place called Sheridan but had found nothing more than a few ramshackle buildings arranged side by side at what amounted to a wide place in the road. When she got off the stage, she had been about to cry. "What time does the stage go back to Laramie?"

"Wednesday." He held out his hand again. "You don't need to be afraid of me, Miss Drummond. I'll stand your friend."

She stared at the eyes and then the hand. Her purse was empty and she was hungry and tired. She really had no choice. She placed her own hand in his. "Thank you, Mr. Wolf."

"Hugh has promised to come for the dedication of the monument." Westfall wrote a note on a sheet of paper and underlined it.

"Monument?"

"As part of the Independence Day celebration, we're going to erect a monument on the site of Fort Gallatin." He looked hopefully at his wife. "I didn't want to tell you anything about it until I could be sure. But now I am."

She looked at him wearily. Her eyes had dark circles under them. Tiny lines had become deep brackets from her nose to her jaw. Her mouth looked as if it would never smile again.

"The names will be on it. Clarendon's and your— Drummond's. All of them."

Still she said nothing.

"Ruth," he whined at last. "I'm trying to do everything I can to make this up to you. Surely, you can meet me halfway."

She nodded. Her mouth tightened, then she smiled. "I'll be beside you, Benjamin. What more can I do?"

He took her hands. She was still a beautiful woman, even with her yellow hair muted by streaks of white. He had killed for her more than once. He would like to tell her so, but she would turn from him. Better to keep her sweet by appealing to her feelings of gratitude. "Be happy for me. I'm going to make my life come right again. It's been off track for so long. All the dreams that I had when I joined the army had to be put aside. I was achieving them, slowly, steadily. Then this disaster. And it wasn't my fault."

She looked at him steadily. Did a shadow flicker in her eyes? Did her mouth move into a hint of disdain?

His eyes narrowed. He hurried on, words tumbling and stumbling over themselves. "I couldn't help it that Clarendon was a glory-hunter. I knew it. Maud Mary—God rest her sweet soul—warned me. I knew it. But I couldn't do anything about it. I sent Drummond out as a buffer, as an anchor. I've never told this to anyone. Your husband was the best man. He should have been the Brevet-Colonel. If I'd only promoted him after that first skirmish. But I didn't. Other than that, I'm blameless in this. Blameless."

He lifted her hand to his mouth, pressed his lips to it fervently. "Ruth, you believe me, don't you? They believed me at the court-martial."

His lips were bitten and rough. They prickled the back of her soft white hand. She gave no sign that they repulsed her. "But why come back to all this?" she asked him frankly. "The court-martial exonerated you. You could go anywhere. I thought that was why you married me, so you could resume your career. The politicians in Washington would see me at your side and know that I had forgiven you. They would reinstate you. You could go anywhere with

405

Senator Butler's recommendation."

He released her and began to pace. "Don't you think I know that? I know I could have had whatever I wanted. But I didn't take the easy way. You should admire me for that. I wanted this post. I had to have it. Until I face this and put it behind me, I can't accept something else. Surely you must see this?"

She shook her head hopelessly. "No, Benjamin, I don't. I think this is a mistake. You're putting us in danger when there's no need. Neither one of us is as young as we were." She put her hand on his arm. "Benjamin, I'm fifty-one, but you're sixty-four."

"I'm hale. I'm in excellent health," he declared, twitching his arm away and straightening the stoop in his shoulders.

She heaved a sigh. "You're sixty-four. Anything could happen at any minute."

He strode to the door. His hand reaching for the knob shook with his perturbation. "I don't want to continue this conversation. I'm in excellent health, and that's the end of it."

"What will you do, Shrevey-boy?" Ada had posed the question from her seat across from him as the train rumbled south to St. Louis.

"Play *Julius Caesar*," came the bitter reply.

"Now, Shreve," George admonished him. "It's not as if she won't be back. We have another week before we play Saint Louis. If she can't make that date, she'll be back in New Orleans for sure."

"I wouldn't take her back. Hell! She's through as far as I'm concerned. Who needs her?" Shreve rose and stomped into the smoking car.

"He's takin' it hard," Ada commented unnecessarily. "But he doesn't mean a word of it. She's set him back on his heels. It's good for him. He's taken her for granted all these years. He never gave a thought to what she might like to do."

George scratched his head. "He sounds like he means it. That's a shame. She was a fine actress and a great little trouper."

"Tush. Don't you be believin' it. Selfish, greedy, self-servin'. That's our Shrevey-boy. Even if he didn't love her all out of reason, he'd still take her back in a minute. Why? Because she's one of the best there is, that's why. He's not much for cuttin' off his nose to spite his face."

"But—"

" 'Play *Julius Caesar*,' he says," Ada snorted. "That's your tip-off right there. No female parts. He's not plannin' on replacin' her. He'll just wait for her to come back. He's full of himself, too. Doesn't believe for a minute she can go it alone."

"I hope you're right."

When Shreve came back, he had had more than a cigar. He dropped into his seat and pulled his hat over his eyes. For a while he pretended to sleep, while Ada and George regarded him stoically. Finally, he sat up. "She's never going to find another partner like me."

"That's true enough, Shrevey-boy," Ada agreed exchanging a sidelong glance with George.

"She's liable to go out there to Wyoming and get herself hurt."

"Maybe even killed," Ada predicted direly. When Shreve threw her a startled look, she lifted her chin. "I may be old, but I'm nary a fool, boyo, and that you know. I've seen the comin's and goin's and I've

407

overheard the conversations. I haven't listened at keyholes, nor sneaked around, but I've brought in the private detectives to talk to her. And back at the theater, everybody was buzzin' with the doin's of Archie Doight and the army officers. I can put two and two together. And four means she's in danger."

"She won't listen," Shreve protested. "I forbade her to go. But she ran away."

"Forbade her." Ada crossed her hands more tightly over her pocketbook. Her mouth set in a straight line. "Forbade her, Shrevey-boy. And who are you to forbid?"

He bristled. "I'm her director. Her producer. Her costar."

"But you're not her father, nor her keeper, nor" — she added grimly — "her husband. She's free, white, and twenty-one. She can do as she pleases."

"But she needs one! She doesn't understand the way of the world any more than a baby. She's going to get herself killed."

Ada pursed her lips, staring at the passing countryside through the big picture-glass windows. "We're to blame for sending her out like that, I'm thinkin'. She never moved a step without one of us by her side. She's never paid a bill, because George was here to be payin' them. She's never bought a dress without m'self standin' at her shoulder and makin' sure she got the right color and fabric. She's never even crossed the street alone. You've always been with her, to put your hand under her arm."

He leaned his elbows on his knees, his hands hanging limply. Ada glanced at him then quickly returned to the passing scenery. His anguish was naked in his dark eyes. "I can't remember when I've been without her."

"We've always been like a family. We've always taken care of each other," Ada's voice continued softly. "She's been part of our family for fourteen years. She's been our baby child. We've watched her grow from a raggedy scamp into a beautiful lady. And she's always been the one to do everything we've ever asked of her."

He nodded, remembering Juliet and Ophelia, Beatrice and Rosalind, Katherine and Isabella, and most recently, Lady Macbeth. More than a dozen parts that Miranda had performed, sometimes under less than ideal conditions.

"And she's never asked anything in return, has she?"

"No, she never has."

Ada smiled. She leaned forward and patted one big hand. "So don't you think we ought to help her when she needs help?"

He stared at her for a full minute, hearing the rumble and click of the iron wheels in his ears, and also hearing Miranda's voice saying *If I have to cross the floor of Hell itself, I'll go to Fort Gallatin.* He looked at George.

The old actor nodded. "I think we should."

He straightened then and flashed them both one of his best heroic smiles. "Then that is what we'll do."

"I can't believe how good the store looks," Wolf remarked. He stood with hands on hips in the middle of the aisle.

"You're just saying that." Rachel blushed happily. "I haven't really done so much."

"You've done a lot."

While she had not rearranged anything, she had

placed it in a more artful display, dusted, refolded, and stacked. He looked at her admiringly as she wiped her hands on the voluminous apron he had given her.

"I really do appreciate your letting me stay here until your father comes."

"By the time he gets here, you'll have this store looking like a department store in Chicago."

"You're just saying that." Her blush deepened as she looked up at him, pride and pleasure in her eyes. Hastily, she concentrated on adjusting a pile of shirts one inch to the right. The dimple appeared beside her mouth.

Victor swallowed. The store's cool interior felt unaccountably warm. Unconscious of what he did, he put out his hand to help her. Their fingers accidentally brushed. The touch sent a shock through him.

She did not move except to draw a quick breath. Her lips parted.

"Rachel, I —"

She took a step toward him, bringing their bodies so close they could almost touch. "Victor."

The sweetness of her lips shaping his name mesmerized him, drew him down, down to touch them, to find the honey he knew waited for him there.

They were bliss. Gentle, yielding, warm. Without breaking the contact, he drew her toward him, or perhaps he stepped into her arms. He could not tell how they came to be together, their bodies touching at all points, his hands cupping her shoulders, urging her to him.

Her own arms spread wide, then hesitantly closed around him. Her hands touched his waist, felt the heat and strength of his muscular body. Alarmed, she jerked them away as if she had laid hands upon a hot stove. But the attraction was too strong. The magic of his lips made tremors run through her body, made her knees weak. She was falling. She had to hold on to him to stand. Her palms slid around his waist.

His tongue flicked at her lips. Startled at the touch, hers parted.

The taste of her was just as he had known it would be — heaven. His heart thudded against his ribs. He felt dizzy. He wrapped his arms around her to steady himself.

Heat, incandescent, molten, engulfed them both.

Her tongue touched his, then followed into his mouth. He felt her tremble, burrow closer. He could feel her breasts, their nipples hard, pressing against him.

She was the sister of his best friend and she was a virgin. The Cheyenne part of him understood the torrent of sensuality that a first kiss could awaken in a young woman.

"No!" Valiantly, he tore his mouth away from her. Throwing back his head, he drew in great gulps of air.

Dazed, she stared up at the brown column of his throat. Her own heart was beating so fast that it shook her body. Tension curled in her belly. Heat stirred in her loins. She had not imagined such desperate pain and such intense pleasure were possible in her body. A force had been building at the very core of her being and he had interrupted it.

To her amazement, he released her and stepped back.

"I don't understand," she murmured.

He backed clear across the store to brace against the counter and run his hand through the shock of

411

blond hair. "No. You sure don't."

She took a step toward him. "Is that what a kiss is like?"

He smiled briefly. "Pretty much."

She touched her fingers to her swollen lips. "I've never been kissed before."

"I was sure of that, too."

She looked around her. The store seemed different somehow. The light streaming through the narrow windows, more golden; the scents of spices, oils, and leathers, sharper. "I didn't know it would be like that."

He straightened away from the countertop. "It isn't all the time." This time he ran both hands through his thick hair. "That was better than most."

Smiling, she took a step toward him. "Then you liked it."

He thrust out a hand warding her off. "Now just stay away from me. Unless you want a whole lot more than a kiss."

She considered his warning a moment. "I think I want a whole lot more than a kiss."

"Don't!" He almost shouted the word.

She froze.

He leaped around the end of the counter, desperate to put a barrier between them. "You don't know me. We've only just met."

"I know that I'm in love with you."

He reeled back against the rows of shelves, clutching at them for support. "You can't be."

"Yes, I can." She held out her hands. "My mother told me once. Like a secret, you understand. She told me that she fell in love with my father the first time she saw him. My real father. Not my stepfather. My real father was a cadet at West Point. He came to visit one of his friends in Chicago. They met at a reception and she fell in love with him over a cup of punch."

"This can't be real."

"I've always known that was the way I was going to fall in love. My mother was crying a little when she told me. She was so sad because he was dead. He'd been dead a long time when she told me. He died before I was born."

"I know."

"That's right. You do." She looked at him a little curiously. "You know all about my family. And I don't know anything about yours."

He gestured with a sweep of his arm. "This is all there is to know. I'm just a half-breed shopkeeper."

"Half-breed?"

"My mother is Cheyenne." He watched her carefully, waiting for the look of distaste to come. Her face did not change.

"Is that why your name is Wolf?"

"That and the fact that my mother and father didn't get married in American style."

"They married in Cheyenne style."

"Yes."

"That's good." She took another step, putting her hands on the counter, running her palms like a caress over the smooth wood surface. "My mother will want to include her when she plans the wedding."

"Wedding?" He felt as if he were on a speeding express train, unable to slow it down.

"I'm afraid we may have to have a rather big wedding. My stepfather has so many friends and political associates. And then I'm sure your father probably has just as many business associates he will want to ask."

413

"My father—!"

"Of course, I'd rather have just a quiet wedding. I suppose if we insisted, we could have just my mother and stepfather and your parents. Wouldn't you rather do that?"

"We're not going to get married."

"Of course, we are. We're in love." She came around the end of the counter trapping him behind the counter and against the wall. Her arms went around his waist. "Kiss me again."

"No."

"Yes."

She was like the winter winds blowing down out of Canada, unstoppable, irresistible. He put his arms around her and kissed her until he thought he would die of wanting.

Suddenly, the front door swung open. "Anybody here?"

They pulled themselves apart to peer into the darkness of the silhouette. The figure was definitely female with a narrow waist and a long riding skirt looped over one arm.

"Oh, no." Rachel pulled away from Victor in disgust. "Miranda."

Twenty-two

Fair madam, kneel,
And pray your mother's blessing.

The figure stopped dead in the doorway. "R-Rachel?"

"Oh no, it's my sister."

Wolf looked from one girl to the other, then his mouth spread in a welcoming smile. "Mirry."

"Wolf?" She stood blinking to accustom her eyes to the dimness after the bright summer's day.

"Yes."

"White Wolf's Brother." His full name came out in a croon.

"Yes." He held out his arms even as she flung herself into them.

"I can't believe it's you."

"I'm so glad to see you."

"It's been so long. You're so tall."

"You're so different. Your voice. It doesn't sound like you at all."

"It's my stage voice. I had to make it big so people could hear me."

"You're an actress?!"

"Yes."

"Miranda Drummond. An actress."

She pushed herself away to arm's length drinking him in while he did the same with her. Then she laughed and hugged him again. "We've both grown up. White Wolf's Brother." She repeated the name wonderingly.

He raised his eyebrows in mock warning. "Let's keep that a secret between us. The name's Victor Wolf now. I'm a respectable shopkeeper and someday soon, when Wyoming becomes a state, I'm going to be one of her first congressmen."

She gasped in delight. "You will. You will. I know you will. You'll make a good congressman. You'll be conservative and careful. You always kept me safe from myself. I'd vote for you." They kissed and hugged again. At last with his arm around her waist, he turned back to Rachel. "I knew you were coming. Your sister came in yesterday. For a minute I thought she was you."

"Rachel?" Miranda's amazement was evident in her voice.

"Hello, Miranda," came the unhappy reply.

"What are you doing here? You should be in school."

Rachel hesitated, then folded her arms across her chest. "I'm here to keep you from doing whatever you're planning to do."

Wolf shook his head in mock exasperation. "What are you planning, Mirry?"

When Miranda hesitated, Rachel answered for her. "She's planning to destroy my father."

"Your father?"

"She means Benjamin Westfall."

"Westfall?" Wolf's confusion increased. "Benjamin Westfall. Your father? But he's the one who—"

"That's right." Miranda interrupted. "He's the one who let her father—her real father Francis Drummond—and Hickory Joe Magruder and all their men die. She calls him Father, but he's really her stepfather."

Wolf's face grew more and more sober as Miranda told the story. Rachel looked from one to the other until she could stand the suspense no longer. She caught Wolf's hand and put herself between him and her sister. "Don't listen to her. Listen to me. She's crazy. She wants vengeance for something that was over and done with years ago."

"If what she says is true, then she may have a case for legal action," Wolf began thoughtfully. "Wrongful imprisonment. Furthermore, if Pinkerton's wants to reopen that case and can dig up proof, then the state will prosecute for murder."

Miranda smiled. "The lawyer and legislator. Keeping busy as a shopkeeper until statehood."

"But that's just her story!" Rachel all but screamed in her frustration. "You don't have any proof, do you?" She threw the words in her sister's face.

"No."

"There. You see." She turned to Wolf. "Oh, look at me." She put her hand on his cheek and turned his face back down to her. "Don't look at her. You must help me. I'm here to see your father. I know he's a powerful man in the territory. Mother was always writing to him. He can help me to put a stop to this."

Wolf put his hand reassuringly over hers. "Why don't we all just sit down in the back of the

417

store and have a cool drink? We can talk this over sensibly and calmly."

"That sounds wonderful to me," Miranda agreed. "I'm dry as a bone and almost too dusty to be in polite company."

He nodded. Taking Rachel by the hand, he led the way back and motioned to the girls to sit down. From the cabinet he took three sarsaparillas, opened each in turn, and handed them around. Miranda turned hers up immediately. "Now, Mirry, what do you plan?"

Rachel shot her sister a dark look. "She plans something terrible. She wants to disgrace my father. I wouldn't put it past her to kill him if she could. She's half crazy. She came to me at school in—"

Miranda lowered the tall brown bottle, checking to see that it was almost half empty. She tilted it up and drank again. While Rachel raged on and on the cool liquid washed away some of the dryness left by the wild Wyoming wind. When her sister paused for breath, she said, "At first I thought I would try to get your father to use his influence to keep Westfall from being appointed in the first place, but I found out about the appointment too late."

Wolf shrugged. "Appointments can be changed."

"But not for years. This is a senatorial appointment. His father-in-law by his first marriage set this up for him."

"If you brought proof of wrongdoing—"

"The chances of getting proof against Westfall at this late date are slim. Pinkerton's didn't even suspect him in the death of Bledsoe, and they investigated thoroughly at the time. A man set fire to the theater where I was appearing just last month, but he said someone paid him to do it as a joke. He had no idea who paid him. No, Rachel is right. There is absolutely no proof."

"So—"

"I have to find a way to make him confess."

Rachel broke in savagely. "He'll never confess to what he didn't do."

Miranda closed her eyes. "No. I don't suppose he will." Her words dropped like stones, cold and heavy ending the conversation. At last she opened her eyes. "There's construction going on at the site of Fort Gallatin."

Wolf nodded. "It's part of the Independence Day celebration. They've put up a monument to the members of the Second Cavalry who died on Lodge Trail Ridge."

"I saw it, but there's more than that. Buildings are going up. At least three. Maybe more."

"The headquarters for the new regional director of the Bureau of Indian Affairs is going to be there."

"And this director is my stepfather." Miranda's voice crackled with sarcasm us she paused for dramatic effect. She cleared her throat. "The Honorable Benjamin Butler Westfall." She looked into her sister's eyes. *For sure he is an honorable man.* Of course. It's what he's planned on all along."

"What has he planned?" Wolf looked at her skeptically. "After all it's been seventeen years."

"He wants revenge." Miranda finished the bottle of sarsaparilla and set it down with a sharp thwack. "He wants every Indian in this territory under his thumb, completely humiliated by him. If he can get them so infuriated that they start a war, he'll call the army in and annihilate them."

"My father will not—"

"When will your father be coming back?" She directed the question to Wolf.

"He isn't going to do something like that," Rachel insisted angrily. "You don't know what you're talking about."

"A couple of days. He's at Laramie right now," Victor replied.

"Then I'd better be leaving." Miranda stood up, stretching her tired back as she did so.

Rachel sprang to her feet. "You're not going to find Victor's father and turn him against my father. I won't let you."

"It's not possible to turn Wolf's father against *your* father," Miranda informed her placing heavy emphasis on the pronoun. Her voice was low, but the intensity vibrated through it. "Adolf Lindhauer rode out in the dead of night to find *my* father and bring him back. He thought that much of *my* father."

"I hate you." Rachel's untrained voice sounded weak and strained.

Miranda set her hat on her head and drew the button up under her chin. "Is that supposed to stop me? You've never liked me." Her mouth looked as if it had never smiled. "If you wanted to stop me, you might try telling me that I had something to live for besides vengeance."

She turned on her heel and walked to the front of the store.

"Mirry, wait." Wolf hurried to catch her at the door. "Don't ride off at this time of day. You only have a couple of hours of daylight left. Spend the night. Rest yourself. Father might accidentally be in tomorrow. Sometimes he comes in early. Besides, if you go now, you might run the risk of missing him.

He might come by a different trail or be camped off to the side of the road as you ride by."

She hesitated in the doorway. While she felt fine at the moment, she knew that her reserves of strength had been deeply tapped. To ride around over the Wyoming Territory on horseback for four days had been foolish indeed. She realized that, as her body protested softly. Just sitting long enough to drink a sarsaparilla had stiffened her joints. Her thigh muscles shrieked in anguish at the very thought of climbing back aboard her horse. Her back hurt low at her hips. Her buttocks were rubbed raw. Even as she shook her head, she knew she would allow herself to be persuaded to remain.

"We've got to do something!" Rachel exclaimed passionately. Her blue eyes searched Wolf's face relentlessly. "You've got to help me."

"Help you do what?" The corners of his mouth twitched, but he managed to keep from grinning. She was so intense. Her blue eyes fairly blazed with righteous anger. The Cheyenne in him responded mightily to that anger. Miranda had never asked him for anything. She had led him into trouble, into danger, into adventure with this same passion and he had carried the memory of it all his life. For that reason he was the despair of his mother and father, refusing to marry either charming white girls or dutiful Cheyenne maidens.

He had thought he was doomed to bachelorhood until this girl—her younger sister—Mirry's passionate twin—had plunged into his life. He shook his head wonderingly.

She misread the movement. "Don't!" She caught

him by the upper arms. "Don't tell me 'no.' She's crazy. I don't care if she is my sister. What she's trying to do is crazy. Stop her."

"We can't stop her until we know what she's planning to do."

Rachel stopped nonplussed. "It's going to be something awful."

"Maybe not. Maybe she's just going to denounce him. Then it will depend upon the people present as to whether they believe her or not." He shook his head. "Chances are, they won't believe her. And even if they do, they probably don't care enough to do anything. What would they do? It was all so long ago."

"Exactly."

"And the court-martial found him innocent, if I remember correctly."

"Of course." Rachel did not let go of his arms. "That's why she's got to do something awful. She's going to do something that will hurt all of us."

White Wolf's Brother took a deep breath. "Rachel, I don't know what Mirry's planning, but I do know this. Whatever she's planning will not hurt us. She's not that kind of person. Never has been."

"You don't know her anymore. It's not sane to keep wanting to hurt someone after so many years. That's crazy."

"Not if there's murder involved." He wrapped his big hands around her upper arms so they were clutching each other. "She loved her father, and he loved her. You don't get over something like that. How would you feel if someone killed your mother?"

"I wouldn't nurse my grief for half my life," Rachel said instantly. "I'd do something right then, or

422

I'd forget it." Her hold on his arms tightened. The fingernails bit into the muscle through his thin cotton shirt. "You've got to help me."

He looked down at her. She sounded almost like Mirry trying to engage him in some harebrained scheme. Except that this was not Mirry. Miranda never begged for anything. If he said no, he got left behind. No, Rachel was not the woman her sister was. Perhaps the difference was the gentler life she had led. Perhaps it was just Ruth Drummond in her rather than Francis. Still, Rachel had left her safe home in Chicago to dare the western frontier, just as determined in her own desperate way. And in that moment he knew. Rachel Drummond was enough woman for him. "Perhaps you don't really need me. You could change this all yourself."

"What do you mean?"

"Didn't you hear her? She said if someone had given her something besides vengeance to live for, she might not want it so much."

"That doesn't make any sense," Rachel said crossly.

"Oh, I think it does. What did you do when she came to see you?"

Rachel folded her arms tightly across her bosom. "I told her to mind her own business. I warned her not to come back and bother Mother."

"Did you think she might want you to love her?"

"I'm sure she did, but she had deserted us. She couldn't just come back into our lives and expect us to fall all over ourselves loving her."

"No, indeed. Why did she come back in the first place?"

At that Rachel looked uncomfortable. "She was just trying to mind my business."

"Why?"

"She thought I might — er — not want to — er — go to Mrs. Wilcox's school."

"You mean she thought she might be rescuing you."

Rachel pressed her lips tight together in a stubborn line.

Wolf put his arm around her shoulders and turned her gently into his arms. "I think you hurt your sister very badly that day. I think she's been hurt most of her life. And she's a fighter. She's not one to give in."

"Then you're going to help her."

"I won't help her. I *will* help you do whatever needs to be done when the time comes, so long as it's not against her. This I promise you." He could see the luminous quality of her eyes, the ripe pinkness of her lips and cheeks. He could see the fineness of her skin.

Suddenly, her lips began to tremble. A wondering look came into her eyes. The grip of her hands relaxed as if she suddenly realized she was holding on to him.

"Rachel," he murmured, "may I kiss you?"

The dimple appeared at the corner of her mouth. She swallowed. "Yes."

"I told you he might be here today." Wolf gave Mirry a triumphant smile. "He likes this store the best. It's where he got started. That's why I manage it for him. He wouldn't trust either of my brothers with it. They're too wild."

Miranda nodded. "And you're not wild."

"Never."

424

Through the open door they could see Adolf Lindhauer climb carefully down from the phaeton. Miranda, Rachel, and Wolf strolled out on the porch to greet him. "Father, you'll never believe who's here to see you."

Adolf nodded briefly to the three. His pale blue eyes did not study the two girls. "Well, now, that's a coincidence for a fact. You'll never believe who's come to see you." He held out his hand to a woman whose face was shielded by a broad-brimmed hat and veiling knotted under her chin. "But if you think right hard, you'll remember this dear lady from a long time ago."

Of the three on the porch Rachel recognized the woman first. "Mother!"

Miranda faltered, then drew back. Her hand extended in greeting began to tremble. She shot Wolf a frightened look.

At her younger daughter's exclamation, Ruth raised her head. "Rachel?"

Adolf threw a glance over his shoulder. "What's this?"

Miranda was backing toward the door, but too late. Ruth Drummond Westfall went white. The hand that clasped Lindhauer's tightened, then began to tremble. "Dear Lord! Who—? Who are you?"

"Mother—" Rachel sprang down the steps to take her mother's arm when the older woman would have sunk to the ground. Her eyes blazed accusing fire at Miranda.

"What's this? What's this?" Adolf's voice rose. "What in hell's goin' on here, Wolf? Who're these girls?"

Ruth shuddered helplessly. As if she had taken a blow to the heart, her mouth gaped open as she

425

wheezed and choked.

"What's goin' on? What's this? Ruth, are you sick? Hellfire!" He motioned to his son. "Wolf, get yourself down here and help me with her. She's havin' an attack of some kind."

"Yes, sir." White Wolf's Brother sprang down and took his father's place alongside Ruth. She looked at him vaguely, then she seemed to be sliding through his grasp. He swept her up in his arms. She twisted trying to keep her eyes on Miranda. "Steady now. I've got you."

"Has she fainted?" Adolf asked anxiously.

"No," Ruth whispered. "No." Her head lolled back against Wolf's shoulder as he mounted the steps, but when she came abreast of her long-lost daughter, she reached out for Miranda. "Who are you?" Her hand wavered; the fingers trembled. *Who are you?*

Too late to run away. Moreover, she would not if she could, Miranda caught her mother's hand. "I'm Miranda."

Ruth's breath slipped out in a long sigh. "Miranda."

"Yes, Mother."

White Wolf's Brother carried Ruth into the store and down the aisle to the back. There he set her in a chair. Miranda, who had followed at his heels, knelt in front of her mother.

Ruth took her daughter's face between her icy hands. Tears spilled out of her eyes and streamed down her cheeks. "I knew you weren't dead. I just knew you weren't. You just couldn't be. I would have known it. And I didn't feel quite that empty. My baby. My baby."

"Mother." Miranda was crying, too. After so long

to be able to see her mother, to hear herself called "baby," had broken her control. "Oh, Mother." She put her arms around her mother's waist.

Rachel and Adolf came up to them. The old man had a flabbergasted expression on his face. "What's goin' on here?" he asked his son. "Will somebody please tell me what in hell's goin' on?"

"It's Mirry," Wolf told him softly. "She's come back."

"I can see that. But where'd she come from. Last time somebody said anything about her, they thought she was dead. Ruth, didn't you write me to find out if I'd seen her?" He did not wait for an answer. "Maybe I'm mixed up. That was years ago. I forget some things occasionally now. But I don't think I'd forget that. Ruth, didn't you write me that she was dead?"

"Yes, Adolf." Ruth was laughing now. She had not taken her eyes off her daughter. Her fingers touched Miranda's temple and smoothed the hair back.

"But she's here now," Adolf observed. He grinned at his son. "I guess you'll explain this to me before too long."

"I promise I will."

"I ran away," Miranda said in a choked voice. "I ran away from home." She hesitated, uncertain what to tell and what to keep secret.

Rachel stepped forward. "Would you like a cold drink, Mother, Mr. Lindhauer? You must be so hot and dry."

"That'd be a good idea. Maybe even somethin' stronger?" Lindhauer looked hopefully toward his son, but Rachel had already crossed to the cabinet where the sarsaparillas were kept.

"Miranda," Ruth asked softly. "Where have you been?"

"All around," came the hesitant reply. She smiled. "I've been all around the world. I'm an actress."

"An actress?"

"Yes, I joined a theater troupe. I've been touring for years."

"But you never sent me word. Never wrote."

"Mother—" The questions were implicit. "I—"

"Was it because of Benjamin?" The words were lightly spoken, but they froze everyone in the room.

"I—I didn't— That is, he wouldn't— We didn't get along."

"But he found you. He told me he found you, but you were dead. He told me you were dead."

Now was the moment to tell about her ordeal. About Benjamin Westfall's vicious cruelty. About what Miranda believed were not one but two attempts to murder her. But she could not. If her plan failed, then her mother would still be married to him. The less Ruth knew about him the better.

"He must have gotten false information." Miranda rose still holding her mother's hand, then stooped to kiss her forehead and hug her hard. "Oh, it's so good to see you."

Ruth stood, too, and hugged her daughter in her arms. She began to laugh a little shakily, then joyously. "I can't believe it. I can't believe it's really you. I just can't believe it. After all these years. It's so good. It's so good."

When Miranda stepped back, Ruth studied her. "You've grown a little bit taller, but only just a little. Your face is just the same. God took Francis away from me, but He didn't take you. He didn't take you. Your voice sounds different though. What did you do to your voice?"

- Miranda smiled. With both fingers she wiped at the tears on her cheeks. "I'm an actress, Mother. This is my stage voice. We have to learn to speak very loudly so people can hear us in a big theater."

"Here's a cool drink for you." Rachel pressed the bottle into her mother's hand.

Ruth automatically closed her fingers around it but ignored it. "I should never have married him. I know that. I knew it even when I was doing it, but — " She gestured helplessly with the bottle, then looked at it in some surprise. "It was so awful in your grandfather's house. We were so poor even with a roof over our heads and plenty of food on the table. I thought Benjamin would be able to give you the things I wanted you to have. You and Rachel. And it all turned out wrong. So terribly wrong."

"Mother, it's all right," Miranda said. "I understood."

"What are you both talking about?" Rachel broke in on the conversation. Her expression was equal parts anger and disbelief.

"Oh, Rachel, I never wanted you to know."

"Know what? What are you talking about? You're talking about my father," she accused. "You're saying you never should have married him."

Ruth bowed her head before her younger daughter's condemnation. "I wanted an education for Miranda. She was so smart. And she'd never had a chance. I wanted her to meet some nice young men and get married. I thought he'd provide that. But I should have known better. I knew what he'd done. We both knew what he'd done."

"What he'd done!"

"We all did." Ruth raised her head to Adolf. The shopkeeper had folded his arms across his barrel chest. The brown sarsaparilla bottle dangled from one hand. "Didn't we?"

He cleared his throat. "Maybe so. Maybe so."

Rachel looked frantically from one to the other. "You're talking about my father."

Ruth shrugged helplessly. She turned her attention from her younger daughter to her older one. "Miranda, have you been—all right?"

"Yes, Mother. I've been fine. I've learned a profession. I've made my own way."

"But has it been hard?"

Miranda had thought about that more times than not. "Not really. It's been easy. I made some wonderful friends, and they made it easy for me."

"I always knew you would. You were just like Francis. He would stick at anything."

"Were you ever in want?"

"Not really. I joined up with a troupe the very first night I left. Stowed away in the back of their wagon. They were half way to Saint Louis before they found me. At first I just helped around backstage, ran errands, took care of costumes. But then the leading lady quit and they needed an actress to go on right away."

"And you were good." Ruth's eyes were shining with pride.

"I was awful, but I was better than nothing. The leader of the troupe, Shreve Catherwood, covered for me and spoke my lines under his breath when I'd forget. He and the others made me look good. I've been on the stage ever since and I've learned to act quite well."

"Just like Francis."

White Wolf's Brother was watching Rachel closely. Her face had gone from white to red. She opened her mouth, her rage ready to erupt, but he wrapped his arm around her waist. She looked at him, her blue eyes flashing fire, but he shook his head. A gentle smile curved his mouth as he squeezed her warningly.

Adolf observed the byplay. He cleared his throat. "So. Who's this other one? I think I recognize this young lady. She sure looks like Miss Miranda. I think I can guess who she is, but I'd still like an introduction."

Ruth remembered her younger daughter for the first time. "Rachel, what are you doing here? You're supposed to be in school."

"I—I just—" White Wolf's Brother's face was stern. Rachel swallowed, then wiped the scowl from her face. She smiled brightly. "I just wanted to be with you and Father. And now I've gotten to meet my sister Miranda."

Ruth put her arm out and drew her younger daughter into the circle of her arms. Her chin began to tremble again. Tears began to pour down her cheeks. "I just can't believe it. I'm so happy. So happy. My two babies back in my arms. I didn't think it would ever happen." She kissed Rachel and then Miranda. "I just knew you weren't dead. I had consoled myself that you were alive somewhere. But here you are and looking so beautiful."

"I'm so happy, too." Miranda buried her face in her mother's neck. "I've wanted to come home, but at first I was scared, and then I had so many obligations. I couldn't let my friends down. They'd worked with me so hard and put so much faith in me."

Ruth smoothed her daughter's hair and patted her head. "My precious baby. Of course you couldn't. Your father would be so proud of you."

Wolf blinked at the tears that tried to form in his own eyes. Adolf was frankly weeping.

Rachel gently but firmly extracted herself from the embrace and backed away. Wolf's broad chest stopped her retreat. His mouth touched her ear. "Be happy for your mother, if you can't be happy for your sister."

"This is making me sick," she muttered out of the corner of her mouth. "She's living with a man. Her father would probably be—"

Ruth's eyes were on her. She stopped abruptly.

Miranda raised her head and covered her face with her hand. "I've got your blouse all wet, Mother."

Ruth laughed. "Those are the sweetest tears I've ever seen. You could soak a hundred blouses and I wouldn't care."

"This is quite a day," Adolf said fervently. "Quite a day."

Ruth took a deep breath. "Yes, it's the most wonderful day. But tell me now, Miranda, why did you come here?"

Twenty-three

The time is out of joint, O cursed spite
That ever I was born to set it right!

"Miranda has taken this upon herself, when I should have been the one to do it," Ruth declared.

"Mother!" Rachel's voice rose in a shriek of anguish. "Mother. How can you say that?"

"Rachel, be quiet!"

"Mother."

"I can say it for the very good reason that my own daughter makes me ashamed of the way I have lived. This monster was responsible in some degree for the deaths of a whole troop of men. I knew that. Never mind what the court-martial found. He came back into my life and my beloved daughter disappeared. Instead of ordering him off and moving heaven and earth to find her, I married him. Now I find that he has destroyed her girlhood and tried to take her life. Oh, I could die of shame." She looked at Adolf and Wolf. "I'm surprised that you would have me in your home."

"Well, now, you're always welcome to what I have," Lindhauer reassured her. He gave a swift encompassing glance around him. His eyes glowed with pride as they met those of his wife. They sat in the parlor of the Lindhauer house in Sheridan. Once it had been a tepee of buffalo hides for Adolf and his young Cheyenne squaw. Now it had ten rooms and a staff of four servants.

Furniture and carpets imported from the East by railroad and then by Lindhauer's own freight wagons had been mixed with the Indian bowls and baskets, pouches and blankets. Blue Sun on Snow, Lindhauer's wife, still wore Indian boots as did her son White Wolf's Brother, but she wore them beneath a fine linen dress with a deep lace jabot.

Under Adolf's approving eyes she sat in a mahogany chair upholstered in a dark floral brocade and served them in china cups from a sterling silver service. What they drank was her own special blend of smoked herbs combined with imported tea.

Blue Sun on Snow spoke English fluently, but she spoke only occasionally. While she listened to the conversation, she watched her son watch the young Rachel Drummond. The barest hint of a smile tugged repeatedly at the corners of her straight mouth.

"I left my daughter to do what I should have done," Ruth mourned. "Even on the day Francis was killed, I didn't protest the way she did. I just stood there numb with shock." She squeezed her daughter's hand. "And you are absolutely right, Miranda. He cannot be allowed to proceed with his plans."

"Mother," Rachel protested. "You don't know what Father is going to do. You can't be serious."

Ruth looked at her daughter pityingly.

434

Rachel burned as she recognized the look as the same one her sister had bestowed on her only the day before. She looked around the room seeking some support. The faces were all equally solemn with a patient air reserved for the very young. She crossed her arms over her chest. "You are all out of your minds. My father is going to be the new Indian agent."

"But he's not talking about ministering to the needs of the Sioux and Northern Cheyenne. He's building a fort, not an Indian Agency. He's planning on bringing in more armed troops," Ruth stated bluntly. "He's going to start a war."

White Wolf's Brother let out a long low whistle. "What makes you so sure?"

"I rode across half this country with him pouring over ordnance maps, making lists of supplies, rifles, ammunition, troops."

"His job—"

Ruth interrupted her daughter. "He's supposed to be requisitioning medicine, food, schoolbooks. It hasn't been that long since Custer's defeat. I can imagine the peace is shaky at best. It wouldn't take much to set the Sioux on the warpath. And"—she looked straight at Adolf and Blue Sun on Snow—"Ben Westfall is looking for a war."

Rachel sprang to her feet. "You're both crazy. Mother, I can't believe you're saying all these things. You're actually encouraging her."

"Rachel, the last thing Wyoming needs is a war. If we can do something to stop it, then we must do it."

"But you're mistaken. My father—"

"He's not your father," Miranda interrupted. "He

killed your father. But the only way you'll believe that is if I force him to admit."

"He'll never admit it because he didn't do it. He didn't do any of the things you are accusing him of." She hurried out the door and down the hall.

Ruth caught up to her and spun her around. Her voice was low but intense. "Miranda is right. You have to learn the truth. I won't have you going through the rest of your life loving this man. If he goes through with his plans, he'll end up causing the deaths of hundreds of innocent people."

Miranda joined them. "You'd better listen to her, Rachel. If he starts an Indian war, our mother might be killed, as well as our friends. If he follows his pattern, he'll probably manage to be on his way back East to get more supplies. He manages to stay out of the way of the action."

"You're horrible!" Rachel accused tearfully. "Horrible!"

Miranda lifted her chin. Lady Macbeth's eyes were chips of cold steel. "The only way I'll ever be your sister is to get him to admit what he did. I'm going to get that confession from him, and then I'm going to end this once and for all."

"You're crazy! Mother, she's crazy!"

Ruth shook her head. "No, she's right. This must end. Seventeen years is too long for justice to be delayed."

"This celebration is going to be the biggest this territory's ever seen." Benjamin Westfall could feel his spirits rise as he stared up at the stone column. A large bronze plaque at eye level listed the names of those who had died that day. Listed first were Bvt.-Col. Robert Clarendon and Captain Francis Drummond. He pointed to the names triumphantly. "There," he said to his wife. "There they are, just as I promised they would be. They'll never be forgotten now. Not some plot among thousands in a military cemetery, but a monument."

Ruth knew he was waiting for her to thank him. She smiled wanly. "It's very nice dear. I hope everything works out as you've planned it."

"It will. It will. With this I'll lay the rumors to rest forever. People will never whisper about me behind my back again. They'll come to see this and go away satisfied. Do you know people are coming from as far away as Fort Laramie and Casper? They're not just the oldtimers but young people who've built new towns in these hills. They'll all be there and I'll put their minds at rest. I'll tell them what they can expect from the new Indian agent."

"The Sioux who need to know that. They're the ones with whom you'll deal," she pointed out softly, but he did not hear her.

"I can promise them protection such as they haven't had since Little Big Horn. They'll sleep sounder in their beds because of the new agency."

"Benjamin—"

"I've saved the biggest surprise for the last. Hugh Butler is coming all the way from Washington, D.C., to dedicate it."

She looked at him incredulously. "Senator Butler!"

"Yes. I knew you'd be surprised."

"All this distance! Are you sure?"

Westfall frowned. "Of course, he's coming. Don't you believe me?"

"But surely this is not sufficiently important to bring him all the way from Washington, D.C. Benjamin, he's an old man. Why, he must be seventy-five years old!"

Her husband stopped nonplussed. She realized that he had never considered Hugh Butler to be old. "Benjamin," she continued softly. "He's too old to travel all this distance. You were exhausted when we arrived. Think how terrible the trip will be for him."

"That's ridiculous. I was not exhausted." He wiped sweat from his forehead and glanced upward accusingly at the sun. "He will come. I've invited him. I've made all the arrangements."

"But you haven't heard from him? He hasn't confirmed his arrival."

"He'll come. He knows how important this is to me. He'll come." Her husband climbed down out of the buggy and strode away toward where the men were throwing up a speaker's platform.

The Wyoming wind blew puffs of dust behind every footstep. She slanted her parasol against the gusts, a move that bared her shoulder and the side of her face to the sun's fierce rays. He paused to light a cigar and cast an angry look in her direction. She watched him, unable to summon up even a trace of pity. His obsessions had led him to this inhospitable spot. All she could pray was that he would be the only one to die.

Shreve smiled down into the dark Indian face

above the starched white-and-green-striped blouse. "I've come to speak with Adolf Lindhauer."

"Why?"

"It's a private matter. I'm looking for a dear friend of mine and, since I understood that she was an old friend of his, I thought perhaps he might have some idea of her whereabouts."

Blue Sun on Snow digested the elegant speech pronounced in the most precise language. She smiled. "Are you an actor?"

His black eyebrows shot upward. Then his own smile spread wider than ever as he swept his hat before him in a courtly bow. "I think you know the friend I'm searching for."

"Come in."

"Thank you, ma'am. My name is Shreve Catherwood."

"I am Blue Sun on Snow."

He bowed again, at the same time moving his lips silently over the name. "Wonderful name. Have you ever considered an acting career?"

She giggled, her dark smooth face breaking into a mass of lines as her eyes crinkled and her mouth spread. "No, sir. I am a wife and mother. Come this way."

He followed her down a long hall, taking note of the blue and red Persian carpet runner beneath his feet. She opened a door. "Miranda, you have a visitor."

The sight of him literally sent her staggering. "What are you doing here? How did you find me?"

He hurried to meet her as Blue Sun on Snow closed the door behind him and left them alone.

439

"Miranda." The feel of her forestalled all explanations. He caught her in his arms and kissed her thoroughly. The only sound in the room for a very long time was her impassioned whimper and his soft moan of longing. At last they tore apart to gasp in great lungfuls of air.

"I can't believe you're here."

"I thought I'd lost half of myself."

"I've missed you so much."

"Whatever you want to do, I'm here to help."

"Kiss me again," she whispered. "Please."

And like the gallant gentleman he was, he could not wait to serve her.

At length they sat together on the brocade sofa draped with a bright Indian blanket. "I can't believe you came after me," she said shyly. "I meant what I wrote. I was going to try to rejoin the troupe in Saint Louis. If this took longer than I thought, I was going to meet you in New Orleans. But I wasn't sure that you'd take me back."

He kept her hand in his. "I canceled Saint Louis."

"Shreve, we've never canceled a show. Never."

"—because of your 'illness.' The manager was unhappy but understanding. We drew up a contract for next fall."

"Then—then—"

"You need us," he told her seriously. "Whatever you plan to do, it's going to be dangerous. That man is a murderer a hundred times over. You're part of the family." He watched her eyes fill with sparkling tears. "And anyway, Mark Antony is not my favorite part."

She laughed, choking a little. "He seems the

perfect casting to me. You've always threatened to play it running naked through the streets, striking women with goat-hide whips. Whenever I was particularly bad, you'd say you were going to do *Julius Caesar.*"

"Yes, but I lied." He assumed a superior attitude. "All those men's roles are hard to cast. And you were never more than moderately bad."

She smiled. "I'll remember that. Did Ada and George go on to New Orleans?"

"Them! Not much. They're over at a most ill-furnished boardinghouse run by a woman named Mrs. Brownboots, who could easily play Third Witch. We're all staying there together, but I notice you're not." He looked around him appreciatively.

"No, I'm staying with friends." She clapped her hands to her cheeks. Tears overflowed and trickled. "Ada and George came with you. You all came to Sheridan, Wyoming, to help me."

"Why, Miranda—" Nothing would do but that he kiss her again, tasting her tears.

"Oh, Shreve. I love you. I love you."

"I love you, too."

She looked at him seriously. "You really do. You don't just love me when you want me to do something."

He kissed the tip of her nose. "I swear I love you even when there's nothing I want you to do. Except make love to me." He waggled his eyebrows mockingly. "Now tell me what's been going on."

She cuddled in the circle of his arm and told him everything—her reunion with White Wolf's Brother, her sister's anger and dismay, the reunion with her mother. "She even apologized to me," she murmured, turning her face up to his. "She said she should have taken care of him."

He kissed her mouth. "And so she should have, rather than leaving it for her daughter to do. However, I'm glad she did. If she had not, you would never have stowed away on the wagon."

"And never joined the troupe."

"And never become the magnificent Miranda." He kissed her again. His heart felt so full he thought it would burst with love. Why had he torn up that marriage license? They should get married immediately.

"And never fallen in love with Shreve Catherwood, Romantic Star of Three Continents."

"This is true." After another few minutes, he lifted his head for air. "A woman ushered me in here. Her name was unusual."

"Blue Sun on Snow?"

"She asked me if I was an actor and seemed to think I belonged in here." He looked around the comfortably furnished parlor. "However, I don't think she would be totally agreeable to my throwing you down on the floor and having my way with you."

"You never know about her. She's Adolf's wife. And he's very proud of her. They have six beautiful children, three boys and three girls. I'm sure they've had their moments."

He kissed her again, trailing his kisses down across her jaw to the delicate corner of her mouth. He caressed and tickled her cheek until the dimple appeared, then plunged his tongue into her mouth caressing her until she moaned in pleasure. When he stopped, they were both trembling. "I have to get you out of this town and into a decent hotel suite."

She sat up reluctantly. "I want to go, Shreve, but I have to go through with it. If he goes through with his plans, there'll be an Indian war. He's reconstructing a fort, instead of building an Indian agency."

"You're right. You have to. But what?"

She rose and began to pace the floor. He watched her, thinking how she had grown and changed, how the thin awkwardness of youth had metamorphosed into the slender elegance of womanhood. She was all in all to him. He swelled with pride as he saw before him his daughter, his student, and his lover. Soon he hoped to take her for a wife.

The love in his eyes must have been shown, for she stopped. A strange look came over her face. "Don't," she whispered. "Don't, Shreve."

He smiled and waved her on.

"I-I'm glad you've come because I've had no time to think. Too much has happened. Too many things are happening all at once. Suddenly, I need a plan, because it must be done day after tomorrow."

He sat up straight. "What? Why so soon?"

"Because tomorrow is the Fourth of July. Independence Day. There's a big celebration planned wherein they'll dedicate the monument."

"What monument?"

"On the site of old Fort Gallatin, they've built a monument to Clarendon and the men who died with him. They're dedicating it that day. Westfall'll make a speech. People will come from miles around. Somehow, someway, I've got to get him to confess his crime before them."

He shook his head incredulously. "In front of an audience? Impossible. We might kidnap him and get him to write a confession and then publish it in the newspaper."

She shook her head. "It wouldn't be the same. He has to say it. He has to admit it. Otherwise, my sister will never forgive me."

He threw up his hands in disgust. "That girl! What's she doing here?"

"She came to stop me." She looked at him ruefully. "And she's furious enough to do it. She's even mad at our mother. Westfall's been the only father she's known. He's never been anything but good to her. She's determined to defend him."

"But surely she won't do anything. She's just a child."

"She got away from school and came all the way from Chicago by herself."

Shreve grinned. "Of course. I forgot she's your sister."

She smiled in return. "Of course. She might warn him. She might attack me. I don't know. But I've got to make her see him for what he is. Unless she hears it from his own lips, she'll never believe it. He's got to confess."

Shreve laughed. "Certainly sounds simple enough to me. Just make your stepfather confess in front of hundreds of witnesses that he caused the death of nearly a hundred men. What about getting him to admit that he murdered that Pinkerton man and hired Archie Doight to set fire to the theater. Sounds simple enough. And while we're at it, we

444

have to make your sister love you? You know, don't you, that even if he confesses at gunpoint, she'll never believe you?"

Miranda pressed her fingertips against her temples. "I don't know anything anymore."

"You can always come away. We can still play Saint Louis. Or take a little vacation until we play New Orleans. This isn't like a tragedy where the hero is damned if he does and damned if he doesn't. If you try to do this, you may succeed in getting yourself killed. If you don't try it, you can walk away and forget about it. Lead a long, happy life. Marry." He paused significantly, but she was too distracted to notice. "Have children."

Her back was to him, her hands thrust into the pockets of her skirt. Her hair tied with a wide ribbon hung in a long skein down her back. The ends curled at her waistband. She looked so impossibly fragile to be plotting such dire deeds. "More and more I've been thinking about what I thought of years ago. I suppose you brought all the costume trunks and everything."

He sighed. He had wasted his breath. "We never know when we'll be called upon to perform."

"Do we still have those army uniforms from the time we played *Much Ado* in modern dress?"

"Yes."

She stared in silence for a long minute. When she turned back from the window, she smiled. *"I have heard that guilty creatures, sitting at a play, Have by the very cunning of the scene been struck so to the soul that presently they have proclaim'd their malefactions."*

"Miranda," he warned her sternly. "Life is not

445

like the theater. A real King Claudius would never have confessed like that in front of everyone." Shreve made a sweeping kinglike gesture. "He would have called for some lights, had the soldiers kill the players, and arrest Hamlet. Or possibly arrest the players and kill Hamlet."

"I disagree. I think he would have done exactly as he did. Particularly if the time were right."

He shrugged. "But how would we get your stepfather into a theater?"

"We won't get him in a theater. He'll be out at the monument. He'll be dedicating it."

He sprang to his feet. "Impossible. No. I forbid it."

She caught his hands. "Think of it. *Nor time nor place did then adhere, and yet they have made themselves.* What great theater! He's there on the very spot where he stood while they died, just beyond the hill. He's trying to assuage his conscience. For seventeen years he's carried this guilt around with him. He's married to the wife of the man he killed. He's tried to kill her daughter. He's trying to make all this up to her. He calls their names and they come. Like Banquo's ghost and Hamlet's father. The spirits of the dead come."

His own eyes took on a faraway look even as he shook his head. "Maybe. Just maybe in the dead of night, you might get someone to believe in ghosts, but never out here in broad daylight."

"You don't understand this country. You don't understand what people who live out here believe. This is a country where spirits walk the ridge lines and the deep valleys. I rode through it a few days ago. I could feel my father's spirit. Not ghosts.

446

Not sheets and wailing. No! Spirits. *I am thy father's spirit.*"

He stared at her. "So you're determined to play Hamlet."

She dropped her hands and stepped back to stand straight and proud. "I am Hamlet. I've known it since I first read the play."

He smiled and bowed. "Fellow player. Then I'll play the ghost."

"You'll do no such thing! In a cavalry uniform with my hair up and a blond mustache I'll look just like my father. No one who ever saw Francis Drummond who sees me coming from a distance can doubt that I'm my father. Particularly, if my mother sits on the platform beside Westfall. When I come over the hill, she'll raise a commotion."

"What if he doesn't flinch? What if he laughs? What if he just demands that someone go out there and stop you from disrupting the ceremonies? What if he draws a gun and starts shooting?"

She thrust her hands back into her pockets. Her mouth set in a straight line. "Oh, I hope he does. *If I can get him within my pistol's length, I'll make him sure enough.* If he does? I'll shoot him."

He gathered her into his arms. She held herself stiff in his embrace; her body trembled slightly. He leaned his cheek against the top of her head and stroked her back under her hair. "Miranda. Miranda. What have I done to you? Teaching you that life is a dramatic scene."

"This will work, Shreve," she said. "This will work."

He found that he was trembling, too. "Miranda. I love you."

Suddenly, she twisted in his grasp, bent herself back over his arm, caught his face between her hands and drew it down. Her mouth covered his, sucking his lips into her own. "This will work." She kissed him again. "It will." Again. "It will." Again. "It will."

Passion ignited between them. She lifted her belly against his loins. "Shreve. Shreve."

"Miranda, sweetheart. Not here."

"Here. Now. I have to. I can't stand—"

She pulled her blouse open, the buttons tearing out of the holes, and lifted her breasts to his face. "Please. Please."

The nipples were already stiff. His own body answered her demand. He could feel himself hardening. He put his mouth to her. She clapped her hands around his head and rose on tiptoe. "Oh, Shreve." Her breath shuddered out through clenched teeth. "Bite me. Hurt me. I can't stand this. I can't stand what I am. Please. Oh, God! *But screw your courage to the sticking place, and we'll not fail.*"

She became a demon in his arms. She bent her head to catch the curve of his ear. Her teeth grazed it. "Please."

"Sweetheart—"

One arm snaked around his body. Her hand slipped between his trousers and his shirt until only his thin cotton underwear separated her hand from his buttock. He had usually taken the lead in initiating their lovemaking. Now he reeled as her fingernails clawed at the material, clawed at his

448

flesh beneath.

Never taking his mouth off her breast, he stooped and lifted her skirts. His hands caught at her drawers and split them wide with a glorious ripping of material.

"Yes!" she hissed. "Oh, yes."

The last word ended on a cry of pain as he bit down hard on her turgid nipple. With one hand he managed to unbutton his trousers and free himself.

"Miranda," he gasped hoarsely. "We shouldn't be doing this. Not here in your friend's parlor."

For answer, she threw her arms around his neck. Her right leg snaked around his waist, spreading the steaming opening of her body to him. Like another mouth it kissed him, hot and wet. She moved, sliding up and down, on him.

"I want you, Shreve. I want you now."

He slid his hands through the torn material over her smooth thighs to her buttocks. Not soft like a woman's when she lies beneath a man on a bed but hard, the muscles tensed, pushing forward, striving.

He lifted her, or she climbed him. He could not tell which. He did not care. For she was suddenly above him, her sheath open to receive his sword. He throbbed, probed, touched her, found her wet.

She shivered. Her breasts arched beneath his mouth. Her eyes were lapis, deep blue with flecks of gold swimming in their depths. Their vision was transcendent, concentrated, set on him.

"Shreve." Did she actually speak his name? Or only think it?

He bowed his back and pushed upward. She

cried out with the glory of it, riding, feeling him to the very center of her, feeling him touch her heart.

He stroked once, stroked twice. The third time he exploded. The very essence of his life and his love, he put into her.

She cried out again, this time a desperate mewing sound. Her hips moved, and around him her sheath moved, caressing him, rippling over him and around him, tightening and relaxing, tightening and relaxing. He groaned like a man in pain as she seemed to draw the very life from his body.

They hung together for a full minute, like a tree. His legs the trunk planted firmly in the ground, their arms and bodies the branches and limbs. Then he felt himself shivering, quaking as if her slight weight and his own were too much for him to support. With a sigh she unlocked her ankles, allowing her legs to slide gently down, caressing him as she came.

He staggered back, breaking their joining and dropped down on a low stool. Her feet touched the floor. She turned sideways and settled over him, her skirts surrounding and covering him. To anyone entering the room, she was sitting on his lap. Her eyes closed, her head sank on his shoulder.

"I love you," she whispered. "And thank you. Thank you."

He kissed her temple, his eyes closed. "Don't mention it. Believe me, Miranda, it was my pleasure."

Twenty-four

*The time has been
That when the brains were out,
the man would die.*

"So that's what we plan to do. George is going to dress as Hickory Joe Magruder. Shreve will dress as a trooper and carry the guidon. And I will dress as my father. The three of us will come riding down off the ridge. The only thing you have to do is recognize us as we get closer." Miranda looked around at the group, trying to gauge their reaction to the plan.

"We'll need someone to send us a signal as soon as his speech begins, preferably as soon as he names her name," Shreve directed. "At that point, someone has to pull out a handkerchief and wipe his face or fan himself with it. I'll have the spyglass trained on the bandstand."

"I'll take care of that," White Wolf's Brother volunteered.

"Victor!" Rachel exclaimed. "You promised."

"I'm not really helping," he objected. "Just pulling out a handkerchief is not like putting on a disguise."

451

"I'll do it," Ruth volunteered. "No one will think a thing about a woman taking out a white handkerchief and fanning herself with it. I'll be sitting on the bandstand above the heads of the people. You can see me easily."

"Remember the timing is important. Be sure and let him announce our names and tell everyone who we are," Shreve directed. "I hope he's written that information into the speech." He looked irritably at Miranda. "How can we do this effectively? We don't even know whether the proper cues have been written in."

She giggled at his fussiness. Shreve's perfectionism had taken over, giving the project an air of professional detachment that she found reassuring. So long as he was staging it, it would be perfect.

He looked around at the older members of the group. "If what you tell me is true, this is a young crowd. Not many of them are people who would have known the soldiers at Fort Gallatin. So it's going to be hard to get their attention. And remember. We have to fool the crowd, too."

"I'll listen to his speech tonight and offer a few suggestions," Ruth volunteered.

"Good. (Should I write down some things?" He turned to Miranda. "No. I suppose that won't be necessary.)" He turned back to the rest of the group. "Now don't forget to shout your lines just as I've told you. Shout them two or three times in a loud clear voice, the deeper, the better. Don't allow yourself to get shrill."

"This is utterly disgusting," Rachel interrupted.

He ignored her. "Enunciate every syllable of every word and pause between each word. Even though you're supposed to be very agitated, you still have to be crystal clear. After the first exclamation, the audience will be noisy. They're going to start muttering and shuffling and turning around, stretching and straining to see what you're pointing to. They'll have a hard time hearing you, and it's important that Westfall believes that everyone recognizes us. He'll be caught up in the hysteria."

"This is the most awful thing I've ever heard," Rachel declared again. "You're directing this as if it were a play."

"It is, my dear," he replied, managing his most charming smile. "Art should never, never imitate life. Life is messy and clumsy. The timing is terrible. That's why things invariably turn out badly. But when things are directed properly, everyone sees a purpose and a pattern to life. Everything is clear as glass to the audience."

"You're tricking him."

"If he's innocent, then he'll be as flabbergasted as the crowd and you'll all have a big laugh," Miranda told her. "And you'll have a real reason never to speak to me again."

"If he's injured in any way, I swear you'll pay for it." Rachel's voice fairly shuddered in its intensity.

"What about those people in the theater? Some broke bones, some were burned, some were crushed. At the very least they were frightened almost to death."

"He didn't have anything to do with that. He was a thousand miles away in Washington, D.C."

The two sisters glared at each other.

Adolf looked at Blue Sun on Snow. She nodded solemnly. "I want to get my hand in this, too," Adolf announced. "I've heard you all talkin' 'bout costumes and sayin' speeches. I can't do much of that. But I've got the horse for you to ride. I just want to say, why settle for that livery stable plug when you can have the real thing?"

Miranda looked at him inquiringly. "The real thing? A cavalry mount?"

"That's right, and not just any cavalry mount, but the real one. You can ride your father's horse."

Cold chills coursed down her spine. "Wellington. But he came back wounded. I thought he was dead."

The old man grinned, obviously enjoying his moment in the spotlight. "That dang-blasted farrier cut the arrow out, but then they said his shoulder wasn't gonna heal right They were goin' to shoot him. Not only one of the best pieces of horseflesh in Wyoming, but your Francis's horse. I couldn't stand it." He looked appealingly at Ruth, who's eyes gleamed with tears. "I bought him. And you know what? He healed up just fine. So if you want him, he's yours."

Miranda hugged the old man. "He'll be perfect. He'll complete my costume." She turned to Shreve. "Nobody whoever saw that horse could ever forget him. Rich dark red mahogany hide. Long black mane and tail and three black points. And—his right front hoof was white, clear to the knee. Daddy said he'd stepped in snow. Wellington." Her eyes gleamed. "Now, I know I'm doing the right thing."

454

"I'm leaving."

Victor caught Rachel's arm and pulled her around to face him. "This is your sister's play. Don't you think you could let her make it?"

"No, I don't. It's not fair. You're all on her side and against him. Even you. Especially you. And I had thought—" She tried to twist her arm out of his grasp. "Let me go."

"Wait. What had you thought, Rachel?"

"Nothing." She shook her head, then faced him defiantly. "I had thought you loved me."

He took a deep breath. She was so beautiful. "I do love you. I can't marry you, but I do love you."

She went into his arms and lifted her mouth for him to kiss. He took it, caressing her sweet sixteen-year-old lips, damning himself for his weak will, for his urges throbbing and boiling inside him.

"Why can't you marry me?" she asked after a long time.

"You have to ask, but you're the only one I know of who would. You've seen my mother."

"Blue Sun on Snow. Of course."

"She's Northern Cheyenne. She's not even a so-called 'princess' or a 'shaman's daughter' or any of those silly labels white men try to stick on to the squaws they take under their blankets. She's just a woman. Beautiful, proud, intelligent. But she's an Indian."

"Are you thinking that because your mother was an Indian, people will despise you?"

He smiled without humor. "I don't think. I

455

know they will. You're so ignorant about things like that, you don't understand the hatred that so many people out here—and in other parts of the country—feel for Indians. I've changed my name to Victor Wolf so that most of the people in the state of Wyoming won't associate me with my father. He's well-known. A lot of people admire him because he's rich and he got that way by being an honest trader."

"That's very honorable of you to want to make it on your own."

He could have wept at her naïveté. "I'm not honorable. Not at all. A lot of people resent my father not only because he's made a success of himself but also because he's treated his wife so well. I'm actually renouncing my father and my mother because I'm afraid that association with them will hurt my chance of being elected."

"I don't believe that. You couldn't do something like that?" Her eyes were luminous with love and faith.

"I could. I have. I've even told my father why I'm doing it. He doesn't like my being dishonest, but he understands." He took her face between his hands and kissed her hard. "But I'm being honest with myself. Important men in this state and in the nation's capital, too, say that the only good Indian is a dead Indian. Generals in the army want to exterminate them like vermin. I wouldn't stand a chance if I confessed."

"Those people are wrong."

"Your stepfather is one of them."

She gulped. "Then he's wrong, too."

"Maybe. Maybe not. The wars have gone on so

long that nobody really knows who to blame. Whites kill Indians, but Indians kill whites, too. For every Indian who can tell a story of rape and murder, there's a white who can match him with torture and massacre." He heaved a deep sigh. "For every tale of Crook or Crazy Horse, there's a story of Black Kettle or Custer."

She wrapped her hands around his arms. "I don't care about any of that. Listen. Why don't we get married and move to Chicago. That's a wonderful town. You could set up a shop there and—"

He put a couple of fingers to her lips. "I want to help my people. Both whites and Indians. In Texas there's a great war chief named Quanah Parker, who's doing that. His mother was white and his father was Comanche."

"Then *we'll* help them. I'll be the best wife you've ever seen. I've watched my mother be a hostess for my stepfather's friends for years."

"No, you can't marry me. Because they'll hate you, too, if they find out that I'm a half-breed. They'll despise you and spit on you. They'll think you're filth because you even touched my mouth or my hand." Sweat stood on his anguished brow.

"I love you," she insisted. "I don't care what other people say."

He shook his head. "You don't care now. But you'd care soon enough if people started being cruel to you. You're still in school."

"I'll graduate soon."

He smiled. "Rachel, that's exactly what I want you to do. Day after tomorrow, I want you to go back to Chicago. Finish your schooling, let your mother introduce you to society, meet some nice young man, marry him, and lead a normal life."

"If you loved me, you'd want to marry me."

"It's because I love you that I won't marry you." He put his arm around her. "Now be a good girl and forget about finding your stepfather and warning him."

"My sister—"

He folded his arms like an Indian. He set his features in stern lines and deepened his voice. He was no longer Victor Wolf but White Wolf's Brother. "Your sister's feet were set upon this path seventeen winters ago. She was only a child of thirteen when she was forced to become a warrior."

Rachel dropped her hands and stepped back, shivering at the solemnity of the words.

"If you had been a boy, the war club would have been passed to you. But you were another girl, so she kept it. The path has been long and winding, but it has never led anywhere but here. When the general meets her, his innocence or guilt will be revealed. Whatever he says will set her free."

Like a knife in the heart, he watched the love fade and be replaced by doubt and fear. She backed away from him a couple of steps, then turned and ran back into the house.

Miranda looked at herself in the mirror and then at the cardboard-backed photograph of her father. Despite the blue uniform with the captain's bars, she did not look like him. Certainly, she did not look the way she remembered her father.

Instead, she looked like a schoolgirl dressed up for an amateur pageant. She felt like one, too. Her hands were cold and clammy. Her breathing shallow. *O cursed spite, that ever I was born to set it right.*

In a room in this very town only a few doors away, Benjamin Westfall was dressing, too. Her mother had told her he had ordered a new blue uniform with a general's stars for the occasion. Undoubtedly someone was outfitting him in gold sash and regimental saber. A saber of her own clanked against the chair as she sat.

Ada quietly opened the door behind her. "My stars, dearie, you're already dressed. And here I was comin' in to help you."

"I couldn't wait." Miranda's voice was breathless and high, just as she knew it would be.

Ada's wise old eyes met hers in the mirror. "It's still not too late to be giving it up. We didn't sell any tickets to this performance. There's no audience stomping and jeering out front. Just say the word and the four of us can be getting in that buggy and taking off down the trail for Casper. And from what I'm understanding, quite a few people at the celebration will just draw a hearty sigh of relief."

Miranda leaned her head against the heel of her hand. "I can't. I can't, Ada. But it's not easy."

Her dresser hugged her charge and laid her cheek upon her hair. "Nothing worth doing ever is."

The door opened behind them. Shreve strode in. "What do you think?" he queried turning from side to side. "All Lindhauer had was a dark blue

459

shirt. The pants with the yellow stripe wouldn't fit me. Do you think anyone will notice?"

Ada stepped back and Miranda rallied. "I think it'll do."

"I hate for my costume not to be right. Makes the whole thing look like a boys' school production."

She gave a hollow laugh. "I was just thinking that I look like the girl picked to play the hero in a girls' school performance. Did Adolf find a guidon?"

"No. We had to make one at the last minute. Blue Sun on Snow sewed it up and we painted the number "2" on it. Again it's a botched-up job. Thank God we only have to do this once."

His fussy complaining steadied Miranda as nothing else ever could. This was just another performance. Shreve was in his element worrying about tiny details that bothered no one else in the world, certainly not the audience. She faced the mirror, a grim smile on her face, while Ada rolled up the coils of bright hair and pinned them securely on top of her head.

Next came dark makeup and crêpe hair for her father's mustache and thicker eyebrows. As Ada worked, consulting the photograph from time to time, Miranda watched her own face disappear. At last Ada took the wide-brimmed buff campaign hat and set it carefully in place.

Shreve was watching in the mirror. "Amazing, Ada. You've outdone yourself. I doubt if his own mother could tell the difference."

"Thank you, Ada." Miranda rose. The saber clanked, caught the chair leg, and almost tripped her. She cursed with great feeling.

Shreve caught her and righted her. Concerned, he scanned her face. "Still want to go through with this?"

"Yes."

"Then come on outside. You have a treat in store. You've got to see George dressed up in a coat made out of a buffalo robe, a fur hat, and a full beard. If he doesn't pass out from heat exhaustion, he'll scare your stepfather to death."

"Gentlemen and you, dear Ladies, who have come such great distances to honor these brave and noble men, I welcome you to what was once Fort Gallatin." Benjamin Westfall gestured stiffly with his right arm. "It is indeed fitting that we honor them on this day, July 4th, 1883. They died fighting in the noble cause of this great country of ours. They died protecting the lives of settlers such as yourselves who came with plow and wagon to — create."

"Lord, I can't stand much more of this." George Windom threw back the buffalo hide coat from his shoulders and let it slide down to rest on the horse's rump. "I'm going to pass out or throw up or both."

"I wish we had a bugle," Shreve lamented. He leaned back at his ease against a boulder, spyglass to his eye, watching the scene below from the lip of the ridge. "A bugle would have made a much more dramatic entrance. Or perhaps a drum. Yes, a drum. A slow and stately funereal beat. Rrrrrum-ta-tum. Rrrrrum-ta-tum. Why didn't you think of a drum, Miranda? You know this could

461

have been much more effective if we'd had more time to plan."

The sun beat down on the three figures. The wind blew hot and dry across barren rocks. Not even a lizard or a ground squirrel moved among the rocks on Lodge Trail Ridge.

Miranda did not answer. She did not hear George's complaints nor Shreve's laments. She did not see the mirages rising off the rocks like rippling water. She did not feel the heat.

Cold as ice, one hand rested on the pistol in the holster on her hip. In her mind she saw her father as she remembered him best. Happy scenes from her childhood. She could almost feel his strong arm lifting her up against him to kiss her mother and him in their triumphal greeting. She could hear the cries of the Sioux as they charged and her father fought, bellowing orders, covering his men's retreat. She could see his poor mutilated body in the frozen room.

She shook her head violently as the whitened skin and gaping wounds came too close.

"Miranda. Miranda!" Shreve was looking at her, the spyglass dangling from his hand. "Are you sure you want to go through with this?"

She nodded vaguely. She could barely see over the lip of the hill. Hundreds of horses and vehicles of every type were drawn up in a circle around the monument. Most of their owners had stepped down and were gathered in front of the bandstand, although undoubtedly some were still sitting under the canvas tops to get away from the merciless sun. If any chanced to look in this direction, her buff campaign hat would look like another boulder.

Her stepfather's words were too far away for even the wild Wyoming wind to carry them up to her. He was a tiny figure a long way away, gesturing occasionally. She could see her mother sitting beside him. Adolf Lindhauer and White Wolf's Brother were somewhere down there, too, among other dignitaries and honored citizens. Blue Sun on Snow would undoubtedly be in the Lindhauer carriage with a very angry Rachel.

Miranda stared unseeing at the scene below her. She would not have heard Westfall's words had she been standing at the foot of the bandstand. Her ears were filled with strange whispers some in tongues she could not understand. Spirits of Sioux and American warriors were in the wind.

She shuddered. They were very close to the spot where he had died. Where the survivors of the first attack had fled, using their Henry repeaters, fighting, fighting, fighting until they had exhausted their ammunition.

Perhaps on this very spot. She gave a quick frightened glance around. The screams were in her ears. The curses. The prayers. The triumphant cries of the Sioux as they rode back and forth over the spot, killing the American dead over and over, stabbing and hacking, taking the scalps, the eyes, the hands—

"Places everybody. Your mother's fanning herself with her handkerchief." Shreve vaulted down from the rock and swung up into his saddle. He set the Second Cavalry guidon in his stirrup. "Curtain going up."

George shrugged the great coat back onto his

463

shoulders.

Miranda leaned forward over the big stallion's withers. "Wellington." She patted his neck. "It's time to bring him home."

The black ears flicked back then forward. The stallion dipped his head and pulled against the slope, mounted the crest, then halted for an instant, looking away to the east. Below in the valley the flag flapped on its pole, the monument intruded into the burning blue vault of the big sky, a cairn of stone that covered no bodies.

It only named the dead.

"O, from this time forth," she murmured, *"My thoughts be bloody, or be nothing worth!"*

Ruth felt her heart rise in her throat. A cold chill swept her as the horse appeared as if by magic on the crest of the ridge. Even knowing she saw Miranda, she could hardly believe she did not see Francis.

Beside her she felt White Wolf's Brother tense. Adolf Lindhauer murmured something under his breath.

Then a trooper of the Second appeared beside him with the guidon, and on the other side a figure like a huge grizzly bear riding a horse. Wellington started down the slope picking his way nimbly, the other two came behind him shoulder to shoulder.

"Private William Kirkendall, Private Matthew Johnson, Private—"

General Westfall's voice droned on. He had not raised his eyes from the roll call. He did not see the figures coming down the draw.

The ground leveled out under Wellington's

hooves. He needed no touch of the spur nor voice command to move into a spirited trot. Close to a quarter of century old, he might be; but his neck arched, his tail lifted. His black flags flying, he came on.

Miranda's eyes burned making the figures on the grandstand swim in front of the gray cairn. In her ears the voices were silent, but it was the silence of hunters waiting for the prey to jump.

The trio reached the outside ring of vehicles. She could see her mother rise from her seat. "Francis! My God! Francis!"

The general's voice faltered. He turned to stare at his wife in amazement and then in the direction she looked.

Adolf Lindhauer clambered to his feet, too. "Hickory Joe. Hickory Joe Magruder. Goddamn!"

"What in tarnation's goin' on?"

"Is this part of the celebration?"

"Where'd they come from?"

"What's it supposed to mean?"

The crowd, as Shreve had predicted, shuffled and strained to get the best view of the proceedings.

"Francis!" Ruth cried again. "Francis!" She put her gloved hands to her mouth. Shreve heard the note of truth in her voice. Miranda had done it again, he thought. She had gotten so deep inside the part that she had lost her sense of herself. He made a mental note to warn her about it. His eyes slid sideways to her face.

The sight of it would have thrown him off if he had had to say a line. Its resemblance to the photograph of Francis Drummond was uncanny. Ada

465

was undoubtedly one of the best in the business.

Westfall caught sight of her face at the same moment. The sheaf of names and the rest of his speech fluttered from his nerveless fingers. He stumbled forward to the edge of the grandstand. His hands locked around the rail for support. The red-white-and-blue bunting fluttered. "Who are you?"

The crowd murmured and buzzed as people shuffled and stretched and strained to see what was happening.

Wellington had slowed to a steady marching pace. Still he brought her on, sometimes straight, sometimes turning sideways and back to get around a buggy or a ground-hitched team. The course had the effect of presenting the figure in profile and then again face front.

"Francis Drummond!" Adolf yelled. "Glory be!"

In front of the grandstand only a few feet from Westfall, Miranda halted Wellington. A sudden silence fell as the crowd sensed the import of the meeting between the two.

"You're dead," Westfall croaked. "You're dead!" he said more loudly.

Miranda said nothing. Her blue eyes, Francis Drummond's eyes gleamed from beneath the buff hat. Slowly, her right arm rose. Her index finger pointed at Benjamin Westfall.

"No." He shook his head violently. His gray beard waggled. "You're dead. I sent you out. You didn't come back. I made sure." He flung an impassioned look over his shoulder at his wife, standing now. Her eyes fixed on the figure in front of her.

466

"Francis," she whispered. Her black-gloved hands went out. "Francis, my husband."

"NO!" A howl tore out of Westfall's throat. He threw himself in front of his wife. "No. You're mine. I couldn't have you any other way. I killed him for you. You're mine. I killed him."

From the deep shade of the Lindhauer carriage, Rachel covered her mouth with her hands. Infinitely sympathetic, Blue Sun on Snow put her arm around the girl's shoulders.

Westfall swung back to the three figures drawn up abreast in front of him. "You're dead!" he screamed. "You're all dead!"

From out of the depths of her throat, Miranda pulled the words. They came out harsh and deep, not a man's tones, but not a woman's either. "You killed us."

"This time I'll make sure. You'll never come back to haunt me again. If I've learned one thing in this life, it's that I must do the important things myself." He slapped at his holster, drawing the old sidearm. His hand was shaking so badly that he seemed to take forever to raise the weapon.

Women screamed. The crowd split on either side, running from the possibility of a stray bullet.

Shreve and George both flung themselves out of the saddles. (A good actor always knows when to make his exit.)

Miranda pulled her own revolver from its holster. With careful precision she raised the Smith and Wesson she had bought for the purpose in Chicago. Westfall's dark eyes were locked on hers.

She could see him struggling, shaking. His mouth opened and closed, working, cursing. He

467

added his left hand to his right, dragging up the old Navy Colt.

"Look out, Miranda!"

She squeezed the trigger. The back kick of the pistol knocked the sight up in the air, but not before the bullet left the barrel. Westfall took the round full in the chest. His arms flung wide, his thin body shot backward, crashing into the chairs on the bandstand and tumbling off onto the ground.

Screams echoed in her ears. Suddenly, Shreve was at her side, turning the horse. "Get the hell out of here," he ordered. "While they're all still trying to figure out what happened."

The trance was broken. She felt a sort of curtain dropping from her eyes. Like water washing a glass clean, she could see him.

"Shreve, I love you."

He flashed his old smile. Romeo's smile. "I love you, too."

"I'll meet you. In New Orleans."

"New Orleans it is."

She bent in the saddle. Her mouth found his briefly. Then for the first time that day, she spurred Wellington. The big horse leaped forward, gathered speed as he passed the buggies and the gaping crowd, and galloped over the horizon.

The drama continues in Deana James's *Acts of Love,* to be published by Zebra Books in December 1992. Here's a taste of the adventure and passion awaiting Miranda and Shreve . . .

Acts of Love

by Deana James

"Shreve, Shreve. Can you hear me?"

He could barely see. His eyes were so swollen. Blackness like slats in a jalousie slid across his vision. His head still buzzed from the many blows. But through the buzzing came Miranda's urgent whispers at his ear. He must be dreaming.

Cool water bathed his face with infinite gentleness.

He struggled to open his eyes. "Miranda?"

"Yes, darling. Oh, yes."

The water dribbled into his swollen mouth. He swallowed. His voice gathered strength. "Miranda."

Instantly, her hand covered his mouth. "Ssssh, darling. You mustn't say my name."

"What're you doing here?" He could barely get the words out through his swollen lips. Dimly, he tried to open his mouth wider. His jaw might be broken. He tried to raise his hand to touch it. His chain clanked ominously.

"I've come to get you away."

Get him away! He must still be in prison. He had been groggy with pain and exhaustion when

469

guards had fastened irons to his ankles and connected his manacles to them by a chain. Then they had put their hands under his armpits and dragged him out of the cell into the blinding glare of the noon sun. Then lifting him by the irons, they had slung him into a closed wagon. As it jolted away, he had been too weak to raise himself to the tiny barred window even if he had cared where they were taking him.

Now somehow Miranda was here with him. She must not be. "Get away," he whispered. "Don't stay."

"Yes, darling." Her lips were next to his ear.

Hair tickled him. He managed to open his eyes. His vision cleared for an instant. Then he saw that she was heavily disguised. The sight of the grease paint and crêpe hair chilled him to the bone. "No. Get away," he repeated, more strongly. He tried to lift his arms. "They'll catch you. Don't want you—"

She smiled encouragingly. "We'll be going together in just a few hours."

"No. You mustn't wait." Suddenly, he felt so damned heroic he wanted to cry. He had hurt so much for so long. He didn't want her to leave. He wanted her to take him in her arms and hold him against the pain that was wracking him. But he couldn't because the woman he loved was going to be hurt if she helped him.

Heroism stank.

Even as he forced the bruised muscles of his face to sketch a travesty of a smile, he wanted her to keep him safe from Trask's beatings. Even as he tried to think of the words to send her away, he didn't want to be slung back into the well. He could feel the tears starting in his eyes.

"Shreve," she whispered. "Oh, Shreve." She put her arms carefully around his face and pressed her lips to his forehead.

"Miranda." His lips formed the word, but no sound came. His fear for himself was magnified to terror for her. He closed his eyes to try to gather strength.

"No one will beat you again. I swear."

He made a tiny shake of negation within the circle of her arms. "You can't stop them. Get away."

"We will. Together." She kissed him again.

The tears were stopping. The trembling in his belly subsided to a persistent ache. At length he released a shaky breath. "Where are we?"

She lifted her head. "In a hotel in Cheyenne, waiting for the train."

He could hear the soft splash of water. A wet cloth bathed his forehead, his temples, his bruised cheeks, wiping away the hot tears beneath his closed eyes. It dipped again, then resumed laving his neck, bestowing blessed coolness to his body that felt burnt and blistered.

"How?" His voice was stronger than he had meant it to be, but his control seemed to have lapsed.

Again she put her finger over his swollen lips. "Don't talk, darling. Don't. We're in danger."

He tried to open his eyes, blinked them twice, three times. Through a haze, he looked up into her face, the face of a bewhiskered stranger. "You look like a man."

She smiled. "Thank God. Ada's makeup is a miracle."

"You're in danger," he whispered.

"Yes, but only a little. We're both waiting for the train. Under guard. Sergeant Trask—"

At the mention of the man's name, Shreve felt hatred course through him in waves. He cursed long and vividly. His body began to shake uncontrollably.

Miranda put her hand on his shoulder. "Shreve, don't get so—"

A knock sounded at the door.

He stiffened, his curses silenced.

She dropped the rag into the pan and slid them under the bed. "Remember, darling. You don't know me."

He set his teeth. "Yes. All right."

Squeezing his hand, she rose. Through the ringing and buzzing in his ears, he could hear her boots tapping across the floor. Even in boots he recognized the rhythm of her walk. The door opened.

"Here's the tray, Lieutenant."

"Thanks, soldier."

"I'll stay with him while he eats and you can go on down."

"You go ahead, Private Perkins. I'll see that he eats and then get him settled for the night. I've got the key to his chains. I want to be sure he's anchored down good and tight."

"Right, sir."

"Come back at eight, soldier."

"Yes, sir."

He heard her footsteps returning. Her weight

472

came down on the bed beside him. She bent over him. Her lips touched his forehead, the wounds in his eyebrows. "Oh, Shreve."

"Pretty bad, huh?"

"Pretty bad," she agreed.

"But they didn't break my nose," he croaked. He tried to raise his hand, but again the manacles connected by a short chain to his ankle irons restrained him. "Feel it."

Her cool fingertip slid down his nose. "You're right. It's not broken."

"I ducked," he said with quiet pride.

She kissed his nose. "Clever darling." And the nasty abrasion on his cheek. "Oh, Shreve, what have I done to you? I never thought they'd arrest you for just riding up on a horse."

He shrugged one shoulder. "You can't depend on the army to have any sense. I told you so. Life isn't like the theater. Real people don't see logic the way playwrights do. Or they do, but it's their own kind of logic, based on keeping their jobs and getting promotions." He stirred trying to find some way to ease his aching body.

She shook her head. "I've made a mess of things. I never really thought beyond confronting Westfall and making him admit that he sent my father out to die. Have I ruined everything for us?"

He heaved a sigh and tried to open his eyes to see her clearly. "Miranda. So long as they don't know who you are, they'll eventually have to let me go. After all, I didn't do anything."

"But they're hurting you." Her voice was strained.

473

"They've about given up on that," he lied, shuddering as he thought of Trask somewhere nearby. He had to convince her to give up this scheme to set him free. It was probably as harebrained as the one that had gotten him caught in the first place. "Look, sweetheart, I love you for coming here. I don't know how you did it. But you've got to go. They'll catch you. And what they did to me will be minor compared to what they'll do to you."

She kissed him one more time and straightened up. "Now don't waste your breath. I've got some food. You must be starving."

He shook his head, then regretted the movement as the pain lanced behind his eyes. "You've got to get out of here."

"*We've* got to get out of here, but we can't go until the train comes."

"They'll find you out."

"How can they, when you didn't even recognize me?"

"I can't see very well. But they'll see right through that costume."

"Shreve. I'm a better actress than that."

He tried to rise, managed to push up on one elbow, chains clanking. Fighting pain in his jaws, in his ribs, in his temples, he stared her up and down. "You look like the lead in a girls' school drama production."

"Only to a trained actor. You know what to look for." She sawed off a tiny piece of the tough steak. "Can you chew?"

He slumped back, muttering curses behind his swollen lips. "I doubt it."

"You've got to try." She held the piece to his mouth.

He shook his head once again, fractionally. "Teeth loose."

She closed her eyes, struggling to keep from crying. She could not shed tears and spoil her makeup. She had not counted on forty-eight hours until the train. The crêpe hair would last, though it would itch like the very devil, but she had not Ada's skill with the paint. "Shreve," she whispered. "You must eat. You have to keep up your strength. At least until I can get you on the train."

"I'll make it," he murmured and turned his face away on the pillow.

"Shreve!"

He had lost consciousness.

For several minutes she sought to get herself under control. First, she performed all the deep breathing exercises he had taught her. As she breathed, she went over her lines and her moves analyzing her performance. So far it had been perfect. Nothing less would have served. She had to remember everything and maintain a consistent characterization for forty-eight hours.

It was the role of a lifetime. Women played men in farce, but never in drama. It would be the performance of her life.

To the Reader

By now you have perceived that *Acts of Passion* is constructed like a play by William Shakespeare. In further homage to the master writer of all time, I have begun each chapter with a quotation to foreshadow what will follow. I hope the sources have piqued your interest. If so, they have served their purpose well. I further thought to allow you the fun of seeing how well you remembered your Shakespeare. Have you tested yourself thus far? Four points for each correct answer. Ninety-six is a perfect score.

Deana James

    I. "Let slip the dogs of war!"   *Julius Caesar*
   II. "O villainy! Ho! Let the door be lock'd
       Treachery! Seek it out."   *Hamlet*
  III. "The valiant never taste of death but
       once."   *Julius Caesar*
  IV. "One may smile, and smile, and be a
       villain."   *Hamlet*
   V. "Few love to hear the sins they love to
       act."   *Pericles, Prince of Tyre*

VI. "No enemy
But winter and rough weather."

As You Like It

VII. "And, most dear actors, eat no onions
nor garlic,
for we are to utter sweet breath.

A Midsummer Night's Dream

VIII. "This may prove worse than
hanging."   *Measure for Measure*

IX. "She has a good face, speaks well, and has
excellent good clothes."

Pericles, Prince of Tyre

X. "—and not so much for love
As for another secret close intent."

Richard III

XI. "But here I am to speak what I do
know."   *Julius Caesar*

XII. "For look you how cheerfully my mother
looks."   *Hamlet*

XIII. "Call you me daughter!"

The Taming of the Shrew

XIV. "The best actors in the world."   *Hamlet*

XV. "The play's the thing."   *Hamlet*

XVI. "Our very loving sister, well bemet."

King Lear

XVII. "Do you call me fool?"   *Cymbeline*

XVIII. "According to the fair play of the world,
Let me have audience."   *King John*

XIX. "The secret'st man of blood."   *Macbeth*

XX. "Good lover, let me go."

Love's Labours Lost

XXI. "If the great gods be just, they shall assist the deeds of justest men."

Antony and Cleopatra

XXII. "Fair madam; kneel,
And pray your mother's blessing."

The Winter's Tale

XXIII. "The time is out of joint, O cursed spite
That ever I was born to set
it right!" *Hamlet*

XXIV. "The time has been
That, when the brains were out, the man
would die." *Macbeth*